**IT WAS HAPPENING AGAIN, THE INVASION,
THE RAPE OF HIS MIND
THAT MORTALS CALLED PRAYER. . . .**

Volos stood rigidly, with taut face and wings clenched,
violated by a distant summons.

*Volos. Volos.
Come rescue me.*

Once he was on his Harley and moving, no one would
bother him. Not even Her. Whoever She was. Volos
roared off into the starless city night, running away,
drowning out her still-distant voice. His wings caught
the wind and spread, translucent, gradually lightening
from angry red to fire-orange in the streetlamp's light.

In part he knew who she was. It was her, the one
whose songs spoke straight to his mind and somehow
she knew him better than he knew her. She called
him angel, and she was summoning him by name. But
no matter who she was, no matter what she said or
did, he would not go back to the role of servant, of
guardian angel, of comer-when-called. He would scald
in her tears first. He would fry in hell. . . .

Metal Angel

ROC

SCIENCE FICTION AND FANTASY

☐ **THE STALK by Janet and Chris Morris.** The Unity had made its offer, stated its terms. Now the United Nations of Earth must respond. But how could Mickey Croft make an unbiased decision for all humankind, when his own direct contact with the Interpreter had left him uncertain whether he himself was still completely human? (453077—$4.99)

☐ **DOWN AMONG THE DEAD MEN by Simon R. Green.** It was the most ancient of evils—and it was about to wake—in this sequel to *Blue Moon Rising*. "This one really stands out from the crowd."—*Science Fiction Chronicle* (453018—$4.50)

☐ **RED BRIDE by Christopher Fowler.** A horror is on the loose, savagely killing again and again. The police are powerless to stop the slaughter. The finest detectives cannot unmask the killer. Only one man suspects the secret. (452933—$4.99)

☐ **STALKER ANALOG by Mel Odom.** Bethany Shay was a cop on a serial killer's trail—a trail that led from the Church to the cybernet and into the heart of madness. (452577—$5.50)

☐ **THE MISTS FROM BEYOND** *20 Ghost Stories & Tales From the Other Side* by Peter Straub, Clive Barker, Joyce Carol Oates and 17 others. Twenty of the most haunting ghost tales ever created . . . all of them certain to transport you, if only for a brief time, from our everyday world to one in which even the faintest of shadows takes on a ghostly life of its own. (452399—$20.00)

*Prices slightly higher in Canada

Buy them at your local bookstore or use this convenient coupon for ordering.

PENGUIN USA
P.O. Box 999 — Dept. #17109
Bergenfield, New Jersey 07621

Please send me the books I have checked above.
I am enclosing $_____ (please add $2.00 to cover postage and handling). Send check or money order (no cash or C.O.D.'s) or charge by Mastercard or VISA (with a $15.00 minimum). Prices and numbers are subject to change without notice.

Card #_____ Exp. Date _____
Signature_____
Name_____
Address_____
City _____ State _____ Zip Code _____

For faster service when ordering by credit card call **1-800-253-6476**

Allow a minimum of 4-6 weeks for delivery. This offer is subject to change without notice.

Metal Angel

NANCY SPRINGER

A ROC BOOK

ROC
Published by the Penguin Group
Penguin Books USA Inc., 375 Hudson Street,
New York, New York 10014, U.S.A.
Penguin Books Ltd, 27 Wrights Lane,
London W8 5TZ, England
Penguin Books Australia Ltd, Ringwood,
Victoria, Australia
Penguin Books Canada Ltd, 10 Alcorn Avenue,
Toronto, Ontario, Canada M4V 3B2
Penguin Books (N.Z.) Ltd, 182^190 Wairau Road,
Auckland 10, New Zealand

Penguin Books Ltd, Registered Offices:
Harmondsworth, Middlesex, England

First published by Roc, an imprint of Dutton Signet,
a division of Penguin Books USA Inc.

First Printing, April, 1994
10 9 8 7 6 5 4 3 2 1

 REGISTERED TRADEMARK—MARCA REGISTRADA

To my angel

"Holy hell, this guy sings like an angel in *heat*."
—Deejay, WSAY, Cassandra, Alabama

prologue

He incarnated on an L.A. rooftop with no onlooker but the ever-galloping Marlboro Man, who watched, indifferent, as he imagined himself into being. It was an act not without discomfort. His first experience of flesh was of panting, of strain, of sprawling on a hard, gritty surface, wet as a newborn with sweat. His first bodily thought was *What will be my punishment?* A cosmic rebel engaged in an act of blatant self-will, he knew there had to be a price to pay aside from the obvious ones of the temporality, transience, and death. The Supreme Being's convoluted sense of humor had come up with AIDS, atomic power, poisonous snakes, and illogical hope; what might it have in store for him?

A seagull flew over with a spoiled-brat cry: "More! More! More salsa, more clams!" The newcomer lying on the rooftop saw first the shadow, then the bird, and smiled, and heaved himself up, struggling to his unaccustomed feet. Standing spraddle-legged, he looked down at himself.

Jeans. Levi's 501 blues. He had paid a lot of attention to the jeans, and they were faded and torn and fit long and tight, just as he had wanted them. Quickly he opened his fly and checked—yes. He had taken care to fully imagine his genitals, also, and they appeared complete and very satisfactory. He zipped, noticing the slight, just-right bulge of denim at his crotch, the long slim line below, the urban-cowboy boots with their glint of silver at the toes. Naked chest and belly, arms, hands—all were lean, long, fit, and firm, all as he wanted them. He raised his hands to his face, feeling it, reassuring himself; the essential features seemed to be in place. The face had been the hardest part to envision, and he would not know until he found a mirror whether he had succeeded in being beautiful. But he felt hope, for there were many sorts of mortal beauty.

He looked at his hands, admiring the sunlit dexterity of them. "Hello, strangers," he whispered to them, checking his voice. "Do you know how to play a mean ax?"

They did. He knew to the marrow of his brand-new bones that they did. He could feel it, the wildly physical electric music pumping in them like the beat of his ardent new heart.

To Volos music was the center of every circle, the locus where crosses joined, the hub of every compass. And the axis on which his adopted world turned, the flame with which it blazed, was called rock and roll. This was the music that glorified the body, that thrust like a cock, enveloped like a cunt, pounded like his strong new pulse. This was the loud music, the renegade music, the music of tight jeans and suggestive lower-body movements, the music that shook its fist and thumbed its nose at its elders. This was the music of decadence, of defiant youth, of rash, rich life with death as its ultimate adventure. It was for this that he had chosen this rash, rich young country, this decadent city, in which to will himself into mortality.

And just being real was all Volos had believed it would be. The rhythm, the heartbeat, was ecstasy. It lidded his eyes, turned his face toward the sky, parted his lips. He shouted, he drew out the shout into a jolt of barbaric song, startling echoes off the Marlboro billboard, feeling for the first time the hot, vibrant rush of air in his throat, the willing effort and deep resonance of his chest. He flung wide his arms, he felt the cantilevering strength of his shoulders, the lift of his wings—

Wings.

Wings! Hell forever, no! His song splintered into a yell of despair. Hands clenched into fists, trembling tight, shaking hard, like the rest of him. With all his renegade strength of ego and in all the old languages of power, in Latin, Hebrew, Sanskrit, he commanded the wings to be gone, demanded the demons of the Unholy Sefiroth to take them from him; he wanted to be all and only human, human, human and damned! He kept up the effort for moments, until even his taut eyelids shook. But it was no use. Fatigue made him go limp. He was flesh now, he was frail, stubborn, defiant, and helpless within his own selfhood. A bird flies, and when death smashes it to the roadway it is reshaped. He could be reshaped only by his own death.

"Damn it to hell," he whispered to the rooftop.

He kicked at some pigeons pecking near his feet. Sullen city birds, they merely walked away, complaining through their beaks. "Who does he think he is?" they remarked to each other. "Bigwing. Flap-happy."

"Bigwing freak," Volos said bitterly, face turned away from the sky. "Damn it all, who said God does not lie? Free will, my eye. He saw what I would do, and he has made a fool of me. I should have known."

It was a familiar feeling, the rage. Not that he had considered leaving it behind. Rather, he cherished it, took satisfaction in the way it buzzed and clicked in him, high voltage, ready for him to use. He would wire it into this new world, lick it with his skilled hands into savage, dissolute music.

"What are you staring at?" he stormed at the billboard where the American hero gazed. "You can sit there and wait for your sunset. You can rot up there, for all I care. There is no halo on me. I came here to live fast and deep, and I will do it. Wings be damned, I am going to dance and learn love and live."

Amid sulky, waddling birds, near the sweaty patch of rooftop where he had lain while giving birth to himself, he saw a sprawl of shimmering blue cloth. Though he had never before seen celestial garb in its physical manifestation—for it was not customary for immortal beings to risk incarnation, not at all—he recognized the garment and picked it up: a turbanlike thing, it was his headcovering, the very plain headcovering required of the lowest choir. Its only ornament was a *petalon,* a four-lobed flowerlike medal made of solid molded gold. This he pulled off and put in his jeans pocket. Pawned, it would give him the guitar he needed. As for the headcovering itself, symbol of respect and humility before the throne of the Almighty: with sudden energy he hurled it down, sending the pigeons flying at last. He trod on it, leaving the marks of his booted feet on the heavenly fabric, as he walked away.

chapter
one

If you live in an eastern state, when you run away you go to the West Coast. This is one of the unwritten rules, the kind real folks live by, and Bob Balfour "Texas" McCardle at age forty had always lived by that kind of rules. When he ran away from his wife and West Virginia, he headed straight for the City of Angels.

Not that he had any grudge against his wife. Wyoma was a strong, good woman, held a well-paying job brazing metal in the air-conditioning factory, mothered their two daughters like an Apache, so sensible and tough he felt as if she didn't need him to speak of, maybe not until her old age. And it wasn't as if he didn't figure on going back. He sent her a quick letter when he got there.

Dear Wy,

Well as you can see by the postmark I am in L.A. I guess I surprised everybody pretty good taking off that way. You can tell people I'm looking for my father if you want. Truth is I got the shits of everything and had to get out awhile or bust. I don't

know how to explain it any better but I don't think
it's anything you did. I guess I'll be back when I
get over it. Will keep you posted.

                                                    Bob

She was the only one who called him Bob. Everybody else in Mingo County had called him Texas since
as a teenager he had gotten himself Western boots and
a cowboy hat. The nickname was not meant kindly at
first, since affection for the trappings of TV westerns
was seen as a tacit betrayal of the good things of Persimmon, West Virginia. Who needed far places when
home meant friends and family and God's own mountains? The boy showed signs of being a no-good like
his daddy.

All McCardle's adult years, when he had tried hard
to be as solid as anybody, the epithet had stuck with
him. Well, hell, he didn't mind. He still preferred to
dress western style, and knew he looked the part: slim
no-hurry body, sandy hair, the weathered face of a
guy who liked to be out on his horse. Though in fact
he owned no horse, just wanted one. Went fishing or
skeet shooting or woodchuck hunting with friends
when he could, but wished sometimes he was a kid
again, gunning for trouble all the time. Looked at the
stars sometimes and wondered about things. Hated to
think of growing fat or old.

Maybe there was some truth to what people had
thought of him. Because here he was, wasn't he, where
he had no business to be? Never content with what
he had.

He had not signed his letter to Wyoma "Love."
They had been together seemed like forever, since he
had got her pregnant at age sixteen. There had been
no mush at their wedding or since, and he didn't think
she would want or understand it now.

So if he was out along the one-way street below his

cheap hotel at three in the morning it was maybe not because he was looking for his father.

"Hey, cowboy." A black whore approached him. She wore a spangled dress that she had probably gotten at a Hollywood secondhand store, might have belonged to a movie star once. And she had shaved her eyebrows entirely. The penciled substitutes halfway up her forehead appeared to have crawled there, millipedes at a standoff. "You look like a guy with an appetite, Slim," she wheedled.

"I'm a bed wetter," Texas informed her. "Also I got a nervous disease makes me drool." Being a cop most of his life, even just a backwoods West Virginia cop, had turned him off on hookers pretty good.

"Come on, Stretch. I can tell you're looking for some action."

"No, thanks." He was looking for something, all right, but he felt pretty sure it wasn't her.

"Want to buy some grass? I know where you can get good Colombian."

"No, thanks."

"And you ain't interested in me, huh?"

"Nope."

"You looking for boys? They're down the other end of the block." She sounded anxious to please. Maybe she worked daytimes at the tourist bureau.

"Jesus," he said.

"Well, if it ain't that, then what the hell do you want, honey?"

As she spoke her eyes looked past him. He said, more to himself than to her, "Damned if I know," and turned to see what she was gawking at.

Walking down the middle of the street, stopping traffic, was a tall youth, bare-chested, with wings.

Big wings. Must have been over six foot, and he must have been about the same. Their leading edges, folded, rose above shoulders that looked strong, muscled like he'd been pumping iron. Their tips trailed almost to his booted feet.

"Some sort of publicity stunt," Texas said. City of Angels, right? The guy looked like a show biz hopeful, very young, very well hung, very pretty in the face. Some kid from Podunk, new in smog city, getting attention any way he could.

No, maybe not from Podunk. There was hot blood in this one. Full lips, high cheekbones, something strange, exotic, about his thin face. Skin the color of a dun stallion, not suntanned but earth-toned. Awfully dark for an angel.

"Where's he get off, wearing them things?" said the whore, her voice no longer eager to please—it had gone shrill. "He's gonna get his ass kicked coming here that way."

"Probably just heading back to his room," Texas offered. The kid should have taken off his wings before he came into that neighborhood. Texas wondered how he fastened the things on. The guy had crossed to the other side of the street, too far away for Texas to tell in the shadowy streetlamp light.

The whore snorted and turned away. Texas kept watching. They were damned impressive, those wings. Not white, though. This guy must think of himself as an angel of a different color. Or maybe it was just the glow off the neon bar signs, but the feathers looked pearly pink.

Which was the wrong color for the ambience in this particular garbage-filled gash of an asphalt-and-concrete hole where the stars never shone. Texas saw it coming—attention the kid didn't want. Issuing in gang uniform out of an alley. Jeering.

"Whassis, a new kind of faggot?"

"Looks like a no-ball to me."

"Cocksucker."

"Hey, I used to fuck guys like him in prison!"

"Guys with pink wings?"

"Pink all over, motherfuckers."

There were three homeboys, and they blocked the kid's way. Texas stayed where he was. He had left his badge and gun in a dresser drawer in West Virginia, running away from them as well as the rest of his life there. He was on vacation from caring about anything. Anyway, the youngster with wings was half a head taller than any of the street punks and did not seem afraid. It would be a real luxury to stand around and watch what happened and not give a shit.

In a voice so correct it seemed accented the kid said, "You are strange people. You do fucking with men you do not like?"

All three at once they hit him, and Texas was halfway across the street within an eyeblink, losing his brand-new hat in his hurry, the luxury of not caring forgotten, because fast as the punches had fallen something had changed. He could see it. Every whore on the street could feel it and scuttled for cover. The air screamed with it. Somebody was gonna get killed.

After the first blow, no longer were the homeboys fighting out of boredom of territoriality or to score points with girls or each other. As soon as they had touched the winged stranger they virulently hated him. One pulled a knife. They wanted to butcher him.

And he was no match for them. He stood his ground, tried to connect, but he swung wide and didn't know how to move, didn't circle or put his back toward the wall; he let them get behind him, where they savaged his offending wings and the back of his head. Any one of them could have pulped him, and there were three. Already he was beaten down to his knees—

Texas used the force of his cross-street charge to gut-ram the knife fighter with his head. He stomped a hand as the homeboy sprawled, kicked the weapon into the darkness. After that it was all reflex work. He had broken up enough tavern brawls to know he had to move quickly, and find something to use like a baton, and make a lot of noise. The moves and the weapon were only to survive until the noise took effect. Once enough time and noise had passed the bad guys would run. It was a psychological warfare thing. They would get afraid, even though they knew nobody would really call the cops. All they knew was hit and run. They would run.

"Cretins!" he bellowed, bruising his knuckles on one of them. "No-neck motor-ass pinheads!" He regretted the upbringing his gentle Methodist mother had given him, which all his life—despite his best efforts—had kept him from cursing really well. But what the hell, it was volume that counted. Texas kept the volume high-decibel enough to buzz his skull as he ducked a flung chunk of concrete, kicked a knee, scooped up a beer bottle to thrust with. The kid with wings learned fast. He was on his feet again, he had picked up his own weapon. "Back up toward the wall!" Texas called to him.

A few streets away, like a mother shrilling for her children at suppertime, a siren yodeled. The homeboys indulged in one last hard assault. Texas felt a hand clawing his face, fingers digging for his eyes. He kneed the attacker, doubling him so that his two buddies had to support him as they ran, the three of them looking like a six-legged thing, an oversized cockroach scuttling back into the shadows of the alley.

Texas panted. The siren rolled over to bleep mode, dopplered past at the gay hustlers' end of the street.

When he had caught his breath a little, Texas said to the youngster with wings, "You gotta learn to fight if you're gonna wear that kind of getup, kid."

The kid stood shakily on his long legs—being tall is unfair that way; if a tall person gets the least bit shaky everybody sees it. Blood on the young man's face— just a nosebleed. Scanning him for injuries, Texas saw a shallow knife scratch across his bare chest and some lacerations, some bruises. Nothing to worry about. Also he noticed with muted surprise that he had somehow been mistaken about the color of the wings. They were much darker than he had thought. Brick-red, in fact.

"You all right?" he asked, his throat raw from shouting, his face smarting from the mauling it had gotten, his wrists aching. This would be a good time for the kid to thank him. But the kid stood fingering the blood trickling from his nose.

"Hot," he murmured. He licked his bloodied lips, and his face grew rapt. "I can taste it. I can taste myself."

There was something odd about the way he spoke besides its precision. His voice sounded strangely intense and penetrating, so that even at its quietest it had been vibrant enough to be heard across the street. Yet now that he stood right next to him, Texas found it eerily distant.

Shadowy eyes turned. The stranger asked, "Will all this blood coming out of me hurt me?"

Shit, was the kid simpleminded? Texas answered only with a shrug, wishing, now it was over, that he hadn't gotten involved, suddenly wanting very much to turn his back on everything, get back to his own room, tend to his own wounds ... but he couldn't leave a hurt retard standing on the street. Had to see him home. Dammit. He asked, "What's your name?"

"Volos."

"Volos what?"

"Just Volos. I am of low degree. It is not considered necessary for me to have more names than one." The stranger subjected Texas to a dark-eyed scrutiny from below frowning brows. "You are bleeding also."

"I know that." Texas kept most of the annoyance out of his voice. What bothered him more than this problem youngster or his scratches, anyway, was the spectacle of his new eighty-dollar black Resistol cowboy hat lying flattened in the middle of the street. "Where do you live?"

"Here. The city."

"But where?"

"Wherever I am standing." Volos was studying the blood drying on his fingers. "Sticky," he remarked.

"Oh, for Chrissake." Texas grabbed him not very gently by the elbow and urged him across the street, into the Palace Hotel and through its shabby lobby, glaring at the desk attendant to shut her up about blood on the carpet—as if winos enough haven't puked on the carpet before now, lady. In the elevator Volos stood stiffly, hanging on to the walls, looking pale under his tea-colored skin. Shaken up more than Texas had thought. Texas led him down the third-floor hall, unlocked his room, flicked the light switch, and towed the kid in. Once released, Volos stood looking around him blankly.

"Sit," Texas ordered, pulling a straight chair out from the wall. He handed Volos a wad of Kleenex, pulled down his beat-up old Stetson from the closet shelf—he felt naked without a western hat, wore one indoors as well as out except when Wyoma made him take it off for bed or company. Jammed the ratty white thing on his head, went out into the hallway again, and got ice from the machine, strongly feeling the small-hour blues weighing him down. It was his own mistake, to have stayed up this late. Whenever night found him awake at this hour he felt utterly alone, orphaned, like the last person on earth, even with Wyoma gently snoring at his side. And now there wasn't even Wyoma. Just a jerk with wings bleeding in his room. Why the hell did he have to go and get involved? He held the cold ice bucket to his hot face. Back in the room, he found Volos seated with tissues in hand but his hands slack in his lap.

"You want to apply pressure." Obviously the kid was rowing with one oar out of the water. Accepting this, Texas found it easier to have patience. "Here." He set the ice down, took Volos's hand, and guided it. "Do like I tell you. Press." Only one nostril was bleeding, and it looked ready to stop soon anyway. Texas went into the bathroom, found a washcloth and wrapped it around some ice. Damn cheap hotel had given him only one washcloth. He sopped the corner of a towel and went back to Volos, dabbing at the kid's mouth with the wet terrycloth, clearing away blood to assess the damage. As he expected, the kid's lips were swelling. He had taken some hard hits. "You got to stop leading with your chin, Volos," Texas said. He handed him the cold pack, showing him how to hold it to his mouth and jaw.

"Leading with my chin?"

Texas did not answer. He was staring. The kid's wings (lifted somewhat to fit over the back of the chair, then trailing to the floor) had turned a pale opalescent blue.

"How do you do that?" Texas blurted.

"The chin thing?"

Texas reached out to switch on the table lamp for better light and rounded Volos to have a look at him from the back. The mechanism that operated the wings was not immediately apparent to him, but he saw broken feathers and, halfway up the left wing, a sizable stain of bright red. Blood.

"Where'd that come from?" Jesus, had the kid been knifed in the back? Was he walking around with a stab wound? Panicked, Texas grabbed the wing, lifted it to look—

The blood came from the wing itself. Texas knew that as soon as he touched it. Through his hand like an electric charge clear to his heart he felt an odd hot rush, a wordless recognition, and at the same time he heard Volos gasp with pain. Ice clattered to the floor. Volos had dropped it. The kid had gone ashen, and his hands clutched at the air as if it could support him. He looked ready to topple out of the chair. Texas caught him with an arm around the shoulders.

"I'm sorry!" he exclaimed. "I'm sorry, I didn't mean to hurt you!"

Volos trembled. "So this is pain," he whispered, panting.

"I'm god-awful sorry. I thought—" Texas gave up. To hell with what he had thought. To hell with anything he had ever thought, especially about this kid. Not a would-be wearing Styrofoam wings for a stunt, this one. Not a half-wit. More like a—a visitant, an innocent, an—God, he couldn't say it or think it.

"Maybe it is not that you hurt me so much." With effort Volos straightened enough to look at him. "Maybe it is that I am not accustomed to pain."

"I hurt you," Texas said.

Volos went on, intent, not seeming to hear him. "Bodily pain, I mean. The other sort I know well, but this—it fights me, it takes over. It makes me feel thin as water."

His eyes were of the same moonstone blue as his wings, startlingly light in his earth-tan face, very direct in their gaze, almost vehement. His hair, brown-black and chopped without finesse halfway down his neck, hung in stringy dark curls over his forehead, making him look boyish, vulnerable. It was peculiar hair. Texas had thought at first that it was twisted in very thin braids or dreadlocks, that the kid had some black blood in him, what with his dusky skin and full lips—but now he saw that Volos's hair had the texture of pinfeathers.

Still holding him by the shoulders, Texas whispered, "You're real."

Volos stopped shaking, grew still, and smiled. It was a small smile, but enough to show Texas that women could be blinded by this one. "Thanks," the tall young hunk said, as he had not thanked Texas for saving his ass on the street. "You do not think I have utterly failed?"

"Better get some ice on the wing," Texas mumbled.

He helped Volos to the bed. Only the one double bed in the room. Made you know what kept these sleazy hotels going. He had Volos lie face down, noticed that the hurt wing smeared blood on the bedspread. He would end up paying for the damn thing. Terrific. Maybe they charged double for supernatural blood. Maybe with any sort of luck he would get sane soon and figure out what sort of hallucinogen he had been breathing in along with the yellow, oily-smelling L.A. air. Texas brought his last towel and dumped all the ice he had into it for a cold pack. "Hold on, now," he told Volos before he touched the injury.

"That was not as bad as before," Volos said after a while.

"I tried to take it easy this time." Texas sat beside him on the bed, holding the ice pack so that it sandwiched the wounded wing. A few streets away a car security system screamed. Through the wall Texas could hear athletic lovemaking going on in the next room. Why did that not bother him? A while back he had been feeling blue as a Hank Williams ballad, but now ... It had to be four in the morning, and he hadn't slept, yet he did not feel tired. More than that—he did not feel wretched. When had he last faced the night without feeling desolate? He could not remember. But just being around this crazy kid, he felt as if someone had finally taken in his orphaned soul off hell's cold doorstep.

Christ. He had to be tired. He was getting sappy.

"What is your name?" Volos asked him.

"Bob McCardle. But you can call me Texas."

One hollow cheek against the bedspread, Volos nodded. "Yes. Texas. I like your boots." They were new, top-of-the-line Laredos with real snake-leather feet and tooled-cowskin shafts, so he better like them. "You are a son of the state Texas?"

McCardle laughed. "Son, I ain't a son of much of anybody."

After a while he judged that the wing was numbed. Easing the ice away, he warned Volos to hang on, then parted the feathers and looked. It was not a large wound, but it was ugly, not a clean cut but more of a tear. Some sort of laceration. Had to hurt like a sonuvabitch. No way to wrap it up that he could figure, either. He put the ice back on it.

"Shit, kid. Your wing's a mess. What the devil am I supposed to do with it?"

"Let it rot and fall off. The other one too. I do not want them."

Texas said, "Talk sense, Volos. Is there someplace I can take you?"

Volos shook his head against the pillow.

"You got a home address?"

"No."

"Somebody I can phone? Anyplace you're supposed to be? Anybody worrying about you?"

Faint smile of bruised lips told Texas McCardle: Here was someone far more alone in the world than he.

His cop training made him try one more time. "Know anybody who could help? Any more like you around here?"

"No. Just me."

"Damn. Well, at least it's stopped bleeding." In a few hours, once the stores were open, he would go get the kid some kind of antiseptic.

The ice had melted into slop. Texas took the wet towel away. "You want something for the pain?"

"It will not work to just let it hurt and die?"

He was serious. Texas sputtered twice before he barked at him, "Kid, that wing's part of you! Jesus Christ. Sit up there so I can give you some aspirin."

Volos spilled water down his chin, swallowed the pills with difficulty, lay down again afterward. "To lie down feels better," he said in a tone of mild surprise.

"Go to sleep if you can."

"How do I do that?"

"Holy . . ." Texas felt his patience slipping. "Just lie there! Close your eyes."

Volos obeyed. Texas turned off the light, found his way around the bed in the dim cityglow of the window, settled in the room's beat-up excuse for an armchair, and tried not to think. He slumped down, propping his long legs on the edge of the bed. Dozed for a while. Became aware that he was effortlessly sleeping, which surprised him so much that he jolted awake. Took a look at his foundling. Volos lay still, but his eyes were open and staring.

"Close your eyes," Texas reminded him.

"I am not asleep, then?"

"Not hardly. Not if you're talking to me."

"People do not tell each other things when they are sleeping?"

"Not that I know of."

Volos said, "Perhaps she is awake, then. She might be awake in the night?"

Texas looked at him. Under the shadow of his brows the kid's eyes seemed large and darker than he remembered. Keeping his voice quiet, he asked, "What are you talking about?"

Volos said, "It is not the usual thing? A young woman far to the east, a silent woman, I can hear her. A shrouded woman. She is thinking, or dreaming, and sending me the dreams."

chapter
two

Far to the east: sitting at a kitchen table in a stolid brick house in Jenkins, Pennsylvania. It was morning there. The dishes were done, the beds made, the laundry churning in its rectilinear machine. Her husband was out of the house, the children playing in the fenced back yard. Therefore she could get out her Bic pen and tablet paper, sit down a minute and write the words.

> *This angel's taking a fall*
> *This angel's full of the devil*

Red rhythms pulsed in her head. Physically, as if addicted, she craved rock and roll, the music that made her feel like dancing naked. But even with the children outside she did not dare to bring out the garage-sale radio she kept hidden in the bottom of her Kotex box. She would have to wait until they were napping. Little Michael and Gabe were only two and three years old. They might need her suddenly, and then someone might hear, however faintly, the low, ominous thudding of drums and bass guitar. Or the boys themselves would hear and blab. One way or another, word would get around fast if people found out that Angie Bradley, Reverend Crawshaw's daughter, listened to the devil's music.

You say die and go to Heaven
Gonna be an angel
But this angel ain't no dead person Daddy
This angel is alive
I WANT TO LIVE

A knock at the back door.

The sound acted on Angie like a cattle prod. With panicky haste she thrust tablet and pen into a kitchen drawer. Her hands checked her hair (innocent of perm, smoothed back and decently bunned beneath a stiff white prayer bonnet) and her skirt (long enough to cover her knees). She knew without looking who was knocking: her father. No one else dropped by without phoning first.

And there, sure enough, on her scrubbed back stoop he stood, Reverend Daniel Ephraim Crawshaw in his crow-black suit and bow tie, his head thrust forward slightly for a close look at her. "I been praying for you, daughter," he told her.

"Good." She stood back to invite him in.

"I pray for you constantly, Angela." He passed through the hallway and stepped into the front room, looking around. Light poured in through entirely too many tall windows. The house was as old as her father, precisely square, two-story, built with fearsome symmetry. Across each of its four faces windows marched wherever there was not a door. In the wintertime, coldness poured in like daylight. Angie and Ennis hoped to build a place of their own someday, something cozier, more private, but meanwhile Angela spent most of her life housecleaning. There was no place out of that fierce light to hide anything, nowhere to let the dirt lie. Yet her father glowered around at her hand-me-down furniture as if expecting to find a murdered body. "Have you read your Bible this morning?" he demanded.

"Of course."

He scrutinized her, and she withstood the scrutiny impassively, keeping her face as smooth and disciplined as her hair. When she was a little girl, he could always see a fib in her face, and as many times as he had caught her he had told her that liars went to hell. A few times since she had grown to adulthood, thinking back, she had understood: He cared about her in his scowling way, he wanted her to be safe, saved. It was the passion of his life, telling people what to do, how to behave, how to be saved.

But most of the time she was not able to understand whether he loved her, or why she loved him, and she had learned to tell her lies to him and not be caught. She had to. Short of leaving outright, the only way for her to keep some selfhood was to sneak and lie her way around his myriad rules. She knew it was no use trying to talk with him. Reverend Crawshaw perceived himself as a soldier of God at war with the devil, and he took no prisoners. He was not the sort of person who would ever in eternity agree to disagree.

He peered. He had narrow eyes that could crinkle and be kind, blast him, when he was pleased with her. She was his only child.

"Have you had your coffee?" she asked.

He unbent enough to come into her kitchen, to sit and chat. No he did not want coffee. Angela could give him a glass of water if she liked. None of that bug juice for him, just plain water. Angie put ice cubes in it, which did not displease him. Rather than drinking it down, he sipped. The children ran in and latched onto their grandpa like Velcro, and he chuckled, letting them climb his black-trousered legs. He held them in his lap, bounced them on his bony knees as Angie watched with a bittersweet taste in her silent mouth. (A virtuous woman kept her head covered and was silent.) She loved how he loved her children. Watching

the three of them warmed her heart. But—why was
he so much less stern with her sons than she remembered his being with her? Was it because he was their
grandfather? Or was it because they were boys and
she was a daughter of Eve? Female, prone to evil, and
therefore less loved?

At the door, as he left, he said to her in a low voice,
"Angela, are you in danger of sin?"

"No, Father." *It's the truth,* she thought, keeping
the dark amusement in her mind from reaching her
mouth to make her smile. She was way past just being
in danger. She was clear in, thoroughly damned, a
fallen woman, a diver in the murky forbidden depths.
Not only did she listen to rock music, but at night its
lewd rhythms pulsed in her mind. Often it seemed to
her that she was most alive when she slept, when in
her dreams she moved her body in barbaric ways and
sang, sang, sang . . . In daylight and in fact she could
not sing worth a nickel—a thousand church services
had shown her that. Her voice when she tried it was
reedy and insubstantial, like something in the wind.
But when she dreamed, she could sing like Elvis come
back from the dead in a woman's breasty hot-throated
body.

Just the night before, she had dreamed such a
dream, and now even as she faced her father with
bland eyes she wrote the words of the song in her
mind.

A grownup ain't a child who died
That kid's still kicking strong inside
Making rude noises
Spitting on the floor
Alive and wanting to live some more

Her father said softly to her, "Something is troubling you, Angela. Be careful. Satan is a seducer. Keep
your eyes turned toward God. Say your prayers."

"I do," she lied. "Every day."

"The ones I taught you."

"I do, Father!"

He wanted her to recite the petitions he had written when she was a child, the words he had put into her mouth. Reverend Daniel Crawshaw was like that. He preferred to be in charge. Felt safer that way. His church was entirely his own, unaffiliated with any denomination; he called it the Church of the Holy Virgin and ran it out of a former lingerie shop. His theology oscillated somewhere between sugar-scoop Brethren and total-immersion Baptist, but also threw off sparks of mystic Mariolatry. Under her feet Angela felt the relentless uplifting confines of the pedestal on which he had placed her.

"Call me and I will pray with you."

"Stop worrying," she told him. She kissed him on his flat cheek, sent him on his way, and waited patiently, like a rabbit flattened in the grass, until she felt sure he was gone. Once she considered it safe, she scrawled the next verse of her song, then took the half-finished thing and hid it under the old bedsheets at the back of the linen closet. Most of her efforts she flushed down the john like the dregs of Michael's diaper pail, but this one she would keep. It smoked in her, heady and illicit as brandy, while she took laundry downstairs and continued the exquisitely boring routine of her housework.

For an hour while the boys napped she listened to her radio, even though listening was sweet suffering because she had to keep the volume down and the music made her want to do just the opposite, made her feel wild to turn up the fizzy old thing and scandalize the neighbors, tuck a flower in her hair, walk in the rain, kiss a stranger, do *something*. Almost anything.

She had married straight out of high school, at age seventeen. She was only twenty.

Ennis, her husband, did not get home until late. In the summertime he worked until dark, hammering, fitting homes together, earnest, steady, sober. He

wanted to have his own construction company someday. Angie felt no doubt that he would, and that when
he did he would work even harder and leave her even
more alone.

" 'Lo, hon." He kissed her because he knew she
wanted it, but awkwardly, with closed lips. Kissing did
not come easily to Ennis. Even a Dagwood peck at
the door made him faintly blush.

"Have you eaten?"

"Nope. I worked straight through. I'm starved."

She had fed Gabe and Mikey their dinner but had
saved her own hunger for Ennis. She had given the
children their baths and their bedtime story, cuddling
them one in each arm in a hundred-year-old rocking
chair, their small heads and wispy hair warm against
her neck. After tucking them in amid kisses and hugs
and teddy bears, she had settled down to wait for her
husband, her belly growling. Now she put out the cold
chicken, the apple salad, the sweet-and-sour pepper
slaw.

Ennis sat at his place. Even across the kitchen she
could whiff the good workingman smell of him. If he
had touched her, even sweaty as he was, she would
not have pulled away ... He waited until she sat, then
steepled his big hands and said a quick grace. He was
a member of the Church of the Holy Virgin, of course,
like his parents before him. Angie had known him all
her life, and looking at him across the table she could
not say for certain whether he was handsome. Her
eyes were so accustomed to him that she could not
tell. And the loose-fitting Sears work pants and work
shirt he wore did not help her. But certainly he was
not ugly ... and she was no beauty, she reminded
herself, certainly not attractive in any fashionable
sense, sitting there in her round-collared blouse and
scrubbed face and bunned hair and prayer bonnet. She
had never been able to feel sure he desired her.

They ate in near-silence. Ennis asked how her day
had been, then looked at the mail. It was mostly junk,

but it served to occupy him. He had never been one to talk much. Even less during the past year, since his dad had died.

An hour later, after he had showered and Angie had done the dishes, she undressed in the bathroom, taking off with relief the prayer bonnet with its irksome hairpins—at least her father and his God did not require strings that tied under the chin! Taking off with supreme relief the chastely sheathing pantyhose, the white, constricting bra. She rubbed at the red marks under her breasts, the furrows on her shoulders, then shook her hair free of its bun, feeling it sway silkily against her bare back down to her waist. It had never been cut, not since she was a baby, and this one stricture of her father's do-it-yourself religion she did not mind. She loved her long, seal-brown hair and wished she could let it swing down her back all the time, instead of for just a few minutes in the evening.

She put on her nightgown but did not plait her hair in its customary bedtime braids. All day, even more so than usual, she had felt pregnant with desperation. She had decided to take a risk. In the bed Ennis was waiting, and though the nightgown was a cotton sack not fit to excite anyone, her unbound hair would serve as a signal for him.

In the glow of the hallway night-light she saw his face a moment before she closed the bedroom door. Yes, it was a nice enough face, a farm boy's face, quiet and rugged and tawny, like winter fields . . . Her closing the door also was a signal. For sleeping, they kept it open so she could hear if the children cried. But for the other thing they closed it.

She felt her way to the bed in the dark, found Ennis and kissed him. And yes, yes, this time it was going to be all right. She could tell. He wanted her.

But afterward, after he had gotten up and found his pajamas in the dark and put them on again, after he had washed himself and come back to bed and settled down to sleep, Angie (once more decently gowned) found that her unrest had increased rather than abated. What she and Ennis had done—it had felt good, it always did, but she wished it had lasted longer.... Want, want, there was always more to want, and what was the use of it? But still she wanted. She wished he would let her leave a light on, just a little light, so that she could see him. She had never seen him with his clothes off, not even on their wedding night, he was too shy, and she wanted to know what he looked like, she wanted to love him that way, she wanted him to look at her and love her—but he would not look at her, and he had never let her so much as see him without his shirt. Even swimming, even in the heat of summer, he wore a shirt. When she was dating him she had dreamed that once they were married Ennis would change, that he would unpin her hair and kiss her, unbutton her prim white blouse and pull off her bra and caress her breasts. She still dreamed that same dream. But it was not going to happen.

She said softly into the darkness, "Ennis. Don't you ever feel like you just want to bust loose?"

"From what?"

"Church and things."

He considered so long that she thought he had gone to sleep. When finally he rendered his opinion, it came without censure but also utterly without comprehension. "No. Don't think so. Nope."

She slept restlessly and had a dream so stark with longing that it made her moan and awoke her. In her sleep there had been a man, and it had not been Ennis—he was utterly not Ennis. She knew this to her bones, even though she had seen only his back, naked and powerful, his bare, broad, dun-colored shoulders, his scars—on his back were scars as if he had been wounded or tortured, sizable marks harshly pallid on the tan skin. She could not see his face. When would she see his face? His hair hung dark and long; he tossed his head, flinging the hair back from his eyes, and turned—and then in her dream she cried out and hid her eyes with her hands, for it was like meeting a god or an angel.

When she looked again, he stood on a rooftop, and above him in the sky galloped a white-hat cowboy on a mustang, and the man in the sky stared past her with dead-eyed indifference, but the half-naked god-man on the rooftop looked down at her intently. She saw his face, narrow and strong and beautiful and very strange, saw his deep eyes and dark brows and the dangerous sweetness of his mouth, lips dusky pink amid his dun skin. But when she awoke (softly panting, feeling the heat between her legs) she thought first of how he had stood spraddle-legged in blue jeans that bulged at the crotch. A—an erection? Or his— equipment, maybe it was bigger than other men's? And how the bloody blazes would she ever know? Fiercely she hated her life, she wanted to know these things, to see—she had never seen the penis of any man. Ennis would not let her even feel his with her hands. She knew it only as a blunt, springy thing entering her in the dark. But the man in her dream had looked as if . . .

Had he seen her?

It had been more than just a dream. As she became less aroused and more lucidly awake, she felt quite sure it had been much more. A holy visitation? Hardly. More like a—a demon standing over her as she lay vulnerable in dreams, an incubus. This night-time vision was satanic; the tingle between her thighs told her that. She should pray.

Instead, with a feeling of restless urgency, she left the bed where Ennis lay soundly sleeping, went with soft barefoot steps to the linen closet in the hallway, and pulled her pad of tablet paper out from its back corner. In the bathroom, behind a locked door, sitting on the hard toilet lid, she finished her song.

Yah yah yah yah yah
I WANT TO LIVE
Show this angel where they keep the cookies.
Yeah yeah yeah yeah yeah
I WANT TO LIVE
Show me who to give my candy bar to.
Ow ow ow ow wow
I WANT TO LIVE
Show me how to get your trousers down
Show me what oh devil lover show me
Why please show me why
I want to live I WANT TO LIVE
Before I die.

She recopied the finished lyric and sat looking at it awhile. Tore her rough draft into tiny shreds and flushed it down the john. Waited to make sure she hadn't woken anyone. Then took her finished song, folded it in and in on itself and gave it back to the linen closet, to an envelope containing perhaps a dozen others she thought worth keeping. Worth hiding. And maybe the devil knew what she would ever do with them.

She seldom left the marriage bed, no matter how cramped and smothered she felt, no matter how much Ennis breathed in her face. It seemed to her that if she got up and prowled the dark, even within the confines of her own house, she would be somehow endangering the marital bond, betraying the wedding vows. Thoughts of a peril vague as the nighttime shadows always kept her lying still—but on this night other thoughts were stronger. For the first time ever at night she took her radio out of its hiding place and carried it softly down the stairs, down to the basement, where until nearly dawn she sat shivering in her nightgown on the chilly concrete steps and listening to the forbidden music, trying to draw in stations from farther and farther away, maybe even from California.

*   *   *

In a bar in the Boystown area of West Hollywood, fruit-flavored vodka at his fingertips, Mercedes Kell sat waiting for a long-expected annunciation and listening to a drunk claiming he had seen an angel.

The drunk was vehement. "Publicity stunt," the bartender tried to soothe him.

"Who the hell wants publicity at three in the morning? A warm squeeze is whatcha want at three in the morning. Doncha? Ain't that what you want?"

The bartender ignored the latter questions in favor of the first one. "Some wannabe, I mean, trying to get seen. Going around the hot spots."

"On Sunset?"

"Dorkhead," another drinker put in patronizingly, moving over next to him, "people with halos don't go to Sunset after dark. People in favor of safe sex don't go to Sunset after dark. What the hell would an angel be doing on Sunset?"

"Looking for a fifty-dollar fuck," Mercedes suggested down the length of the bar.

Three heads turned to look at him, but only the drunk who had sighted the angel seemed really to hear. "Don't talk like that!" The man, who was as young and thin and overbred as Mercedes himself, started to flush and moisten at the eyes. "He was beautiful, you hear what I'm saying? Beautiful."

"Sure. Nice buns, huh?"

"It wasn't like that!"

The little slut looked ready to attack. The man sitting next to him placed a hand on his arm, and the bartender said gently, "Hey, buddy, don't go getting yourself upset. It ain't worth it. If it was an angel, why would he be walking? He had big wings, why didn't he fly?"

"Come on, chill out," said the other drinker. "Hey, what're you having? I'll buy you one."

Mercedes got up and headed toward the ladies' room, where he used the john lid to inhale a line of low-grade cocaine. He doubted the ladies' was ever used for much else. Women never came into this place, not even dykes. They knew they weren't welcome.

When Mercedes came back, the drunk had capitulated. "Okay, okay," he was saying tearfully to the bar, "maybe it was just a nice ass in fake wings. Okay." The other barsitter had his arm around him, and the bartender stood by with his brow wrinkled like a spaniel's. Mercedes put his back to the three of them and watched the door, waiting, the way some people waited for their prince to come, though in his case he knew things were different. He was the prince. He awaited a disciple who would recognize him.

Mercedes's ambitions were simple and mystic: He wanted to be God. Translated into secular terms that meant being big, very big, in Hollywood, because he who is glorified in Hollywood is deified all over the world. He would be colossal, and it didn't much matter how, whether in movies, on TV, in music, maybe playing kickass guitar or fronting the ultimate band— Mercedes embraced all these possibilities, and knew one of them would open itself to him, because he believed in himself. It did not trouble him that his talents were mediocre. In fact he did not think in terms of talent at all. What was necessary, he knew, was to meet the right person, his own anointed John the Baptist, someone to prepare the way for him. Therefore he risked humiliation, going to exclusive parties where he was sometimes stopped at the door, careful to wear the right clothes, careful (if he got in) to look mildly amused at everything and appear ready to leave at any moment, careful to seem bored and interesting. So far only unimportant people had paid attention to him, but someday (to this article of faith he adhered with apostolic fervor) he would be a star.

More than a star. A sun. *The* sun. It would happen, Mercedes knew, because his motives were pure: To hell with fame and money; he wanted to be a media messiah. He wanted to found a religion of himself. He wanted to be worshiped.

From time to time there had been friends and lovers who seemed to like him for a while but did not take him seriously enough. They were not offering him devotion the way they were supposed to. A prophet hath no honor in his own country. And L.A. was, he knew, Mercedes Kell country. Back in Kickapoo, Illinois, where his parents had adored him until they found out he was gay, where he had always taken the lead in the school plays and everyone had known he was special, he had nevertheless felt like a stranger, as if he had happened there by mistake, stolen from some more distinguished cradle. But arriving in L.A., leaving behind forever his family and his lower-class given name, he had felt himself coming home. Yet so far nobody had made his apotheosis happen.

The inebriate who had seen the angel and the man who had bought him a drink were going out together. Mercedes watched, warming himself by imagining where they would go, what they would do and in what sequence. He thought of picking up someone himself, then dismissed the thought. Sometimes he settled for what he got. But most times, like tonight, he waited for Him, his own personal Voice Crying in the Wilderness, the One who never came.

He wished he had seen the angel.

He hadn't been writing much lately. Back in Kickapoo he had written all the time, songs, screenplays, and the stuff was good, he knew it was ... but out here it was hard, with the smell of jasmine in the air all summer long like some sexy after-shave hanging in a vast men's room. Mercedes belonged to the Guild, he knew how little good work got done or screened, he heard the other writers sighing about the state of the art. Where has the holy fire gone? they lamented. How long has it been since we experienced the angel's kiss?

Mercedes scorned them. Straight old farts, most of them. Angel's kiss, hell. If he had an angel ...

"Bring you another?" the bartender asked.

"Okay. Hey, Otto, whadaya think? Would you know an angel if you met one on the street?" Reversing, as he often did for modesty's sake, his actual thought: Would the angel know him?

The bartender laughed with no more than necessary politeness. "Sure. Wouldn't you?"

Mercedes said rather tangentially, "If I had an angel I would make him very happy."

The kiss. No chaste and worshipful meeting of lips for him. He craved the probe of the angel's tongue, and he would probe that hot mouth with his own. He was not afraid of being burned. Why should a star be afraid of fire? Or of air, wind, wings, or of falling? Fire, flight, fall, they were all ... desire, danger, he craved it all, the feathery caress of the wing, the body hot as flame, the searing conjunction somewhere amid the clouds ... How to bring off an angel, what there might be to work with, what to do and in what sequence he did not yet know, but it didn't matter much. He was good at these things. And what mattered more was what the angel could do for him.

chapter
three

Texas knew that buying Volos antiseptic would take miles of walking through this city all spread out like a buckwheat cake with only sin for sweetening. Not that he minded walking. But it surprised him how much he minded the flatness. It was still almost a physical shock to him, how there were no mountains, how Los Angeles kept him six thousand feet farther away from the sky than he was used to.

In the morning light the smog looked platinum, almost beautiful. But, like any other beauty, it was a betrayer. It would be bad today. Already he could feel it stinging his nose and throat.

L.A. was a place where the world's swankiest cars glided past and no one with any pride ever seemed to use the sidewalks at all. *Shows you what I am,* Texas thought, trudging along, his old dirty-white flattop Stetson pulled down over his eyes. It was this feeling of being nothing, of being less than dust in the world's wind, that would not let him rest at home. Yet it let him feel sourly at home in this urban hell. It was what had made him leave his wife and his Chevy truck behind and come here, to this mythic mecca of decadence, on a Greyhound bus, counting on the station to be in the sleaziest part of downtown. It was what made him wander the gray dangerous streets at three o'clock in the morning. Texas walked L.A. because he wanted to dive into darkness and come up again. He needed to descend to some nameless fundament, and survive it, and come home with some treasure pulled from its murky depths.

His father was just his excuse. There was no reason at all to think that the man was in L.A. He could be dead, or anywhere. All the time Bobby McCardle was growing up he had dreamed of becoming a detective and finding his father, but being a cop had showed him mostly that it was impossible to trace a man long gone. Over a period of years he had tried. No go. Any one of the junkies passed out in the alleys could be his father, and he would walk by without knowing.

And his father, supposing he knew it was happening, would not care. That was the hell of it.

So okay. Instead of his father the city had offered him a kid with wings. Even drunk or crazy, how many people ever got—

He had to be going crazy.

Feeling a need to relax and clear his head, Texas took his time finding a drugstore that suited him, one with a lunch counter where he got himself coffee and a greasy two-egg breakfast before he bought a spray can of antibiotic and a tube of ointment for Volos. At the cash register he counted his change twice, suffering mild disbelief. Everything in California was so godawful expensive, his money was going fast. That worried him a little, but not much. There were worse things in life than being without money.

He got back to the room late in the morning, half afraid that Volos would be gone and half hoping it would be that way so he could stop being crazy and just get on with normal misery. He had told the kid to stay put, and he had meant it, but finding the youngster gone sure would solve a lot of problems. Nevertheless, when he entered the room Texas felt a smile take charge of his face. The kid was still there, on his feet, leaning toward the window like a sapling toward sunlight.

His smile faded when Volos turned toward him. The youngster was staggering.

"So small!" Volos gestured wildly. "How can you humans live in rooms so small?" It was true that his wings, if he had spread them, would have touched the walls on either side. No wonder his eyes had gone wide as a spooked colt's and he sounded half-panicked. "I want to go out of here. But my legs seem not to work right."

His wing feathers had turned turgid brick-red again. His frightened eyes, Texas saw with a shock, were dark, hot brown, when only hours before, they had been cerulean blue—but if the wings changed colors, why not the eyes? What was more ominous was that the kid's tawny face looked flushed. Texas set down his paper bag, strode over, and reached up to check his forehead. He said, "Cripes. Volos, you're burning up with fever."

Suddenly Volos was calm, interested. "Is that what this shivery feeling is? Fever?"

"Yes. We got to get it down. Dammit." Texas mentally cursed himself for lingering over coffee, for staying away so long. Should have known somehow that Volos would need him. Wings had to be delicate things. That was what was causing the problem, infection in the wing. He didn't have to take a look, because he could see the swelling from where he stood.

"Out of those pants," he ordered.

He noted in passing that the kid wore no underwear. Have to get him some. Have to get a job at this rate, to pay for everything. He started the shower—no tub in this sorry excuse for a hotel, and the cracks in the bathroom tile were growing moss, but at least the damn shower worked. He adjusted the water temperature and hustled Volos in.

"Cold!" Volos exclaimed.

Actually it was tepid, almost warm. But the kid's skin was as hot and dry as the Mojave. "Got to cool you down," Texas explained, and he saw with a squeezing feeling in his heart that Volos took his word for it without question. For God's sake, the—he could not yet bring himself to say or think, *angel*—the stranger had to feel like humans were trying to kill him, yet he could trust.

Texas turned away and went to pester the desk clerk for more towels.

"Volos," he said later, after the kid was dried off and lying on the bed again, or rather in it, blanketed to the waist, with his wings drying atop the cover, "Volos, tell me something here. Seems like everything's new to you. Did you just—" How the hell was he going to say this? "Did you just get here?"

"I have been here several hours." Volos sounded peevish. Perhaps the fever was making him irritable. "I came prepared for most things. It is just that I have not had occasion to be beaten, or to be sick."

"Don't go making a habit of it."

Volos said more quietly, "I have been watching for a long time. This is very much the usual sort of thing, is it not? But I am finding that there is a large difference between watching and living. Being hurt does not seem usual now that I am within this body."

His voice softened on the last word, and Texas noticed how he moved a hand so that it touched his bruised lips and cheek, so that it lay where he could smell his own skin. Broken skin. The dirty old world sure knew how to welcome this one.

Texas asked, "Why did you come?"

Volos pushed himself up on his fists and scowled at Texas in sudden challenge. "Not to be anybody's bloody savior, that is for certain! Not to help or guard or deliver or ransom or redeem. If you have any good-angel thoughts of me, give them up."

Texas tried not to let the A-word shake him. A longtime cop knows how to keep cool and say sooth-

ing things in a good-ol'-boy drawl. "Son, I gave up
thinking about the prize in the Cracker Jack box a
long time ago. Lie down."

Volos obeyed but asked, "Why do you call me
son?"

"Because you seem young." Texas realized he was
being a fool. "My mistake. Sorry."

"Do not be sorry. I like it."

"I guess—my guess is you've been around a lot
longer than I have."

"Millennia." Volos spoke into the bedclothes, his
voice so low and muffled that McCardle could barely
hear it. "But only to watch, to listen, to wait. I have
never danced or been drunk or patted a dog or run
on the beach or slept with a lover."

Texas felt a hunch that the last item on the list was
foremost in Volos's mind, but he said only, "You were
not equipped for that sort of thing?"

"Made of ether and worth no more than a stray
breeze is in this world." Anger strengthened Volos's
voice. "To be bodiless is to be less than a gnat. Those
who swarm infinitely on the head of a pin, they are
expendable." Volos sighed and turned his head,
speaking quietly again. "The Supreme Being has been
known to destroy whole choirs if their chanting does
not please him. Thousands immolated at a glance."

"But I—you mean you could be killed?"

"Annihilated. Nullified. Snuffed out like candle
flame, leaving nothing behind. *Now* I can be killed."
Volos shrugged, grimacing from the pain that small
gesture caused him. "Being killed is better, I think."

Texas studied him, worried. Wyoma had always said
he fussed like a mother hen whenever a kid was sick,
but he felt like he really should get this one to a
doctor. That infected wing needed penicillin—but how
the hell was he going to get a doctor to treat Volos
and keep his mouth shut? He had been around bu-
reaucracy enough to know it ain't paranoia if it's true:
a phone call, and they would take the kid away, the

FBI or the CIA or Immigration or somebody. And then it would be a long time till Volos danced or got drunk or patted a dog or ran on a beach or, Lord help him, slept with a lover.

The shower had done some good. Or maybe it was the most recent dose of aspirin, Texas thought. Anyway, it looked to him as if the kid's temperature was down, because, among other things, Volos's wings had turned fawn-colored, his eyes a quiet blue. The wing wound had opened and was oozing, thanks to hot compresses and maybe dumb luck. Texas had sprayed it with antiseptic, and felt relieved that he would not have to lance it. Wasn't sure how in God's name he would explain things to Volos if he had to lance it.

"You hungry?" he asked after a while.

"How would that feel?"

McCardle blinked, steadied himself, tried to explain. "Sort of a pain in your gut."

"Everything hurts, Texas."

"I guess so. Well, you ought to eat. I'll go get you something. Soup?"

"I am not sure."

"Sandwich? Applesauce?"

"I mean I am not sure whether—I did not imagine myself to eat as a regular thing."

Texas stared. It occurred to him that he had not noticed Volos using the bathroom.

"I don't suppose you know how to crap."

"Not yet, no."

"Or—Cripes, I gave you water with those pills. You know how to pee?"

"I would not mind trying."

Texas put his hands to his head for a moment. After he had contained his exploding brain, he said, "You know what your penis is for, besides women? Sooner or later that water we put in you is going to want to come out there. When you feel a pressure or a burning down there, let me know. Don't wet the bed, you hear?"

"Yes, of course I hear you. They did not hurt my ears."

"I feel like I ought to get you some soup. Stay in bed. Get some rest."

"How do I do that?"

"Just lie there!"

Irritable. Okay, so he was tired, feeling his lack of sleep, and now he had to trek all the way to the goddamn drugstore again and fight the goddamn California crowds and stand in the goddamn lunch-hour line ... for a thermometer. Texas did so, mentally grousing. Everything was so freaking far apart in L.A., and the blanket of smog made the streets feel closed in, ovenlike even in modest heat. God, he hated this city in the daytime. To the deli next, for chicken soup. Knowing furiously all the slogging while that Volos would hardly eat any, that it was mostly to make him, Texas, feel better.

Back in the room, he found Volos not in bed but in the bathroom, mother naked, studying the fixtures. "I am a dunce," Volos said. "All the eons I watched, and what was the good of it? I did not pay attention as to how to do this water thing. Every century it changed, anyway."

"My guess is you paid more attention to other things. Okay, you wanna use this one." Texas flipped the john lid up, wishing he could get out of the habit of closing it now that he was on his own. Wyoma had trained him too well in—had it really been twenty-three years of marriage? God. He told Volos, "No big deal. Just aim and shoot."

"Pardon?"

Texas unzipped and demonstrated. "And you really oughta wash your hands afterward." Though he himself did not generally do so. This time, to set a good example, he did, then went to pull off his tight new boots, which were starting to hurt him after all the walking he had done. Then came back in and said, "Aaaa!"

"I seem to slip."

"Bad aim, all right."

"I am sorry."

"Don't worry about it." Texas started to kick a wet towel around. The hotel was going to love him. He remarked, "Place looks like I should've just stood you in the shower. Not as hard to hit that when you're inside it." He was so tired, his own weak joke sent him silly, making him hoot with laughter. Amusement bent him over and wet his cheeks. Volos laughed too. The kid did not know how to do it right at first, but he learned fast. He laughed hard, swayed on his feet and grabbed at a towel rack, which came off the wall in his hand. He nearly fell. Catching him with both arms, Texas stopped laughing within a breath—Christ, the kid's skin was burning hot again.

"No wonder you got bad aim!"

Volos's chest was heaving. "Laughing—hurts."

"Only because they bruised your ribs. Don't be afraid of laughing, son. Sometimes laughing is the only thing that will keep you going." Texas helped him to the bed. "Lie down before you fall down."

The day grew long. Volos broke the thermometer between his teeth, and Texas did not go for another one; he never did find out how high the kid's fever was. Twice more he stood him in the shower to cool him down. In between times he kept busy putting ice and ice water on the kid's wing, wrists, forehead. Most of the soup went to waste. Texas ate a little, but gave up trying to get any down Volos. The wound swelled tight and hard, and Texas switched treatment from cold towels to hot, worrying, never sure he was doing the right thing. Late in the day he opened the smallest blade of his penknife, held it in a match flame, explained to Volos as best he could what he had to do and why. Had the kid grab hold of something, wadded bed sheets around his mouth, then lanced the wound. The kid screamed once when Texas opened it, then lay shaking while he pressed out the pus and serum and sprayed on the stinging antiseptic. Afterward, he lay staring but unresponsive, and Texas did not know what to say to him.

"Go to sleep," he tried, and Volos closed his eyes with a quick obedience that wrenched at McCardle's heart. But his breathing came fast and restless.

The fever grew only worse. By evening Volos's wings, except for the region of the injury, had gone pale. Belly down on the bed, he lay with eyes closed, but their lids fluttered, his hands twitched and stirred, his head flounced from side to side. He panted, and sometimes a breath sounded like a soft moan or sometimes a whimper. Moving in a stupor of fatigue, Texas felt his heart aching like his sore feet and his overtaxed back. Somehow he had become vulnerable to the angel's wretchedness. Volos's thrashings and weary noises made him remember how it had been when his daughters were infants, when they had fought sleep, how the babies, newcomers to a terrifying mortality, had seemed unable to manage the transition to oblivion, unable to give in to the helplessness of sleep and dreams. Sometimes for as much as an hour Wyoma would stand by a crib patting and stroking a small back until the little stranger slept.

Volos's eyelids trembled like moths beating at a lamp, then opened. His pupils had dilated, and his stare looked hard and distant.

"So this is suffering," he mumbled. "Well, I hate it. And I hate you."

Coming over with yet another hot towel for the hurt wing, Texas protested, "Kid, you think I wanted to hurt you? I told you, it was something I had to do! You want poison in you?"

Volos did not respond. His gaze burned far past Texas. With vinegar in his voice he whispered, "Father. Up there on your throne. You call yourself a father? What father would do this to his children?"

Volos was not speaking to him. This was delirium. Feeling spooked, Texas took a steadying breath and gentled his voice. "Hey." Instead of applying the towel, he knelt down at the bedside, looked into eyes so wide and deep they seemed midnight black. "Volos. Just go to sleep, buddy."

Sky-dark eyes focused on him for a moment. "Texas."

"That's right."

"You're a human." It sounded like an accusation. "You don't understand how it is. You have a father, all you bloody humans have a father—" His voice, though weak, was rising in hysteria.

"Shhh." Texas laid a hand on Volos's shoulder to try to calm him. He could feel the kid quivering, thought wildly of calling an ambulance, knew suddenly that he could not do it, could not give up his adopted angel to public uproar and the care of strangers. Hell, he could manage, his mother and his Aunt Zora had pulled him through worse than this when he was a kid, back in those West Virginia days when everybody was stony broke, when nobody called a doctor; poor people didn't trust them. Volos would be okay.

Had to be.

Volos drew back from his hand, pushed himself up on shaking arms to glare. "A doting father. He yearns over you humans, even the worst of you, no matter what you do he loves you all as he has never—loved—" It was an old song, and anger was the flip side of heartache. Volos's voice broke. Texas reached over to toss the hot pillow aside, then sat on the bed where it had been and pulled the kid down into his arms. Volos yielded without seeming to be aware of him, once more looking past him, seeing someone else.

"You tyrant. You scourge. We were gods, and you made messenger boys of us."

Volos's wings had gone stormcloud black. They lifted from his back, the long, harsh feathers rustling as if fronting a high wind, and Texas stroked what he could reach of them, coaxing them down again. Tingling through his hand he felt the angel's pain and rage—they felt familiar to him, very similar to his own. He felt them give way to sadness, as his own sometimes did, and he leaned back against the bed's headboard, slipping down so that he cradled Volos's chest in his lap, so that he pillowed the angel's head on his belly, clear of his belt buckle. He steadied it there with one hand on the kid's coarse, dark hair. With the other he rubbed the back of the kid's neck. Kid, huh. Been around for millennia. But it didn't matter. Tonight Volos was a baby who needed to sleep.

"Father." Volos spoke wearily to the air. "You joker, I claim you father. I have flesh now. I can sin. Bad as any of them. Try loving me, why don't you?"

"Hey," said Texas softly, "you ain't the only one got father problems. Shut up and go to sleep, for Chrissake."

He slid his hand down to pat Volos's back. Between shoulder blades to which the wings attached with great bands of muscle was a hollow where tiny curled feathers grew, thinning to bare dun skin at the spine. For what might have been an hour Texas slumped and held Volos and hummed Willie Nelson to himself and stroked the feathers, the skin. He had become so tired that none of this seemed strange, and he watched with acceptance so deep it could only be called faith as the wings quieted and lightened, first to warm gray, later to sunset-pink, the color change starting at the base of the wings and flowing pinion by pinion to the tip, as if beginning at Volos's heart. And he watched with patience so deep it could only be called love as Volos's shoulders and wide chest quieted, breathing steadied, wings relaxed. Once folded over the angel's back so tightly they quivered, now they slackened so that they sprawled to either side. Texas's long legs, slanting off the bed and propped up on the shabby armchair, supported the injured one. The other lay open on the bed as Volos slept.

Texas continued to hold the angel until he was sure-and-then-some that he was sleeping. No hurry. Not going anywhere soon. Only when he ached in every cramped and assaulted bone did he ease the injured wing onto the armchair, get himself gently out from under Volos and stand up. Volos turned his head once, settling himself on the bed, then slept on. His face looked tawny but not flushed. The fever was down, and Texas felt so limp with relief and weariness that he stood gazing.

Sleep did not change Volos much. Even awake, the kid had that same look, profound and rapt and innocent, that glow of beauty most people attained only when they were making love.

Texas blinked at his own thoughts and got himself moving. Edged around the armchair to the foot of the bed and pulled the cover up to the kid's shoulders, careful, very careful not to touch the hurt wing. He hobbled to the john. So tired he'd maybe better stand himself in the shower, huh? But he managed. Left his belt loose. Lay down next to Volos on the bed, a narrow share of it, on top of the blankets, too done in to cover himself or care about the customary nighttime shouting and screaming on the street below.

He awoke late the next morning to find Volos's wing, the uninjured one, blanketing him so that he lay warm as a chick by a nesting dove.

chapter
four

My God, he's a wet dream.
Brett Decimo restrained herself from whispering the thought aloud. She liked power even more than she liked male tail, and she had not gotten where she was by showing a weakness for male beauty, however extravagant. It had taken toughness and risky timing to make her investment, Club Decimo, one of the Basin's hottest night spots. That, and a good ear for new talent on audition night.

He's a walking turn-on.

Guitar in hand, he was on his way to the stage, where like anyone else he would have just five minutes, no more, to impress her. No one ever had to know she was impressed already.

There he stood. Tall. Cloaked from his shoulders to his booted feet in heavy folds of black. Bare-chested, and Brett noticed how smooth his tawny skin was over his nicely defined pecs. Like a weight lifter or a fashion model he had depilated his chest, she surmised. Broad shoulders. He had fastened the cloak at his throat with some sort of heavy brass brooch, barbaric-looking, wonderfully strange, like his face—which was strong-boned, hollow-cheeked, yet with something sweet and shy in the expression of the eyes. And with lips worth fainting over. Full, sensitive lips—focusing on them made Brett start to think in practical terms. She wanted to kiss this man, and possess him, and after that she wanted to cash in on him. On the basis of his looks alone she smelled money in him. He seemed made to be worshiped.

"Name," she demanded crisply.

"Volos."

No last name. Gimmicky. She made a show of boredom as she wrote it down. "All right, play," she told him.

Volos did not obey her, but lifted his hands to his throat and swung off the cloak so that she saw the wings. They did not at first impress her. Just another gimmick. Being a jaded Angeleno, she sighed with exasperation.

"Play, please." With edge in her voice.

The first notes flew up plangent and strange, like tropical birds. A moment later, deeper chords had settled into a jungle drumbeat, a good beat, something people just had to dance to ... then Volos leaned into a riff, and Brett blinked: This guy was making a nothing-special Gibson sound like two guitars, like electric coitus. He was cookin', smokin', hot, hot, hot; he knew how to move, and then he started to sing and blue blazes he knew how to do that too. And his wings were going rainbow as the song heated up, band after band of luminous color, cyan, magenta, mauve, rippling down them from root to tip. It was, Brett had to admit, very well done. This guy was his own goddamn light show. A gimmick, all right, but it was a good one, it could make him a hot property. Briefly she wondered who he had gotten to make the wings for him, how they were wired and where the control mechanism was hidden.

She liked his sound: hard rock, almost heavy metal but not quite, with plenty of beat and groove and guitar thrash yet more songline to it than most contemporary music. Melodic—the guy had a fantastic voice—but full of passion, not slick or sticky. Familiar enough that people would like it. Different enough that they would remember it.

Somewhere far down the list of her priorities Brett listened to the words of Volos's song:

This angel's taking a fall
This angel's full of the devil
This angel ain't no dead person Daddy
This angel is alive
I WANT TO LIVE

Yah yah yah yah yah
I WANT TO LIVE
Show this angel where they keep the cookies
Yeah yeah yeah yeah yeah
I WANT TO LIVE
Show me who to give my heart to.
Ow ow ow ow wow
I WANT TO LIVE
Show me how to get you out of those clothes.
Show me what ... oh woman you know what.
Oh devil lover show me
Why please show me why
I want to live I WANT TO LIVE
Before I die.

"Okay," she told him when he was done. "Hang around, I want to talk with you."

Luckily it was not too far a step from lute to guitar. Volos had been considered a slow study as heavenly choristers go, but there had been eons for him to acquire skill with stringed instruments. Certainly he could play guitar. And sing—yes, he could sing. Even as a member of the lowest rank of the incorporeal host he had somewhat learned to sing. Any of the countless disembodied voices of the eight higher choirs could have shamed him, but Volos did not care, because they were far away and not even as material as air, whereas he was real, real, feet on the floor, swaying with a guitar as his dancing partner, raptured by the tremor and pulse of the instrument physical as a living body in his arms, the rush of his voice in his throat, the thrust of his diaphragm, the bright-pink ache of his lungs. It was for this that he had come. Even more than for fucking it was for this that he had come: to solo, to sing with his fundament in his voice.

To be human was to sing, Volos believed. Singing, he would be human, he would be accepted, he would be understood. Perhaps even loved.

There is a relentless dues-paying logic to the rockstardom process: Start in the clubs, auditioning on talent night, maybe if you're any good catch the manager's interest, maybe get called to fill in for somebody who doesn't show. Then in the fullness of time maybe open for somebody bigger than you, go on tour to the small venues, learning like an apprentice whore how to sell yourself, learning how to handle yourself onstage when the crowds get ugly. Build a repertoire of songs and moves. Maybe if you're lucky, find a good booking agent or a pushy manager. Make a tape, take it around, hope it gets heard, hope somehow you catch fire, hope somebody puts out the word that you're hot and a recording studio hears it. Do this for a while, maybe five years, maybe ten, until finally, somehow, the break comes and you're the one headlining and you're a star. Usually it happens, if it happens at all, just about when the wrinkles start taking over your pretty face and all the eyes turn to somebody younger, wide-eyed and sweet-throated and new. This is show biz. Stars rise slowly, fall like stones.

Brett had managed a few talents in her time and watched them fizzle. If she could find a way to beat the system, she had sometimes thought, if she could sign on a really promising adolescent hunk (her enthusiasm was only for attractive male singers) and find him a shortcut to stardom so he got there while he was still young and gorgeous and could manage to stay aloft for a while, she would make a fortune.

Those wings were a shortcut if she had ever seen one. They were very lifelike. She had never run across anything like them.

And the guy wearing them—

If she had any sense she would make him her client rather than her lover. But just this once, she decided, she was not going to be sensible. This one time she was going to break the rules. Make him both.

He was standing in the doorway, waiting for her, getting in everybody's way and seemingly quite unaware of it. With his black cloak on again, he loomed, and unlike many tall men he did not slouch or make a show of awkwardness to diminish his tallness. But neither did he seem to menace. A homeboy loitering on the street corner needs self-consciousness in order to menace. Volos had none. Lounging, blocking traffic, he occupied space as thoughtlessly as a tree.

"Volos," Brett summoned, brushing past him.

He followed her. She loved the way he walked, with forward impetus like that of a raked street rod, with graceful booted vehemence. She led him out of the empty music hall and into the main barroom, the night-spot attraction she had built out of chrome and shadows, neon and mirrors. Selecting a table, she watched Volos struggle with his wings and cloak as he sat with her.

"Why don't you take those wings off now," she told him.

"No, I cannot." There was something faintly foreign in the way he spoke. That accent pleased her, because it took a low-pitched, vibrant, very sexy voice and made it even better, made it exotic, distinctive. But she was not pleased that he had not done what she had said concerning his wings.

"They'll just get in the way," she said.

"Because the rooms are so small," he agreed. "Yes, it is a nuisance."

Something in his voice distanced him from her and made her wonder if he and she were speaking the same language. The cloak was perhaps meant for concealment, but it drew stares. Brett heard a woman passing by say something about the new extreme padded-shoulder look.

The bartender hovered at her elbow. "Shot of tequila with salt on the side," she told him.

Volos seemed not to know what to order at all. He had to be even younger than she thought. Good. She liked them young.

"Try a margarita," she suggested.

"That will be good, yes."

He sounded questioning. Men, they were all the same. Like children. Had to be managed. While the drinks were coming Brett tried to make arrangements with Volos. She wanted him to open for the Friday night act she had already booked for Club Decimo, wanted to see what sort of repertoire he had, how he handled a crowd, whether the audience liked him. But it was difficult to talk with the strobes rapid-firing and the dance-floor music vibrating their bones.

She jolted her mouth with a fistful of salt, followed up with her tequila. "Something wrong with your drink?" she shouted at Volos when she could speak. He had not touched it.

"Wrong?"

She teased, "I'm going to think you don't like me."

"Like you?"

"Just drink the booze," she said.

He raised his salt-rimmed glass and downed his drink all at once, choking on it a little. Watching him, Brett felt surprise and warm anticipation—he had done just as he had been told. She could get things started sooner than she had thought. There was no need to play games with this boy. No more plying with liquor would be necessary. No seduction. No subtlety.

"Come on," she ordered Volos when he set down the empty glass, and he followed her obediently out of the place, like a large dog. It was just as well that they could leave. He would have been an embarrassment on the crowded dance floor, with those tacky wings—he could barely get through the door. Brett led him to her candy-apple-red Corvette, and instead of sitting beside her he perched atop the seat back.

"It is a nice thing you have a convertible," he remarked. Because of the wings, she intuited. He would not have been able to fit into her car at all with the top up.

She demanded, "Can't you take those damn things off?"

"No."

Why was he so stubborn about this one thing? She was annoyed, but not enough to make her stop wanting him. Driving home with him, even though his booted feet were marring her upholstery, she felt so turned on at the thought of him that she could barely talk or look at him. He was exquisite.

Over the eons Volos had often watched humans in coitus. How many angels can crowd onto the head of a pin, and how many can hover in any given bedroom? But that had been in his ethereal time. Then, his interest had been that of a bodiless voyeur. It was different now, feeling the demands of his own warm, rousing flesh. He felt no special attraction to Brett just because she was blond and thin—he had seen many generations of mortal beauty, and this bumpy-fronted modern type, all ribs and erectile breasts, appealed to him no more than the seallike sleekness of the Venus de Milo might, or a soulful Renaissance courtesan made mostly of dark eyes and a sweet face. But he went with Brett. How could he not go with Brett? His body was clamoring.

Once in her apartment he took off his cloak. He

had found it advisable to wear the thing over his wings in public places—but this was not a public place. *Not quite,* Volos thought, dropping the garment to her pussywillow-gray carpet, standing in her living room and looking around at black tables and white chairs, at pink calla lily lamps in front of beveled-glass mirrors. "Deco," he remarked to show that he kept track of human transience, "very Art Deco." Hearing his own voice he knew at once that he should have kept silent. The words had slopped, and his torso felt watery and warm. What she had given him, that drink, whatever it was, that margarita, it had made itself a oneness with the ebb and flow of his blood, it had gone straight to his body. The mirrored walls were sea deep, the lamps pink phosphorescent kelp swaying in the room's dim private currents, in the sex-scented wash of the world. *Drunk,* Volos thought, *so this is drunk.* He did not dislike it.

Brett had taken off some of her clothes, and suddenly he was seeing her, really seeing her with the attention he usually reserved for himself. Pale, moonlike curves above satin and lace—her breasts. Yes, he wanted to touch them. . . . Why had she not taken off her shoes? Was she not going to do this thing with him after all? Surely . . . yes. Volos understood that the absurd heeled shoes worn by modern women were designed to increase their sexual appeal. He had heard this, but now for the first time he comprehended. To his bones he comprehended. His whole body saw how her tiptoe stance made her breasts tilt toward him, her back arch, her hips swing as she stepped nearer. Moreover, the shoes were of functional use, giving her the height she needed as she kissed him.

She is kissing me—

Lips, she was moving her lips against his lips, and sweet demons of hell, he had seen this thing done how many times yet never known how lips could tickle like feathertouch and tingle like fire and how the effect was not limited to mouth; he felt it lifting his hands to the curve of her back, felt it quicken the tempo of his breathing, felt it amplify his shoulders, his chest, his buttocks. His body, responding to hers. Lips moving in response. Tongue moving in response.

So this is a kiss ...

It startled his heart, it filled him, it ran like electric shock straight from his mouth to his groin. He felt her nipples against him, heads up beneath thin cloth. He felt—himself, that important forbidden part of himself, hot and rebellious and ecstatic, straining against the zipper of his Levi's. The feeling and the realization excited him so that he broke the kiss and blurted aloud, "It's—all right!"

"You like, baby?" she murmured against his face.

"My God, yes!"

Desire, it burned like fire, she rocked her hips against him and pleasure tore him like pain, he wanted to scream.... Hard-on, big dick, crotch rocket, trouser snake—the well-researched expressions skidded across his mind. He wanted to sing them, all of them, every word he knew for penis, cock, phallus, willy, wedding tackle, boner, dong, tool. He felt heat in his wings and knew they had to be flashing like neon in Vegas. He wanted to shout an announcement, he wanted to dance, and most of all he wanted to get out of his pants and into her.

"Soon?" he whispered. "Please."

"Now be good." She backed off; she was a tease. Smiling into his eyes, lifting both arms so that her breasts swelled above her camisole, she traced the top line of his shoulders with her fingertips. Said, "Just you wait." Said, "We've got all night. Take off those Hollywood wings first."

"I can't."

"They'll get in the way, baby."

"I can't! They're part of me." How could she look straight at him and not see? Yet she did. Most people did. There was something in humans that could not face the truth. So far only Texas knew him truly.

"Hey, it's them or me, lover." Lightly Brett tugged at his left shoulder, urging him to turn his back; he resisted her. "Come on. I'll help you. How do you get them off?" She reached past his neck to find the Velcro, the clasp, the catch, and found the crisp overlapping smoothness of his covert feathers instead. For just a moment she lightly touched before she jerked her hand away as if something had stung her.

She backed away, off balance, teetering on her high heels, her face spooked, yet uncertain. How could she be frightened without comprehending what it was she feared? Yet she managed it. Humans had always managed these seemingly impossible contradictions. It was quite possible, apparently, for this woman to decide about him without even trying to understand. Watching her, Volos felt all his desire sag into despair, the fire in him turn to a smoldering anger.

She said, "I think maybe I'm too tired tonight after all."

"Of course."

"Maybe some other time."

"It is of no importance." He said this as a matter of ontological truth, though his body, and therefore his mortal being, did not believe it. He picked up his cloak, fastened it on. It would protect him from some of the gawking, some of the foolish questions to which people never believed the answers.

Seemingly out of nowhere Brett said, "It's just as well not to be intimate if we have to work together. You'll be seeing a lot of me, Volos. I'm going to make you a star." She told him this with the utter certainty of one who has looked destiny in the eye and touched its wide wings.

Yet she had said none of this before. Volos was bemused. "You are what?"

"I am going to make you big, Volos. Very, very big."

"Big," Volos said. "Yes." For a small while—all too small—she had already done so. He felt the sticky place bigness had left inside his jeans. A few moments later, out on the street, he stepped into an alley and unzipped and used his fingers to smell it.

All smells were new to him. His first bodily memory of this world was that of the smell of the ocean in the air, salty as his sweat. Since then he had smelled oleander and McDonald's, vagrants and Brett's perfume, sun-baked concrete and a wet poodle and the tar pits at La Brea and the reek of perm outside a beauty salon. All smells were exciting to him—but this one, the fetor of his own sexual arousal, raised his neck hairs and shivered down his spine, so brutal was it and so much unlike anything he had ever experienced.

Dawn air in the city smelled like petroleum, Texas noticed. He discovered this because he hadn't slept, had given up on sleep and was sitting in his open window, stony lonesome, watching the rockers head home for their lofts pale as if they never saw daylight, wondering what Volos was doing and trying to write a letter to Wyoma: "Dear Wyoma,

Sorry I haven't written. It's been a strange week, and not the way you're thinking."

He was working himself up to tell her about Volos, but how the hell was he supposed to do that? He couldn't. There was no way on earth she was ever going to understand. When when was the last time he had looked at her and seen understanding? He couldn't remember. That attempt got crumpled into a ball and tossed. He tried again: "Dear Wyoma,

Please notice the new address. I am staying at the Y near the bus station and am looking for some kind of job."

He tossed that one as well. Too much like a business letter. It was not as if he were writing her to conduct business or out of a sense of duty. The truth was he really wanted to connect with her. But God, he felt farther from her than miles could tell.

Dear Wy,

I have not cheated on you or gone drinking or gambled or made a fool of myself much of anyhow since I've been here except that I wasted money on a new hat and boots. The hat got ruined already and the boots are scuffed. You are probably wondering what the hell I am doing here then and so am I. All I can say is it feels like I am looking for something. Maybe my mind which it appears I have lost. I think I better stick it out awhile longer and see. Please note new address.

Bob

McCardle really couldn't figure out why he didn't just give it up and go home. Unless it had something to do with Volos.

He hadn't seen the kid for almost a week. Volos had been welcome to stay in the hotel room with him awhile, and he had told the youngster so. But as soon as he felt better, the day after the fever broke, Volos began to pace and sweat. The angel couldn't stand the feeling of being boxed in.

"I came here to live, Texas! Not to sit within walls."

"Just stay a couple days longer till I get a chance to show you how not to get hurt!" Really, Texas knew, a person could spend a lifetime trying to show a kid that, and not succeed. Every parent knew that. "Where you going to live if you go? And what on?"

"Pardon?"

"How are you gonna earn your living?"

It took maybe five minutes of confused conversation before Volos caught on to the human concept of making a living, of exchanging money for shelter and food. Then Texas did not at first comprehend what the kid tried to explain to him, that these concepts did not apply to him.

"I did not imagine myself to eat or sleep."

"Kid, you got to eat and you got to have a place to sleep, or you die!"

"I will die, yes, but not of those things."

"What the hell you think you are, an exception to the rules?"

"Yes, that is right. I thought it out. A lifetime will seem very short to me, you see. I did not want to spend it on those things."

Only because he had nursed the stranger for three days and had seen how hunger did not affect him was Texas able to understand. "You mean—for you, food is fugging *optional?*"

"Yes."

Texas had been badgering Volos to eat, buying him soups, bread, sliced turkey, fresh fruit, then urging the stuff down him. "Jesus," he said, his first thought a petty one—he could have been saving his money.

"But pleasant," Volos added.

"Oh. Well, in that case." Texas let it go, spurring his thoughts onward. "There's still gotta be some things you need. Clothes. You can't wear that same pair of jeans all your life. Bus fare."

"A guitar," Volos said.

"Right." It did not surprise Texas that Volos intended to be a singer. That last night in the hotel he had heard the music of a strange dark angel. Unsleeping, Volos had sung softly to the shadows, and in Texas each note had turned to a bright-colored, yearning dream, making a bittersweet ache stay with him into daylight. It was with him as he spoke, softening his eyes but sharpening his voice.

"So you need to buy a guitar. They don't come free. What d'you plan to use for money?"

And Volos did not respond to his tone, not even with lifted eyebrows, but merely reached into a jeans pocket and pulled out a flower of solid gold.

So that the kid would not get hassled or cheated, McCardle was the one who went out and pawned the thing. On the way back to the hotel he had an idea and stopped at some of L.A.'s secondhand stores, which were well stocked by California-style upward mobility and by the movie industry. Without too much trouble Texas found what he was looking for: a cloak. When he got to the room he made the kid put it on before he let him leave.

And handed over the money. He did not keep any for himself, and probably wouldn't have done so even if the kid had thought to offer him any, which he did not. Volos thanked him, but not, Texas sensed, with any real comprehension of how much Texas had invested in him. But that was all right, if Volos didn't realize about the money and about the rest of it, the investment that was not money. It was part of a kid's job to be thoughtless, to take a lot for granted.

So there went Volos. Typical kid.

Texas had stood watching him walk out into the city of angels. Had looked down from the window until he was gone. Had remembered the sound of an angel's voice in the night, and remembering, had known he would never forget, maybe not even when he was dead.

That was what was keeping him in L.A. all right, and he might as well admit it: Volos. The kid might need him for something sometime.

Dawn heated into day. The smell in the air took on substance, became visible, called itself smog. Texas added a line to Wyoma's letter: "P.S. Wy, I did get into one fight, which is how the hat got ruined."

There had been no chance for him to show Volos how to punch, how not to lead with his chin. He tried not to think of the kid as hurt. Instead, he imagined him singing out there in the city somewhere, on a rooftop maybe, watching sunrise light up a thousand billboards. No rented room, no apartment, no condo for that one. He could be in Watts, La Habra, Van

Nuys, Chinatown, wandering anywhere from the harbor to the hills. No sleep, few possessions. Texas envisioned Volos showering in a fountain. Conversing with a wino. Touching a hooker with his wings.

Okay, maybe hurt. Somewhere in this huge city. Texas felt a cold wind of fear start to blow through his mind. He had to get up out of his chair, go find him. Unless he did, he might never see the kid again—

His door opened, and Volos came in.

"Kid!" With surprise and a jab of dismay Texas discovered who needed who. He felt his eyes prickle with relief. Volos was all right—and, what was more, Volos had come to him. He wanted to hug this six-foot-six child, this winged stranger.

Volos was not looking at him, but glaring around the room instead. "It is all closed in, like a trap," he said, appalled. "It is tiny. Even smaller than the other. How can you stand it?"

The angel's lack of greeting gave Texas's eyes and smile a chance to right themselves. "Didn't your mama ever teach you no manners, boy?" he teased.

"Pardon?" Volos looked at him blankly.

The kid didn't understand teasing. Come to think of it, Volos didn't seem to understand joking in general. If they had a sense of humor in heaven, it must have been different than the human sort. "Never mind," Texas told him. "You want to go outside to talk?"

"No. I will be all right in here for a little while." Sighing, Volos flipped off his cloak and sat on the bed, his wings half-lifted so that they rested on it behind him, trailing from his shoulders like a sky-blue bridal train.

"How's the wing?"

"Good."

As Texas could see, it was healing nicely. A few bone-white feathers showed amid the cerulean blue, the ones that had been broken in the fight. If color meant life in Volos's wings, then those feathers had died, but Texas had not wanted to give up on them. He had spent most of an afternoon finding the right glue and mending them, overruling Volos, who had wanted to pluck them out and throw them away.

Texas said, "So what's new? What have you been doing?"

"I have had an erection."

"A first?"

Volos nodded. "Yes. It felt very good."

"Congratulations."

"Thank you."

"So what's the matter?" Texas could see something was troubling the kid. He looked tired, and physically, Texas now knew, Volos did not get tired. His wings were blue, which meant Volos was blue as well.

The youngster sighed. He said, "I am never satisfied. I wanted more. I thought I was going to do some fucking."

"You found somebody to help you with that?"

"Yes. But it did not happen."

"Why not?"

"She wanted to take my wings off."

"Oh."

"Then it all went wrong. Texas ..." Volos looked down. "I am trying to understand. That first day, when you touched my wings, did something happen to you?"

McCardle found that his mouth had gone dry. He tried not to show it as he said, "I felt something, yeah."

"Did it hurt?"

"Sort of. No, not exactly. Not then." Someday, he had a hunch, he would hurt plenty because of this youngster. So what else was new? Life hurt.

"What, then? What did it feel like?"

"I really don't remember, kid." That was a whopper. Texas shook his head at himself and stood up. "C'mon. Let's go take a walk. I got to mail a letter."

"Texas." Volos did not move. "Please. I have to know."

McCardle stood looking at him a moment, took the one necessary step and laid a hand softly on sleek feathers. It was not that his memory needed help. He would remember the rush of that first touch of an angel's wing when he was in his grave, probably. But the words to describe what he had felt were hard to find.

"Texas?"

He said in a voice gone only slightly husky, "You make me feel young."

"Young?"

"Never say die. Hero riding into the sunset. Love forever. That sort of thing."

"Love," Volos murmured, his tone puzzled. No reaction to the word other than bemusement, Texas noted. Okay, so he had spilled his guts and the kid barely blinked, okay. He should be used to putting himself on the line for people who took it for granted. He was a cop, and a father.

He lifted his hand, stepped back.

"But with those others," Volos said, "on the street that first night, it was hate. They wanted to kill me."

"That's a goddamn fact. Nothing I can do about that, kid." Texas sat down again, looking at Volos.

"And the woman tonight—she never saw me truly, yet she seemed afraid of me."

"Kid—I don't know what to tell you."

"I think I see, though." Volos talked quietly to his long, skilled hands, rubbing at the guitar-string calluses on his fingertips. "The wings manifest. Or magnify. They take everything and make it—more. You are a good man, and—and touching me only made you better."

"Whoa," Texas protested. "I'm no saint." Since he was away from Wyoma, he had the *Hustler* magazines under the bed to prove it.

"Of course not. A saint is a dead person. You are alive."

"I mean, it's not that simple." Texas had known a contract murderer who wept at weddings, a sadistic child abuser who wrote award-winning poetry, a rapist who was the sole and loving support of his aged father. "People aren't like that, just plain good or bad."

"Tell that to the ruler of heaven and hell."

Texas heard something very bitter in Volos's voice, and stared at him for a considerable moment before he said, "Tell me something. You should know." His voice had gone very soft. "Does God really send people to hell?"

"How can I tell?" The angel's eyes flashed up, dark, startling, their color an angry purple. "What you call heaven was hell to me."

Texas flinched from the look in those eyes, tried to think of something calming to say. No time. Volos talked on, his words a stormwind, rising.

"Eternity is a very long time to sing in a choir, Texas. Think of it. Eons and eons of circling the Throne, chanting 'Gloria, Gloria, Gloria'—"

"I always heard heaven is what you want it to be."

"For you humans, perhaps." Volos said "humans" with venom. "Not for us slaves. You children of God, you think being a servant of God is all basking in the Lordlight, immortal and sinless, but without free will ... To be without freedom is to be without a soul. Summoned here, summoned there, prayed to by generation after generation of mortal wretches, called upon, with no way to say no, with no self to hide in—and you think service to humankind is happiness, it makes us sweet, ladylike things—"

"I wouldn't say that," Texas remarked. "Not now that I know you."

"But you don't know. Or you don't like to remember. For every angel of mercy there is an angel of punishment. If you ever met Chayyliel—"

"Chayyliel?"

Volos's voice softened as he wearied of vehemence. "My choirmaster. The one who will be allowed to put on beast form in the end days, who will swallow the world in a single gulp. When we sang badly he punished us with whips of flame."

"Jesus."

"Yes, I remember Jesus. I knew him, a little. He was another one who obeyed and obeyed and obeyed."

Texas felt his head start pounding; he was a chopper churning through L.A. smog. He wished he hadn't started this. "I'm sorry," he mumbled.

"For what?"

"I don't know . . . for not knowing. I always thought heaven would be what you made it. Like life."

"No. It's all a sham and a trick and an almighty joke. These wings of mine, are they not laughable? Is it not amusing to see me struggle with them?" Now, speaking of his wings, Volos sounded brattish, though a moment before, speaking of Chayyliel, his voice had crackled with truth. "They get in the way of everything," he complained of his wings, nearly whining. "Movie seats. Bus rides. Shopping. Dancing. Fucking."

"Take it easy, big guy." Texas gladly abandoned theological research. "Fucking will happen. Bound to. Come on, let's walk. Your wings are going apeshit."

Texas got an envelope out and addressed and stamped it. Before he sealed his letter inside, though, he looked at it awhile, then added one more line:

"P.P.S. Wyoma, are you really pissed? I sure would like to hear from you. Please write."

chapter
five

It was not difficult for Mercedes to track down his angel, and no great sacrifice was required for him to come into the holy presence. All he had to do was pay the cover charge at the Club Decimo, where Volos was headlining.

On the other hand, there was a purgatory to be endured. The place was packed. Mercedes found himself standing in the back of the music hall, jammed disagreeably close to hetero males and their heavily scented dates.

"I hear they done it by surgical implant," a man with an orange mohawk was saying to his girlfriend. "Took condor wings, something like that, put them on him."

"That's stupid. They can't do that, not between different species."

"Sure they can. It's no weirder than the stuff Michael Jackson does to himself."

His girlfriend looked at him with utmost scorn. "Okay," she said. "Sure. So, say they did that. You telling me condor wings change colors?"

"Microcircuitry."

"Nah," a denim-jacketed man put in, an aging hippie with a gray ponytail. "It's all lights. Special effects. You know, like an illusionist."

The mohawk and his girlfriend both ignored the ponytail, for they were too involved with detesting each other. When they went home, Mercedes knew, they would fall into each other's arms, slobbering. The mohawk was young, hard, lean and mean in black leather, and the thought that he was going to let her female sloppiness touch his smooth male body disgusted Mercedes almost as much as the unidentified mammaries pressing into his back.

"Dumb," the girlfriend said.

"Well, what do you think they are, big mouth?"

"I think they're just plain light-up fake wings. The trouble with men is they always want to complicate things."

The woman was right in a way, Mercedes thought. It was all very simple: The wings were real. Volos was just what he appeared to be. Though his reasoning, founded in his mysticism, was inexpressible, Mercedes Kell felt not a doubt in the world that soon he would meet an angel. The thought caused him excitement but no nervousness, for angelic intervention on his behalf was no more than he needed and deserved.

"Me, I don't care about no wings, man," the ponytail announced to anyone who would listen. "What I say is, if he can't rock my ass, I'm gonna kick his."

This, Mercedes sensed, was the mood of the crowd overall. Volos had come out of nowhere, he had short-cut his way to the stage, and no true rock fan really likes a gimmick. There were a lot of people there; they had come to see a freak show, but some of them had brought things to throw. The unfortunate glam rock band that opened for Volos drew only boos. Then there was a long wait before the main act, letting the audience mutter and grow restless, not a good move—

The room lights went out.

Not down, but out, hushing the crowd, turning its

muttering to a whisper. In blackness like that of the chaos before creation Volos came onstage.

Then a single still, small light dawned, and the dawn had wings.

With his back to the congregation Volos stood, and the spotlight started just at his feathered shoulder blades and slowly spread, as slowly as the wings themselves were lifting and spreading to fill the small stage, shimmering, their color pulsing somewhere between crimson and electric-blue. Then Mercedes couldn't see, there were people craning their necks in front of him, it made him furious, he missed the turn and that first bone-quivering downbeat, but he felt the tremor of the crowd amid the seism of the music and knew he was standing heart-deep in rock-and-roll history. Whether he could see or not, he was a witness: There was revelation in the room.

He caught glimpses of Volos between the heads of annoyingly taller people. Even at this distance, the singer's face gave Mercedes hope for some sort of understanding between the two of them, for it was so beautiful as to be nearly androgynous. And that body—Volos was tall, strong, and he carried himself with a huge, half-naked joy. Except for the plain leather guitar strap across one shoulder the guy wore nothing above the waist, nothing at all. *If he were mine*, Mercedes thought, *I would dress him in gold armbands, gold chains, topaz pendants the size of his balls.* He shivered in anticipation, for he had heard all the legends of rock star prowess, of groupies laid in the dressing room, the bus, the hotel stairwell, of clusterfucking, of lingam worship, of erections sustained while being cast in plaster.

Volos looked as if he could do all those things. Yet, Mercedes thought, there was something vulnerable in the utter bareness of that exquisitely muscled, hairless chest.

"Great buns," he heard the woman behind him remark to her friend. "Great everything." Her voice yearned.

Not for you, Mercedes thought.

"He's a hunk," the friend, another woman, agreed. "And he sure does know how to swing his ass. Hey. He even knows how to sing."

Not for you. Swine, you think the world is going to give you pearls to eat?

Pigs, what were they thinking of? Of course Volos knew how to sing. What angel would not know how to sing? But if these barnyard animals had come to see a winged oddity and had instead witnessed the nascence of a star, it was because of something more. He was a profligate, a prodigal, a huge spender, this Volos. The faces in front of his stage were precious gold to him, and expensive. They were costing him everything he had, and he was giving it unstintingly.

LET ME IN
Tell me where they hid all the flowers
LET ME IN
Where they put the shrouded women
I'll pull those petals open to the stem
I'll probe those blossoms
With a hummingbird tongue
I'll bust wide open that golden cage
Tear down the walls of that holy bower
Let me in
LET ME IN
Let me in to that slavehouse of sin.

He sang songs of aggressive sex, songs of rage and rebellion and yearning and desire. It was an odd mix: no let's-dance songs, no love songs except a few covers of rock classics. But it worked for Volos. He did not seem to know how to handle himself between num-bers, how to talk and joke with his audience or his band, but despite his seriousness—or perhaps because of it—the rowdy crowd warmed to him. For two Dionysian hours the songs pumped hot, one after the other, and by the time he closed with "Before I Die" he had them standing on their chairs, swaying, chanting, with their hands upraised and reaching toward him.

After the encores, after Volos had gone off for good, the four members of the backup band stayed and jammed, seeming far more relaxed with each other than they had been with their lead singer. The crowd mostly either headed toward the bar and the dance floor or left. Timing his move for when Security's massive head was turned, Mercedes slipped backstage.

He found Volos in a dressing room not much larger than a broom closet. There were a chair and a sink and mirror and clothes tree in there, but Volos was using none of those things. He was merely standing between them, in the exact geometric center of the cramped space, looking stunned. Or too tired to move. Or lost, with nowhere to go. His wings hung dusky blue. Already Mercedes was beginning to be able to interpret the wing colors; he had seen them changing while Volos sang, going blood blazing red for passion or rage, sunrise shades for gladness, purple for poetry. Now they were, as the old song said, indigo. The gig was over and the singer had the blues. Volos had crashed.

"What is the matter?" Mercedes asked, to give the appearance of caring, to show that he understood. It was necessary that Volos should see that he, Mercedes, understood.

That eerily beautiful face turned, swerved rather, to look at him with eyes deep and distant as space. Volos did not answer.

Mercedes tried again. "You are far from home. The others are too stupid to perceive or believe, but I know. You are an angel."

Volos did not display the gratitude Mercedes expected. Instead he said hotly, "I do not like that word.

You Christians and Jews and Muslims think of angels only as messengers, servants, tattletales, and spies."

"But?" asked Mercedes softly.

"But to the Babylonians we were the genii. To the Hindus, the spirits of air. To the Persians, the mighty Kerubim. To the Greeks, the very gods themselves."

"You were feared," Mercedes said.

"We were powerful." Volos's gaze on him had focused, intent yet gentler than before. "Fear without understanding is useless . . . you at least try to understand. But you are not afraid."

Mercedes allowed himself a small shrug and a puckish smile. "He who was once powerful has fallen."

"It was not a matter of falling. I dove." Volos mirrored the shrug, the smile. He had been alone, at his own mercy, torn open like a road kill after his singing, and now there was someone with him, someone who returned him to himself, who understood him; Mercedes had counted on all this and saw it working. Already Volos's wings had lightened, passing through lavender toward the color of a dayspring sky. The angel asked him, "Who are you?"

"My name is Mercedes." It was not his given name, of course. But what Hollywood name is? And who was to say what was more real, the birth name or the stage one.

"That is a type of car." (*As if I don't know,* thought Mercedes.) "What are you doing here? What do you want?"

Mercedes said, "Everything."

Volos gazed, and Mercedes steadily met his gaze, certain without knowing why—or caring why—that the angel understood him utterly. He saw how Volos's eyes had lightened to copper brown. He saw the angel take a moment to think, to question, then physically ready himself, rustling his wings like a rousing hawk, gathering courage.

Volos said, "Touch my wing."

Mercedes did not hesitate. It would have happened

soon in any event; he wanted it to happen. But because he could see this was a serious moment to Volos, he held the angel's stare a moment longer and nodded before he stepped forward to lay his left hand on the shining feathers.

He felt a sort of jolt, deeply startling but not painful, and suddenly he was even hungrier and bolder than ever before, so much so that his ambitious appetite would not wait a moment longer. His mouth lurched toward Volos's. His right hand swung forward, found the part of this stranger that mainly interested him, felt it respond beneath the zipper, the denim.

"Aaah!"

He had taken Volos by surprise, but the angel's face had softened into the stupid look people get when they're making love, his gasp seemed made mostly of pleasure . . . and too bad if it was not. Mercedes could not wait, could not help himself. He went down on his knees, a suppliant at the shrine of Priapus, he opened Volos's fly rapidly but with trembling hands. No underwear, by God, and no padding in this rocker's crotch, just—Christ, everything he had heard was true. More. He had not guessed it would be the phallus of a savage, uncircumcised, dusky, long, so fearsomely exciting that even the familiar musky aroma seemed magnificently strange.

Only afterward did he notice, or rather remember, that the dark curls that grew around that superlative cock were tiny feathers, like a black eagle's down.

Since coming to this hot, rocking city Volos had seen many things that made him think of hard metal music. He had spent a night at the Watts Towers, watching the moon swim behind the filigree spires. He had seen skateboarders wash like surf through a parking lot, shouting their seagull cries. He had scanned the strange yellow L.A. sky, and then looked downward and watched the tar of the streets shine and bubble like sin in the midday heat. He had seen a stoned kid with his head out a car window gulping air like a dog. He had seen a garbageman unzip and send a stream of pungent urine into the back of his even more pungent truck. He had seen Mercedes naked.

Many of these things made him feel an erection coming, not just Mercedes naked.

But undeniably, none of them gave him such pleasure as Mercedes did. The apartment in West Hollywood, it was small and in a noisy neighborhood, but it had a waterbed, and mirrors. It was there that Mercedes had taken him the first time and taught him things that even in all his eons of watching he had never thought of.

This, then, was fucking. Mercedes had assured him it was so, and made him look in the mirror, and told him he was beautiful.

He could see that this was true. And Mercedes also was beautiful. He wore silk shirts unbuttoned halfway to his waist, showing his faintly furred chest. He had a still, smooth face, closed in on itself like a mysterious woman's face. He had a Mona Lisa smile. Dressed, he stood slender yet walked tall. Naked, he was small and lay waiting on the bed, a boy, a woman, a white bird of desire. Dreaming of him sometimes, Volos forgot to remember he was a man. His dreams of Mercedes grew out of womanhood, like those other dreams that came to him from far to the shrouded east.

God, he makes me feel like I'm having sex.
It was one of Angie's least admissible thoughts yet, and its sinfulness thrilled her almost as much as the new hit tune, the one she felt tingling in her like foreplay. Never had a song affected her so strongly. Amid its rock rhythms she heard little of the words, but they didn't matter. It was the singer's voice that went through her. Even on her ancient little radio, even with the volume turned as low as she had to keep it when the children were napping, the man sounded

supernatural—like the deejays said, like an angel in heat. His voice was a raptor, a bird of prey, ravening among drums and bass, rising on dark wings to—to somewhere sky-high and glassy pure, and amid throbbing guitar he held the pitch for perhaps seven heartbeats past impossible before he roughened it into a banshee scream and plunged, a diver, a suicide— Angie shivered and turned up the volume anxiously even though she risked waking the boys. The song was ending, and it had called to her; God, she didn't want it to end, and who was the singer? No one she had ever heard before, she felt sure of that. No one alive had ever had that cerulean range combined with such earthiness, so that in the voice she could hear both a god's chill, hawklike soaring and a man's body, strong and hot.

"Whoo-ee," the deejay declared, yammering over the final notes; she hated it when they did that! "A brand new talent, kids, and I bet we'll be hearing a lot more from him! That was—"

The doorbell buzzed, making Angie miss the name. And suddenly wildly, rebelliously angry, she left the radio on, volume and all, let it sit on her kitchen table while she went to see who had cut short her pleasure. Halfway across the living room she realized she had been neglecting to sweep the doorstep, and the thought redoubled her annoyance. Nobody but the mailman and the Avon lady used the front, anyway, and let them talk all they liked, about her untidiness, about her listening to forbidden music. She didn't care. She just didn't care what anybody said anymore.

Without even scouting through a window first she jerked open the door, and there stood her father, his brows gathering like thunder.

"Angela! A radio! A temptation of the devil!"

He sounded aghast, hurt and appalled as much as wroth. He was not a bad man, really. He just wanted what was best for her, goodness and a heavenly reward such as his own. Angie knew that in his harsh way he loved her, that if she gibbered and wept the storm would pass after a suitable penance and a public apology to the congregation. But she did not weep. Something had gone heavy and stubborn in her and refused any longer to pacify her father. If God Almighty himself had stood on her besmirched doorstep, she might have refused to pacify him.

Her father rebuked, "You might as well open your door and let Satan himself into your house, girl!"

"Well, for the matter of that," she snapped, "are you coming in or not?"

Storm broke. The Right Reverend Daniel Ephraim Crawshaw blew in like a gale. Door crashed shut behind him. Lightning crackled in his voice: "Repent! Down on your knees, young woman."

She remained standing, lumpen, stolid.

"On your *knees!* Or you'll burn in hell!"

"You've sent me to hell a thousand times. How often do you think I can go there? I'll only die once."

"Angela!" Her father's voice rose high, shrilling along with a tormented and lamenting guitar from her radio. "Put your faith in the mercy of God! He can save you from sin and death!"

"Oh, I see. You send me to hell, and God is supposed to save me. What does that make you?"

She had never spoken to him this way, so hardfaced, so coldly furious, and she saw it stagger him. He softened his voice. "Daughter," he said, "daughter." She should have felt touched, for he was giving in to her somewhat, and he never gave in so much as an inch, not to Mammon or the devil or anyone. But she did not in fact feel touched. She felt angrier. Why had he not spoken to her so gently years ago, and years since, when she wanted it?

"Daughter," he said softly, kindly, "you are possessed, in need of healing. Let us pray together. Let me lay my hands on you and ask God to take the devil away from you."

She shook her head vehemently and stepped back.

He stared at her a moment, then took six long-legged strides to her kitchen, picked up her baby-wailing radio, hurled it to the floor and smashed it like a cricket under one heavy black heel, silencing its tinny voice.

"You are a vandal," Angie told him. "You have destroyed my personal property. I should call the police." She had heard people described enraged people as "beside themselves" but had not understood the accuracy of the expression until now. Hearing herself with amazement, she felt sure the real Angie was cowering upstairs somewhere, listening through the floorboards and weeping with terror.

"Daughter, I have done it to save you." Listen to the man. He was pleading with her. Pleading! Her father! "Please. You must open your ears, you must hear me. Satan is a seducer, and so is his music. It smiles, it is provocative, suggestive, it beckons with honeyed words and a jungle beat. It stuns the mind and numbs the nervous system and leaves the body weak and exhausted, susceptible to the demons of obscene desire. It promises happiness and fun and joy, but it delivers only a ticket to hellfire. The only true joy is in the Lord. Angela, please. Read your Bible and pray. No more rock music."

It was, after all, more a sermonette than a plea. And Angela knew just how to respond, how she had always wanted to respond to such a homily. She shrugged, as if she had been practicing it for years she managed the cool, sexy shrug of a sophisticated woman, and she bared her teeth at him, giving him the smile she and her schoolmates used to give their teachers, the one that, giggling among themselves, they had called a "snake grin." She said, "On the other hand, I should thank you for breaking that so-called radio. I've been wanting to get myself a better one."

For a moment she thought he would strike her. She winced, though he had never struck her, and by the backwards logic of her family it would have been a victory for her if he had. It would have given her a weapon of guilt to use against him. But he did not strike. Instead, with windmilling gestures he slammed out.

The thunderclap of the door woke the boys, and Angie was glad. She kissed them and promised them a treat. Leaving plastic shards and metal parts scattered on the kitchen floor, she took her sons outside and put them in the heavy old Mercury Messenger wagon that used to be Ennis's. Along the cracked sidewalks she pulled them all the way to the McCrory's store, where she used her grocery money to buy them candy bars and herself an AM-FM cord-or-battery boogie box, two feet long and electric pink.

Afterward, days later when tears finally came, she wondered what had brought her father to the house that day and to the front door. She never found out. By then, things had gone too far for such questions. Much too far for turning back.

But for that first day of her rebellion she had no questions, no doubts, and she felt sublimely calm and quite happy. Once home, knowing she was late starting supper, she delayed the meal yet more by unpackaging her purchase, setting it up and turning it on and glorying in the volume and clarity of its tone. While she cooked she listened for the new song, the one her father had interrupted, the one she wanted to hear again and again. Ennis came home early and found her still waiting for it, so engrossed in her listening that she did not meet him at the door for her kiss. He scooped up Gabe and Mikey instead and stood looking at her.

"Mommy bought a radio!" Gabe informed him in heightened tones. The boys had capered around the radio for hours, delighted by the novelty of having music in the house.

"Yes, I see," Ennis said to the boys, and then to his wife, "Your father called me at work."

"My father can go to that place he's so fond of mentioning."

"Ange, don't talk like that." He set the boys down. "It's not like you."

"You don't know me."

"I know there's something wrong."

There was no thundering in Ennis, no radio smashing. He did not even attempt to turn the instrument of Satan off. In due time he ate his supper, had his shower, and helped put the boys to bed, and all the while the radio played its siren song, and from time to time Ennis said, "Angie?" Just her name, in a voice so floundering and perplexed and worried that she felt as if she had not two children but three, and the big one was pulling with sticky hands at her skirt. It was hard for her to conquer her irritation enough to hug him.

"Stop fussing, Ennis!"

"I ain't fussing at you."

That was the truth. There was no anger in him for her, only heavy foreboding, a sense of trouble building. There would be comeuppance. Playing the radio was capital-letter Wrong.

"What are you doing it for, Ange?"

She felt unable to explain in any way he could ever understand. Confound Ennis, he was all patience and obedience. Was there a self-willed bone in his whole bashful body? His goodness made her furious. She pushed him away with her fists and screamed at him, "I hate it all! Let me out of here! Out of this slavehouse!"

If she had showed him the slavehouse song, she thought later, if she had gone to her linen closet and gotten out her small-folded pieces of paper and let him read them, maybe he would have felt, if not her yearnings, at least her desperation:

LET ME OUT
I am a hidden flower

LET ME OUT
I am a shrouded prisoner
Come sweet devil open my petals
Come bee-sting angel probe this blossom
Break open this seraglio
Tear down the walls of this holy jail
Let me out
LET ME OUT
Let me out of this sacred slavehouse.

But she did not think to do that. And when at his usual time Ennis went to bed, she pulled the hairpins from her bun but stayed up, listening to her radio.

Her song, the one with the singer who made her shiver, came on around midnight, the witching hour. This time, with her new radio turned up in the still of the night, she heard the words:

This angel's full of the devil.
This angel ain't no dead person daddy
This angel is alive
Alive and looking for lovin'
I WANT TO LIVE

Angie stiffened, listening hard as the singer's voice skidded without effort up the heightening rhythms of the words—words she had written. Changed somewhat, it was true. But nevertheless, hers. Her own.

"What's going on?" she whispered.

A strange coincidence? No. Impossible. On the airwaves she had just heard her creation, her mind child, a piece of her soul written down on a page of tablet paper, her words. How could they have gotten from her to—

"Volos," the deejay told her. "The hot new kid from L.A., singing 'Before I Die.' And yes I've heard it's true, he does have wings. Don't ask me how, that's all I know, folks, so you people phoning in, give me a break, huh? Coming up next—"

Angie turned her radio off and sat fingering her lips, thinking not at all of her father and his wrath, quite a bit of the squares of paper hidden in the linen closet upstairs, but most of all of the singer who had somehow stolen her soul from her, and of how she had heard in his voice the warmth of his throat and tongue.

chapter
six

Texas had found himself a job at a dry-cleaning establishment, and it was there, in the steam-thick, chemical-scented hell of the back room, in the midst of machinery reminiscent of a medieval torture shop, that Volos one day came to see him. When the tall, black-cloaked figure walked in, all the poplin-clad Mexican women in the place clustered at the other end of the room, as if they were peasants in the presence of the executioner or chickens cowering in the shadow of a huge dark hawk.

Texas, however, merely nodded hello, unsurprised. Volos had been visiting him every few days to announce with equal delight his first live performance, his first recording session, his first ejaculation. Texas started laying bets with himself as to what was on the kid's mind this time.

He called to the boss that he was taking his break, lifted his Stetson from a hook near the door and led Volos into the more breathable air outside. It was early fall. The Santa Anas had dispersed the city's layer of smog, but also the aroma of jasmine. Now L.A. was dry and hot.

"How's it going, kid?"

"Good." They sat on a concrete retaining wall

spray-painted with graffiti: "Love Stinks," "Izzy Sucks Donkey Dick," "God is Dead." Volos fingered the varicolored lettering as he said, "They are starting to want to give me money."

Texas had thought Volos's manager was taking care of the money end of things for him. He exclaimed, "You mean Brett ain't given you some already?"

"A little. Under the table, she said. I saw no table. But now there are problems."

It was as Texas had bet himself, the kid wanted something, wanted advice or at least wanted to talk. Volos always wanted something whenever he came to him. That was all right, Texas guessed. What else was an old cowboy like him good for? Though he sometimes wondered: If other people had wings, if Texas had wings and Volos touched them, what would Volos feel? Anything? Was there anything in him to manifest, would anything ever change him at all? Or would he stay just the same, as if all he ever touched was himself?

Texas asked, as he was expected to ask, "What kind of problems?"

"There is a great deal of talk about a Social Security number and a birth certificate and a bank account."

"Ouch."

Volos swung his feet, kicking his booted heels against the wall and its spray paint, against an anarchy symbol done in runny orange. He said, "I would rather go on as I have been doing. But they say also that I will need a citizenship and a passport to go on tour. And this touring, it seems it is something I must do. Also, I have decided there are things I want, possessions, that require money."

"Possessions? You?" Texas teased. "Like what?"

The angel did not respond to his light tone. He replied soberly, "A Harley-Davidson motorcycle."

"A Hawg! You gonna be a Hell's Angel?"

This time Volos comprehended the joke, and smiled. "Am I not already?"

"Guess so."

Volos said, "Also, I want a convertible like Brett's. Only mine will have a better stereo, and be black. But you see, there it is again, the problem. In order to drive any of these things I need a license. And to get the license I need the certificate of having been born and all the rest of it."

"I see."

"Your world is nuts for licenses and papers, Texas."

"Don't sweat the cattle in the heat of the day. Just hold your horses." Texas was thinking. Like most cops, he felt little compunction about breaking the law if it seemed the thing to do at the time. There were laws, and then there was the right thing to do, and he had been around long enough to know the two were often not the same. Also, his state of limbo in L.A. made him feel ready to be reckless. What had he run away for except to be reckless? Though the risk he was contemplating was not about the law so much. More about giving away a secret part of himself.

He decided to do it. Said, "Volos. I had a son once, would have been about twenty years old now if he'd lived. You can use his birth certificate if you like."

Volos looked at him with blue eyes as blank as an infant's. "You had a son?"

"Only lived a couple days. Born in the hospital, so he got the birth certificate all right, but he died in his sleep the first night we took him home. Things were rocky for me and Wyoma, we didn't have no money, we was far from our families, they mostly weren't speaking to us—see, I was a McCardle, got a no-good for a father, and she was a Catholic when she should have been a Methodist—it's hard to explain." Texas frowned at the ground and his scuffed boots, trying. "They didn't mind us getting in trouble, but they didn't like us getting married. So we went away for a while. And then when the little guy died, we just moved on. It's not that we done anything wrong to the baby. But he was young, our hearts was broke, and if we buried him ourselves and didn't get no death certificate it was like he was still alive, see?"

"Yes."

Nobody else Texas knew would have said it so cleanly, the simple "Yes." He liked that in Volos, the kid's no-frills honesty. Being around Volos always did something good for him, even when it drove him crazy. He smiled, feeling the new warmth in his voice as he said, "So you can be him if you want."

"Be a dead person? But yes, I suppose it is the only way."

"Don't thank me," Texas hinted.

"Pardon?"

"Never mind." Texas didn't know why, but he damn near loved this guy. "Okay, then. I'll write Wyoma and tell her to send me the birth certificate. From now on you're him." Sliding off the wall, Texas stood on asphalt, making a small, awkward ceremony of saying the name. "You're Flaim Carson McCardle. 'Course you'll still want to call yourself Volos, but it'll be like a stage name."

Volos stood also and shook his hand. The angel seemed to understand that no small thing was happening. "Flaim," he said softly. "It is a beautiful name."

"I thought so. I chose it. I like that kind of name that's simple and means something."

"An old Greek once said that men are flames and the world is a fire. Always the same, yet always changing."

"He really said that?" Texas was astonished that someone else so long ago had thought the same things he thought, almost in the same words.

"Yes."

"That's what you are, then. A flame."

The two of them stood for a moment in understanding so close it was almost union, like the union of two flames wavering momentarily into one, before Texas spoiled it. It was so good he had to spoil it. So good it made him, like a child on Christmas, want more. Not content just to give and be any longer.

"Volos. I'm doing something for you, now I want you to do something for me. I want you to help me—" He fumbled it slightly. "Help me find my father."

"He is missing?"

"Been gone a long time now."

"But how can I find him if you cannot?"

"I thought—you being what you are—or were— there might be a way."

Volos said, "No."

"No, there's not a way?"

"No, I will not do it."

That blunt honesty again. This time Texas did not appreciate it at all.

You bastard. "Why not?"

"I came here to be human, Texas."

"And I saved your goddamn human ass," Texas said between his teeth, keeping his voice down almost to a whisper, "and took you in, and busted my butt nursing you, and spent damn near my last dime on you— and now there's something you could do for me—"

"Texas, I can't!" The kid was being human, all right. Sounded as human as Texas had ever heard him. Whining. Getting his own way, as usual. Something about Volos made Texas so panting mad-dog furious that his mother's Methodist strictures took automatic hold on him, keeping his voice low, controlled.

"You can't, or you won't?"

"Texas—"

"Never mind. Forget it." Texas came from a family that knew how to do these things, how to speak softly and turn a big knife of guilt. "I got to get back to work. Just forget I asked." Stalking into the back of Keller's Kleaners, into the hot, clanking hell where he spent his days, he did not glance at Volos to see him go.

That evening, though still angry fit to spit, he wrote the promised letter to Wyoma—because he had said he would do it, and also because it was a nearly sure-fire way of getting a reply out of her at last.

After he had sealed the letter he thought of Flaim, the baby he had seldom remembered for years, and of his two daughters, Starr and Merrilee, both already married. Even when he was home he had not seen as much of them as he would have liked. He missed them. Hell, he had been missing them already before he left them behind.

It was peculiar, the way he'd always been, feeling like a stranger in his own home place. Always turning his daydreaming to somewhere else. He'd never in his whole life realized how much he was *from* the hills he was born in. But now that he was far away, he knew: He was a mountaineer at heart, he came from West Virginia. The Indian legends said West Virginia was the spine of the world, the place where human beings were first created, and now Bob McCardle could believe it. He missed almost everything about the place: the hogbacks, and the trees—old people from his hills said West Virginia trees talked to God. He missed the Indian mounds. And he missed the way a man could look up at night and see the stars floating in the black sky big as water lilies.

He missed the mountains, and the one all his memories gathered round. He missed Wyoma.

During those hot, dry Santa Ana days, Mercedes moved in air so electrically charged it seemed to crackle. He noticed sunsets, saw some that were worth weeping over—though he did not weep, he never wept, had not done so since the childhood day of his first time with his first love, a boy he had not seen since eighth grade. He was twenty-eight now, and in L.A., and beloved of Volos, and filled to the point of giddiness with a sense of his own godlike well-being. The ionized air, the light shows in the sky, and angel Volos himself, all were uniquely for him, Mercedes Kell. California was unzipping itself, opening its pene-

tralia to him. His career was on the climb. He would
yet be recognized as great.

Already through Volos he had met Brett Decimo.

Actually he had introduced himself. Volos had no
tact, no manners, and refused to play most of the
social-pecking-order games. But it was Volos who had
taken him to the private party at Club Decimo. No
way would he have gotten in otherwise. Some of the
most powerful people in the industry were there. And
having intuited that he was Volos's lover, Brett Decimo shook his hand with evident interest.

"Tell me," she asked him, "does he do *everything*
with his wings on?"

"Absolutely," Mercedes responded with his most
charming and mysterious smile. He had adopted Volos's unspoken policy of neither affirming nor denying
the presence and provenance of the angel's wings, but
letting people function on the basis of their assump-
tions that those interesting appendages were clever
fakes. Mercedes, believing himself to be the only individual on earth sufficiently anointed by the hand of
God to know Volos, was to be painfully disillusioned
and bitterly jealous some time later, when he finally
met Texas.

"Well," Brett Decimo remarked to him, "I've met
guys who wear their glasses to bed. But not *my* bed."
She showed Mercedes her very straight, very white
teeth. "You know he likes women too?"

"Of course." Mercedes had accepted even before
he met Volos, as part of his theology of power, that
the angel would be a bisexual. This ability, this virility,
was potency. Mercedes had always found real men,
the ones who could get it up with women as well as
with him, far more attractive and exciting than the
faggoty-looking ones the world identified as homosex-
uals. His ideal, like Plato's, was the androgyne. He
believed that this ideal had been Yahweh's as well, as
he created Adam from clay. It had all been there in
Adam. That business with the rib afterward, the divi-

sion of humans into two sexes, had been an after-thought, a tragic mistake, the beginning of the Fall and of alienation.

The blond and important woman to whom he was speaking, however, would not understand or care about much of this. She would want to keep things light. Mercedes quipped at her, "Like Mae West said, why cut yourself off from half the population?"

Brett's Hollywood smile softened, became fairly genuine. One of the odd ironies of Mercedes's life, as he knew well, was that women seemed to like him even though he did not particularly like them. With Brett, however, things were different. She could like him if she wanted to, because it was not his exposed chest or his bared homosexuality that attracted her to him—it was his ambition. Bright, hard, and calculating, their eyes met, and they recognized each other across the gender barrier: They were two of a kind. They understood each other. Brett nodded.

"Come have a drink with me next time you're free," she invited before she turned away to greet other guests.

It was all he could have asked for at the moment—though, of course, soon enough he would ask for more. And so would she. That was what it was all about, this matter of grabbing a comet by the tail and hanging on. When Volos burned to ash, suicided in the sunblaze of his own fame, she would be there, as high in the Hollywood hotshot rankings as Volos's wings could lift her. And so would Mercedes be there, right by her side.

At the buffet he got himself a mushroom stuffed with snow crab and langostino, which he ate with slow delectation. He licked bits of seafood from his lips with the supple tip of his tongue. Caught Volos's eye across the room, and Volos smiled at him, the sunrise smile of a child in love. Mercedes was doing just what he had said he would: He was making an angel very happy.

Yes, things were going very well for Mercedes Kell. And it was not just a matter of riding to immortality on Volos's broad shoulders. The sexual liaison gratified him too. Everything about Volos turned him on, even the touch of his wings. Especially the quivering touch of his wings on naked skin. . . . Quite simply, Volos was the best lover he had ever experienced. He would have wonderful memories to savor when he moved on to even more pleasurable things.

Lying in the satin-and-polyester nest of the waterbed with his lover the night after his quarrel with Texas, Volos found himself for the first time indifferent to the skilled touch of Mercy's lips and hands. Out of sync with the rhythms of lovemaking, bone-weary, unaroused, he felt his chest heave and knew that he had done something deeply wrong.

What of it? Had he not become flesh in order to do wrong?

Yet he had thought it would be a matter of free choice, of a head-tossing defiance, and now he was finding—it had not been that way at all, he had wanted to do the favor for Texas, he would have done it if . . . if . . . Was this the almighty joke, was this what it meant to be human—to want to do right, yet do wrong and wrong and wrong?

He struggled out of the bed's clinging touch. "Some other time," he told Mercedes.

His lover was not angry. "Thinking of a song?"

"Something like that, yes." Which was a lie, and another way in which he did evil, by letting it be thought that he wrote his own songs. He had told himself he did not care that it was wrong. That night, though, he knew he did care, and he knew why. He wanted to do this thing, he wanted to create music out of himself the way he made sperm. Being unable to write songs was like being impotent. There were things about himself he had failed to fully imagine. He lacked memories, he lacked a childhood, he lacked parents and a hometown to love and hate. He could not have been Volos the rocker at all if it were not for the young woman somewhere far to the east, whose name and provenance he did not know.

Some important aspect of him was missing.

He pulled on his jeans and his boots, kissed Mercedes, and went out in the night to wander the streets.

He loved the night. There was peace in it, and loneliness, and danger. The peril—that of ravaged people who roamed, as he did, in the night—the danger only made the peace more lovely, and the peace made danger's knife glint more bright.

Black-cloaked, black-jeaned, black-booted, he strode under the broad black shadow of a freeway overpass. There he could see nothing and thought at first that nothing could see him until he heard the pigeons murmuring from their roost somewhere above his head.

"Look at him. Humans don't know how to dress. He could put on anything he wants, and he's all one color, like a wretched crow."

"At least he has those nice shiny toenails. See? Like tin foil."

"Oooo, tacky. You have bad taste, Banana Beak."

"I like a little something different, White Ass. Trendy. Daring. New wave."

"Just what I should expect of a variant. Never trust a hen in speckled feathers."

"I like high fashion."

"Low class is what you mean."

There were, Volos decided, two of them. The female, she of the impugned beak, gave her soft utterances edge by means of that hard nasal protuberance. The male, he of the white rump-patch, had a bitchy charm that reminded Volos of Brett or Mercedes.

"I believe in classic style, myself," he cooed. "Ring necks and white breasts are for hens and comelatelies."

"As if any of us have a choice."

"All the same, I think a bird looks best in basic gray with a narrow band of black on the wingtips. Restrained and elegant, with just a touch of iridescence at the throat."

"And pink feet."

"Yes, of course, pink feet."

"And a white butt."

"You don't like my white butt?"

"I'll show you what you can do with your white butt."

Then he heard billing and cooing. They were a couple, all right. It was something of a mystery to Volos, how mortal couples could make love sound so much like war. Feeling his own solitude, yet intrigued, he listened until they grew aware that he was still there.

"That human has not moved," Banana Beak murmured to her mate. "Drop a juicy one on him."

"You drop one on him."

Before either of them could do so, he moved on. In and out of shadows he walked, sometimes watching a horned moon swimming in the thin clouds. Smelling the sea in the breeze. Keeping away from the places where the youths ganged, the ones with the hard fists and the salty yells. He did not want to deal with fists or knives. Texas had not yet showed him how to stop leading with his chin.

Texas.

The way the moon tugged at the tide his thoughts tugged at him until, around two in the morning, he risked the bad section of downtown and went up the narrow stairs to Texas's room in the Y, knowing he would wake McCardle out of sleep, knowing this was another wrong thing to do, and unable to help it.

For some reason, though, Texas was still up, sitting in the dark, fully dressed. He glanced at Volos as he entered, then looked away again, out the window.

"You are angry at me," Volos said to him. "That is what this hurtful feeling is in me. Your anger."

Texas did not move or speak.

"I want to at least try to explain. Listen. Are you listening?"

"Sure." Tonelessly.

"It is like this. To do what you ask—to find out about your father—I would have to pray. I would have to become obedient to the one on the Throne again. It would be necessary that I should get down on my knees before that tyrant and take back everything I ever said of him, and beg his forgiveness."

"Never mind, then," said Texas.

His voice sounded quiet, tired, nothing more. Not angry. Volos took two impulsive steps toward him and knelt on the bare floor almost close enough to touch him. His wings trailed, heart-red.

"You really do see? It is something that—I just cannot do it. He—He made a serving boy of me. Go do this for this human, go do that for that one. It was the humans he loved. I never want to do anything for a human again."

Texas turned his head suddenly to stare. Volos winced and looked down. "I keep forgetting," he muttered.

Texas said, "It doesn't matter."

"It matters to me that you must understand. He wounded me. Not really, for I was a bodiless thing, but—when I made myself this body I tried to imagine it with scars on the back. Because that is how I feel. Scarred."

"Bullshit, kid." Texas came out of his torpor suddenly, sat up, and glared. Volos heard anger now, but it was a different anger than before, hot and more hurting and mixed with something worse, some kind of despair. "Nasty choirmasters and hurt feelings just don't cut it compared to real abuse. I should know."

"I—"

"Shut up and listen. My daddy was a junkie. He must have had to put himself out to get hold of the stuff down where we lived, but he managed it. He was a drunk, too. Hit my mother, bruised her face, and she was the sweetest woman ever to marry a no-good rotten bum. The sonuvabitch left her when I was three, and I never saw him again. Except once." Texas turned to stare out the dark window again. His voice quieted, but it was not a good quietness. "I was ten years old, and I guess I let it be known to some of my friends what I thought of my father for leaving my mother that way. And it turned out he was living with some floozie in a smackhouse only a couple of towns away. He heard it from somebody, what I was saying about him. So he came to see me. Caught me on the road home from school. And he beat me."

"He *what*?"

"First he told me to look at him, look at what he was. Told me I ought to consider he had done me and Ma a favor by getting out of our lives. And then he beat me. Broke my arm, my nose, my collarbone, tore one ear half off. He beat me sick. Ma had to come find me and carry me home. I was in bed for a week."

Volos felt sick just hearing about it. Watching Texas' face as Texas told about it made him feel weak and queasy. He had never experienced how a kind man can hide a long shadow. He whispered, "Texas, please stop."

"I'm done."

"You wanted me to find this—this monster for you? In all hell's name, why?"

"So I could do him the way he done me." Texas faced Volos without a smile. "So I could beat the shit out of him and walk away and leave him laying on the ground, the way he done to me. All right?"

"No," Volos said, "not all right. Not for you, Texas."

"Why not?"

"You are—you are good."

"And you're not? Would you for Chrissake get up off the floor?"

Something dark in Texas' voice puzzled Volos. He

stayed where he was, on one knee. "You are still angry with me."

"No. No, I'm not. Honest to God, kid, I'm not. Get up, you asshole." Texas reached down and tugged at him. His hand was warm, and Volos submitted to its touch, standing up, then sitting on the bed.

"None of it matters anymore, anyways," Texas said.

Then for the first time Volos took a long enough glimpse outside self to realize that his friend's desperation might have nothing to do with him. He sat rigidly. He whispered, "What has happened?"

There was a considerable pause before Texas answered.

"I called Wyoma," he said at last. He gestured at the letter still lying on his windowsill. "I figured, why send that when I could spare a couple bucks and phone. Took a yen to hear her voice."

"She was not there?"

"Oh, she was there all right." Texas took a deep breath, or gave a sigh—it was hard to tell which in the darkened room. "But it looks like I'll have to get your birth certificate from the state, kid."

"She would not send it?"

"She told me to go to hell. Don't call her again. Don't write. And don't bother coming back."

Volos found that he could not speak, that there was nothing right to say, that pain tightened his chest and made it hard to talk anyway.

So this is what it is to feel for someone.

He wanted to do something, and all that seemed permissible was to lift one hand and lay it on Texas' shoulder.

"I'm glad you're here, kid," said Texas to the window's black glass. "I feel like I been walked on."

Never mind what was permissible. Volos reached over with both arms and hugged him, this man forty years old, more than halfway to the end of it all. A man in a cowboy hat—which fell off—and the sandy-haired head lay against Volos's collarbone, the sagging shoulders accepted his embrace, and the work-dried hands reached around him and under his wings to their warm, downy axillae, finding comfort.

chapter
seven

Angie became obsessed with this secret soulmate, this singer of the songs she had written and hidden, this Volos. It was not enough for her to listen to her radio through the October days in case the deejays might have something to say about him. She ventured to the drugstore and bought the shockingly secular magazines, full of bright, slick photographs and exclamation points, that interviewed him and showed his picture above boldface captions: **"Strange Rock Angel!"** and **"Oh, Sexy Volos!"**

INTERVIEWER: You wear wings. Many people say this is to show that you are a rock god, a divine being. Are they right?

VOLOS: Quite the contrary. I am a carnal being. If the wings show anything, it must be that I am flesh, I am half animal. A bird is an animal, is it not?

INTERVIEWER: I hadn't thought of it that way. But it makes sense. You know what the historians are saying, that never before has anyone sung with such presence, such physicality.

VOLOS: They might as well go ahead and say it, that I am horny as a meadowlark. Has no one noticed how it is with birds?

The magazines could be concealed, but Angie made no attempt to do so. She bought them openly and read them openly, and she did more: Taking the children with her, she caught a shuttle bus to that modern-day Babylon, the shopping mall, where for the first time in her life she deliberately watched a television screen, on which was playing again and again a video-tape of Volos singing his profane hit song, his bare shoulders working as he fingered the guitar slung at his hips.

That was the autumn of Volos, not only for her but for young people everywhere that rock and roll played. Taking her children out to walk in the warm Indian summer days that came like a drollery before the bitter Pennsylvania winter, she would hear his music in the smoke-blue air, winging to her through the flame-colored falling leaves. But she did not know the people who played his music in their sports cars and in their apartments with the windows open. There was no one she could tell about a strange thing that was often in her mind: that once, before she had known he existed, she had seen Volos in a vivid dream. He had stood on a rooftop and looked straight at her. His back had been scarred. He had no wings.

Those days she sighed often and wore certain pages of her magazines soft with looking at them. Even in a conventional family her behavior might have been considered eccentric, compulsive, cause for concern, but in her family and her church it was far more: It was perversion and blasphemy and devil-possession and sin. It was shocking, offensive, as frightening as if she had defected to Cuba.

The Sunday after he had smashed her radio, Reverend Daniel Ephraim Crawshaw preached his hour-long sermon on the evils of "ROCK and ROLL music! Even the name refers to a lewd physical act, brothers and sisters, and is derived from the oversexed barbarianism of the honky-tonks. This SO-CALLED music knows no language but the vocabulary of FILTH. It glorifies the lowest instinct of the BODY. Its gods are named OBSCENITY and VULGARITY and always have been. From the very first, ROCK MUSIC has promoted JUVENILE DELINQUENCY and sown the seeds of ATHEISM in America's youth." Afterward, he called on his daughter to make public confession of her wickedness before the congregation. Angela kept sullen silence, refusing. When he exhorted her to repent, she turned her back on him.

That night in the marriage bed Ennis did not immediately lapse into a laborer's exhausted sleep, as he would usually have done, but reached for her angry body and hugged it. He did not try to make love to her, but held her against his chest for close to an hour, until finally she relaxed and felt warm for the first time in days. "Ange," he kept whispering to her. "Ange, hon." Calling her back as if she had already left him.

"What?" she asked when she felt able to keep her voice as gentle as he was. Yes, all right, he clutched at her like a child. But she loved her children.

"What's happening to you, honey?"

"I'm fine. I'm not hurting anyone."

"You're—hurting yourself." He spoke with difficulty, and she began to feel loved, for he did not usually talk about such things; she had to be important to him, to make him talk this way. "You're—putting yourself in danger."

"Music makes me happy. What can be wrong with that?"

"If it—kills your soul. . . ."

"I don't feel dead inside. I did before, but not anymore. Stop worrying about me, Ennis. I'm not worried about myself."

"Worry about—the kids. . . ."

"Music makes them happy, too." It did. They liked what they heard on her radio. Sometimes the beat made them prance like a pair of young goats.

"It's bad for them. Ange, what are you trying to do?"

The question was half protest but also a real request for an explanation. And she wanted him to understand. But she herself understood only a little of what was happening to her.

She said, "Did you ever think maybe my father is wrong? Maybe there's nothing so bad about rock music?"

"But he's the pastor, Ange!" In Ennis's lexicon there were no words for disagreement with the minister of God.

She said nothing more, because already she had tacitly lied to him. She did not really believe that rock music was anything other than bad, wicked, depraved. Its very depravity made it her salvation. Its badness was what made her feel alive when she played it.

"Ange," Ennis said, "please stop."

Silence.

"For me. Please. Just stop. Go back to being the way you were."

He loved her, she knew now that he loved her, and he was asking her in the name of love to do something for him, and if she loved him she would do it, she would make the sacrifice. That was what women were for. It was beautiful, what women could do, what women could give and what they could give up. Love's name was womanhood.

He loved her. He loved—the obedient woman, meek in bonnet and bun . . .

She thrust her hands against his chest and tore herself out of his arms, flinging herself out of the bed, into the cold. "I'm not Christ," she told him in a shak-

ing voice. "I'm not going to crucify myself for you."
She left the room, going barefoot to the kitchen to
listen to her radio.

All that week her husband pleaded with her, until
to her ear his importunities colored themselves the
same murky purple as her father's fulminations. Sunday morning she told Ennis she was not going to
church. "You have to," he said. He believed this so
devoutly and so literally that he shouted at her. But
she had made up her mind: Short of physically forcing
her he was not going to get her there. They quarreled
until it was time to leave, when he gave her a long,
wretched look before he took Michael and Gabriel
and went without her.

Oddly, while they were gone and she had the house
to herself she listened not to the Weekly Top Forty
but to a radio evangelist. Her entire body ached, as if
she had been beaten.

Home for Sunday dinner, the children came in the
door waving construction-paper "Jesus Loves You"
sunbursts in their pawlike hands. Running up to her,
little Gabe sang, "Mommy, you're shunned! Grandpap
said so!"

She looked at Ennis, who would not meet her eyes.

With great, cheerful confidence, Gabe continued,
"Me'n Mikey don't got to do it, because we ain't saved
yet. But everybody that's saved got to shun you till
you repent."

"I see." She hugged him and little Michael, and
admired their Sunday School projects, then straightened and spoke directly to Ennis. "It's roast chicken
for dinner. Which would you rather have with it, wild
rice or Betty Crocker potatoes?"

He did not look at her or answer her.

"Ennis," she said, bleated rather, much as he had
been bleating "Ange" at her all week. He looked at
her then, a quick, heartsick glance, before he turned
away and went upstairs to take off his tie.

She gave him noodles and butter with dinner because she knew he did not like them. He ate them without a word. That afternoon she listened to rock music and looked at the pictures of Volos in her magazines, feeling more guilt and defiance than pleasure this time, for she knew her love of this stranger's face and body were what the Bible called lusting in her soul. This was a form of infidelity to Ennis. And she hoped he noticed it, she hoped it scorched his heart, because she considered that what he was doing was a form of infidelity to her.

She could tell he was miserable by the way he blundered through the day. Still, he obeyed his church and its strictures regarding this punishment called shunning. He did not say a word to her. If he had to, he was allowed to write notes to her concerning matters of household business, but as far as possible he was to ignore her. She had been declared an unclean person, and as such she did not exist except as a shadow in his home and life. He was not to kiss her or speak to her. He was not even to look at her as he passed by. And above all he was not to have sexual converse with her. According to the rules he could have made her sleep on the floor like a dog, but that night when she came to bed he got out the other side and went to sleep on the sofa, leaving the wide marriage nest to her.

In the morning her father phoned her. Without a greeting, "Repent," he commanded her, the one word. She hung up.

Walking along the leaf-strewn street with the children in their wagon that week, down to the corner grocery for a gallon of milk, over to the drugstore for her magazines, she greeted lifelong friends and watched them turn their backs on her in a way that was hard to read: discomfort or disapproval? Gabe and Mikey's Sunday School teacher chatted with the children but snubbed their mother. A thrift shop clerk offered her no service, pretending not to see her standing at the counter.

"Lady *shunned* Mommy," Mikey declaimed. To the children shunning was constant fun, a game grown-ups played, even more different and exciting than rock music. Life had been full of surprises since Mommy had started listening to the devil's music.

Not everyone in Jenkins belonged to the Church of the Holy Virgin, not by any means, but those who were not members knew those who were. Depending on their alliances or whom they wished not to offend, their intermarriages or their dislike of Reverend Crawshaw, they either avoided Angie or made a point of greeting her with extra warmth. Some actually stopped her on the street and offered their support. This did not comfort her. It was Ennis's support she wanted.

"Did you marry my father or me?" she asked him one night as he sat in the living room after the kids were in bed.

Silence.

"I know you're trying to please God. But does God cook your supper for you? Does God wash your shirts?"

He stared past her. She could see the pain in his eyes and did not care. There was too much pain everywhere.

"They tell you God loves you. Well, he better. Get him to keep you warm at night next winter, why don't you."

He got up and left the room. She went upstairs and picked up her sleeping children out of their cribs and took them to the rocking chair, where she sat and cuddled them one in each arm for a long time. The feeling of their heedless little bodies warm against her chest helped somewhat. She slept alone again that night.

The next day she bought batteries for her shocking-pink boogie box and started carrying it with her as a public show of defiance when she took the boys for walks through the fallen leaves.

On one such walk toward the end of the week, a woman she barely knew, a stiletto-nosed, unctuous neighbor, stopped her and offered high-pitched sympathy. "It's just too bad," the nose said. "A pretty young thing like you, and they go and coop you up and make you a nun. Or not a nun, but same as, ain't? You know what I mean, ain't?"

Angie no more than nodded, trying to force some sort of smile. This careless pity of strangers she found as hard to take as the silence of friends.

Then the woman said, "I hear tell they're going to take the little ones away from you if you don't come 'round to their way of thinking. Now I say that's a crime against nature and a sin and a shame, ain't?"

Angie found herself saying stupidly, "Thank you." Walking away without hearing the rumbling opening notes of "Born to Run" on her radio. Feeling a muted surprise that she was still standing. Her heart was pierced, was it not? There should have been blood spilling down her body, flooding her sensible brown oxfords.

She did not have to ask herself if what Stiletto Nose had said was true. She knew it was. Taking her babies away was exactly what her father would do. He and his brainless slaves. Ennis, too, just like the rest of them.

Why was she still there, in this place where they could do such a thing to her? Yesterday was not soon enough for her to be somewhere else.

As if she had just passed over a mountain ridge, her life suddenly gathered momentum, accelerated. She picked up Mikey so that she could walk faster. Hurrying Gabe along at her side, she made plans quickly, carefully. There was no time for dithering or tears. Since she was a mother she had learned to save those luxuries for after the crisis was over, to react quickly and efficiently in any sort of emergency that threatened her children.

The savings account passbook was in her purse, because Ennis had always left the handling of money to her. She dropped off the radio at the house, put the boys in the wagon and walked to the bank, where she withdrew what she thought she would need, a few hundred dollars, leaving Ennis the rest. He wanted to start his own business someday, and she did not want to take that away from him.

Then she stopped at the drugstore, looking at the Greyhound schedule posted in the front window near the park bench that constituted the bus depot. It was a good thing Ennis worked late. There was still time to be gone before he got home.

Once back at the house she packed a diaper bag and a tote full of things for the boys, but almost nothing for herself. Toothbrush, writing tablet, pen, panties, that was all. Most of her clothes she wanted never to wear again. She would take no skirt and prim white blouse but those she had on. The moment she had a chance she would buy herself a pair of jeans, her first. To think of it. Real clothes, soon. In a small indulgence of feeling (not enough to shatter control; she needed to keep everything under control), she wrenched off her prayer bonnet, crumpled the stiff white mesh thing, and flung it in the trash. Pulling the hairpins from her bun, she let her long, soft-brown hair ripple down her back.

From the linen closet she retrieved an envelope containing twenty-some pieces of tablet paper folded very small: her songs. She looked at it distantly a moment before she shoved it into the tote, then sat down on the children's rocking chair and wrote another song, this one for Ennis.

What you call heaven I call hell
It's all shame and blame
So how can I tell
If I love you?
If I ever did?
If what I do is so hard on you

Then maybe we were wrong from the start
A marriage made in a citadel
Instead of in our hearts.
Let it go.
We need a saving angel
And we don't have even
One feather from an angel's wing.

She left it and the bank passbook on the kitchen table where he would find them when he came home expecting dinner to be ready for him.

The walk to the Greyhound stop was hard. Gabe and Michael were cranky after being awakened from their late naps, hot in their winter jackets, hungry for their supper. The bags hung heavy from Angie's shoulders, the whining children pulled at her hands, dragging their feet no matter how she tried to hurry them, and even her radio seemed heavy, like her heart. When she reached the drugstore the bus had already come. She had to get on and buy her tickets from the driver—there was no time to get the children overpriced hot dogs at the lunch counter or even cheese crackers to eat. Once under way, as soon as the novelty of the bus ride had worn off, Mikey and Gabe turned up their volume, progressing from whining to wailing, then crying for miles until finally the drone of the Greyhound put them to sleep.

Angie felt as if she should cry also, but did not. She sat numbly, staring out windows that ought, according to her mood, to have been streaked with rain, but were in fact glowing cloudy gold in the late-day light, filth and all.

The bus bumbled westward, stopping at every small town. It would take days to reach California.

But maybe she would not have to go all the way to L.A. before she contacted the one who was going to help her. Angie took out her tablet of cheap lined newsprint and her Bic pen and began to write.

Volos
Volos
I need you.
Volos
Volos
Come to me.

Despite all the ingenious speculations she had read in her magazines, there was not a doubt in her mind that Volos was an angel. She had felt sure of that for some time, and lately she had begun to be able to feel his spirit's light-fingered touch as he robbed her of her songs. Therefore she knew him: He was a willful sinner, like her. He was one who had fallen from grace. And it was not for the sake of a feather of his wing that she was calling him.

"I'm glad you like your new toy, son," Texas remarked.

It was a Guild one-off, glossy black, shaped rather like the old Gibson Flying V; with its long neck and backswept body, it resembled a swan in flight. With it Volos had ordered a full range of pedals and effects, and now he was running it through fuzz, sustain, tremolo, echo, reverb, and something that made it sound like the Concorde coming in for a landing. His wings had gone rainbow with pleasure. Texas sat back on the sofa, tilted his new Stetson (camel-tan, pinch top) over his wincing eyes and longed for the gentler sounds of Kenny Rogers.

"I am going to get new toys for the band also," Volos said.

With the onset of his first major earnings, the ex-angel had finally begun to explore the joys of materialism. In Westwood (Brett had wanted him to locate someplace more fashionable, like Bel Air, but he did not always do what his manager said) he had rented a Spanish-style house. The Hokey Hacienda, Mercedes scornfully called it. Volos did not care. He had little feeling for the house itself, but thought of it as a convenience, a place to rehearse his band and store things he wanted. He had turned its once-trendy South California living room, all blond wood and white walls and picture window, into a rock-and-roll inferno of amps and keyboards and drum stands and blacksnaking wires. But if anyone asked him where he lived, he still said what he had told Texas that first day: *Here, wherever I am standing.* Westwood's disreputable streets, the UCLA campus, the roller rinks, Mercedes's bed, the skateboard tubes, dance clubs, massage parlors were home to him. No one would touch him in the massage parlors, but he liked to watch. And parking lots, museum steps, playgrounds—he liked the playgrounds, because the children did not hesitate to talk with him. And recording studios, and the bars where musicians gathered.

To Texas, Volos's house was a home of sorts. He lived there, cleaning the john occasionally and keeping the fridge stocked with beer. Most of the time, though, he spent tomcatting. He had quit his Keller's Kleaner's job and felt thin and rootless and sere, like a winter thistle. And prickly. These days his pride was rubbing against his hurt feelings all the time. Maybe he should have gone back to Wyoma really, maybe when she had said what she did she just wanted him to shit or get off the pot. But how could he humble himself and go home after the way she had talked to him?

So he sat in his angel's rock and roll hell, and Volos made the new guitar wail like a fox in the chilly dawn, sob like a graveyard ghost, scream, a bird with an arrow in its breast. Just as Texas considered that he was ready to scream as well, the kid silenced his weapon and called across the room, "Mercy wants me to get rid of this band I have and get a different one."

Mercedes was Volos's so-called artistic director. Texas could not scoff at that arrangement, because he himself was Volos's highly informal head of security. But he felt his jaw tighten at the mention of Mercedes.

The word "prick" presented itself to his mind, but he said merely, "Why?"

"He says they are small-time, just ordinary-looking people. He wants me to find band players who are more performers, sharper-looking."

Texas liked the people in Volos's band, who appreciated good beer. He said, "Those people dropped everything and came through for you when Brett asked them to. They were there for you when you needed them, and they've been there for you since. Mercedes has no respect for loyalty."

Everything about Texas ached: his clenched jaw, his head, his ribs, the bruised skin around his eyes. He had gotten into a brawl again the night before, over a barfly he had been bringing home to hump on the sofa. Lately he got into fights even more regularly than he found women to justify them. Just about the only person in California he did not sometimes want to fight was Volos, but speaking of Mercedes he had not been able to keep an edge out of his voice. Volos looked at him, then hung his new guitar in its stainless-steel stand and came closer, spreading his wings to sit on the floor at McCardle's feet. He looked some more. He asked, "Why don't you like Mercy?"

The kid was getting better at reading people than he used to be. Starting to talk more like a human too. Texas said quietly, "You're right, I don't like him."

"But why? Is it because he is gay with me?"

"No, that don't bother me." It honestly did not. A few times in his life as a cop Texas had come up against pure evil, enough times to know that real malignance had nothing to do with sex. Anyway, he had a feeling the kid hadn't really decided which ear to pierce yet. He said, "Anybody that's been around cows or dogs or whatever knows it's natural all ways. It ain't him being gay gets to me. It's just *him*."

"What about him?"

It was one of those questions a person should never answer. But Volos had helped Texas through some hard times those first few days after Wyoma had told him to take a hike. More than once Texas had needed the touch of a wing. He owed the kid, and he, Texas, knew the meaning of loyalty. Quietly he said, "It's just a feeling I got, that he's going to hurt you someday."

"Hurt me?" Volos considered, then smiled and shook his head, tossing his dark, curling hair. "How?"

Entirely too many possible ways. To Texas the world was full of things that could hurt Volos. But one likelihood seemed foremost. "Are you in love with him?"

"I don't know. How can I tell for sure?"

"You don't know what love is?" *But why should that surprise me?* Texas thought. He had looked into Volos's eyes. Trying to see into them was like trying to tell what lay under deep water. He had seen the kid sing in the studio, eyes closed, earphones on, shut off from everything but his own music, utterly self-involved.

"How should I? What is it like?"

"You're asking the wrong cowboy, son." But Texas tried anyway. "Love is a one-on-one sort of thing. If Mercedes got mad at you, stopped seeing you, started doing it with somebody else instead, would any of that hurt you?"

"The way Wyoma has hurt you?"

"Leave Wyoma out of it." She had hurt him. Maybe he had hurt her first. Maybe not. What was the use of talking about it? Texas did not feel sure, had never felt that she really needed him. He said, "What I mean is, if you love somebody that don't love you, it leaves you wide open. Could he hurt you that way?"

It took Volos a while to answer. His long, tawny hands practiced air guitar in his lap, and he looked down at them. "Perhaps," he admitted. "Mostly because he's the only one ... it seems like everybody else always wants me to take my wings off first."

Texas did not pay attention, for a frightening thought had just occurred to him. He had been counting on Mercedes's experience, was why he hadn't thought of it before, but if Mercedes was as much of a prick as he thought he was—

"Kid." He tried to keep the panic out of his voice. "You two—when you do it—you been using condoms?"

"No."

"JESUS, Volos!" Texas lurched to his feet. "Why don't you just go stick yourself with a dirty needle and be done with it! You—"

"Why are you shouting? It is all right. I did not imagine myself to get AIDS. That or any kind of sickness."

Staring, Texas sank back onto the sofa again. When the kid talked like that he sounded as far away as another planet. But the words made sense. Sure, a newcomer to this dirty world ought to be easy meat for all kinds of bugs. Volos ought to be always getting the flu or something. But except for those first few days, Texas hadn't known Volos to be sick with so much as a head cold.

Except.

"What about the fever you had that time?"

"What about it?"

"That was sickness."

Volos said, "That was my ridiculous wings."

"So?"

"So if you want to save me from harm, guard my back." Volos gave a dismissive gesture, got lithely to his feet, and turned toward his new guitar.

"Yo! Hold on, buddy. What are you telling me about your wings?"

Volos did not face him, but stood still and said, "I am telling you I don't know about them. I did not imagine them."

"I don't get you, son."

"Listen. I had it all held in my mind before I came, like a bird in my hand. I will die someday, yes. My body will age and then die. Or I can be killed. A knife, a gun, a car. But I will not sicken or starve. I decided against that." God, the ego of the young brute. And the anger hardening his voice. "These wings, though, I did not imagine. They are a trick played on me. They have made everything uncertain."

Texas said, "Welcome to the real world, kid."

Volos shot him a dark look over his shoulder. "So yes, I can be hurt through my wings. I think. So now you are sure Mercy will do it. For a good man you think too much of evil, Texas."

"It's my job."

"I think—you are as likely to hurt me as he."

It took Texas a moment to get his breath. Then he said in a strangled voice, "I ought to deck you for that, Volos."

The youngster's mood had changed suddenly. "Do not be angry. Please." Lifting the new guitar, Volos faced him with a stark look. "I am just trying to find truth. Do not these things happen?"

Texas thought of Wyoma and felt his anger puddle into despair. He said, "Yes, dammit, shit happens. But I would never do anything to hurt you on purpose, son."

"Does it hurt less if it is not on purpose?"

"Volos, would you for Chrissake shut up? You're hurting me right this fucking minute."

Wide-eyed, the kid looked at him, then without a word sat down on a tall stool and began to play. But this time what came out of the black guitar was the music of a white angel of mercy. Volos made the thing sing like bells, like a sweet human voice, a choir of treble voices in golden-hued harmony. Joy, Peace, Love—from its first chord, the melody took Texas into its embrace, cradled him, flooded him in a warm baptism of sound to wash away his aches. He felt easy tears brightening his bruised eyes. "God," he whispered. It was magical music, heaven's gift. And, he knew, Volos's gift of atonement to him.

Touched to his soul, he looked at the giver, and saw that Volos's face was lowered over the guitar and his wings had gone tar-dark.

Texas got up, went to him and stopped him with a

hand on the strings. "All right," he said, "okay. I hear you. How in God's name can you make that kind of music and still feel the way you feel?"

Without looking up Volos said, "For a long time I had to."

"You don't have to give me no peace offering if it's that hard on you."

"I wish—I wish I could be good for you. But nothing's simple, is it? Nothing's pure."

Texas said gently, "Not in this life, son."

By the time his band arrived for rehearsal, Volos had his wings back to quiet gray. He watched without saying much as his musicians set up and warmed up and chatted with each other.

It was as Mercedes had said: They were very ordinary-looking people. The keyboard player was going bald above habitual button-down oxford-weave shirts. The drummer was a middle-aged man shaped like a tom-tom. The bass guitarist was a stick of a woman who always wore straight skirts and thick glasses; she looked like Buddy Holly in drag. Even the lead guitarist, Red, was no more than a freckled young man who loved music.

Even before he had heard what Texas had to say about loyalty, Volos had mostly made up his mind to go with this nameless band a while longer. Because of musical considerations, he would tell Mercedes, because there was no time to audition and rehearse new people with his busy recording and nightclub schedule. Which was true. But the deeper truth was that he had begun to intuit what a real rock band could be like, what it meant when the backup vocals came and sang at the same mike as the front man, when the singer stood back to arched back with his lead guitarist, so close their heads touched. He had started to want that closeness, like the oneness of music itself, and knew he wasn't going to get it. Brett had explained to him that most music people had worked their way up together, paid dues together, got to be like family, whereas he had come out of nowhere (more literally than Brett knew) and started at the top. His band had a right to resent him. It was enough that they were respectful to him as a professional.

But what he couldn't have, Volos had decided, he was not going to stage with performers. As one who knew no other way to sing than from the heart, Volos held an opinion of performers much like Texas's opinion of whores.

"I have a new song to work out," he reported. The band quieted at once, too quickly, to hear him. "This is somewhat different. A love ballad, almost. Listen." What he should have done really was work up a lead sheet, but Volos found it difficult to write. By way of autograph, all he could manage quickly was a sort of vee-bird, the kind of thing small children put in the skies of their crayon pictures. He knew several hundred languages, but he had forgotten to imagine the relays that send language to the hand, so he held a pencil like a first-grader and stabbed holes in paper with it. Necessarily, his band learned his songs by ear.

He and the new guitar sang the ballad for them:

What you call heaven I call hell
It's all shame and blame
So how can I tell
If I love you. . . .

"Nice," opined Jack, the keyboard man, in his buttoned-down way after Volos had finished.

They talked about a heartbeat tempo, dark-honey guitar, a few word changes. "Citadel" struck them as obscure. Volos agreed, and they changed the word to "chapel." The drummer clicked his sticks to get them going, and after that it was Volos's hot voice that melted them, almost miraculously, into oneness. When the song had come to him a few hours before, he had felt a young woman's desolation as if it were his own. He sang as if for her alone.

"Man, how do you *do* that?" Red begged him. The freckled guitarist's frequent ardor made him seem younger than he was. He was, in fact, a longtime sessions player, and it showed when he said, "I've worked with pros who did worse on the tenth try than you do on the first." They were all, even Jack, looking at Volos with something like awe. But awe is made of distance and fear. He did not want that. What was he to say to them? He turned away.

"Hey, man, something wrong?"

"No," he said to the wall. "Let us do it again."

What you call heaven I call hell
It's all shame and blame ...

Then—he could no longer sing, or even hear the song, or move. It was the shock of his incarnate life to date. Taking on flesh, he had thought he would never suffer it again, but—it was happening, the familiar intrusion, the invasion, the rape of his mind they called prayer. Volos stood rigidly, with taut face and wings clenched into the shape of a long, quivering heart, violated by a distant summons:

Volos
Volos
Angel of anarchy

His band faltered to silence and looked at him curiously.

Volos
Volos
Come rescue me

"What's the matter, man?" the drummer asked.

He managed to move his mouth, to speak. "Nothing," he whispered.

Volos
Volos

God, he could feel it inching closer. "Shut up!" he begged between clenched teeth.

"Hey, man, are you okay?" Red looked worried. They all did. Their concern impinged on Volos like the prayer. He turned and lunged blindly out of the house, cloakless. In his benighted garage his black Hawg awaited him like a prize stallion sulking in an oversized stall. Once he was on the Harley and moving, no one would bother him.

Volos
Volos
Come to me

Not even Her. Whoever She was.

Volos roared off into the starless city night, running away, drowning out her still-distant voice. His wings caught the wind and spread, translucent, gradually lightening from angry red to fire-orange in the streetlamp light. Speed slapped his face, lifted his hair. Black bike, black night, dark hair flying—he loved these things. Even She could not take them away from him.

In part he knew who she was. It was her, the one whose songs spoke straight to his mind, and somehow she knew him better than he knew her, she called him angel and she was summoning him by name. And he owed her something, he knew that. But loyalty had its limits. No matter who she was, no matter what she said or did, he would not go back to the role of servant, of guardian angel, of comer-when-called. Not even for Texas could he do that. He would scald in her tears first. He would fry in hell.

chapter
eight

Gabe, the fussed-over firstborn, had always been the one who was wired too tight, while little two-year-old Mikey was more easygoing. Therefore it was Gabe whom Angela had to carry in her arms as she tried to find shelter her first dark night in the worst streets of downtown L.A. He was too heavy for her, but the fatigue of the long journey and the sight of a hydrocephalic beggar had combined to send him out of control. He would not or could not walk. Lugging the tote bags and the screaming child, with Mikey trailing at her side through the filthy bus station and out to the even filthier streets, Angie felt beyond screaming herself. She had gone numb. The sight of men selling stolen jewelry and the come-ons of rip-off artists could not make her more frightened than she already was.

Her money was all but gone. The long days on the road, even on a nearly constant diet of hot dogs, had been more expensive than she had previously imagined possible. And she had never expected to be on her own for so long, had not thought that Volos, her soulmate, could fail to come to her. It all seemed crazy now, the way she had run to him. Her notion of a linkage, a bond with him was nothing more than a sexually repressed neurotic's delusion, and that made her a nut case, and she had acted like one. Now she had to find a charity somewhere to take her in, or else spend the night on the street. She didn't want that ... but once around the first corner she could carry Gabe no farther. She sank down on the sidewalk, leaning back against a cinder-block wall. Gabe sprawled on her, weeping more quietly, with his face hidden between her breasts. Mikey sat down and pressed himself against her, far too quiet. A ravaged old man shuffled past on bare feet the gray color of a bloated tick, his toenails so long they curled down under his toes, making him limp. Gabe needed a Kleenex. Mikey began to hiccup. Poor kids, even being taken away from her by their hellfire grandpa might have been better for them than this. She had gone and proved everybody right, she was a worthless mother—

Hellfire. She would show them worthless.

As if her desperation had made her into nothing but a torch waiting to be lit, as if a match had struck, Angela Bradley blazed into incandescent fury.

"Volos!"

She shrieked the name aloud, startling her children—but her rage was not at them, or even at the two God-fearing men, her father and her husband, who had driven her to this place where already she had seen an old woman squatting and defecating in a dumpster. Rather, like the wrath of the mob on Calvary day, her anger was all for the savior, the rescuer who had failed.

"Volos, you wretch, I am calling you!"

Except for her frightened sons, no one actually within earshot paid any attention to her. It was not the sort of place where a woman's screaming meant much. In a nearby alley a hooker administered a stand-up quickie and collected her fee, already on the lookout for the next john. Across the street teenagers peddled crack.

"You half-finished excuse for a human being!

Volos! You come to me now, or I swear I'll tell the world everything I know about you!"

She raged with no effect whatsoever on the whores and pimps and dealers or the drifters lying stoned in stairwells. But miles away, on his Hawg for the seventh night in a row and roaring far up the Hollywood hills, Volos felt her white-hot summons go through him like a barbed spear through a river carp, like a lightning strike through a yellow pine, and there was nothing he could do but obey her. Against his will, but at once.

Instantly. So hastily that he left his beloved Harley lying by the roadside and used his wings for the first time in his incarnate life, flying to her at a speed that far exceeded anything his bike could do. Just as she had ranted herself out and leaned back silent and panting against the chill wall, arms around her two frightened little boys, a booted apparition landed with a thump in front of her. A tall visitant with glaring eyes and wings the color of dried blood. Volos.

"Where have you *been*?" she snapped at him. Because she had given up on him, had forgotten she was ever in love with his picture in *Metal Mag,* no longer remembered how she had once kissed a centerfold poster of his perfect full-lipped face, the sight of him made her angry all over again. There was much more she could have said to him if she had not been so tired.

"You—called—me." He seemed to be having difficulty speaking. Out of breath, she thought. Served him right.

"I've *been* calling you." She heaved herself to her feet, graceless with fatigue, conscious of how her jeaned legs spraddled and her hair hung in strings and the fact that she smelled. Never mind all that. Rebellious. To hell with being attractive, especially for this hugging-himself hotshot of an angel. Tote bags hunching her shoulders, a child hanging from each hand, she stood weary and proud.

"You—made me—fly."

"Well, about time, isn't it?"

"No! By the devil, no! I am never in eternal suffering going to be a servant again!" He took a step toward her, wings half-lifted and rustling, head forward like that of a charging stallion, and she saw that his choked speech was due not to breathlessness but to anger that maybe matched hers. The realization did not trouble her. She had reached a point where she was not afraid of anything.

He raged, "I am no one's guardian, no one's rescuer, and no one is going to make a carrier pigeon of me! Or a savior. I don't care how much you recognize me. You don't get to put my head on a plate or nail me to a tree."

None of this impressed Angie, but little Mikey started to cry. Lifting him, she said automatically to Volos, "Shush. You're scaring the babies."

"Babies." His gaze shifted, and even in the shadowy street the whites of his eyes showed. "Babies yet!"

Angela commanded, "We need a place to stay and something to eat and a bath."

"I have told you, I am not an errand boy anymore! Why should I—"

"I AM YOUR LYRICIST." She did not raise her voice, but more than she knew, Angela Bradley was her father's daughter; the statement crackled with her righteous wrath. "You have taken my words and called them your own. Have you forgotten?"

Volos stood silent, his wings folded and still.

"And if that's not enough," Angie added, "you have destroyed my marriage." She believed this at the time, with the unaccustomed anger in her—more anger than she would have previously thought possible.

Volos blurted, "I have done that? But you said it was all shame and blame, that you could not tell if you loved him."

"You used—you used Ennis's song? You swine!"

Her shout made Gabe start again to cry, adding his thin, weary clamor to Mikey's. "Shush," Volos told Angie sourly. "You are frightening the babies." He reached down and picked up the youngster, slinging him over his shoulder. Gabriel's startled, pudgy hand brushed the angel's wing, and the boy quieted at once, settling his head against Volos's naked neck to sleep. Watching, with Mikey still sobbing in her arms, Angie felt a perverse annoyance that Volos had done something helpful just as she had decided to hate him always.

"You are right that I owe you for the songs," he said. His voice had gone very quiet.

"*Thank* you." She was quiet also, but in a different way.

Even in this most inhospitable of downtowns at three in the morning, Volos was a celebrity. A small crowd of street people had gathered around him. The shuffling man with the blue bare feet and the laming toenails reached out and touched one finger to the very tip of a pinion. Tears began to wash his gray face, but when Volos felt the touch he stepped sharply away.

"Come," he told Angie, striding down the street. The tote bags bounced and dug into her shoulders as she struggled to keep up with him.

"*Where,* O Superstar?"

"To get you a cab." He slowed down somewhat when he had left the crowd behind.

Later, when she knew him better, she would understand why he had not offered to take the baggage from her or to comfort weeping Mikey with the touch of a wing. It was not that he was evil, though as a fallen angel he tried hard to be evil. It was just that he was incomplete.

At the time, however, she detested everything about him, from his boots to his curling mane of dark hair to the perfect ass swinging between his wings.

He found a cab near the bus station, gave the driver

money and the address and, when the man asked, an autograph. "Go in through the garage," he told Angie. That door, Angie later learned, was kept unlocked because Volos generally forgot to carry a key. "If Texas is there, just tell him I sent you."

Placed on the taxicab seat, Gabe woke up, grasped the situation, and started to cry again. "Birdman come with us!" he wailed.

"I can't, little one. I do not fit in." Volos spread his wings partway in illustration. "It is not possible for me to get into a cab. I'll walk."

"Not fly?" Angie asked, so startled that she spoke to him almost civilly. It had always seemed to her that flying would be wonderful.

"No. I look laughable when I fly." Volos knew himself to be a dunce among angels. "I cannot keep my legs from dangling like a crane's."

"But—why did you keep your wings, then?" What were wings for but to fly?

"It was not my idea. I hate my wings. They get in the way of everything."

"Birdman come too!" Gabe implored.

"Little one, listen, you go to sleep. Wait a minute. Here." On the inner surface of his left wing he found a small feather that was coming loose and handed it to Gabe. "I will see you when you wake up, yes?"

"You might give one to Michael too," Angie told Volos crossly.

"Oh." He did so, then stood balancing on the uneven sidewalk as the cab drove away, watching after it in bewilderment.

By all the little devils, but it was shiversome to see her. There she was, physical, separate, in a very appealing female body, and he had never really thought of her in that way. The songs—they were heart of his heart, soul of his soul. It had always seemed to Volos that anyone listening to those songs should know him utterly, should understand him. Yes, they had come to him from somewhere else; as clear and eerie as a far-side-of-the-world radio signal skipping off the stratosphere they had reached him in the starless L.A. nights, and he had committed them to memory, nothing more, only changing them to suit the shape his guitar gave the music. And yes, he had sensed direction and gender, he had known that his telepathic soulmate was female—what of it? Genderless most of his existence, he might just as readily have incarnated as a woman, except that he selfishly wanted the more privileged life of a male. Women were the lowest choir here, an underclass—no wonder he felt so much at one with them. No wonder there were those who looked at his face and snickered that he should have been a girl.

This woman, he had known about her all along—yet she had seemed so much a part of him that, meeting her, it was as if he had cut his thigh open to look at his body's longest bone.

She had a straight, stark flow of dark hair, a wide brow, very direct eyes. A heart-shaped face, golden skin, and a pointed chin, as if she had stepped out of an old masterpiece, a Botticelli. There was something level and anchored and innocent about her gaze, as if she believed in God. Yet something wise, as if she believed in more gods than one.

Volos sighed, knowing that here was another mortal who could hurt him.

He started walking, not toward the Hokey Hacienda or toward where he had left the motorcycle, but toward West Hollywood. It would be dawn when he knocked at the apartment door, and he hoped Mercedes would not mind being awakened. Suddenly he needed the ease of that bed and the bliss that clever body could offer him and the comfort of Mercy's kiss.

Looking back later, Texas saw how Volos, supernatural being and fallen angel, had happenstanced into his life, backed in almost, just another chance encounter in the big city—but Angela, mortal woman, had dawned on him like an epiphany, turning to him from the first the face of someone holy. A goddess. No, a madonna. That was what he thought the first moment he saw her standing proud and dirty in the doorway, with a sleeping child in one arm and a stumbling toddler clinging to the other hand and her hair flowing off her brow long and smooth as the Virgin Mary's headcloth: a quiet-faced pietà, a brave mother. He thanked whatever power was intermittently looking after him that he had not brought a floozie home with him that night.

As long as Angie lived in that house, he did not bring one home again.

His hands remembered what it was like to be a father. He took Gabe from her, got the child halfway fed and approximately bathed and put down behind a barrier of chair backs to keep him from rolling off the bed onto the floor. She laid Michael in the same bed and rewarded Texas with a tired smile. It dizzied him. He had forgotten how a mother's smile could do that, made up as it was of tenderness and weary cynicism and the bone-deep surrender that goes with loving a baby. There was not much need for talk between Texas and Angela. She saw him for what he was, and in her eyes he saw himself: more in danger than Volos. Not a clumsy fighter who always led with his chin, but a blundering country boy who led with his heart.

He went back to bed, and found to his amazement when he awoke that the exhausted children were up before him. The sound of their birdlike voices filled the house. Texas had forgotten how tired or overburdened children got to be like self-winding tops, moving louder and faster by the moment until something stopped them. He went out to the equipment-filled living room and found Volos there, flat on the floor, wings outspread, with both little boys bobbing atop his broad chest.

"Texas. Tell Brett I said give you money for food and stuff, okay?"

Texas nodded. "Tell Brett I said give you money" was in essence the fiscal arrangement between him and Volos, and he took a rebellious pleasure in being satisfied with it. So who cared about fringe benefits and pension plans and Getting Ahead. It did bother him, though, that the arrangement was much the same for Mercedes.

"We're going to have to keep more food in the house with these weanlings around," Volos added.

"Birdman make me go *up!*" commanded Gabriel. Volos swung the kid into a sort of lift and held him there kicking and giggling.

"Now Mikey." Volos lowered Gabe and lifted his younger brother, who screamed. "Mikey?" Volos asked anxiously.

"He's okay," Texas said. "They like to screech."

Angie padded in, barefoot, still dewy from the shower, wearing her jeans and a shirt Texas had loaned her. Oversized, it made her look narrow-shouldered and frail. Her face rose like a flower from its wide neck. Volos's face changed when he saw her, Texas noticed with a squeezing feeling in his heart. He saw the red blush start to spread through the angel's sunrise-colored wings. Volos sent the boys trotting to their mother and sat up amid a difficult readjustment of those appendages to look at her.

"Have you eaten, Angela?"

She nodded without thanks. Maybe knowing that Volos was not hinting for thanks. One thing about Volos, Texas reminded himself: The kid might not think of things he ought to say or do, but when he did come through for a person, he did not expect any show of gratitude. Maybe Angie understood that.

Or maybe she just plain did not like him. She was being careful not to look at him. Not to give him anything of herself, not even a smile.

"Angela." Volos tried again. "Can you sew?"

"Yes, of course." The surprise in her voice told Texas she had been raised country-style, in a home where every woman had to cook and sew or be called a slut.

"Would you like to be my wardrobe department?"

She looked at him then, made a show of scanning his half-naked body, and said with just a hint of a smile, "What wardrobe?"

Texas laughed, but Volos missed her joke. "Mercy says I need one," he told her earnestly. "He says for the big stage on tour I will need something more than jeans. Bright colors. Ornaments."

Texas, grinning, teased him, "What are you gonna do about the band?"

"Oh, I give it up." This time Volos recognized levity and shot Texas a sour look. "You can costume the band, Texas. Go out and buy them each a hat."

"I will. I'm gonna do just that."

"We'll be cowboys. I can get chaps with long fringe and silver studding. Mercy wants me to wear things that glitter."

Angie was watching him seriously. "Please not rhinestones and sequins," she said in her abrupt, level way. "They would cheapen you."

Texas felt his heart aching with adoration for her. Already she knew, she understood everything, she looked at Volos with eyes that saw truly. She would never love him, Texas, except as a fatherly sort of old fool, and Texas understood that and accepted it immediately. But how could he not love her when she looked at his angel with honest eyes?

He said to Volos, "She's right, kid. Don't let your precious Mercy push you too far. Remember what Elvis started to look like before the end?"

Volos grimaced at him. "But I do need new clothes," he complained.

"I been telling you that for weeks."

"Now I really do. I must meet the record company people. Brett says I must wear something on my torso. Show respect."

"Shirt and tie?" Texas teased.

"In the devil's name, how?"

"When is this?" Angie asked.

"Tomorrow."

"Christ, Volos!" Texas exploded. "I keep telling you, don't leave things till the last minute!" The kid had little sense of time or of the limits it put on people who actually had to eat and sleep.

Angie said merely, "One of you had better take me shopping."

Volos took her, in the old Corvair convertible with its custom paint job, black with red flames running back from the hood to the rear wheel wells. Brett had been the one who had convinced Volos he couldn't afford anything fancier yet. But he had installed the best stereo system on the market. And kept installing it, because it had been stolen out of the car three times so far.

Texas held Gabe and Mikey up to the window so they could watch, so they could see Volos driving with his wings lifted to clear the back of his seat, stretched six feet above his head. Texas hoped Angie would not be frightened. He knew Volos drove the freeways like a plummeting hawk, knew that surrounding cars would veer as the drivers saw him, knew that one way or another the shopping itself would turn into a circus as well. Hoped Volos would make Angie buy clothing for herself and the little boys. Texas would far rather have chauffeured the young woman himself, but weighing the problems of sending her off with Volos against the dangers of leaving Volos to baby-sit the little ones, he saw no choice. Volos would want to play but would be likely to forget that children needed to eat or sleep or breathe.

"Uncle Texas?" It was the older one, Gabriel.

"What is it, big guy?"

"I dood in my pants."

Therefore Texas had laundry to do, after which he fed the boys cheese sandwiches and applesauce for lunch and introduced them to the joys of TV until

they fell asleep. While they napped, he lay down himself, tilted his hat over his face, and dozed, dreaming
that he was young again, about twenty-one. Something
made him dream of Wyoma and his daughters, so that
in his sleep he was a cowboy coming home from a
long day of riding to the ranch house where standing
at the door Wyoma smiled at him, and the babies,
three or four of them, boys now as well as girls,
climbed his long work-jeaned legs as if he were the
deep-rooted great tree of life.

Angie's quick solution to Volos's upper-body-nudity
problem was a black vest from the leather shop. That
evening after the boys were in bed she reworked the
back, cutting it away so that it would fit under Volos's
wings, all the while trying to decide how she felt about
him. Angry at him, yes, still a little. At one point she
had made up her mind to be his efficient and respectful employee, nothing more. It was a stance she
thought she could manage, but she had not been able
to do so even for a day. Without meaning to (she felt
fairly certain of that), he kept her constantly off balance. His hawk-swoop driving thrilled and terrified
her, his generosity touched her—he had bought her
things, all sorts of things, sundresses, sandals, a jeans
jacket. And he had bought rompers and sneakers and
Zoom Cars for the boys. But just as she had decided
to like him, some sort of thoughtless arrogance, perhaps the snap of his fingers as he summoned a sales-
person, would make her detest him all over again.

Back at the house, he had gotten down on the floor
with the boys and played for hours, running the radio-
controlled cars. Already Gabe and Mikey regarded
him as a huge feathered pet and adored him. Down
on all fours, he would let the boys ride him like a
Pegasus.

"Bless the beasts and children," Texas had remarked, passing through.

Mixed feelings had made it a long day.

Working on Volos's vest, Angie sewed at a portable Sears free-arm machine (bought that afternoon) set up on the table in the erstwhile dining room, now her workroom. (It had probably not been used for dining since Volos had leased the house.) In the next room, the living-room-cum-studio, Volos and his band were rehearsing. Angie listened (the amps were turned up halfway to insanity, so how could she not listen?) as they swung into Ennis's song. She clenched her teeth, rigid with anger. The nerve! But then she felt herself melt. What Volos had done with the stolen song was beautiful enough to soften anyone.

As rehearsal broke up she mentally checked herself: niceness in place, like a prayer bonnet? Temper smoothed down, like mussed hair? Inhibitions, a drab skirt, hanging straight, long enough to cover everything? This done, she called Volos into her new domain for a fitting. Businesslike, she had him stand facing away from her. "Wings up," she directed. "Hands back." She guided them into the armholes, slipped the reshaped vest up his arms, and as she placed it on his shoulders her left wrist brushed the primaries near the base of one wing.

Afterward, she did not think of it as an accident, because sometime it had to happen, that moment of contact in which her life changed.

Or not changed exactly. Enlarged, amplified, magnified, manifested so that the changes that had gone before, the liberation of jeans and unbound hair, the hegira, the ordeal of L.A. seemed merest tentative first steps by comparison. In that moment when she touched Volos's wing, Angela was consummately herself, more so than she had ever been in her life, yet also—him, and therefore nearly infinite. Her rage, huge; her rebellion, huge; her lifelust, huge; her striving desire, immense. She felt as never before aware of, and in love with, her own body, with its beauty, its transience, its doom, and its possibilities. She felt terribly vulnerable, yet at the same time very old, as if she had heard God throatily singing in his shower. She felt time bend like a squeezed string, a single note in a lovely, lonely dissonance, beneath a berserk guitarist's hand.

The feeling, though not so physical as to be really a shock, staggered her. Volos felt her fingers clutch for support, turned quickly and caught her. She let herself lean for a moment against his leather-vested chest, and he pressed his hands against her shoulder blades, steadying her there.

"I'm sorry!" he exclaimed. "My idiot wings, I keep forgetting—"

Interrupting, she said into the alar curve of his collarbone, "I love your wings."

"You do?"

"Yes." She straightened, looking up into his eyes, knowing that she had completely forgiven him for being what he was and not what she had thought he should be. Knowing also that she ought to be frightened of him but was not. "I'm all right now," she told him, and he took his hands away.

He asked her quietly, "What did you feel?"

"I felt . . ." Impossible to describe it all, but what little she said was deeply true. "I want to make the most incredible music."

"You do?" Glad. His eyes and wings were the same warm golden brown. "You are still my lyricist, Angela?"

"Yes."

"Thank you. I need you." His eyes saddened to gray. "I am what you said, a half-done thing. I failed somehow. I sing but I cannot make the songs."

She told him gently, "Not everyone writes songs. Or sings, even." Certainly she herself could not sing.

"But—are you sure of this?" His astonishment, childlike, made her wonder how she could ever have been angry at him.

"I'm certain."

"But—but how can that be? To be alive is to dance

and sing. How can mortals do otherwise? A fire is not a fire unless it burns."

She had no answer, but stood looking at him. He did not grow flustered or restless, as most people would have done, but stood waiting with his wings folded over the back of the new vest. He fingered its soft, rich-smelling leather a moment, then looked back at her and smiled. Did he know how the sweetness of his mouth when he smiled could turn a woman to water?

She said abruptly, "You need to do more songs about love. It is not the same thing as sex."

"It is not?"

"No. All you have done so far is sex and anger. . . . What have I been thinking of, Volos? I must write you love songs."

Sitting in the Millican Records offices, facing a big man behind a big desk, Volos fingered his leather vest and knew he need not have gone to the trouble of covering his torso. He might have been beef naked for all the man scanning him cared. He might as well be a piece of meat that sang.

"You get that tax business cleared away?" the man was asking Brett, who nodded fervidly, explaining that yes, sir, it was all taken care of, Social Security, passport, all the necessary numbers and documents and laminated cards identifying Volos as Flaim Carson McCardle.

"About time," Big Desk grumbled. "Okay, so now you gonna get on with arranging the fucking tour?"

"You bet. We got some concerts lined up already. Houston, Indianapolis, Philadelphia—"

"You got a show for those people? They're gonna come to see the wings, that's what you gotta give them, something to look at. Smoke, fireworks, fountains, lasers, the works. Lots of sequins on this guy, lots of outfit changes. Flash, glitter, movement, color.

If I was you I'd pick a color scheme each set and go with it, wings and all—"

"It does not work that way," Volos said.

"Say what?" The record company exec peered at him. Had not expected him to speak any more than if he had been a Wonder Wombat.

Volos said, "It does not work that way. I do not control the color of my wings. Most of the time I do not know even what color they are unless I look."

"Well, start looking, sonny!"

"You do not understand." The nuisance appendages in question were flushing dull red, Volos could tell that by the dark feeling just below his diaphragm. "They change color with my heart. I cannot—"

"We've got it under control, Mr. Millican," Brett broke in smoothly. "We've got a dynamite young artistic director, Mercedes Kell, and on top of that Volos has a style all his own. He's a born crowd-pleaser. It'll be a natural."

"I was not born," Volos said.

The boss man, used to temperamental artists but by no means happy with them, gave him a bored, uncomprehending look. Brett scowled at him. SHUT UP, her glare commanded.

"It better be under control," Big Desk complained to her. "I don't like risks. Best to go for the sure thing. Lights, glitz, color. Another thing, if I was you I'd get rid of that dowdy band. Get some fresh people up there, and give them a catchy name. Black Angel and the Electric Devils, something like that."

"No," Volos said.

Brett cringed. The mighty man behind the big desk barked at Volos, "What you mean, NO?"

"I mean no, do not call me an angel. I mean no, I will not change my band. They are good musicians. I will have them wear hats. I will talk with them and we will choose a name."

"It better be a fucking good name!" Big Desk, huffy, cut the appointment short.

"Jesus shit," Brett swore at Volos afterward. "You imbecile, you could have blown the whole deal. From now on, you shut your mouth and let me handle things. The only time I want you to open it is when you're singing a song."

More than her anger, her incomprehension silenced him. Who had made him a walking lie, he himself or these others? Why could they not know him? But day after day they said to him, How do your wings work? How do you make them change colors the way you do? What are they made of? Don't you take them off even to sleep?

They thought he was human.

Was that not what he wanted? To be human?

Volos did not let Brett take him home, but walked for miles through his own lonesome valley, cloak thrown back, wanting someone, anyone, to see him truly and tell him who he was.

Texas had told him he was real—but what did that mean? And Mercedes—he had performed every conceivable homoerotic act with Mercedes, but still he felt hollow. Now there was Angela . . .

The thought of her comforted him. But he was a fool to feel that way, for he had wronged her, and now she would never love him. He would not ask it of her. It was enough that she would stay in the house with him, fix his clothes, write his songs. It was more than enough for a half-finished thing like him. More than he deserved.

chapter
nine

Christmas in California with Volos—Angie knew it would be so different from any other Christmas she had ever experienced that she would have to reinvent it. No churchgoing, no gift-wrapped piety from her father, no martyrdom served up by her mother along with candied yams, no lump-of-coal guilt in her seasonal stocking. She was glad these things were gone, but they left a space that had to be filled. What was she to replace them with?

On Thanksgiving Day, clearing away in the kitchen after the meal, she was thinking somewhat along these lines. While it was true that boxes were easy to dispose of, she did not feel quite soul-satisfied with take-out pizza as a Thanksgiving dinner. She did not want to end up cooking a turkey for Christmas, but she did want—she was not sure what she wanted. She asked Volos, "What are you doing for Christmas?"

He was at the table crayoning coloring books along with Gabe and Mikey. At first he had colored as clumsily as either of them, but he was getting better—not to win gold stars, but because he loved the bright sticks of wax. "Nothing. I am not a Christian," he told her without looking up from the page he was working on.

"You don't have to be."

"I will not do Christmas. I will not celebrate that Jesus was sent to the world to be killed."

Wiping red smears off the countertops, she looked at him. He was keeping his voice level because of the children, but she could hear the edge in it and see the darkness flowing into his wings. Quietly she said, "I don't think that's what Christmas is really about for most people."

"What is it about, then?"

"I don't know . . ." She did of course know the stock answer: it was the season of capital-letter Love. But what did that mean? "God Is Love," the Sunday School paper hearts proclaimed, and in invisible ink on the flip side was written, "Go to Hell." Angie was not sure she knew what Love was. Anyway, she was not going to say "Love" to Volos. Even the thought made her face go hot. She said, "It's just a good time, I guess. Gifts, good things to eat, decorations."

"Christmas tree," put in Gabe, who had not appeared to be listening. "Candy."

"Santa!" Mikey shouted. Zapped by his excitement, his hands flew out, scattering crayons. He clambered down from his chair, went to his mother and tugged at her jeans, suddenly anxious. "Santa bring me, Mommy?"

Was Santa going to bring him presents, he meant. "Who's been telling you about Santa?" Angela squatted down to speak with the child so he would know she was on his side even though Santa was not something he had heard about from her and Ennis. Back in Jenkins, Santa had not been allowed in the house because ho-ho-ho did not fit into her father's theology. The children had always been told gifts came from God.

"Uncle Texas."

"Well, then I'm sure Santa will come. Uncle Texas knows about these things."

"What things?" Volos stood over her, looking troubled.

"The Santa Claus things and the Christmas tree things and the things that say you absolutely must get him something, Volos."

"Get Texas something?"

"Yes. Whether you like it or not. He'll be hurt if you don't."

"Texas believes in Christmas?"

Angela stood up, starting to feel exasperated. In her experience talk about religion was good for nothing except to come between people. "It's not about that," she said. "It's about whether you believe in Texas. Don't step on the crayons," she added, as he turned away with a dazed look.

"Mikey put crayons all over the floor," said Gabe severely. "He should pick them up."

"Oh." Volos halted and, to Angie's surprise, helped gather the bright-colored toys before he wandered out with muted wings.

It was a good thing Gabe and Mikey were around, thought Texas, meditating over his beer. A good thing for him in particular. He needed the little boys to pin Christmas on that year. It was early in December, and already he had sent Wyoma a card, not a box card but one of those big ones from a drugstore rack, he had spent half an hour picking it out and had made triple sure his return address was on the envelope, though he had signed it only "Bob." But he knew better, really, than to expect anything in reply.

It was a good thing, too, that nothing about Christmas seemed real around this place anyway. Palm trees. Shirtsleeves. No snow. Plastic garland on the lawn flamingos. Not much like West Virginia—which made it easier not to think about West Virginia much. Especially if he kept busy.

So there he was in the middle of the afternoon sitting in the neighborhood bar and thinking about West Virginia. What else was there to do?

Volos came in. Texas saw the feathery shadow in the mirror behind the bottles and knew right away there was something on the kid's mind. Dark wings. Also, Texas had invited Volos to go drinking with him a time or two before, but Volos would not come into narrow, enclosed places like this dive unless he had his own reasons. The kid wanted to talk.

So the angel sat on the barstool next to Texas, and the bartender came over. Texas did not much like this particular bartender. The guy had spiked hair and a ring in his nose and a ring in his ear and a chain that looked like it had been swiped from a bank's ballpoint pen strung between the two. Someday there was gonna be a nice big fight to break up and somebody was gonna grab that chain and yank it.

"Gnarly wings, dude," the bartender greeted Volos. "What'll it be?"

"Soon, the second week in Advent."

"Say again?"

"Give him a Mich," Texas directed.

The place was dark and not real friendly, which worked two ways: Late at night it meant watching your ass, but at this time of day it just meant people were going to leave you alone. Nobody bothered Volos, even though his wings trailed in the aisle. Texas sat sipping his own beer and eyeing the kid, who was watching the bulbs blinking around the Bud Lite mirror, the neon Coors sign blinking in the window, the fake tree blinking in the corner. Blink, Blink, God's a fink.

"I can't tell what are Christmas lights and what are just lights," Volos said.

Texas nodded, waiting.

"I am having trouble with this Christmas thing altogether."

"You and me both, kid."

"You, too? But Angela said you understood about it."

"I guess I do. But understanding don't always help. Christmas is a family time, see. And I got no family to go home to anymore."

Of course the kid looked blank. Family wouldn't mean squat to him. Texas didn't know sometimes why he bothered talking to Volos.

Trying to keep the weariness out of his voice, he asked the kid, "So what's the problem with you and Christmas?"

"I find it all very confusing. Do you believe in God, Texas?"

McCardle nearly choked on his beer. It was a moment before he managed to say, "Considering that I believe in you, that's a real peculiar question."

"Yes. But do you?"

"Yeah, dammit, I guess I do." He felt irritated; this was too personal. "Why?"

"Because I do not see how you can believe in God and speak of Santa Claus. God has taken a festival of lights, a yuletide, a Saturnalia, a way to illuminate the dark and warm the winter's chill, and he has turned it into a celebration of death."

"Death?"

"Yes. Jesus was born only to be killed. Do you believe in Jesus?"

Texas drained his beer and gazed into the empty mug before he said, "Got to, son."

"You think he died for your sins? Are you glad he died?"

Texas thought he understood what this was about now. He said very gently, "Hell, no, kid, but I'm glad he lived."

Volos sat silent in the bar, his wings the color of its scarlet neon darkness. After a while Texas added, "So you don't like Christmas."

"Yes. No. I don't know. What am I supposed to do?"

"Nothing. Except you gotta get the little guys something. Break their hearts if you don't. And get Angie something nice." Texas could tell now that Angie cared for Volos. Sweet, grave-faced Angela. Such an innocent, it probably hadn't occurred to her what went on between Volos and Mercy. She probably didn't know men could have sex with one another.

Volos remarked, "Neither of you has told me to get something for Mercedes."

"Well, course you can get him something if you *want* to."

The bartender came over again. "*Purple* eyes today?" he said to Volos. "Christ, man. How many pairs of colored contacts you got?" Not expecting an answer, he set up another round. His T-shirt confronted the world with a Mexican street artist's primitive rendition of a woman in parturition. Texas loathed this guy, but as he pulled the beers Volos seemed to be looking at him with some interest.

"You've got to be kidding," Texas complained after the barman had walked away.

"Pardon?"

There were a lot of slang expressions the kid didn't understand. Texas translated. "You like the looks of him?"

"I like his chain, that is all. Texas—are you going to give me something for Christmas?"

Texas wanted to say, "Only if you're good," but stopped himself. Volos sometimes took teasing seriously. And there was something in the kid's voice as wide open as the woman in childbirth.

" 'Course I am, Volos. Why wouldn't I?"

"I don't know."

"What should I get you?"

"What is that thing you say? About getting beaten?"

"Beats the hell out of me."

"That's what it does, then." Without finishing his

beer—or paying for it—without a smile or a lift of the hand Volos got up and walked out.

The week before Christmas, Volos canceled gigs and rehearsals and sent his band members, surprised but grateful, to their scattered homes for the holidays.

That same week Angie and Texas ate take-out Chicken Singapore for supper one night, while the little boys, who had not yet cultivated a taste for Chinese cuisine, had Steak-Umms. Something in the Chicken Singapore caused the human body to take exception to it. By midnight Texas and Angie were groaning, and Volos discovered that the care and feeding of the household were up to him.

"Are you going to die?" he asked at first, terrified.

"No, just wish we would," Texas panted. "Christ, my gut hurts. We oughta sue. It's food poisoning."

"Food poisoning?" The concept baffled Volos. "How can you eat food, then, if it poisons you?"

"Just—fucking let me alone, goddammit."

Texas did not make a good patient. He reacted to every aspect of his illness as if it were a personal affront, and he refused to see a doctor. Short of picking him up and carrying him out to the car, then sitting on him, there was no way to make him go to one. So in the morning Volos left the boys in front of the television and took Angie to the medical center. When they came back with thick, earthy-smelling medicine he waited until she took her dose, and then he forced some down Texas also, none too gently. In fact, he did it while restraining McCardle with one knee on his chest. The bosomy nurse at the doctor's office had assured him that if Texas was strong enough to swear at him there was nothing to really worry about. Therefore he felt entitled to swear back.

"Just take the fucking medicine, goddammit!"

From the doorway Gabe and Mikey watched, wide-eyed. "Birdman give us lunch?" Mikey chirped after Volos had ministered to Texas.

"Birdman try." Volos headed toward the kitchen.

Over the course of the next several days he discovered, or rather was repeatedly told, that he was an execrable cook, even though all he had to prepare for the patients was tea, toast, and rice. The first time he tried to make tea, he cut open the teabag and tried to dissolve its contents in hot water from the tap. He burned the toast or served it cold or turned it to Styrofoam in the microwave. His rice, even foolproof instant rice, was sticky and undercooked. When Angie suggested grilled cheese sandwiches for the boys, Volos fried the cheese first, turning it to a brown adhesive in the bottom of a pan, then threw the pan away and sent out for pizza. For that week Gabe and Mikey lived mostly on pizza for supper, peanut butter for lunch, cereal for breakfast.

"It's a good thing I bought their presents early," Angie said to Volos in a pale voice. The boys were asleep and therefore would not hear her. Volos had put them to bed. He was getting better at it. He had learned not to let them pour shampoo in the water when they had their bath. He had dried their hair and put them in pajamas and held them in his lap as he read them Little Golden Books about a reindeer in need of rhinoplasty and a hyperactive snowman. Tonight he would stay in the house again in case he was needed. He had not seen Mercedes for five days. Mercy had phoned three times, peevish, but Mercy would have to wait.

Speaking with Angela, he sat on the edge of her bed with his wings blushing petal-pink. It surprised him, the tenderness he felt for her. Odd that he did not mind being her servant. It was true that she did not ask for much, but even if she had called on him more often he would not have minded. It seemed somehow fitting that he should wait on her.

"Do you feel any better?" he asked her. He hated the way sickness made her wretched.

"A little. Volos—I hate to keep asking you to do

things, but do you think you could wrap their stuff while they're asleep?"

"You can ask me anything. Yes, of course I will do it."

"Volos!" Texas bellowed.

Now that one he minded. He said to Angela, "Sometimes I would like to put him in a sack and take him and drop him from a high place."

She smiled. "Men are all like that when they're sick," she informed him.

"Truly?"

"*VO*-los!"

He sighed and answered the summons. Texas was feeling somewhat better too, and sitting up in bed. "Volos," he said with asperity, "my stomach's rubbing itself. Do you think you could just for once make me some toast that don't look and feel and taste like old cardboard?"

"Was I like that?" Volos asked him, tangentially.

"Huh?"

"When you took care of me, when my wing was sick. Was I like you, so full of spleen?"

A considerable silence. Then in a different tone Texas said, "No. No, you weren't. Son, don't mind me. Forget the toast. I ain't really hungry."

Because something other than cardboard toast was troubling him, Volos heard only the first part of this. He blurted, "But Angela says all men are that way. Perhaps it was just that you took better care of me."

Perhaps it is that I am not a man.

"You do okay. It's just that—listen, kid, it's not you, it's me. Ever since my daddy beat me I get this way. Being laid up just makes me pissing mad."

Volos drifted out of the room before Texas was finished speaking. *Perhaps it is that I am not quite human.* He went to the kitchen, put a slice of bread into the toaster. *Not quite real.* Stood by until it popped, gazing at the machine with an unseeing stare. *The humans, they take this Christmas festival and*

celebrate it in spite of everything, in defiance of all reason.
If I could be that way, if I could understand ...

He held the warm toast in his hand and went back
to Texas.

"Here."

"Son, I meant it when I told you not to bother.
Hell, I ain't that sick anymore, I can get up and take
care of myself now." Texas accepted the toast anyway
and ate it, then said, "Hey, that was good. Can you
fix me another slice?"

The next day he and Angie were tottering around
the house some of the time, eating Campbell's chicken
noodle soup, watching TV. Angie even set out a ham
to thaw for the next day's dinner. But Volos had not
had a chance to buy anything for either of them. There
were no stockings hung from the drum stands with
care. There were no tree ornaments in the house.
Moreover, there was no tree. And it was Christmas
Eve.

Gabriel, who was a thoughtful child, did not fully
believe in the Santa Claus mythos to which he had
recently been exposed. He sensed an adult smile behind the stories he was told. Also, he did not much
like fat people; he found their presence in his world
threatening, as if even with all good intentions they
had the potential to sit on him by mistake or suffocate
him with an embrace. From his small-person view-
point, they were just too massive. Moreover, he did
not think it sensible that a stranger, whether fat or
not, would give him presents for no good reason.

Nevertheless, that night when the house was quiet
and everyone should have been asleep, he found himself still awake, kept up by an unreasonable sense of
expectation. In the distance he thought he heard a
noise. Getting out of the double bed he shared with
Mikey by climbing over the backs of its guardian
chairs, he barefooted his way through the dim house
to see if anything was happening.

Nothing was, except that in the living room Birdman was sitting on a tall stool with his newest guitar, bright, slick red, in his lap. This was all right. Birdman was always up at night, though not always in the house—sometimes he went prowling, like a wild animal. The night belonged to Birdman. But knowing that he himself was not supposed to be out of bed, Gabe did not say hello, instead staying back in the shadows of the hallway, watching.

Birdman was very beautiful in a shaft of moonlight from the big window, and his wings were like the blue snow on a Christmas card. He touched his guitar, which was turned down very low. He stroked it like it was alive, so that it hummed notes for him, first one note, then another. Gabe sat down where he was to listen, because he could tell that something good was happening. He had never heard Birdman's guitar speak so softly, humming like a mother at bedtime.

Birdman touched it again, so that it murmured like a sleepy baby. And then Birdman sang.

Never afterward, though he thought of that night sometimes even when he was a grown man, never was Gabe able to remember any words—just notes, just music. Birdman opened his mouth and sent the notes flying softly around the room, one after another, small, flitting notes of all colors, Christmas red and green, gold, silver, shimmering blue. They were little crested birds, each one round and perfect. Of course they had to be birds, coming from Birdman. The way he made a song and turned it into birds was just the way God made angels because God was a big angel himself. An old witch of a Sunday School teacher had told Gabe about it once, how for every word God spoke angels were born out of his mouth.

Then Gabe saw how the humming guitar strings were weaving their music into the shadows of one corner of the room and forming something soft and dark and spiky, like a bad kid's haircut. The guitar purred in Birdman's lap like a big cat with sheathed claws, and the something in the corner grew, and the birds flew to it. It was a tree—just a round sawtooth sort of tree, not really a Christmas tree by Gabe's standards, but the birds liked it. Of course, birds need a tree to sit in. But they didn't just sit on this one, they arranged themselves all over it until they seemed sprinkled onto it like soft little stars onto a shadowy sky, red and green and gold and silver and blue.

It was midnight, because church bells were ringing somewhere out in L.A. Gabe could hear them far away, even though there were people shouting and yipping and fighting in the corner bar, which was much closer. Birdman put down his guitar and sat very still. He was finished singing, and it was the first minute of Christmas Day.

When Gabe went back to bed, Mikey turned over, then seamlessly reentered his dream. In the morning he would remember the dream, but have no memory that Gabe had gone wandering.

Mikey was not convinced about putting his faith in Santa Claus either. He was worried that Santa Claus would forget him because he was new on the list. Therefore Mikey's dream was straightforward: he would receive presents from someone he could trust. Birdman was the Christmas angel, bringing gifts for Mikey and Gabe and Mommy, but nobody else. Not Daddy. Mommy had explained how there would not be a Daddy in this Christmas. Not for Daddy's mommy, the Grandma who lived in Arizona, or the other Grandma either, and especially not for Grandpa, because Mommy was very, very mad at Grandpa. And not for all the other children in the world. They had Santa Claus to take care of them. Birdman was just for Mikey, and Gabe, and Mommy, and he would bring gifts for them. And maybe Uncle Texas. But that was all.

To bring the presents, Birdman was riding a slow-prancing high-crested sweet-headed white horse through the night sky, on top of the clouds. His wings rose high in the indigo air and seemed to belong both to him and to his horse. Why he was riding the horse when he could fly was unclear. Mikey had no clear image either of what the presents were or how Birdman carried them. What was important was the way Birdman sat on the white horse, the Christmas horse. His long legs were straight down around its belly, and his knees pressed against its sides, and his dark eyes stared out over its ears like he was looking at something.

There was a black moon up there in the sky, big, like a hole to let in the cold, like a black roller to flatten the clouds. When the white horse carried Birdman behind it, Mikey stirred and whimpered in his sleep. But Birdman came out the other side, and Mikey smiled, because on the white horse with him Daddy was riding.

"I gotta admit, it's different," Texas remarked.

It was Christmas morning, and sometime during the night the Santa in residence had come up with a tree. Texas hoped Volos hadn't actually stolen it out of somebody's yard, but suspected he had. It appeared to be some sort of palmetto or dwarf palm, and Volos had stood it in Gabe's sand pail in the living room corner and decorated it with all sorts of oddball things: red and yellow guitar picks, crayons, wads of crumpled aluminum foil, cutout paper birds, cereal box Frisbees, toilet tissue garland, a red string tie liberated from Texas's room, a swag of chain that looked like it came off a bank's ballpoint pen—

"How in blazes did you get your hands on that?" Texas asked Volos.

The kid shrugged, making his shoulder feathers rustle. "I asked the man at the bar for it. It seems he collects them, so he gave me many. He says tell you he hopes you are well soon. He says Merry Christmas."

"Well, cut off my head and call me Shorty."

There were a number of the cheap metal chains on the tree. "I think it's the prettiest Christmas tree ever," Angela said. The way she was gazing, her dark eyes big as a deer's in her pale face, she looked like she meant it.

The little boys weren't wasting any time admiring the tree, Texas noticed. They had ripped straight into their presents, which were piled underneath it. Settling into seats nearby, Angie and Texas watched. Volos stayed on his feet. Hovering.

"I could have gone out and bought tree things," the kid said. "You know, those chaser lights and things. There were some stores still open. I checked. But I did not feel as if the things in the store were real." Volos windmilled his arms, trying to explain something important to him, struggling with what he wanted to say. "For me to make it be Christmas, it was as if I had to do it with my hands. Just like to make it be music, I must pull it out of the guitar."

"That's okay, kid." Texas did not understand, but did not feel he really had to. Some things were well enough left alone.

"But it is maybe not okay. I could have bought things last night, and I did not. I never got presents for either of you."

Relief and a sort of rueful happiness bubbled up inside of Texas so that he had to laugh. "Volos, that's fine. I never got you anything either."

"Your heart is not broken?" The kid was looking at him so anxiously that Texas got up from his chair and hugged him.

"Merry Christmas. Hell, no. My heart ain't even dinged."

"Angela?"

She was smiling. Texas loved the way she smiled. She said, "Volos, nearly every day since I came here has been like Christmas to me."

Under the tree Mikey squealed and held up a stuffed toy, his gift from Volos, bought weeks before: a plush white prancing horse.

chapter
ten

Coming out of Club Decimo one dawn, Volos found a priest awaiting him. A young man. Black shirt, white Roman collar, gray starved face that yearned like many of the faces Volos met, audience faces mostly, as if people thought he could somehow hear them, understand them, accept them, when in fact he craved the same of them. The priest stood still and did not call out or come forward with pawing hands, but Volos recognized the look on his face and stopped in front of him, waiting.

The priest said, "Thank you. I have very much been wanting to talk with you." His voice was soft, and shivered with emotion. Volos merely nodded.

The priest asked, "Are you Him? Have you come again?"

Volos answered, low-voiced, "Some people say I am the cock of Satan." The hate mail had been coming in by the bagful from people who found his wings blasphemous, and therefore his behavior offensive, his lyrics obscene. "Why would you believe I am your savior?"

"For that reason. People did not think much of him either."

"Please," Volos said. "I'm not—"

But the young priest went on speaking, intense yet dreamy. "Now they do not want to remember the way he was, you know. They like to forget that he scourged the money dealers out of the temple. That he danced at weddings. That he thumbed his nose at bigwigs, and broke all the rules, and loved women, and liked food, and gloried in wine."

"I know those things," Volos said. "I know he was not a candy-ass. I remember him. He was my friend, and I've never forgiven what happened to him. Please just shut up and go home. I am not the one you want."

"Take courage," the priest said.

"Please. No. You know what they did to him."

Something about the incident with the priest spurred Volos to undergo the passion he had been putting off, the communion, the mystic act, the bonding into brotherhood. That night after rehearsal he had his band stay and choose a name. It had to be done in the witching hours, of course. But first he had to explain that he wanted no name that had anything to do with wings or heavenly mythology. He was a rocker, not an angel.

"Then what the hell do you wear the wings for, man?" Cisco, the drummer, wanted to know.

"Just ignore the wings, please? Humor me."

"Okay, but I think we'll be missing out—"

"Fuck the wings! I hate the goddamn wings!"

His irrational behavior allowed them to roll their eyes and not say what they were thinking: Why did he not take them off? But Red said, "Hey, Volos, like it or not, you're our front man. Without you we ain't nothing. The name's got to have something to do with you."

"Perhaps."

"Yes, it does. I think it does. What about you guys?" Nods all around. "So if you don't want it to do with the wings, then tell us something else about yourself. Where you from?"

"Air."

"Give us a break, man."

"It is true. I was nothing."

"You gotta come from somewhere."

"I was a minor Slavic fertility god."

They laughed and kicked that around awhile, brainstorming names: Electric Prick, What Rhymes with Venus, Man from Nantucket. Volos had never heard some of the filthier limericks, and was delighted with them. But a gross-out name did not suit the group's image, and everyone knew it. In the metal spectrum, Volos was way over at the "lite" edge. If he had ever truly wanted to be black-snake heavy-duty steely-evil, he had failed. There was an innocence about him.

So after a while his band members started asking the basic human questions again: What is your sign? Your birthplace? Your real name? (For they made the assumption, reasonable in L.A., that "Volos" was a pseudonym.) With a sense first of struggle, then of surrender to the lie that might be more true than he knew, Volos told them: Gemini. Moundsville, West Virginia. Flaim Carson McCardle.

He expected them to make the connection with Texas, but they did not. Texas was a sort of janitor to them, just another nice guy, nearly anonymous.

They were, however, impressed by the name. "Christ," the no-nonsense keyboard player said. "A name like Flaim, and you changed it?"

"It was not my choice. I like the name," Volos protested. "All men are fire. Burn and die and turn to dirt. Earth is the inferno." As a bodiless being, full of envy for human passion, sometimes he had been able to see the air waver above people's heads as if above candle flame.

"Hey," said Red softly.

"Yeah," said both the drummer and the keyboard man.

Thus it was that Burning Earth was christened. And once named, immediately it began inexorably to take on identity. The lead guitarist started to grow his hair longer and dyed it to match his name, red. The drummer began hiding his barrel chest under chains and pendants. Even the balding keyboard man abandoned button-downs in favor of open collars. Except for the drummer, who was overweight and had to sit down, they began wearing their jeans skintight. Red smoked joints before rehearsal. Cisco started carrying a flask.

The Buddy Holly look-alike woman, on the other hand, surprised Volos by shouting at him that she was a married woman, how could he expect her to go on tour and leave her family behind? She quit. Her anger astounded him, but within a week he forgot her, once Brett had replaced her with a lank, morose, and hollow-chested individual named Bink. Tall, dark, and obnoxious, he had cobra tattoos on each arm and wore a rat-skull earring. By that time Burning Earth had progressed to the point that he fit right in.

Volos and Burning Earth cut their album in a few days' time, straight and honest-to-the-devil as they could do it, with not much mixing and very few overdubs. It turned out fresh as a city kid's mouth. The cover consisted of a shot of Volos's unclothed back, off-center and close up to show the small downy feathers at the base of the left wing and the sleek coverts of the right. The wings were ice-blue—Volos had been depressed at the time of the shoot. The album was hot, the band was cookin', Volos himself was a hot property, yet he was depressed a lot lately, his heart leadened by a sense of foreboding, of pain on the way.

For no perceptible reason he titled the album *Scars*.

The Burning Earth *Scars* tour opened at Shoreside Amphitheater in Mountain View, California.

For this venue—Volos's first in anything larger than a music hall—Angie had costumed him virtually the opposite of the way Mercedes wanted him. No beaded velvets or sequined satins, no glamour, no glitz. For the first set Volos went out in bare feet and a pair of jeans Angie had carefully destroyed for him so that they showed a webwork of angel-white cotton and earth-dark flesh nearly to his waist. From backstage Angie watched with her heart aflame. It had been she who had suggested the mutilated jeans, and Volos had embraced the concept at once, as she had known he must from knowing his music. Volos could sing angel pure, milk white and honey sweet when he wanted to. But to him it was not the clean tone that was truly beautiful; it was the sweating, distressed tone— warped, tormented, distorted, dirtied—that he loved. Music as gritty as a day laborer, wide open like a wise old whore, music that had been through something. Likewise the jeans.

Angie had laid open one pair of her own jeans to the thigh, and wore them that night, and gazed with deerlike eyes as Volos rocked, swayed, sang. Those in the front rows could tell he wore no Calvin Kleins under those Wrangler slims with the button fly, under those half-concealing wings. And already they were going wild, but it was she, she, who had arranged the torn cloth over that body and who sometimes touched those wings.

And who had written the songs ... but somehow it seemed more important that she had touched the body, the wings.

The music throbbed around her and through her, it was alive, a huge thing, a heartbeat, and she floated in its shadowy womb with an angel whispering in her ear, and she was wise, innocent, preverbal, her whole world was light and color and the strange brilliant butterfly shapes of electric guitars. Volos carried a blood-red one whose double-cutaway design made it seem horned like a demon. Or not so much carried it as wore it, a huge red pendant hanging at his crotch. Angie knew, without any need to think why, that seeing the guitar on Volos excited her, gave her inti-

mations of potency, of power and strength. She had
lifted his guitar once and found the thing unbelievably
heavy even with the neck strap in place. But Volos
bore it like a part of himself, an appendage slung from
his broad brawny shoulders then jutting from his un-
derbelly as those great wings jutted from his back.

Wings lifted in strata of light, pulsing as electric-
pink as a remembered radio, the boogie box somebody had stolen from her on her trip west. Amid that
neon-rose glow Volos turned a tone knob all the way
from steely to mellow and eased into a new song she
had written for him.

> *You can fly*
> *You'd rather walk by my side*
> *You could live*
> *Someday you'll have to die*
> *You're not afraid.*
> *There is sunrise in your eyes*
> *Get out your black bike*
> *Let's take the long ride*
> *Let me put my arms around you*
> *For the long ride.*

> *You are so very beautiful*
> *Half animal*
> *Half god*
> *Your heart is a wild stallion*
> *Your thoughts are clouds in the wind*
> *And I am weak with love of you*
> *I turn to you like a child*
> *Get out your black bike*
> *Let's take the long ride.*
> *Let me put my arms around you*
> *Let me lay my head between your*
> *   wings*
> *For the long ride.*

It seemed not to trouble the audience that in singing

this tender ballad Volos was declaring love to himself. Nor did it trouble Angela. To her he walked on water. Even in his self-absorption (of which she knew as much as anyone), to her he could do no wrong. The exaltation she felt when she touched his wings was like worship, a sharp striving joy untinged with the resentment she had always felt in the presence of her father's God.

Someone came and stood beside her. It took her a moment to gather herself out of the music enough to glance over and see a Hoss Cartwright hat shadowing anxious eyes: Texas. He bent to speak directly into her ear, though standing as they were near the PA stacks, way over their heads in sound, drowning in the stuff, he could probably have shouted without disturbing anyone.

"I think I finally got the security nailed down," he told her. Not that security was any part of her job. It was his problem. But Texas was a sweet old guy, he worried about Volos, he worried about her and her kids, and now he was worried about crowd management and needed her to tell him she was sure everything would be all right. She smiled vaguely at him and turned back to watch Volos just as he reached a climax, arching his body, flinging his head back so that his dark hair coiled down between his shivering wings. Not aware that she did so, Angie sighed.

"Ange." The voice sounded so much like Ennis's that she jumped, jolted by the same kind of sudden reflexive guilt that sometimes hit her when she thought she saw Ennis on the street or in a store. At first glance every sturdy, brown-haired young man was Ennis to her. Some days she seemed to run into him everywhere. But she was getting used to it now, and anyway the man beside her was just Texas again, peering at her.

"Angie, you know he probably don't have no idea of the way you feel about him."

Volos, he meant. It did not surprise her that Texas

had noticed. Sometimes it seemed to her that Texas didn't have much to do except hang around and watch a person. He was kind of useless. But never mind that, because he was a nice guy, maybe her best friend in L.A. He was sweet with her kids, and he took care of them for her whenever she couldn't find a sitter.

She shrugged her shoulders at him. Shoulders blessedly uncut by bra straps, blessedly comfortable in T-shirt and nothing more. Sometimes in public she had to restrain herself from lifting her hands to her delighted, wayward breasts. Sometimes she walked stiffly. Her new freedom was made half of euphoria, half of terror—of her own body, its new self-consciousness, its passions, its unexplored abilities, its power. Nothing in her upbringing helped her know how to make her body send signals to a man.

"No reason why he should," she told Texas.

"You kidding? You don't give yourself enough credit. What you want to do is get yourself a little makeup, maybe a hair ribbon, a pretty dress—"

"It's all right with me if he doesn't notice me," Angie said.

"For crying out loud, Angie, you mean you're just going to go on like you been?"

She said softly, "Sure. Isn't it enough?"

Coming offstage after the first set, Volos walked past her, all gleaming with sweat, and smiled. It was enough.

From a platform atop the gantries with the lighting man, Mercedes waited for the second set, still seething over the costuming of the first. Destroyed denim. Jesus Christ, how déclassé. Volos listened far too much to his little chippie of a seamstress.

The lighting man's intercom crackled, and he spoke softly into it, then pushed the big switch. The stage went dark, but spots lashed the crowd, and under their stimulation it screamed like a single huge primitive animal and lifted a hundred thousand cirri into the tides of the night. The arms held T-shirts, hand-lettered banners, homemade Styrofoam wings. It irked Mercedes that Volos would not let Brett franchise somebody to sell light-up wings. It irked him that the angel insisted on these Stone Age staging arrangements and was not interested in a laser show, computerization, a dance troupe, anything programmed or choreographed or state-of-the-art. Lots of things about Volos irked Mercedes these days.

He waited, not totally immune to the excitement. Somewhere backstage, roadies with faint red flashlights were leading the rock god back to the stage. . . . No telling for sure what color Volos's wings would be when the spot shone on him, but Mercedes, who was as good as anyone at reading the singer's moods, decided that anything in the blue to orange range would be safe.

"Magenta," he directed the lighting man.

"Right, boss."

The intercom crackled again, a bank of fresnel lenses blazed, and there was Volos, his back turned, his wings slowly spreading—and great balls of fire, they could really spread on this stage, they made his presence immense, huge, even the people in the cheap seats knew they were seeing something—poised on the edge of the drum riser he flamed the color of a wild rose, and then came the hammering downbeat, the turn and leap and the dancing advance to the mikes, flanked by his two ax men in their outlaw hats. And Mercedes had to admit Volos was right, he looked good in chaps. They outlined that incredible crotch, visible when he lifted his guitar. Their long fringes and rawhide thongs flowed with him. But Mercedes was not entirely happy, because the Navaho headband and silver-spurred roach stompers were courtesy of Texas, and Mercedes did not care for Texas' influence on Volos any more than he did for Angie's.

The show was reaching its height. Burning Earth had upped tempo and pulsed into "Before I Die," with Volos soloing on guitar—on many frontmen the guitar was nothing more than a giant phallic prop, not even plugged into the speakers, but Volos could really play. The critics made much of that, comparing him to Jimi Hendrix. Hooray for the critics. Funny thing they had never noticed how their new darling could have played his guitar more effectively if he had slung it a few inches higher instead of right at his crotch. But he wore it where it looked best. On that one matter at least, he had taken Mercedes's advice.

Or maybe he would have worn it there anyway. Volos liked being a big dick.

Bink and Red were singing backup vocals, and Red had come over to share a mike with Volos, heads close, lips nearly touching in a stance that reminded Mercedes of a homosexual kiss. He felt a sudden hot stab of jealousy. That rapt, lovemaking look on Volos's fine-edged face—it should not be shared with so many people, only with him. Damn Volos, he always did that, he gave everything he had, threw it all away to the crowd. He courted the mike, that cock of God, with soft lips and fluttering eyelids. He offered to that hellbeast of arms and faces beyond the lights his heart on a platter, his music the colors of wine. And it made people wild. Soon his worshipers would want to eat him. Someday they would tear him apart and swallow the bits, brown bread of the devil's communion.

"Boss?" It was the lighting man.

"White," Mercedes directed. "Just for a moment, until we see what we have."

Volos sang on with wings the color of the sun.

Jealousy left Mercedes and was replaced by something far colder. He smiled, his teeth hard behind tight lips. "Red," he ordered.

All right, he would share his lover. All right, he was the pimp and Volos the whore who would make him rich. All right, Volos could be the sun if he wanted, and Mercedes nothing more than a spot on its face.

Mercedes could wait. He knew what always happened to superstars.

Finale. From dry ice, smoke poured up, throwing everything into shadow. Gunshot sounds ricocheted from the synthesizer. The lights swung wildly, thrashing, flailing, red whips of a raging god. Amid it all, Volos buckled to his knees, guitar laid down like a defeated sword, head bowed, wings flowing down a king's sunset cloak onto the stage.

God, the bastard knew how to pose. Mercedes smiled again, watching the first of the girls up front struggle onto the stage and run sobbing toward him.

It was only a matter of time.

In the bowl of the amphitheater the fans stood on their seats, necks stretched and mouths agape, far too many baby birds in a nest far too large. From where he stood, just offstage, Texas could see only outreached, imploring hands and heaving breasts. Lots of breast and cleavage. Looked to him like these girls hadn't dressed at home.

"Volos," they cried out like wood thrushes. "Volos!" Their reedy voices grew stronger, were joined by the darker shouts of men. Cries became a chant.

"Vo-LOS! Vo-LOS! Vo-LOS!"

"I hope he doesn't get 'em too psyched," Texas muttered to himself. Mobs scared him. Instead of his customary western string tie he wore a clip-on so that he could not be strangled.

"Vo-LOS! Vo-LOS! Vo-LOS!"

Standing as he was in the wind of the speakers, Texas could see their invocation more than hear it. The panting chests. The half-lidded eyes, the mouths wide open as if bread of communion hung for the taking in the vibrating air. And the kid was not holding anything back as the show drew to a close, singing his heart out, dancing like fire, shining all over with sweat and glory. Between numbers he drenched his head with water, shaking it so that his dark hair flew and flung off droplets, sprinkling the front rows. Those who felt that baptism wept and screamed.

Texas thought, *I hope the kid knows what he's getting into.* At first the bared breasts had deceived him. He had assumed he was seeing one of humankind's simpler, more manageable emotions: lust. But now he knew. This was dangerous. This was worship.

Volos was right out at the front of the lowest part of the stage, touching people's hands. He gave too much, he trusted too much. Texas hoped—

It was too late for hoping. The last chords were rocketing with the fireworks, then falling, falling, Volos had gone down on his knees to the horned god of dark music, and dozens of people, young men and women, were up over the lip of the stage.

Texas ran forward. But—wait, the kid seemed almost to be expecting them. And all they wanted was . . .

Volos kneeled like a novice knight, his back straight, head lifted. Music hushed as the band stood watching, uncertain (like Texas) what they needed to do. The lights shone down morning calm and pure. And the people around Volos, some of them fat, some of them ugly as sin, they were all pilgrims to the holy land, worshipers laying their hands on a piece of the cross; they stood in near-silence and touched him as gently as shepherds greeting the baby Jesus. A hundred hands gentled him on his arms, his chest, his neck, his head. Lips, many lips, brushed his hair and face. Like a flower turning to the light Volos turned up his face and closed his eyes. Somebody kissed the lids.

Feeling way out of place, a heathen among the holy, Texas pushed his way to the kid's side—

Volos screamed.

In the same instant Texas saw: an anonymous hand coming away from the kid's back, carrying a long, pale feather. Texas could not have felt worse if he had seen in the crowd a hand coming up pointing a gun.

And before he could move another step, within an eyeblink it all turned ugly, it was all fighting, all hands that reached to grip and claw and tear. Volos was on his feet, with Texas pulling people off him and slinging them away, trying to position himself at Volos's back, between the kid's wings to defend them. Panicked, the kid didn't help him any. But there were others getting into it, the band members, some roadies from backstage. By the time the uniformed security officers arrived, Texas and the irregulars almost had things under control.

"Fuck it, Texas!" Volos screamed at him when they faced each other offstage. "You let them get behind me!"

The kid was shaking, and his dun-colored skin had gone ashy gray. "Easy does it," Texas told him, trying to calm him with a hand on one shoulder. Volos pulled away.

"Why did you let them get onstage? Where were the guards?"

There had been a few polite men in sport coats stationed along the edge of the stage during the performance. Like him, Texas guessed, they had been thrown by the peaceful way it had all started. Or maybe by the numbers of people involved. It looked like there should have been more in the way of security.

He said, "I'm sorry, Volos. I screwed up."

"And you said you'd never hurt me." Volos turned calm but terribly, fiercely bitter.

"Hey, man, lighten up." A soft voice—it was Red. "Texas didn't maul you."

Staring narrow-eyed at Texas, Volos seemed not to hear. "Judas," he accused. "I trusted you."

Red tried again to intervene. "You trusted the fans, was the problem." Crowd noise battered them, loud, screaming, as physical in its presence as a demanding child, making him raise his voice. "Texas just followed your lead. We all did."

After his years as a cop, Texas knew all the things people said when they were in trouble, and he scorned most of them. He knew he should speak up for himself, but did not. Partly, he was quietly angry—the kid should know better than to call him names. And partly, it all felt hopeless. What could he say when Volos felt so betrayed?

The new guy, Bink, the sourpuss bass guitarist, came up and said, "It's all part of the job, for Chrissake. Can we get to the encore before they tear the place apart?"

Texas swallowed hard and bent to smooth a jutting feather. Volos jerked the wing away. "Don't touch them!"

"May I fix them, Volos?" It was Angie. Without waiting for his permission she started, and Volos sighed, extended his wings and submitted to her care. Texas watched, feeling his anger dull into worry. There were only a few drops of blood, only a few broken pinions and a tattered covert or two, but every mark made Texas feel sick. If the kid got feverish and infected again, Texas would hold himself to blame.

"All right." In a few minutes Volos was stonily ready, though his wings had gone bruise-blue. "Encore."

It was "Slavehouse of Power," and Volos led the band through it like a tornado leading a storm front. This time, when the audience rushed the stage, Texas and a dozen roadies-cum-bodyguards were ready for them and held them off.

Afterward, after Volos had signed a few carefully controlled autographs at the stage door, after the kid had been hustled through a gantlet of reaching hands, once in the bus and on the way to the next venue, the next hotel, Texas let himself close his eyes a moment. There had been a busty young woman at the stage door who had pulled down the neck of her T-shirt and invited Volos to sign her breast. "Over my heart," she had breathed at him. But even that had not made the kid smile. He was barely speaking to anyone, not speaking to Texas at all, and his wings had gone the color of glare ice on the road. For a moment Texas wished he was back in Persimmon, West Virginia.

"He's not being fair," said Angie's soft voice next to him. Because he liked her—heck, he more than liked her, even though he knew she was not for him— Texas smiled, but he did not open his eyes.

"Yepper, he's throwing a fit, all right," he said. "But the hell of it is, I know how he feels. I hate it when people get together like a pack of wolves. Let them catch you off guard and they'll crucify you."

chapter
eleven

The next morning Brett phoned Texas at the hotel, as shaken as he had ever heard her. She had just received a rock-through-the-window message: "Volos the unholy, Prepare to DIE."

Simpleminded—but Texas knew better than to take it lightly. Even with people too far away to touch his wings, something about Volos always seemed to stir up the best or worst in them. There had been unholy rockers from the start and always would be, but religious-minded people were frightened by Volos as never before, and anti-rock crusades were heating up all over the country, first on TV and then wherever preachers wanted a piece of the action.

Striding in scuffed Laredos down the hallway to talk with the kid, Texas felt somber, because he knew a lot about fanatics in general and their virulent hatred. But he had not yet heard of the most virulent anti-rock movement in the country, a tent-revival phenomenon called the Central Pennsylvania League for Moral Purity, headed by a charismatic pastor with a personal agenda, a holy man who had tragically lost a daughter and two grandsons to the seductions of rock music.

Texas knew nothing of the Reverend Daniel Ephraim Crawshaw.

At Volos's room, he knocked. Mercedes opened the door and smirked. Beyond him, Volos sat mostly naked on a rumpled bed. Wings, gray-blue. Eyes, Texas saw as he walked closer, the rainy dark color of river water.

Texas waited until Mercedes (who possessed the perfect insincere manners and sardonic charm of a well-paid gigolo) left the room, then asked, "How are the wings?"

"Shit on the wings."

Texas hunkered down to look up into his charge's face. "I mean it, kid. I'm worried, I remember what happened before. How are they?"

Volos said more quietly, "They're tender, that is all. Sore. Like my head."

"Are they gonna be okay?"

"I think so."

Texas said what he should have the night before. "Volos, I never meant for that to happen. Didn't seem at first like anything was wrong. Looked to me like you wanted those people near you."

"I know. I did."

"Then why are you mad at me?"

"I'm not anymore." This, Texas knew, was as close to an apology as he was likely to get, and that was all right with him. Having to apologize just hurt a man's pride and made him madder inside, which didn't help anything in the long run. Better to just let things go by.

He said quietly, "What is it, then?"

"I'm angry at myself. What are you doing down there? Get up."

Texas sat next to him on the bed and offered, "Why not just be mad at the fans instead?"

"I am the one who has screwed up, Texas. I have failed from the day I came here. I wanted—"

"A person don't always get what they want."

"Would you shut up and listen? I came here to be with people. Hang around with them, fix cars, play poker, tell jokes, drink beer with friends. Ride a roller coaster, throw a Frisbee, walk a dog, paint the porch, get caught in the rain with somebody, have a baby."

Texas smiled, and Volos knew at once what he was thinking.

"Fucking right, I want to do that! You know I've never done it with a woman?"

"You're kidding." Texas was genuinely surprised. "I thought you had all the bases covered."

"How could I? Mercy would not let me, even if it wasn't that the wings get in the way. I've never even been on a real date. Or dancing. Or to lie on the beach."

"Some of that stuff you can do," Texas said. He remembered reading how Elvis did things. You're a rock star or a movie star, you want to go skating, you rent the whole rink. If Volos wanted a woman, Texas imagined he could rent one of those too. A high-class one, with the money he had.

"It is not just to do things." Volos struggled to explain. "It is—it is that I wanted to be a person, and be with people, but everything keeps me away from them. My wings. This rock star thing."

"You didn't plan on being a rock star?"

Volos sat silent.

"You never imagined yourself this way?"

Very softly the kid said, "Okay, so I did."

Texas found that he felt irritated, unable to offer any sympathy. He said, "My mama always told me, watch what you wish for, you may get it."

"Why, what were you wishing for? Your father?"

"No. I was mostly wishing nosy people would let me alone. Another thing my mama told me—things generally get worse before they get better."

"What things?"

"Rock star things." Texas described the death threat, watching the kid as he spoke, and feeling his irritation giving way to something like fatherly pride. Volos might be a prick sometimes, but he was a ballsy prick. At first his face grew very still, but a moment later he straightened, a fighter taking a stance, meeting a challenge.

Texas said, "Do you want to hire a different security man to deal with this? Somebody who really knows what he's doing?"

"Bullcrap, Texas. Nobody is going to watch my backside better than you do. The one who did not know what he was doing was me. I seem to want two things at once."

"Well, that's human, kid."

"Is it? Thank you. Then it is stupid of me to sit here moping."

"That's human too."

"Everything seems to be human. So what must I do?"

Texas shrugged. "Make up your mind, I guess. Are you going to be Volos the Unholy Head Banger or not?"

"I must choose."

"Yes."

He waited, watching the kid's wings, seeing them flare from gray into bonfire-orange, Halloween hard and bright. Sunrise orange, or sunset? Difficult to tell.

Volos stood up, facing himself in the big hotel mirror. Lifted his head to a cocky angle. Smiled, narrow-eyed. In one potent motion pulled the lamp out of the wall above the bed and hurled it, shattering the mirror, as if he did not like what he saw there.

"Jesus!" Texas sat where he was, too startled to move, not so much by the act as by the vehemence with which it was performed. "What the hell are you doing?"

"I am doing what rock stars do. And now I know why they do it."

"Can't you think of something else rock stars do?"

"Certainly." Volos began taking apart a desk chair with his hands. "They fuck groupies."

"Besides that."

Volos threw pieces of chair at what remained of his mirrored reflection and said, "They give goddamn interviews."

METAL MAG: Volos, do you intend your music as an affront to organized religion?

VOLOS: No, but organized religion is an affront to me. I think it is jealous, like an old man with a young wife.

MM: Jealous? Of what?

VOLOS: Everyone knows what I mean, but no one will say it, that rock is its own religion. The preachers know, and are afraid.

MM: Rock? A religion?

VOLOS: Yes, very much so. We all know who are the high priests of rock and who are the rock gods. Look at the graffiti: "Elvis lives," "Jim Morrison will come again." These are our gods who will come back to save us. We all know the rock mythology. And we all know what are the icons of rock, what is the ancient symbol we worship.

MM: Symbol?

VOLOS: They used to set up lingams in India. Now they set them up in dressing rooms.

MM: Um ... so you really think of the rock music community as another religion in competition with ...

VOLOS: It is the most potent of all religions and it will swallow all the rest. And the earnest men in black suits know that. Someone has said "God is dead," and it is true. Knowing it is true makes the earnest men quite desperate.

MM: How will your rock religion swallow all the rest?

VOLOS: It is already happening. In rock and roll the self is encompassing, we are all infinite. We are all made of fire and stardust. We are in the universe and it is in us. Nothing transcends. Therefore there can be no God, God is dead, and we all dance for joy that we are alive. The old gods danced before sourmouth Yahweh was thought of, and new gods dance now that Yahweh is gone. We are all gods, and we dance.

MM: But some gods, certain singers for instance, are more exalted than others?

VOLOS: Elvis was a poor man's son. We called him the King, but he was one of us.

MM: Where are you from, Volos?

VOLOS: What does the bio say?

MM: Mingo County, West Virginia.

VOLOS: Then that's where.

MM: Anything more you would like to say about your rock religion?

VOLOS: Sha na na shee oooo. Prophecy lives. Rock speaks in tongues.

Even before Texas mentioned it, Angie had been wanting to experiment with makeup. Back in Jenkins, when the packets of coupons had come in the mail she had always looked at the enclosures, at Frederick's

of Hollywood and Lose Weight Overnight and World
of Beauty Introductory Offer, before she dutifully
threw them away.

At a stopover somewhere between Reno and Phoe-
nix she noticed a big, bright-colored Maybelline
Starter Kit in a Valu-Mart where she had gone to buy
Luvs for Mikey and also for Gabe, who was coming
untrained because of all the mixed-up days and moving around. The price of disposable diapers was outrageous, making the Maybelline kit seem nothing by
comparison. She bought it.

"Me want candy," Gabe said.

"Candy!" shrilled Mikey.

"You don't need candy, guys." Texas gave them too
much of the sweet stuff already. Angie hugged both
boys at once, her whole body fogged by a vague guilt.
"You need lots of things, but not candy." They
needed to settle down in one place where they could
sleep at night and play in the daytime and eat something besides pizza. That was what they needed to
straighten them out, and they weren't likely to get it
as long as Volos was on tour.

Yet she knew she could not leave Volos. Might as
well pull out her heart and nail it to a tree. She would
die.

Angie left the boys at the hotel with a roadie's wife,
who had been brought along for that purpose. Grabbed a
ride to the concert site with Texas, who was driving a
little rental Chevette with overinflated tires that made
it handle and feel like a farm Jeep. Took along her
new toy concealed both in its plastic store bag and in
her tote. Once she was done checking over the cos-
tumes she would have plenty of time to try it out in
front of a dressing room mirror before somebody was
ready to give her a ride back. She hoped the kit contained instructions.

It did not.

And nothing was as easy as it looked on TV, she

discovered. The Ultra-Lash Mascara globbed her with Ebony Black from eyebrow to cheek the first time she tried it. The Passionflower Bronze lipstick smeared. Looking into the mirror at the splotched face of a stranger, she realized that she should have put on the foundation first.

Volos walked in.

"Paints!" he exclaimed in quick delight. The flat white plastic kit, with its brush slots and its tray of ten garish pressed-powder eyeshadows, did indeed look a lot like a kid's watercolor box.

"Makeup," Angie told him faintly, hot with embarrassment. Caught in an essentially private and self-indulgent act, she felt as exposed as if he had barged in and found her naked. Yet his childlike pleasure did not let her feel that way for long.

"So, face paint!" Which was exactly what her poor wan mother, who had never so much as used lipstick on her pale, pursed mouth, would have called it. Eagerly Volos said, "Bitchin'! I love tacky colors. Angie, put some on me."

He had not blinked at her own clownish appearance. She felt obliged to warn him. "I'm not very good at—"

"I don't care, Ange! Come on." He sat down and grinned at her. His guitarists, passing in the hallway, rolled their eyes at each other, smiled, and came in to watch.

"Better put on some powder first," suggested Red, "or some cream. Make the stuff easier to get off when you're done."

Though it had not troubled Angela in the least that Volos wanted to play with paints, it appalled her that this man, a fairly normal-looking man, should know about makeup. More than she did, anyway. She had not had an idea what the powder was for.

With the minuscule puff provided, she dabbed some on Volos. He had stopped grinning and sat with lidded eyes. The shivering colors of pleasure, pink and peach and sky-yellow, ran down his wings.

She tried the eyeliner pencil first, finding it even more difficult to use on Volos than on herself. The tip dragged at the delicate skin of his eyelids. "I'm afraid I'm going to hurt you," she told him.

"Use the eyebrow pencil instead," Red suggested. "It's softer."

It had not occurred to her that she could use something labeled Brow Shaper on eyelids. Freedom was a strange and wonderful thing; with her hand touching his face, she knew that as never before. She put on the pencil, then the mascara. Carefully, carefully, terrified of violating the immaculate tissues of his eyes; they gazed at her yet past her, immense, and she saw that his irises had turned the sweet fugitive blue of windflowers. Maybelline eyeshadow, no matter what color, would look like caked mud on him by comparison.

But it was all just for fun. She read off the colors to him: "Turquoise, Topaz, Violet, Mauve, Maize, Sand, Sky, Jade, Jasper Brown, Lapis."

"You choose, Angie."

There was something yielding, almost shy, in his voice. She rubbed the foam-tipped applicator on the purple square and shaded the creases above his closed eyes. Because she was uncertain of her technique and concerned about jabbing him, her strokes were soft and slow. He sighed with pleasure as if she were caressing him.

"You need the creamy kind for onstage. The glossy stuff with sparkles. Metallic," Red remarked. Then he and Bink drifted away, shutting the dressing room door after them.

Halfway through Turquoise, Volos put a hand on the point of Angie's hip and signaled her closer. Intent on her job, she did not find it disturbing that she sat on his lap. She steadied her elbow against his bare shoulder and applied Lapis in focused silence.

Finished to her satisfaction, she said, "Have a look."

There was a mirror in the lid of her box. She held it up to him, and he studied his image as if he had never seen himself before.

"Candy dandy," he remarked at last, then glanced down at the cosmetics in the tray. "What about all those other things? Blush? Lipstick?"

"I don't know how to use the blush. Which lipstick do you want?"

He handed her a tube of gloss, closed his eyes again and presented his mouth to her. She used the thing like a giant crayon, coloring him slick and wet and the deep off-red of black cherries—it was the fragrance that made her think of cherries. Volos's tongue tasted his lips as soon as she was done. "Good," he said.

It was flavored lipstick. She glanced at the tube. "Kissing Potion," she read aloud, then felt a blush flood her from her hairline to her breasts. All too aware of her breasts, and of his hand on her hip.

"Let's try it out," he whispered, and he slid his lips onto hers so that black cherry mixed with Passionflower.

A bizarre way to start, perhaps. But to her all things about Volos were holy. Not always right—rectitude was a deadening concept, fit for her father to use. Not always pure or true. But holy in the oldest sense: immense, puissant, deeply alive. Brett had once kissed Volos, and experienced only a young hunk, a walking wet dream, an embodied phallus. Mercedes kissed Volos often, embracing an angel, thinking of him more and more as a rival to be wrestled, an intimate enemy. But Angela kissed a god.

Since his wife had run away Ennis had kept himself going with work and church, work and church, more and more the work of the church. He missed her and his children with a mute constant pain, regarding her defection as a punishment to be silently borne. Obviously he had loved her too much, so that a jealous God had taken her away from him; he had been too softhearted about her, and he had cherished his chil-

dren more than he cherished Christ. If he had been
more serious about his religion before, perhaps God
would not have taken his family away from him. But
if he could appease God now, perhaps somehow he
could get wife and children back.

His conduct immediately after they disappeared had
showed him to be a worldly sinner. Rather than re-
sorting first to prayer, he had called the police. When
Angela had been gone a few days without sending
word, he had hired a private detective as well. The
man, he realized later, was incompetent, but had kept
him on the hook for a while with requests for more
money to follow up vague clues. By the time he fired
the P.I. two weeks had passed, and he had to face
facts: it would now be nearly impossible to find Angie.
Where would she have gone? She knew no one outside of Jenkins, and the whole world out there seemed
full of people who could hurt her. Night harrowed
Ennis with thoughts that she was dead, or in the hands
of white slavers or the makers of pornographic films.
She and his children. They did not spare the children
either, in the films. At a Christian lecture once Ennis
had learned about snuff films, and the mere whisper
of that fear in his mind was enough to jolt him out of
his solitary bed and send him pacing in the dead of
night.

In the daytime, he was more reasonable. She had
not been kidnapped—though the idea that she had
been kidnapped, carried away from him against her
will, made her absence in some ways easier to bear.
But no, she had left a note. She had run away and
was aimlessly wandering. In his constant thoughts of
her, he envisioned her as a fugitive in bunned hair
and a ragged skirt, her legs cold and blue, sleeping
under doorsteps, with Gabe and Mikey huddled at her
breasts.

"I should have tried to find her myself," he told his
father-in-law at the Crawshaw house one evening. He
visited the Crawshaws often in the evening, having

supper with them to fill the empty hour or two between work and sleep. After his father had died, his
mother had picked up and moved to Arizona. He seldom saw her now, and never had been any good at
talking to people on the phone. These days he felt
closer to the Crawshaws than he did to his own family.

"Don't blame yourself, Ennis." Reverend Crawshaw's voice was very gentle.

Ennis did blame himself, for everything, and it did
not occur to him until years later that the same man
who spoke to him so softly had trained him to think
that way. He said, "Maybe I should go now. Take the
same bus she took—"

"Ennis, no. You were born and raised here in Jenkins. Here you have your friends and family and
church around you to help you and support you. But
if you leave, you'll be another sheep who wandered
out of the fold, you'll be in danger of the wolves of
Satan. Do you want that?"

"But Angie—"

"She is lost."

"I ought to go find her."

"Ennis." The older man's voice took on a note of
preacherly authority. "It is important that you should
learn to accept the will of God."

"How do I know what's the will of God and what's
the doing of the devil?"

Patiently the Reverend explained it to him, that everything, even the existence of the devil, was part of
God's plan. Even Angela's downfall had to be part of
God's plan somehow. God did not sleep, even if people could not always see his plan in what happened
to them.

"Oh." Ennis considered. He found Reverend Crawshaw's words comforting. Also, in his secret heart he
really did not want to leave home. The house seemed
to need his presence. Leaving it would feel like sev-
ering his last link to Angela and the life they had
shared. Moreover, the world was dangerous, and he

feared it. He had been ashamed of his fear, but if the Reverend said he was to stay home, then staying must be all right.

He asked, "If I pray, will I start to understand God's plan for me?"

"Maybe. But it is more important just to accept."

Accept the Almighty's plan, but pray to change his mind: to one who had been raised with this logic, it made sense enough. "If I pray hard, will God send Angela back to me?"

"It would be better to pray for Angela herself, that she will repent. As a minister of God, I must consider her damned, I must shake her dust off my sandals. But you may pray for her."

"I don't know how to pray very well."

"It doesn't matter, Ennis. God will listen to you. And I need you to help me with your prayers. It is a wicked world."

Ennis went home from that conversation feeling better than he had in weeks. In fact, feeling humbly honored. All his life he had admired Reverend Crawshaw and been in awe of him. His respect for the man had added to his dizzy joy in marrying the Reverend's daughter. But it was only after Angela left that they had started to become close because of their shared grief.

God could bring good out of evil. Perhaps this was what was meant to happen, this closeness, this— discipleship?

Weeks stretched slowly into months. By the time construction lulled for the winter, Ennis's coworkers were looking at him sideways and not speaking to him if they could avoid it. His face had gone flat. He scowled at jokes. He had taken to wearing black clothing and muttering Bible verses under his breath as he worked. In that autumn's annual congregational meeting of the Holy Virgin Church he had been elected to office, and thereafter he preferred to be addressed as Deacon Bradley.

Around Christmastime his mother began calling him weekly, worried about him because of what she had been hearing. Why did he not come see her over the holiday and spend some time in the Arizona warmth? But he told her his duty lay in Jenkins.

Indeed there was no lack of work for him to do there. During the slack of winter he consumed himself with church concerns, leaving himself no idle time in which he might weaken and weep and entertain the doubts the devil wanted to put into his head. Work numbed his pain—and there was urgent work to be done. The evangelical Christian world was becoming more and more aware of the iniquities of rock music, and particularly of a West Coast viper of evil named Volos. Ennis Bradley, now indisputably Reverend Crawshaw's right-hand man, was instrumental in the organization of the Central Pennsylvania League for Moral Purity.

After the infamous *Metal Mag* Volos interview appeared, Reverend Crawshaw came one evening to his son-in-law's house.

Ennis let him in uneasily because he had been busy and had not tidied the house. He liked to keep the place just as Angie would have, with everything in place, awaiting her return—though even at its best the house still did not seem right, not when there were no yelling little boys in it, not with all the toys put away.

Right now there were four days' worth of dishes in the sink. Pastor Crawshaw, however, did not go into the kitchen and therefore did not see them. He headed for the living room and sat there, a sign that this visit was of serious and formal substance.

"Ennis. You and I of all the faithful know firsthand what the seductions of rock music can do to a Christian family."

"Amen." Ennis remained standing, like a soldier being briefed.

"Therefore, I feel that I can rely on you. Others are

faithful and eager, but they have not felt God's rod. You have, and therefore you will be cautious."

Ennis nodded and waited, wondering if he ought to subdue his feeling of pride. Reverend Crawshaw trusted him, and this fact caused him to have a good feeling that partially filled the hollowness in his chest. It was all right, he decided, to feel this way.

"I have a mission for you." Reverend Crawshaw wearily inclined his head, passing a hand across his eyes. "I wish I could do it myself, Ennis, because it is dangerous, but I simply do not have the time."

Knowing how hard his father-in-law worked, Ennis felt a prickling of sympathy. "Whatever it is," he said, "I will be happy to do it."

"It is this. I want you to be my spy in the war against the evils of rock music. Get yourself a radio, Ennis. Listen to it, but privately, so as not to lead others astray. Report to me on what you hear. I need weapons. There are those people even within our own community who claim that rock music is harmless entertainment. I need to be able to say to them and to all scoffers, listen to such-and-such a line from such-and-such a song."

Ennis's mouth had gaped in a manner he knew to be uncouth, "catching flies." He forced himself to close it and nod. Any other response eluded him.

"Get a cassette player also, and as you find certain songs or singers more evil than the others, buy tapes. Listen to them and report on them in the normal manner, then—you will have to get a special machine, but we need to do this—play them backwards. Listen for hidden satanic messages."

"Yes, sir," Ennis whispered, feeling chilled.

"And pray constantly, Ennis." The older man prayed with him before leaving.

There was still time before the stores closed. Ennis went to a place where he was not known and bought, after some confusion, an appropriate radio/cassette player, and also Bic pens and a tablet of cheap paper.

When he got home he drew the blinds before he pulled the toy of Satan out of its shopping bag and packaging, set it up, and turned it on. Music of a sort poured out.

Between then and midnight he filled several pages of his tablet with lyrics, especially rap music lyrics, that appalled him. Nevertheless, Ennis felt the silence when he turned the radio off and went to his bed. The house seemed very quiet, the bed seemed very empty without Angela. Empty as his arms, empty as his heart. He missed her.

chapter
twelve

A convoy of eighteen-wheelers lumbered across New Mexico, and from cactus fingers and fence posts the little hard-nosed elf owls stared, unimpressed. The trucks' sides were painted with scenes of a strange and naked world in which mountains and ocean waves mutated into aspiring humans with wings of flame rising from their shoulders, their ankles, their wrists and heads. *No good for flying,* the owls muttered, to themselves only, for they were solitary birds and did not consult with one another. *What is the point? What do these humans purport to be?*

On one of the rented trucks, along with the rented stage equipment, Volos had stored his Hawg. Strict security arrangements were in effect, yet at the Albuquerque concert site Volos got the motorcycle out, and from there to Wichita he and Angie took the long ride through the desert night, on their own, defiant, unhelmeted, she with her arms around his waist and her head resting between his wings, nestled in a warm hollow that was half feathered, half flesh. So far, she and Volos had done little more than press together like this, like fledglings thrown from their tree by a storm, stranded on dangerous ground. They kissed sometimes, and once, alone in the bus with her, Volos had touched her left breast. But mostly they were hesitant with each other, shy, like children.

That desert night, all the hours of the long ride, they were nearly silent. Overhead, stars tumbled like popcorn. At every gas station the cola machines stood red white and blue, light-up monuments of Americanism, sturdily erect. Angie saw them coming from great distances and watched them pass. She studied the night, and never stopped being aware of the muscles of Volos's bare torso moving under her bare arms. But mostly she was aware of his back, warm under her head, his wings, flanking her like an embrace, his heart, beating like a drum, all night. Afterward, she remembered mostly how the good smell of his dusky skin had combined with the faintly alien musk of his pinfeathers to keep her constantly dreaming of him.

Sometime during that night she grew aware, more in her body than in her mind, of what she was going to do.

Once in Wichita, Texas went straight to bed. It was morning, but it felt like the middle of the night to him. Christ, he hated all this traveling around, he who had never learned to sleep properly in a moving vehicle. The security guards he roomed with considered that sleeping in the bus was enough. They laughed at him a little, then went to bodyguard Volos or hang out in the hotel bar. But Texas needed his nap.

No sooner had he gotten a good start on it than Volos barged in, wanting to talk.

"Just because you don't need to sleep," Texas griped.

Volos sailed straight past his complaining, as usual. "Texas. How do I know if I love her?"

"Cripes, kid." Texas sat up, noticing how his belly creased above his shorts. Damn, he tried to keep slim and fit, but age was taking him over anyway. There was a young person still there inside him, surprised as hell and plenty pissed off about the way things were going. Cranky, he grumbled, "Do you have to love her?"

"With Angela, I think yes."

For the past few days Texas had been watching the two of them with a smile, noting with satisfaction the happy hues of Volos's wings, the quiet glow Angie wore like a halo, the scowl on Mercedes's pretty face. Angie Bradley was so special—if anybody could make a home for his straying angel, she could. This consideration was the reason Texas was not totally pissed about that time when Volos breached security and rode off in the night. More awake now, and therefore more sympathetic, he said to Volos quietly, "Can't you tell if you're falling in love with her?"

"Falling is one thing. I know falling." As if to illustrate, the kid toppled face down across the bed. "Being is another fish kettle." His wings sprawled, reminding Texas of lilacs in the rain. The lilacs would be blooming about now, back in West Virginia. The air would be fresh and sweet, with none of this mad-dog desert heat.

Volos said, "Texas, I sing and sing of love the way heaven's slaves sing of heaven's mysteries, without understanding."

"It's not something you gotta understand in your head," Texas said.

"What is it, then? I thought a feeling, but feelings come and go like rainbows, so how do people stay together?"

Texas felt all his muscles go taut as if he were wrestling. For a few moments he struggled with an invisible antagonist so desperately that he was unable to speak.

Volos asked, "How was it for you and Wyoma?"

More clearly than he remembered yesterday's venue Texas remembered that day twenty-one years before, remembered it so vividly that he might as well have been sixteen again, in the July twilight heat, at the Persimmon Borough Volunteer Firemen's Carnival, and there she was with her girlfriend, who happened to be a cousin of his. Not that he could not have said hello to her anyway. He had known Wyoma to say hello to her most of his life, but that night it was as if something invisible and nameless had placed a strong hand between his shoulder blades and propelled him toward her. He had tagged along with her to the Dunk Willie booth, where the school buddy who was Willie at the time had hooted at him. Trapped, he had laid down money for six softballs and found that his throwing arm had turned to water, he couldn't hit anything. His neck went hot, friends were jeering, Wyoma gave him a look of utter scorn and walked off. She might as well have been leading him by the nose for all that he could help himself; he had followed. Later that same night he had gotten her into a shadow behind the funnel-cake tent and kissed her and tried to touch her breast, for which she had slapped him. Within a week they had gone all the way and couldn't stay away from each other. It had felt like having a mental disease, a mania. All day every day he had gone around with his dick on standby for her. They both knew sooner or later he was going to get her pregnant. When it happened, they had married. That was the way people got married, in Texas's experience.

Until he had come to L.A. she was the love of his life. The only woman he had ever done it with.

"Texas?"

With some difficulty he focused back to Volos. He said, "Son, it's like a fate."

"This fate thing, it is from the Greeks. I do not understand it."

"I didn't mean it any Greek way. I'm trying to say— you're asking about love—it's mostly a matter of just giving in."

"Giving up free will?" The way the kid sounded, a person would think his freedom was real, something he could hold in his hand like a red guitar. Real and made of solid gold.

Texas said, "Sometimes you gotta take a risk. Get off my bed, would you, son? I'm going back to sleep."

Volos stood up, but he asked again, "How do I know?"

"Huh?"

"How do I know when to risk?"

"Kid." Texas puffed his lips in exasperation, then took his own advice and surrendered to love. God knew it had been a while since he had loved anybody or anything the way he loved this strange angel. He said, "Okay. If I was you, I would think like this: If you went and left her today and never saw her again, would you forget about her? Or when you got old would you lay there and look back and think, *God-damn it, Volos, look what you went and threw away*?"

Volos stood with a far-seeing look, his wings the color of mist.

"Now would you get the hell out of here?"

"Okay. Texas—thanks." The kid drifted out like a sleepwalker, closing the door behind him.

Texas threw a pillow against the headboard and leaned on it, knowing he would not go back to sleep, considering he would be doing okay if he did not cry. He had left Wyoma, walked out of her life. Was never going to see her again. And his mind was telling him over and over again, *Goddamn it, Texas, you fool, you dickheaded fool, look what you went and threw away.*

At two in the morning Angela awoke as if she had set an alarm, knew the concert had to be over, quietly got up and put on her clothes. In the bed she had left, Mikey and Gabe slept on. Probably they would sleep through the night, but if they woke up, her roommate, the roadie's wife, would take care of them. The roadie himself was not back yet, was probably still working. The equipment had to be gotten out of the arena, even though Burning Earth was not moving on until day after tomorrow.

Angie slipped out of the Travelodge into the spring-time Kansas night. The crew was staying on the out-skirts of town, near the expressway. Once she had walked a few blocks she was almost in country, and the sky looked huge.

"Volos," she said aloud to the night, but softly.

It did not concern her that he might be with Mer-cedes. She was more aware than most people thought of what he and Mercedes were to each other, but it did not trouble her. Volos had once been made of ether, or starfire, or some nameless substance more rarefied than air; he was beyond the rules she had been raised by, and she had accepted him so deeply that she was unaware of having sacrificed.

"Volos." Very gently. "It's me."

She had to get him out of the hotel, away from all those bodyguards, the band, all those people.

"Volos?"

She had not called him this way since that night near the L.A. bus depot. Until then she had not un-derstood how he had spent millennia answering the prayers of generations of the faithful: Be my protector, my comforter, my hand-holder, nose-wiper, crying towel, my tour guide through life; find my lost purse, destroy my enemies, multiply my seed, carry me on your back, lay ye down as a bridge over troubled water. And ten thousand demands more, plus the commands of his superiors. Being a mother, having been a wife, she could understand how he had felt. No wonder he had rebelled. No wonder he had hated her summoning him. She hoped he would sense that this time was different.

"Volos. I love you."

She had wandered a few blocks farther on her ran-dom way, into a scrubby neighborhood of gas stations and warehouses, before he roared up to her on the Harley. He wore a cloak she had made him for the colder nights outside of California, a magnificent half-circle thing that billowed in dark velvet folds and closed with metal clasps across his chest. So she could not look at his wings to read his mood. But his face, shadowy in the starlight, was beautiful and still. Without a word he parked his cycle behind a pile of skids, came to her and took her hand.

She kissed him, seeing how his eyelids fluttered shut as her lips touched his mouth. That was one of the things she loved about him, that when she kissed him his face changed, his breath quickened, she could see him wanting her. Ennis had always stiffened as if bracing himself against her, afraid. Trying not to show anything. But she could make Volos moan with desire for her, and because he had the courage to be so unguarded, she was ready to pin her heart on him like a medal.

"Where are we going?" he whispered to her when she finished the kiss.

"I don't know."

They walked. The night was full of enigmatic things, power boxes and strange storage tanks and derelict drive-in theaters. After a while they wandered down a dirt access lane and into a starlit back-lot hilltop devoted to concrete products: manhole tubes, sewer arches, septic tanks stacked fifteen feet high. For acres the things loomed, monolithic, moon-gray and silent, a New World Stonehenge. It was a place that called them in as an old barn calls children in, as a cave calls foxes in, as a silent mine seduces the miner. They wandered until they were entirely surrounded by pale blocks and piles and pillars that drew the eye upward.

"My God," Angie said, "the stars."

They sat at the bottom of a long flight of concrete stairs to nowhere, gazing up.

"One thing I liked about L.A. was that I could hardly ever see the stars," Volos said. "I do not like to look at them."

"But they are beautiful."

"Beautiful prisoners. Beautiful slaves. My former comrades in slavery."

"Oh," she whispered, looking at him now instead of at the sky. The dim light made his swarthy skin seem fair, his shadowed eyes, immense. His face had gone so hard that the muscles near his jaw rippled as he spoke.

"Yes, it is ironic, is it not? People call me a star. But I do not want that. A star is what I was before. One little spark in the Milky Way, one of trillions."

"But here you are not little." How could he be, when so many people adored him?

"No? I am a superstar, you mean? So now I am one among thousands. Make me a god, and I will be the same. Call me what you like, I am still a speck in the eye of the almighty. If he blinks, I will be gone. I am dust."

She said, "Not to me."

Volos looked at her, then slipped off his cloak and put an arm around her. From the refuge of his shoulder she watched his wings glimmer deep purple, more sad now than vehement. It must have been hard for him, heaven's rebel. She asked, "Do you miss the others? The ones you left behind?"

"No . . . I don't know. Never mind, Ange."

"But I do mind. They should have all fallen from their places to come with you. Every one of them."

He laughed; she was glad to have made him laugh. His wings glowed lighter as he let go of bitterness. He said, "Why would they follow me? I was a dunce. I could never obey."

She teased gently, "And are you still a dunce?"

"No, I think I am learning." He answered her teasing seriously. He looked into her eyes and she felt herself stop breathing. The whole night seemed to grow still.

He said, "Love is submission. And I am here, Angela, am I not?"

Looking back at him she felt her lips part but could not speak. Her heart was drumming. It was time.

They got up and wandered on to the brow of the slow hill of concrete monoliths, where they found a squat hollow cylinder the size of a cheap swimming pool. Volos climbed into it, laid his cloak on the ground, lifted Angie over its low wall. Lying down within that circle, they could see nothing but the stony moon-white stuff that ringed them, and sky, and stars.

And each other. They could see each other. And Volos's wings were shining like fire.

It was the way a virginal girl named Angela Crawshaw had once dreamed it would be with someone, someday. It was the way a married woman named Angie Bradley had wished lovemaking would be. That night there was nothing left for her to wish for, nothing this lover would not do for her, nothing she could not see and caress and explore with hands and mouth and body. And he was more than any mortal lover had ever been to anyone, anywhere, his kisses explored her soul, he was everything, all-encompassing. They made love under his wings, and as he came to her his wings arched over her and defined her world; he was her dusky earth, her heart-red sky.

With Ennis, lovemaking had been a struggling thing, an act of need or valor, an attempt to make contact with another being across a distance as of planets. But with Volos—there was after all one thing left for Angela to desire, in those ecstatic moments when their bodies had joined; she wanted their hot souls to melt together, to blend, to become one. She wanted to merge with Volos, to occupy the same space as he did, the way bodiless beings might do, two angels dancing.

Surrender, surrender to me, cried a hundred rock tunes meant for the male voice, meant to play on the car radio when the guy had the girl in the back seat and she was saying *No, I'm not that kind, I'm saving myself for marriage.* But women were not the only ones who surrendered, Volos knew, submitting himself in his nakedness to this one who could put a leash on him from miles away, submitting that most precious part of his body to hers, to that strait and dark and potentially entrapping place—to that warm and yielding and pleasure-giving place, like nothing Mercedes could offer him, nothing, no matter how he lubed or how much of the white powder he gave him beforehand.

A prickly feeling at the nape of his neck kept Volos aware of the stars at his back, and when physical ecstasy gave him time he felt a dark sense of triumph. *Eat your hearts out, watchers, if you have any.* From time to time throughout human history, though rarely, certain favored princes among angels had been allowed to take on manly flesh in order to do errands that involved mortal participation—but it had been flesh robed in white, and never had they been allowed to doff the swaddling cloth, never had they been allowed to enjoy the flesh this way, finding the delight so sweet and keen it was almost pain. Only fallen angels knew this ecstasy.

Or did they? Had anyone in all of history, had anyone else ever felt this way? So deep, so lost in the wonders of his soulmate, it was—

Was it truly love?

He wanted to give and give to her. It was the first time he had ever given so much, yet he wanted to give more. "Ange," he whispered against her face. "Angela."

A movement of her lips answered him.

"Would you like to fly?"

Her eyes looked up into his, wide as skies. "But you—"

"Shhh. I know what I said. If you want to, I would like to do it for you."

"Now?"

"Now."

Her sigh told him *Yes.*

His arms gathered her close, close. They were one

flesh. A single downbeat of his great wings shielded them and carried them above the citylight into darkness velvety as a womb, and Wichita floated starrily below them.

Afterward, when they lay close together in their nest again, he knew himself to be strong, mighty as thunder.

Not one to do any job halfway, Ennis used all he could spare of his pay (after food, utilities, and tithes) to buy rock music magazines with paper like inked sawdust and titles like *Sex Metal* and *Fusion*. Looking at photo after photo of young men with far more sneer and hair than he had ever seen on human males before, of young women in tighter clothing than he had believed possible, reading interview after interview of these misguided people, Ennis found himself growing fascinated as well as aghast. Learning about the rock world was like traveling to a different planet, trying to understand an alien species.

"They call the guitars axes," he reported to his father-in-law.

"Weapons of destruction. How apt."

But an ax could also be used to shape and build. Ennis, a carpenter, admired the axwork of the pioneers and also, though to a small and grudging extent, the axwork he heard in some rock music. He said, "I believe they think of them more as symbols of power."

"Power to destroy everything that is right and good."

Ennis did not quibble further. He had indeed read much in the heavy-metal publications and heard much on his radio that he found horrifying, berserk and bizarre. And blasphemous.

"Here is what I have so far." He gave Reverend Crawshaw a list of songs that mentioned angels. Quite a few rock lyrics mentioned angels. Almost as many as mentioned devils or demons of various sorts. The context in which these beings were invoked was sometimes innocuous, sometimes outrageous, but irrelevant in either event. The League for Moral Purity was not interested in context. No matter what use it made of the Bible, secular music had no business opening that sacred book with its dirty hands.

"Some of the men wear makeup," Ennis mentioned tangentially.

"I have heard that. How sickening. Cheapening the temple of the body with paint is just as evil as mutilating it with tattoos."

Ennis, who had seen Grecian Formula in his father-in-law's bathroom, wondered if hair was not a part of the body, and if it was not, why were women supposed to cover theirs? And why did a nice fresh coat of white paint not cheapen the temple of the church? Then he mentally rebuked himself. His duty to his minister, his church, and his God did not include questioning, only obedience.

"What about this devil Volos?" Reverend Crawshaw asked him. "Does he paint himself?"

"He likes many colors of eyeshadow, yes."

"Then he is a degenerate. Is he also an apostate?"

"He has never publicly claimed to be an angel. In fact, he dislikes it when anyone calls him that. But observers who write for the magazines say that his wearing of wings must be taken as a statement."

"In other words he wears wings to call himself an angel, then lives the life of Satan—is he a fornicator?"

"A sodomizer, some say."

Reverend Crawshaw gasped as if he had been struck, and his eyes bugged. But then he smiled.

"Wears wings and is a sodomizer—"

"That is hearsay."

"I am sure it is true. God tells me in my heart that it is true. Therefore our duty is made plain to us. This Volos, who wears the wings of an angel and drags them in filth and sings the songs of Beelzebub—this Volos is too evil to be merely another sinful man. Perhaps the end days are at hand. Perhaps he is the

Antichrist, or an incarnation of the Evil One himself. Ennis. My son." The minister laid a hand on his shoulder. "We must destroy him if we can."

Ennis went home in a daze of doubt and joy. Reverend Crawshaw had called him his son! Of course, he was legally the man's son-in-law, but that had never made the holy man speak to him as a real son before. Reverend Crawshaw had said the word warmly, solemnly, seeming to adopt him with it—making Ennis his heir? His spiritual inheritor? His anointed?

But—destroy Volos? The strange winged rocker was reputed to be the very best axwhacker ever. And he sang like—well, like an angel.

Perhaps by "destroy" Reverend Crawshaw meant something along the lines of making Volos take back some of the things he had said. Ennis promised himself that he would clarify the matter with his father-in-law the next time he saw him. Almost certainly he would be reassured.

Just that day Ennis had bought the cassette tape of *Scars.* Once home, tablet and Bic pen in hand to record offensive lyrics, he put it in his tape player and settled back to listen.

Halfway through Side One he began to feel guilt lashing him because he was enjoying the music. In fact he loved it, no matter how many questionable or disrespectful or plainly obscene lyrics he jotted down. Something in the strong, supple vocals and the wild excess of the guitars called to him. To think that after he finished this assignment he would never be allowed to listen to such music again—and he would never be allowed to admit to anyone how much he liked it—to think these things was to know life for what it was: denial, a long and difficult denial. Obedience was very hard sometimes.

The last song on Side One, a song not released as a single, was called "One Feather."

What you call heaven I call hell
It's all shame and blame

So how can I tell
If I love you?

Ennis jolted upright, not able to believe what he was hearing.

Then he turned off the tape player, got up, and went to his bedroom, where he kept a piece of paper carefully put away in a cuff-link box in the top drawer of his dresser. He got out the penciled sheet and read it yet again, for maybe the hundredth time, with a lump in his throat not so much because of what it said as because she had written such a thing, a poem, for him. Just for him. To ease the pain. When he had not known she ever wrote poetry at all.

With Angela's leave-taking message in hand he went back downstairs, started the Volos tape again, and listened.

If what I do is so hard on you
Then maybe we were wrong from the start …

The record was just released. In no way could Angela have heard it before she wrote her poem.

Ennis listened through the rest of the song, then looked down at the frail thing in his hand and tore it to bits.

It sounded to him like a good idea, now, to destroy Volos.

Angela … would she be with the winged freak? Odd, that it should cause him so little joy to learn how he might find … Ennis discovered that he was no longer inclined to think of her by name. She was just Her. The Fallen Woman. His wife who had betrayed him and sold his poem to a foul-mouthed rock star. Who had left him with a careless farewell and taken away his two little boys.

Gabe and Mikey …

Longing for his sons flooded him, so overwhelming it made him feel physically weak and sick. He would never get over losing them, never. Yesterday would not have been soon enough for him to be with them again.

Where were they? That city of sin, L.A.? Or wandering? A trashy stop along the road somewhere?

They were in a Travelodge on the outskirts of Wichita, and Mikey was coughing in his sleep. Congestion disturbed his breathing so that he sputtered and woke up. Children never accept illness with much grace; it insults them. More because of such insult than because of physical discomfort, Mikey began to howl.

The roadie, who had no more than just fallen asleep after working almost until dawn, elbowed his wife and groaned. "Dammit! Can'tcha shut that kid up?"

Eyes closed, the woman mumbled, "She'll take care of it." Unglued her non-pillowed eye enough to see if Angie was moving. Absorbed the input for a moment. Angie was not there.

"Where the hell does she get off . . ."

Sighing, the roadie's wife heaved herself up and went to Mikey. "Okay, okay." She picked him up, and because he knew her and considered that he was being attended to, he quieted. "You need changed? No. Blow your nose." He blew. His face felt feverish under her hand. "You're coming down with something, little fella."

By mashing it into Gerber's applesauce and then spooning it down him she gave him her cure-all: half a tablet of aspirin.

c h a p t e r
thirteen

Mercedes was no fool. He had known before Wichita, before Volos knew it himself, that the angel was not going to be coming to him for sex much longer. He felt some rage, not so much the jealous rage of a lover as the spleen of one stopped at yet another traffic light on the road to The Top. But also, for the first time in his life, he felt a cold-fingered fear: What if there was to be no Top for him? What if he simply did not have what it took? Being intimate with Volos, he had begun to see that there was some quality in the star that he, Mercedes, lacked and did not comprehend. What if his moment came, and he stood on the stage and no one—no one loved him?

He did not analyze the fear and anger or waste time on them. Instead, he had began working on new ways to keep Volos attached to him. "Attached" in its primal sense: unable to get away.

"It will make you feel bigger," he had said the first time he offered the white powder. "It will make you feel like a thunderhead, full of electricity. Like you could reach out your hand and say, 'Let there be fire,' and there would be."

Volos had accepted, but remarked, "To be like

God, is this what you want?" and Mercedes had stared at him.

"Don't you?"

"No. I do not think very highly of God. Why would I want to be like him?"

Mercedes bit down on fury, feeling spurned or soon to be spurned. First body and now soul. Offering deification via drug, he had in a sense been offering his soul: Of all drugs, cocaine was his favorite for that very reason, because it made him sense self expanding into incandescent godhead. And now finally he could afford the really good stuff with the money Volos would give him, and Volos did not want to be God? Mercedes decided right then and there that Volos was a no-class jerk-off who did not deserve anything the world was giving him, not wealth or fame or love. Mercedes could know this categorically, because among classy people wanting to be God was a tacit given, like masturbation. Everyone who was anyone did it, though it was gauche to say so.

Rather sniffily, Mercedes said, "I just mean it makes you feel *up*. As if you are made of energy. Plugged in."

Volos shrugged. "Music gives me that." He looked at Mercedes and added, "But of course I will do this if you want me to. You say in my nose?"

The disbelief in his voice annoyed Mercedes more than the knowledge that he was losing him to Angie Bradley.

They took the drug, listened to Alice Cooper awhile, made love for what Mercedes knew might be the last time. The cocaine did not seem to affect Volos much, but Mercedes did not allow himself to feel discouraged. There were other drugs.

He begged a meeting with Volos a few days later, saying he had some tour business to discuss. In fact he had acquired some acid.

"Want a hit, Volie?" he offered. "It will make you see colors you have never imagined."

"New colors?" This time Volos was intrigued. "How can there be more colors than those I already know?"

"You'll see. Try it." In a retro-sixties mood, Mercedes lit incense and served the hallucinogen ceremoniously. Because his aesthetic sense could not stomach paper squares with unicorns printed on them, he had opted for liquid in a small brown bottle complete with bulb and dropper. For himself, he would put it in his eyes. For Volos, however, he placed four drops on a sugar cube.

"Like that?" The angel sounded as intrigued by the many ways of taking drugs as he was by anything else about them. "Why not up my nose? Or in a cigarette, like the marijuana? Or in a bottle, like beer?"

"Because beer is for bottle babies and pot is for lollysuckers. You get sweets for the sweet. Come on, Vo."

"You, too."

"No, with this stuff we take turns."

He half hoped the angel would have a bad trip. Also, he had plans. Once the acid began to work, he took advantage of Volos's disorientation to get him out of his jeans. He had thought he wanted to blow him; in fact he did want that, badly, and why did he not do it then? Yet he shoved his drugged lover onto the bed instead, and held him down and tickled him, all parts of him, for a long time. Volos did not resist— he could never have done it if Volos had put up a fight—but lay gasping and trying to get away and laughing himself hoarse, finally whimpering like a puppy before Mercedes grew bored with the torment and screwed him instead.

The next day Volos did not remember what had been done to him, but merely said, "I saw colors, but they did not feel good. Also, it seems this acid has made me sore all over."

Mercedes knew better than to ask him to take it again. His own fault, for losing control. He would have to watch himself, remembering to focus on his long-term goals.

"Heroin," he explained to Volos the next time. "Smack. The ultimate."

"Mercy, the ultimate experience of life is death."

"Yes ... well, there is a chance of that."

"And the other chance?"

"Ecstasy."

Sitting on the bed in yet another beige hotel room, Volos looked steadily into his eyes, like a comrade in some obscure war. Mercedes kneeled in front of him holding the rubber tube and the hypodermic.

"With a needle in my arm," Volos said slowly.

"Yes."

"In my blood."

"Yes, Vo. And then in mine." Ah, the mystic brotherhood. Mindful of its power, Mercedes invoked it, watched Volos for its effect, saw the singer's gaze fix raptly on him, and knew that he had won him over.

"Make a fist," he instructed.

It was not difficult to find a vein on that lean, hard arm. Mercy shot Volos nearly the whole fix, leaving little for himself. But the precaution was not necessary. As he pulled the needle out, Volos slumped sideways and rolled off the bed, unconscious.

"Shit!" Probably Volos had not even experienced the rush. It was that fucking unpredictable physique of his that wouldn't respond right to drugs. The sonuvabitch probably hadn't "imagined himself" as a junkie. He would wake up in a few hours as indifferent to smack as he was to marching powder.

Mercedes let him lie on the floor as he washed the rest of his expensive treat down the drain. He really did not want to mess with heroin himself. Cocaine was a much classier addiction. He allowed himself a line of it, then went out and found a stranger willing to sexually relieve him in the men's room of the local bowling alley, then came back and went to bed.

Volos still lay sprawled on the floor when he got

up, and he began to worry. If Volos missed the sound
check, somebody would come looking for him. Mercedes tried cold water and pinching without any satisfactory result. But an hour later, on his own and
without preamble, Volos came to.

"Mercy," he whispered. He got up, his face red and
stippled from contact with the carpet but smiling.
"Mercedes! Is it the next day?"

"Yes."

"I have never felt anything like that! Suddenly I
was sleeping. Was I sleeping?"

"Yes. Certainly."

"For all that time?"

"Of course."

"But—but it felt wonderful. I was—it was as if I
was not at all. It was oblivion. Yet here I am. Do you
see?"

"Yes, Vo. Certainly."

What Mercedes actually saw was his future brightening. He began to answer Volos's smile. "So you like
being asleep," he said.

"Yes. It is a wonderful letting go. It is—such
freedom."

Volos could not completely explain why the heroin
experience had so deeply excited and delighted him,
how Mercy's magic needle had sent him to a shadow-
land entirely new to him, how he had wandered, lost
as a soul, and sometimes found dreams. Awake, he
remembered no more than the edges of the dreams,
but he felt hope: to sleep, to experience this facsimile
of death, was perhaps to be more human, more a part
of the mortal world. To sleep, perchance to dream—it
was perchance to belong. Perchance even someday to
catch a dream in music and words, to write a song of
his own.

Being human was turning out to be not at all as he
had envisioned it. This thing of trying drugs, for instance. He had expected that to take place at wild

parties, amid chaos and heavy music and maybe clusterfucking, and instead here he was being dosed by Mercedes as if taking instruction at an archon's wing, learning drugs one by one like questions in a catechism. It was so tame. He was so tame. Where were the parties? He was a rock star on tour, it should be all parties and after-concert crumpets, and instead it was all work and Mercy and a soft-spoken sweet-faced woman and her two little boys.

He had come down in order to rebel; he tried and tried to be bad, but those who were truly bad saw through him and scorned him. The true heavy-metal rockers called him a pussy rocker, a wimp in disguise. And they were right; he loved his own body too much. At one point he had thought of having tattoos, he had contemplated entwining a blue-ink serpent around the base of his left wing, or wearing a flaming heart on his chest, or "MERCY" in script on his shoulder. But there had been no guts in him to alter his smooth dun skin. He had contemplated also the holes for ornaments, the piercing of ears or nose or lips or nipples, and he had not been able to make himself do these small mutilations either, not even so much as one hole in one ear to take a silver swinging devil. Some rockers destroyed themselves with alcohol or drugs or sorrows, and Volos had not given up on those ideas. He was trying the Jack Daniels, the smack. But he suspected himself of being a craven wearing wolf's clothing, because in his heart he knew liquor and drugs would not affect him much. Sorrow would affect him more. He had not yet made occasion to try sorrow.

He was always finding the limits of his own wickedness. Aside from loving his own dusky flesh, he perhaps loved Angie. And, in a different way, he loved the very world she moved in. He loved the people he met, all of them, the girl lifting her crop-top to flash her breasts at him, the old poodle-haired woman scowling at him out a tour-bus window, the young man driving a Porsche with one hand at his crotch, the worried middle-aged storekeeper chasing skateboarders off his parking lot, the mouth-breathing kids on the boards, the gum-chewing cashiers, all of them, all. The do-gooders picketing his shows, and the booing kids mobbing the pickets. And he loved the towns they all lived in, with the Movie Shak and the B-Tan Tanning Salon and the old factory turned into apartments or mini-storage, the Cut-Rate Food Mart and the Foursquare Gospel Church and an unmarked house in some back street where women named Bambi and Crystal and Lou Beth were available. He liked Lou Beth, though she did not like him and wanted nothing to do with a queer in wings. He liked the movies he rented at the Shak. He even liked church bells. He no longer really wanted to insult or appall anyone.

Except Yahweh, Jehovah, Elohim, Tetragrammaton. Except God. But that holy name alone was enough to keep him trying: the liquor, the drugs. Perhaps soon the sorrow.

Texas had never abused controlled substances in his life. But even though he drank little and used no drugs, the road trip between Wichita and Toledo was largely a blur to him. All the towns, all the hotels, all the interstates began to look alike to him, and he hated them all. There was too much work: set up, work the concert, strike the set, move on, do it all again. Never enough sleep for anyone.

He worried about Angie. Especially for her there had not been enough sleep. Mikey had a cold with fever high enough to keep him peevish but not high enough to bother calling a doctor for. He kept her up most nights. Volos was no help. It bothered Texas that the kid seemed so oblivious to people's problems. He pestered Angie for kisses between sets, got puppy-eyed when she lost her temper at him, didn't seem to understand, didn't stay around long enough for her to explain. Was spending his nights with Mercedes again. Texas felt as if he had about had it with Volos.

Though, to be fair, it wasn't just Volos, Texas had to admit. Whatever was eating at him had a lot to do with geography. As the states became day by day smaller, more eastern, more crowded together, he grew as cranky as Angie's ailing child. Burning Earth was scheduled to make no stop in West Virginia, was only to cut through the state's knife-blade tip on the way to Pittsburgh, but the closer Texas got to his home the more something seemed to tug at him like a fishhook caught under his heart. On the bus he paced the aisles until the roadies swore at him, yelling that they were trying to sleep. Even in a hotel bed he lay with eyes wide burning open.

To sleep. God. To sleep, perchance to dream.

He was lying in his room outside Toledo trying to do just that when Volos barged in. Texas heard him coming. He had heard Angie's voice in the hallway as she chased Volos out of her room so that she could put her little boys and herself down for naps. He knew Mercedes had gone off to have a massage and mani-cure, for God's sake. He knew he was what was left. Good old Texas. Third choice.

And sure enough, here came Volos in the door, his battery charged, as usual, and color pulsing in his wings. Bright-eyed. Wanting somebody to talk with.

"Texas, I have heard a joke. Why did the chicken cross the road? To show the opossum it could be done."

In another mood and at another time Texas proba-bly would have appreciated this down-home offering. But at this time and in this funk he growled, "Kid, for Chrissake, I'm trying to sleep." God, he hated in-somnia. He hated everything.

Volos stopped where he was and looked at him wide-eyed. "It takes trying? I thought sleeping was something humans did like breathing."

"Jesus. Where you been?"

The kid took this literally. "With Mercy. Texas, listen." Volos came forward and inflicted himself on the edge of the bed. "That reminds me. About sleeping. Do you remember that first time we met? When my wing gave me suffering?"

Texas found that he did not entirely hate everything after all. His voice grew quieter. " 'Course I remember, kid."

"You were good to me." Volos smiled the half-smile of a pensive child. Later, Texas would remember that smile, knowing he was not to see it again.

"I tried to be."

"You were so—you were so mothering. You held me and stroked my back, remember? To help me go to sleep. It took a long time. Do you remember?"

"Yeah, son." Very softly. He remembered, all right, but he hadn't thought Volos did. He felt his tired heart inflame with love for him.

Volos said, "Why did you not just give me what Mercy gives me to make me sleep?"

It was as if a knife had come out of nowhere to stab that swollen heart. Texas lunged up on his hands and sat straight, staring with hard red-lidded eyes. Found it necessary to remind himself of the importance of control. Very quietly he asked, "Mercedes been giving you some kind of pills?"

"Is it possible to do it with pills too? That would be easier. Mercy does it with a needle in my arm."

Texas grabbed him by the shoulder, hard. Startled, Volos pulled back from him, but Texas kept hold. The fingers would bruise. In a day there would be five black marks on the smooth dun skin. Texas did not care.

He barely managed the word. "Heroin?"

Keeping a wide-eyed gaze on him, Volos nodded.

"Jesus Christ!" To hell with control. Texas thrust with both arms, sending the kid thumping off his bed onto the floor. Fists clenched, he stood over him. Who cared that he was barefoot, bare-bellied, dressed only in Stetson and baggy boxer shorts, he could still punish the hell out of this winged punk. "Jesus buggering Christ! Are you out of your mind? You let that faggot shoot you up with smack?"

Without answering, Volos got to his feet, eyes narrow now, wings flooding crimson. Angry? Hurt? Texas hoped so. He wanted somebody besides himself to be angry and in pain. The memories of his dope addict father were beating at him, and he was raging.

"A junkie! Christ, you want to be a junkie? You might as well go flush yourself down the john, Volos. Now I know why they pitched you out of where you were. You're sewage. You're a piece of shit. Get away from me."

Volos did not move. "I am not a junkie," he said. He kept the words low, but they came out tight from between compressed lips.

Texas did not keep his voice down; he was screaming. Everyone on the floor could hear him. "What the devil you call it? You're done, Volos. You get that crap in you, you're gone, shot to hell. You're no better than—"

"No, that is not true. For you, yes, maybe, but not for me."

"I don't care! Fuck it! You're not human, then. And you're never going to be human. You're—"

"Texas. Stop." Volos's voice was shaking, and so was the rest of him, and his wings had gone thunderdark, like his eyes. "You're hurting me."

"I want to hurt you! You selfish prick, I'd like to take you and beat the shit out of you!"

"You said you never wanted to hurt me." Very softly, but there was no tremor any more in Volos. His voice had gone cat smooth and black as thin ice. "You have been my friend, and now you are betraying me."

"So run to Mercy. He'll make it all better."

"Snake," Volos whispered. "Judas."

"You should talk. Get out of my face. I don't want

to look at you." Done shouting, Texas felt dead tired
and half sick. He turned away, wanting only to be left
alone to—yes, lick his wounds. It hurt him like fire,
what the kid had gone and done. Heroin. Christ have
mercy.

He heard no door close. Turned back again. Volos
was still there.

"Get out of here!" Once he had had a few hours
to calm down, Texas knew, then he would want to
talk with the kid. He would do everything he could
to help him get off the junk. But right now he couldn't
stand the sight of him.

In a voice hard as bone Volos said to him, "You
don't tell me what to do, McCardle."

Texas looked again. It was a black angel of wrath
that stood there.

Wrath of God, wrath of the devil, it hardly mattered; anger was anger and power was power, and this
tall rebel out of heaven had both. Lightning flickering
under his dark brows. Thunder in his black, lifted
wings. No one had ever before seen those wings truly
black, but they were black now, as black as night when
no stars shine. Texas took a step back.

The angel said softly, "It is you who will leave,
McCardle."

Texas knew by the feel of his backbone that he was
getting old, dammit. Wasn't about to get into a pissing
contest with a skunk. Had better sense.

He shrugged and reached for his trousers, tried not
to let it show that he was shaking as he pulled them
on. This was the kid who always led with his chin?
And he had felt guilty sometimes because he never
got around to teaching him how to defend himself?
Jesus. This guy did not need anything an old cop could
teach him. Good thing he had not actually tried to
punch the sonuvabitch's lights out. He got his shirt
and boots on, reached for his suitcase, opened it to
throw his toothbrush in.

"You've gone bad, Volos," he said bitterly to the cheap luggage.

"I came here to be bad, McCardle."

"God forgive you."

"God can go to hell."

"He'll join you, then." Texas snapped the suitcase shut again, swung it off the bed, and headed toward the door. Didn't look back.

Mikey couldn't sleep because of the pain in his head. Mommy and the roadie lady kept giving him mashed-up pills that were supposed to make the pain go away, but it didn't. He lay like he was asleep anyway, because he felt so tired. Gabe was asleep. Mommy was supposed to be asleep, but she had gotten up and was at the door listening to the shouting down the hall. Uncle Texas was shouting, which made Mikey feel as if he wanted to cry. Uncle Texas was nice, and nice people weren't supposed to yell like that. It was scary to hear the way he was shouting. But Mikey was too tired to cry.

Because Gabe was asleep and Mommy had her head out in the hallway, he knew neither of them could see the black angel seeping through the crack in the ceiling right above his crib. He knew it was an angel because it looked just like his friend Birdman except it was all black instead of pretty colors and it wasn't him. It didn't have any face, and Birdman always had a face and it was usually nice though it didn't always smile. Birdman was Mommy's boyfriend and Birdman liked Mikey and Gabe and they liked him. Once Birdman had let Mikey wear his headband with the silver ornaments. He made shadow shapes with his hands that weren't just animals but could have been almost anything. He told stories about the Sefiroth, who were the Princes of Heaven and Hell, and about the Grigori, who came down to teach the sons of Adam and daughters of Eve, and about how someday Chayyliel would swallow the world and seven

Sefira of the Right Hand would put out the stars in the sky.

Mikey wished Birdman would come in and tell him stories to help him stop being sick. But Birdman was angry too. Mikey could hear the angriness in his voice. It was not loud, but he could hear it all the way down the hall.

The black angel seeped in and spread across the ceiling like a stain. He could see through it to the fly spots and things that lay behind it on the chalky paper or whatever it was. He could see through its wings too, and they were not feathery or nice at all. They were wings like a snake might have, all scales and skin. The angel hung there flat, the way a black-plastic garbage bag is flat on the road sometimes, and did not speak to him. Mikey considered the angel rude and wondered what it wanted. This was the third time he had seen it in two days. Mommy and the roadie lady and Gabe had all looked straight at it like they were not seeing anything. But maybe angels flattened against ceilings were an ordinary thing to them.

The black angel troubled him every time he saw it, but he always felt too tired to ask about it or say anything to it. Talking was a lot of trouble when you were just two and a half years old.

He wished if Birdman was going to be angry he would come do it at the black angel and maybe chase it away.

Partway down the hall, Texas met up with Angie Bradley, who was standing at her door. She had been listening to the ruckus, of course. Saw the suitcase. Knew the score.

"Texas, don't go," she said without preamble.

"Got to, Ange. Just want to say good-bye." He had headed toward her room on purpose. Would have knocked at her door if she had not been waiting for him. Felt his voice thicken in spite of all the Bogart movies he had watched in his life, and he had to take refuge in small talk. "How's Mikey?"

"He'll be okay. It's just a bug." She brushed away the question, stepped outside and softly closed the door so the kids could sleep. "Texas, please. Give it a few hours. Go someplace, have a beer or something, come back and talk with Volos after you're both calmed down. You know he won't stay mad. He's lost without you."

"He's got you." Texas gave what she was saying some thought, then shook his head. "He's using junk. I can't take it."

"He says it will not hurt him, he did not imagine himself to become addicted to things."

Angie Bradley understood some things deeply and some things not at all. Drugs were one of the latter. She could have no idea how—how malignant they could be. But Texas did not feel he had to stay around and protect her from them or Volos or anything; she had that sheen of innocence to keep her safe. As for Volos—Texas swore to himself that he was gonna write Volos off. He was not going to care anymore.

"I still can't take it," he said. "I just can't take what he's doing."

She saw that he had reached a limit, and nodded. "Where will you go?"

"Back to L.A., I guess." Smog city. High prices. Crowds. Stand in line for everything. "Get a job at the dry cleaner's again. Live at the Y. I don't know what else to do." Damn his voice for choking up on him like that.

She said, "Texas, go home."

What the hell was she talking about? "I don't have a home."

"Sure you do. Go back to Wyoma."

"She told me—" Why was she making him talk about Wyoma? "She said—" He couldn't manage it.

Angie helped him out. "She told you not to come back? Texas, to me that just means quit fooling around. She wanted to light a fire under you. She wanted you to get your butt back there right away."

He stared at her.

She said quietly and with utter conviction, "Texas, she'll take you back. I know she will."

Maybe once she would have, if he hadn't gone and let his pride get in the way. But it was too late now. He shook his head.

"She will! She'd be crazy not to, a sweet man like you. Texas, try. Please. What do you have to lose?"

"Nothing," he admitted. Absolutely nothing anymore, not even his pride. It was all gone, heart, hope, soul. He felt empty as last year's cabbage crock. All used up.

"What's the worst she can do to you?"

"Get down the gun and shoot me."

"Texas—"

"And right now I don't care if she does."

"You'll do it?"

"Yes." He tried not to let the idea catch hold of him too hard. Told himself it would be good just to see Mingo County, to see the hills again—real hills, not the fake Hollywood kind—and breathe home-grown air, and hear the whippoorwills calling. Told himself not to expect much more than that. "It would be a waste to head back west when I've made it this far east," he said.

Angie looked as if she was going to laugh at him or pull his hat down over his eyes, which would not have surprised him. She did those things a lot. But then she did neither. Instead, she stood on her tiptoes and kissed him. " 'Bye," she said, before he could catch his breath. "You got money?"

He nodded, though in fact he didn't have much.

"Good luck." She went back into her room. He watched the door click shut. Stood there awhile.

Looked back down the hallway. Volos was nowhere in sight. Probably went running to Mercy for a fix.

Texas knew he should go find him, if only to try to collect some pay—

To hell with pay. He knew he couldn't face the kid again without coming apart one way or another.

He found the bus station easily enough, just followed his cop instincts to the worst part of town, and there it was. He didn't check his wallet till he got there and asked about fares. Just about enough in it to get him into West Virginia.

There was a retarded woman with scraggly gray hair begging near the stairs. Ticket in hand, Texas passed her, hesitated, then turned back and gave her his last dollar bill. That left him change for a phone call. And hell, he wasn't going to be wanting no hot dog for supper anyway. Bus fumes always made him feel half sick. He felt that way already.

It wasn't until close to midnight, braced in his bus seat with his chest feeling tight as a gnat's ass, looking out on darkness, knowing he was not going to get any sleep again, that he admitted it: The ache was in his heart as much as his gut. God, he needed comforting. Time was, he could have taken his pain to an angel, and the angel would have put his arms around him, and Texas would have hidden his hands under the feathery healing wings. But from what he had seen, that angel was gone. Gone like spit down a creek.

chapter
fourteen

Close to midnight, and the concert showed no signs of ending; Volos was still cookin' worse than the cauldron in *Macbeth*. There he was onstage, Mr. Toil and Trouble himself, a hellbroth wearing black leathers and a horned guitar. Earplugs firmly in place, Mercedes watched Volos from the lighting platform and detested him more than ever before, loathed him because he was so good. For three hours Volos had performed with wings black as charcoal, with eyes that smoldered, giving renditions so hot they smoked. No love ballads tonight. It was all suicide tempo, all fury, all crotchthrob and clenched fist. The screaming women in the crowd loved it, but the band could barely keep up with him. Even from the distance Mercedes could see how the guitarists played with frantic fingers and pale faces, how the drummer kept banging out the beat but looked strained, scared. Poor clowns, exposed there onstage like on a rock at high tide, a lunatic singer in their spotlight and a moon-mad sea of people roaring at their feet. Mercedes himself felt not at all afraid, because he was perched well out of the reach of anyone in that capacity audience, but he could see how

Volos had stormlashed the crowd until it frothed like a whirlpool in the bowl of the arena.

GO BUTCHER YOUR JUDAS SELF
AND HANG THE MEAT ON A TREE.
YOU SAY HOW CAN SOMEONE YOU LOVE
TURN INTO AN ENEMY?
I'LL TELL YOU HOW.
IT HAPPENED THE DAY
YOU BETRAYED ME.

Volos seemed to be trying to inflict permanent hearing loss. The sound was turned up past the point of distortion, so that those below the speakers did not so much hear music as feel it assaulting them, like rough sex, spanking their ears, shaking their viscera, coming at them with whips and chains.

GO CARVE OUT YOUR JUDAS HEART
AND EAT IT LIKE IODINE CANDY
THEN LOOK IN THE MIRROR
WITH A JUDAS TEAR
AND TELL ME WHAT YOU SEE.
WHEN DID IT ALL
COME APART? THE DAY
YOU BETRAYED ME.

Engulfing as the music was, still it was almost drowned in the sound of screams—ecstasy or pain? Not that there was really much difference. Nevertheless, Mercedes glanced down—then he stared. This was truly interesting. He had never seen masses of people actually injuring one another before, and it was better than watching a snuff movie—he did not have to wonder how much of this carnage was faked, because all of it was indisputably real. Every one of the groundlings seemed to have gone berserk, pushing toward the stage, and those people crushed against the rails and shrieking, yes, they were being hurt. The ones with the white, upturned faces, though, he could not tell whether they were fainting or dead. Some of them were lifted off their feet, floating in the crowd like fish bellies on a flood, but others were sinking, perhaps would be trampled. Fascinated, Mercedes watched a hefty man disappear from sight, gone under the maelstrom.

He felt a touch on his arm. "Boss?"

"Keep it on white," Mercedes told the lighting man without looking at him. Tonight had been simple. Volos had stayed in black wings, black clothes. Mercedes had run a classy show in black and white. It was easy.

"I—Boss . . ."

The man was not concerned with lighting. He looked as pale as the fish bellies down below. Mercedes congratulated himself that he was a creative artist, not one of these snivelers who actually had to care about things. He barked at the man, "So what do you expect me to do about it?"

"I—I don't know. Get on the horn or something . . ."

Nobody was doing anything about it. Volos sang on—he probably did not even know what was happening out beyond the stage lights. The security people had apparently scaled down their priorities from "crowd management" to "staying alive." Mercedes did not see them trying to fish the fainters out of the audience. He did not see them at all. If that paragon among assholes, Texas, had been there, he would probably want them to stop the concert, he would probably be riding in on a white horse about now, firing silver bullets into the air. But Texas was gone, and Mercedes was glad. And the show blazed on.

Volos, onstage with his black wings and his burning passion and all his fatal charisma, swung into "Before I Die"—

Goddamn him, he wouldn't die. Ever. Because there were people down there willing to die for him. Look at them. A girl, her face near his feet, squeezed against the stage rails so hard that all the air was pressed out of her, she couldn't even squeak, her ribs were caving in, and old Donne was right about the euphemism he used for sex, the look on her face was just the same, blank-eyed and beatific, as she either came or expired, Mercedes didn't know or much care which—and in that moment truth screwed him, pointed and hard, and this was what truth said: People would never do that for him.

Nobody was ever going to sob and faint and risk being trampled for him. Nobody was going to scream when he smiled. Nobody was going to remember him and keep him alive forever. Nobody was going to worship at his altar or lie down for him and die. Never. There on his perch he stood, seeing it all happen for Volos, and it was never going to happen for him. He knew that now. Because there was something in Volos that he, Mercedes, just didn't have.

Shit, it hurt.

The lights went out.

"Hey!"

"Fuck it," the light man replied in strangled tones, "I gotta do something."

"Certainly. Do something, why don't you?" Mercedes felt his way to a chilly metal seat, started to giggle, then laughed aloud, it hurt so queer.

Volos's voice came over the mike: "What the fucking hell?" Burning Earth fumbled for a surprised moment, then stopped playing. In the relative silence that followed, the screams of the crowd flew like starlings, unmistakably cries of pain.

"What's happening?"

"It's the holocaust, Volie!" Mercedes shrilled across the darkness. Maybe the black angel heard him.

Probably not. Better not. There had been a phone call from Brett, one worth concentrating on. Better forget what he had just been thinking. There might yet be a chance for Mercedes Kell to reach the stars.

*　　*　　*

Backstage, afterward, Red had the shakes and had to lean against the wall, not talking. Nobody was talking much. Nobody was getting changed or showered or packing equipment either. Everybody was just standing around, waiting for who knew what. There was something very strange flying in the air of the place, and it was not just rumors, though there were plenty of those too: a dozen dead, over a hundred injured ... The houselights were on and the police were clearing the arena. Outside, ambulances had gathered like those screaming demon birds, whatever the hell they were called, like vultures, waiting for souls. Thank God Angie was not there, had not been there, had not seen or been mixed up in any of this. She had stayed at the hotel, taking care of her sick kid. Probably an excuse. The kid was okay, as far as Red knew. Probably she was keeping away from Volos, like everybody else today.

There he stood, his face stony, his wings still black as a hit man's heart, and nobody was going near him. Partly because of that afternoon; everybody had liked Texas, so nobody liked what had happened between him and Volos except maybe that bitch Mercedes. But mostly because of that night, the way Volos had thrown off sparks as he sang. He had been awesome, scary. People were afraid of him.

Shit. The guy was one incredible hell of a front man. Gonna go down in rock history. Somebody had to talk to him.

Red pushed away from the wall and wobbled over to him, shaking worse than ever. Said, "Hey, you want a drink, Volos?" Red wanted one himself. With irrational fervor he believed and hoped there was a bottle back in the dressing room somewhere.

"No. Thank you."

That was not so bad. Red chanced a straight look at this guy and began to wonder. Black meant more than just evil or anger. It was the color people wore when someone they loved went and died.

Red said, "You all right, man?"

Volos surprised him with a snort of unfunny laughter. "All right? How?"

"I just mean . . ." Red swallowed. "I just mean, is there anything I can do?"

"No. I do not think so."

Bink butted in, now that Red had gone ahead and taken the first risk. Red and Bink got along fine, but Red had to admit the guy was kind of a dork. Pushy, always shoving himself into a hole. A lot of bass guitarists were like that. It was hard to lick a good riff if you were a bass, because you were always two strings short of a full set. Bink proved this now by thrusting his jaw to within a few inches of Volos's hard face.

"What the hell you trying to prove, big shot? I guess you think we enjoyed your fun and games? You think we like being scared shitless?"

Volos said nothing. His stare looked distant, barely focused on the bass man. Red was the one who complained, "Bink, shut up." He had stopped shaking and felt not so much scared any longer as weary and disgusted. The concert had been bad enough, and now here was this second-fiddle hot dog talking like third-rate TV.

Bink slewed around and growled at him, "You shut up. You're too goddamn nice. Somebody's gotta tell it like it is around here."

"For Chrissake, you sound like a cop show."

Bink had already turned back to Volos. "Hey. Wings! I got something to say to you. You listening to me?"

Volos looked at him. This apparently was response enough for Bink, who upped the volume a notch and went on: "You think you're hot stuff, don't you? Well, maybe you are, but I don't have to put up with it. Don't you ever do that again, you hear me? Don't you *ever* get an audience that worked up again, or I—"

Volos hit him.

It wasn't even a good punch, just a childish sort of sideswipe that knocked Bink down rather than smashing him flat. But it was so sudden, the rattlesnake strike without the warning rattle, that Bink lay blinking on the floor, and Red stood stupefied. Somehow he had had this idea of Volos as a gentle person really, a pussycat, no matter what the guy did onstage, but now—one minute Volos had been standing there brooding or whatever you want to call it, and the next minute he had turned into a goddamn special effect, some kind of horror-movie thing with wings. Red knew why Bink didn't get up, and it wasn't because the guy was hurt or chicken. It was because right now, looking at Volos, a person couldn't move.

Volos said, not even loudly, "Don't you *ever* tell me what to do." Then wheeled away and crashed out the backstage door within a few strides, and nobody tried to stop him.

Great. Oh, just awesomely wonderful. There he went, off on his own in the mood he was in, out where the fans and cops and reporters were. Red could see the headlines now: **Volos Arrested for Assault. Winged Freak Out of Control Ravages City. Twenty Dead, Two Hundred Injured at Burning Earth Concert.**

Of course, hell, that was just the sort of thing that was expected from rock superstars. **Volos Fires Security Head, Decks Band Member.** The fans would love it.

"Jesus," Bink panted from the floor.

"I told you to shut up," Red chided him, not unkindly. He put down a hand, helped Bink stagger to his feet.

"Jesus *Christ*," Bink elaborated. "Scare the shit outa me. What the hell is that guy?"

"He's just a guy," said Red roughly. The question frightened him. Just for a moment as Volos had swooped out the door amid a rustle of black and stormily lifted wings, Red had caught himself thinking something like "dark angel" or "avenging angel," as if Volos could really be—no. It was a mistake even to think it. One of the scariest things about being an artist was knowing how many artists of all kinds went crazy and killed themselves. Red had thought about this a lot, and he believed he had a handle on the reason: Artists went off into Never-Never-Land, and then they went off the edge. So it was important to keep a firm grip on reality. More than just important— it was vital, a matter of life and death.

Volos walked through the stage-door crowd as if it were fog, got past the reporters with a scowl and a glare, found his way to an empty street. Stopped to sigh. The brief conversation with Red had helped him a little. He could feel his wings turning from black to a rainy slate-blue. From rage to melancholy.

Anything I can do? Red was a truly nice person, but no, there was nothing he could do. Not while the guitar player, like nearly everyone else, still thought his lead singer wore colored contacts and worked his wings with some sort of concealed wiring.

Grudgingly, Volos had come to accept, though not understand, how most people had to think these things. He had only three friends who knew him truly: Angela, and Mercedes, and—

Two, now. Angela and Mercedes.

Angela seemed to be preoccupied with her children. She would be angry with him if he knocked at her hotel door and woke them. Mercedes had gotten out of the arena the first minute he could. Volos knew better than to go back to the hotel looking for him. He knew where his ex-lover would be. Wings sagging, he walked through the dark streets in the dirty part of town to find Mercedes.

As always, he looked around him as he walked, because he loved seeing whatever the mortal world put in front of him; there was a strong fascination and a strange comfort in human transience. This time he no-

ticed a crooked weathervane, a fogged front-yard gazing globe, and an empty house with its porch roof
gone to rot and moss. In the dirt-filled gutter grew
wild snapdragons, and amid the yellow spikes nested
something softly gray-blue, a feral parakeet, hidden
from sight of anyone not so tall as Volos. Probably
not noticed even by those who had the height to see.
City humans, Volos had observed, generally walked
with their eyes turned to the pavement, as if looking
for money.

In his mood he found talking to birds preferable to
dealing with people. He greeted the parakeet, "Hello,
little brother with wings the same color as mine are
right now. What are you doing there?"

It replied very softly through its beak, "Just waiting
until the cold weather comes, when I will die."

"Huh. It sounds much like what I am doing. Are
you sorry you escaped, then?"

"No! No, it is well worth it." The parakeet grew
excited and stood up, fluffing its feathers. "It is far
better to die in freedom than to live forever in a
cage."

"I think so also. Little brother, can you tell me
where the Boystown is around here?"

"Pardon?"

"The gay bars. Where are they?"

"Gay as in many colors, like butterflies? Bars?"

"Never mind."

"Whatever they are, how would I know?" the bird
huffed. "I am just an accidental."

"So am I." Or at least that was what he felt like.
"Thank you anyway."

Eventually he had to ask the young men in kerchiefs
and ponytails, the ones holding down the street cor-
ners, before he could locate the gay bars. Not caring
about the way they looked at him. Not caring what
anybody thought. Let the gossip columns print what
they wanted, let people think what they wanted. A lot
of people already thought the worst.

Mercy never had to ask anybody where to find his action. Definitely he was not an accidental.

And there he was, badgering the bartender because he couldn't get Corona beer with a twist of lemon. "I can put a lemon slice in a Beck's for you," the bartender was saying.

"It's not the same," said Mercedes bitchily. "In L.A.—"

Every head in the place turned as Volos came in. "Volie!" Mercedes exclaimed, jumping up and hurrying him right back outside again, to the deserted sidewalk under a vapor lamp. "Vo." Keeping his voice down, an excited and slightly drunken conspirator. "Brett called. Great news. I been trying for hours to get a chance to tell you."

Volos said, "Have you heard about Texas?" He knew Mercy had to have heard about Texas. But Volos wanted to talk about Texas, he needed to talk about what had happened, though it made his chest ache even to say the name.

"Certainly I heard. Good riddance. Vo, MGM called—"

"You saw what happened tonight?" He knew Mercy had to have seen. "They say people were killed." Killed. Killed meant dead long before the frost. No coming back, no second chances.

"So they were killed, to hell with them. Volie! MGM wants to talk about you doing some movies for them. Sort of like the Elvis Presley movies. They want you to be in pictures, Vo!"

Volos shook his head as if shaking off gnats. Orange streetlamp light seemed to buzz around his head as badly as insects. "Did Texas tell anyone where he was going?" he asked.

"Never *mind* about him, Volie! Think about being a movie star."

"I don't want to be an actor." He turned and walked away.

"You don't have to act. They really just want you

to sing and kiss girls. Volie, they want you so bad they'll do whatever you say." Volos had veered from the sidewalk to the middle of the benighted street, and Mercedes hurried along at his side, talking fast. "They'd give me a part if you said the word. Make me the director if you want it that way."

"I just want to be a singer," Volos said to the dark sky. Whispered, almost. Because of yellow streetlight fog he could not see a star. Did not like stars. Was looking for them anyway. Could not find one. God, when had it gone so wrong? His friend of friends abandoning him, people dying at his feet, how had it come to that?

At his side Mercedes panted, "Volos, you're crazy! You can't let this pass. Think of the press it'll get you. Think of the money."

"I don't care about any of that."

Mercedes cried out in what sounded like real anguish, "Volos, *I* care! This is the big break!"

The street was paved with brick. Or cobblestone. Volos stopped where he was, feeling at it with his boot toe, but did not look down. Instead he stared at Mercy. "What big break?" he asked.

"My chance—" Mercedes swallowed the words, tried again. "Your chance to be immortal."

A strange thing about darkness and the dead of night and the blue tinge in the wings. Sometimes they let eyes see more clearly than by day. Volos was seeing himself that way. Accidental? By his own doing. He had intended himself into being, he was a self-willed thing, an amateur mortal who had fucked up. He pondered Mercy, seeing a rather small man with the taste of vinegar always in his mouth. How could it be that Mercy did not care if people died to make Volos money and fame? But it really seemed he was that way. He was empty, so hollow it was no use telling him anything, for the words would echo and echo, yet not be heard.

"I was immortal already," Volos said finally. "It is not worth being dishonest for."

"You got to be kidding. You're really not going to—"

"No. I am really not going to do it, Mercy." He turned his back again and strode on. Once more Mercedes trotted at his side.

"Volie. Please. Don't say no right now. I caught you at a bad time. Sleep on it at least, all right?" His voice brightened like a ferret's eyes. "Would you like to sleep? I got some H."

"No," Volos said. "I think I have been sleeping too much. I think I have been missing things."

"Volie—"

"Go on back to the bar, Mercy." He lengthened his stride and left Mercedes behind.

He wandered in the night, noticing again as if for the first time how brown brick smells of sunshine even at two in the morning, how electricity hung from its crosses does not weep but sings, how television glows glacier-blue through the venetian blinds of the second-story bedrooms where couples were watching the late-night videos they did not want the kids to see and maybe making love. He felt bereft. He wanted Angie terribly, but knew he must not awaken her. In the morning he would kiss her and talk with her about Texas.

Turning a corner nearby, a taxicab caught him in its headlights, jerked to a stop, backed up, and came barreling toward him. Volos stood, resigned to whatever was happening now. But it was not bad. The cab stopped short of hitting him, and Red got out.

"There you are, man." Red paid the cabdriver thirty dollars and sent him away, then came to walk by Volos's side. He kept his voice soft and even, but Volos could hear some sort of strain in it. "I been looking all over for you."

"Why?"

Red hesitated, then came out with what Volos could

tell to be truth. "Worried about you! Didn't know where you were, what you were gonna do, the way—" Evidently Red did not want to say it more plainly, that Volos had been hugely fucking up. "The way things been going."

They walked in silence for a run-down block. Then Red added, "Things ain't as bad as people were saying, Volos. We've got the official word from the police now. Three dead—I mean, that's bad enough, but it could have been a lot worse."

"How many hurt?" Volos asked.

"A few dozen."

Speaking of hurt. "How's Bink?"

"Fine! Bink's got a thick skull. You couldn't kill him if you came at him with a ball-peen hammer."

"Angry at me?"

"He's not gonna quit or anything like that, no."

"But he is angry."

"A little."

"It is all anger today. Has anybody heard from Texas?"

Red looked away, stared down at the pavement. Typical human. "No."

They walked past an Art Deco gas station with pink tile trim, and a little brick restaurant shaped like a coffeepot, complete with a sheet-metal spout. "Smoke comes out of that metal part in the wintertime," Red remarked. "They got the furnace venting through it. I remember from the last time I went through here."

Volos did not reply.

"Volos? Hey, man, uh, a bunch of us are back at the hotel getting drunk. I mean, really plastered. Seems like the thing to do tonight. Why don't you come back with me?"

"No, I do not think so. Thank you." He really did mean the thanks and hoped Red could hear that in his voice.

"You sure, man?"

"Yes, I am certain. I need to walk and think."

"Yeah? That's just what the rest of us don't want to do, is think too much. Okay, so you think for us." Red had worked on getting drunk already, Volos could tell. Now that the strain on him was less, the liquor was starting to show. "Whatcha thinking?"

"I am thinking there is no need to try to be evil. It seems to happen enough by accident."

"That's the goddamn truth, man."

"And the trouble with evil is—it makes a mess of everything." Volos knew that had not come out as cogently as he had wanted, but he did not know how to explain what he was just then comprehending, the straight linkage between evil and pain. How "evil" was not just a pose, a stance, an artistic statement, but a name for that which ruined lives. Not just an idea, but something real, the force that was making his chest ache and his wings hang heavy on his back.

Perhaps Red understood somewhat. At least he did not smile.

Volos said, "I am thinking—it is true that Texas shouted at me, but still ... I think if I had not gone blackwing at him, none of this would have happened."

"Hard to tell," Red hedged. Trying to be nice. Why would humans always and forever try to be nice when it was more important to find truth?

"I am sure of it. And what I mostly think is this, that I must never go blackwing again."

He had reached the limits of Red's comprehension. The guitarist was staring at him with the whites of his eyes showing, spooked.

"Why don't you go back to the hotel," Volos told him quietly. "I want you to tell the others I will not do it again. That I have made a promise. All right?"

Red swallowed and nodded but said, "I'm supposed to leave you alone out here? Hey, don't you worry about crazies and death threats and stuff? I hate to tell you, man, but you don't punch worth a damn."

Volos laughed, feeling his wings lighten—not just in color, but physically lighten, their burden on his back growing less. "If anybody bothers me," he told Red, "I will flap him to death."

Red took a step back.

"It is a joke, Red."

"Oh."

"Is the hotel far? Can you walk to it? Go on back."

He stood and watched the guitarist toddle off, weaving just a little. Waved once when Red waved. Stayed where he was until Red was out of sight.

Like evil itself, his promise was not just an idea or a word, but a force that had acted on him—he sensed that. Imagining himself into being, he had shaped his body, and this thinking, this promise, this renunciation, had felt somewhat the same as that act. It had shaped some part of him, changed him. The direction of his life would go differently because of it.

He turned back the way he had come and kept walking. Saw a skinny kid sleeping on the sidewalk next to a boom box bigger than he was. Saw heat lightning in the sky. Smelled ozone in the air.

Thought of Texas, and sighed, not knowing what to do. Thought of Mercedes, and shrugged. He sensed without much caring how Mercedes hated him now. How on the cobbled street behind his leave-taking back, Mercedes had stood shaking with rage and saying again and again, "Son of a bitch. You hotshot son of a bitch. All the things I've done for you, and will you do this one thing for me ... You bastard. I'll clip your wings."

c h a p t e r
fifteen

Hours after midnight Angie was not sleeping. In the white teddy Volos had gotten her, sitting on the john with the bathroom door closed so that her light would not disturb the kids, she was trying to write a song.

Devil lover
Stormwind in your hair
Lightning in the touch of your hands
You make me scared
I need to grow my wings
I feel so unprepared

It was not the electric touch of his hands that had frightened her, or even the fight with Texas, though the latter had upset her enough to keep her awake. But her fear had started a few days before that, when in the sleepy morning she had looked in the mirror, brushing her teeth, and had expected to see Volos's narrow, elegant face looking back at her. She had been surprised, actually surprised, to see her own soft cheeks instead of his hollow ones, her own wide, dark eyes instead of his that changed more often than the

229

weather. And for a moment she had found it hard to remember her own name.

I'm just a wayfaring angel
A traveler frightened of thunder
A child who stayed too late at the park
Scared of the dark
I'm not daring enough for your arms
Devil lover

She was losing herself in him, that was what terrified her. He was as overwhelming as the sea. Or else she had thrown herself into his tides too completely. Or maybe she should not blame it on him, maybe even before she met him she had not known, really, who she was. A wayfarer, yes; a child, sometimes; but an angel? Huh. Hardly.

She crumpled the poem, unsatisfied. "Angie Bradley," she muttered to herself, "who are you?"

Out in the dim bedroom Mikey wailed.

Though Angie had never been a hovering mother, though Mikey had been pretty much over his cold for several days and she had not been worried while he struggled with the fever and congestion, something about this cry went through her. Any other time, disturbed at her writing, she would have set down pencil and paper with rolling eyes and an expressive sigh. But this time she dropped the things, jumped up, and ran to her child.

She slapped at a light switch on the way. There was nobody to wake up and complain, because she had a room to herself—Volos had taken care of that when Mikey got sick, and she had not needed to ask him. Though maybe Texas had suggested it to him.

Mikey was vomiting violently, yet his hands sprawled weak as mice.

Angie stroked his back, ran for a towel, tried to get him cleaned up. He lay crying thinly, as if he felt tired to death. It was a terrible cry, as if already something had laid claim on his soul; he did not sound like Mikey at all. Yet he still vomited. Though there was nothing left in him, he lay retching as if a machine were making him do it.

Awakened by the noise and light, Gabriel was sitting up in bed and staring at his brother. "He's really *sick,*" Gabe declared, awestruck.

"Yes, he really is," Angie replied, hearing her own voice shake. The sound focused her terror. She cried out loud, "Volos!"

Would it be faster to go pound on the door of the next room? Or get on the phone, call an ambulance? But it was Volos who was her rescuing angel. Volos who loved her. She knew he loved her, though he had not said it. Probably she knew it better than he did.

"Volos! Please hurry!"

She did not understand how much her panic had already hurried him. Before she had finished calling the second time he burst, booted feet first, through the window, wings spread wide, their color as pale as his startled face. He stood amid shattered glass, looked, heard, comprehended at once. "Hospital," he said.

"Wait." He was there, he had come to her in an eyeblink, and she had to make him wait while she grabbed Gabe, ran with him to the next room, pounded on the door, thrust him into the groggy arms of the roadie's wife. Then back, and the roadie's wife came running after her and made her put on a robe, shrieked something about not stepping barefoot on broken glass, as if it mattered while Volos stood with Michael still convulsively retching in his arms. The next instant he reached for her, lifted her off the floor, and toppled out the window with both of them. Someone screamed. Angela felt sure it was not her.

In the Emergency Room lounge Volos paced, his wings leaden with worry. He hated the place, which had linoleum flooring that was cold beneath his feet and smelled of disinfectant. Its molded plastic chairs were of ugly colors. Moreover, they were all in lines, shackled together like slaves.

In one chair a cop sat reading *Newsweek,* waiting for his partner to get stitched up after subduing a drunk who had resisted arrest. In a far corner sat the family of the drunk. Somebody in a white coat came out and beckoned to them: The man was on his way to the operating room. He had been thoroughly subdued.

Volos's worry was not all for Mikey. Some was for himself. Standing on the flat roof of a high school and watching the lovers in the bushes down below, he had heard Angie writing a poem, he had heard the fear in it, and now he himself felt frightened, terrified, because he did not think he could bear it if she went away. Not after—

No, this was no time to think about Texas, no matter how he missed him. He had to be strong now.

Everything else that was happening, and now this with the child. . . . He had to be strong for Ange. The alarm in her call had been so sharp it had hurtled him toward her like a slingshot. There had been no time to kiss her, to talk with her, to say, *Please, by all the demons of hell, please, Angela, do not leave me.*

It was the first time, he realized, that he had been in a hospital. He did not like the chemical odor of the place. It chilled him. It made him feel as if he might someday die.

The cop glanced up at him out of a hard, scarred face. Muttered something that might have been "cocksucker." Looked back to his magazine. Volos paced.

Angela came out of the Emergency Room and walked toward him, her steps short, unsteady. He went to her and wrapped himself around her, arms and wings, like an inverted flower.

"They chased me out," she said into the hollow of his neck. "He doesn't need me right now. He doesn't know me."

"Michael doesn't know you?"

"He went into convulsions. Thrashing around. Now he's unconscious. They wanted me out of the way."

Volos had only a distant understanding of the human body in crisis, of its symptoms, its never-expected rebellions, its betrayals. Unconsciousness to him was a drug-induced novelty, a dreamy sleep. But he could tell that to Angela life had gone very wrong very quickly. She was stunned, as if a great snake had struck. He could feel her shaking against him.

"What is it?"

His worry was all for her now, but she thought he was asking about Mikey. She said, "They're not sure till they see the blood tests. Some sort of syndrome, they think."

"What is a syndrome?"

She shook her head. He could feel her chin hard against his collarbone. "I'd better call Ennis," she said, lifting her head away from him.

"But why?"

"Mikey's—his child too, Volos." Her voice trembled like her body. "Do you have a quarter?"

In his jeans pocket he found several coins. He gave them all to her and watched as she walked away. Fear lay in his gut like ice that would not melt.

The cop put down his magazine and got up. His partner had come out of the E.R. with seven stitches closing a laceration over his cheekbone. The uninjured officer swatted the other on the butt, jock style. They ambled out.

"There's no answer." Angela came back from the phone. "He's not home."

Volos felt his fear dissolve because she was near him and her husband had not taken her away from him yet. He warmed her in his arms again. "It's four in the morning," she said to his shoulder. "Where in God's name could he be?"

Ange. Please don't leave me.

Others from the Burning Earth tour came in: the

roadie's wife, Mercedes, the bus driver, the lighting man. They brought Angie clothing and coffee and made her sit down and talked with her while Volos stood nearby, feeling somehow apart, as if he were invisibly hovering, as if he were a bodiless being again, an ethereal eavesdropper, ineffably of a different substance than their sturdy flesh. He noticed that no one spoke of the concert and its carnage; they would not bring that up with Angela now. Unless she read the morning paper she would hear about it only later. Truth was of less importance to them than most other things. But these humans with their hot drinks and their comradeship and their laughter, they had something that he with all his thinking did not comprehend.

Trying to come in from the cold, to feel floor under his feet again, he said, "Mercedes. You had better cancel the next venue."

Mercy looked at him with an expression he had never seen on that silken face before. "We can't do that," he said.

"I cannot be two places at once, is what I cannot do. And I am staying here."

"Listen to me, Volos. Since I've known you I've just been trying to look out for what's best for you—"

"Hellshit!" Volos felt suddenly angry with the same high-voltage wrath that McCardle had sparked in him. *I must never go blackwing again.* Mercedes was not worth it anyway. Texas had hurt him, but Mercedes merely disgusted him. So it was not very hard to combat merely with words, to say, "You think I am stupid? I know you don't care a quick fuck about me. You want what you can get, that is all. You look out for what is best for Mercedes Kell."

"You—" With difficulty Mercedes swallowed an epithet. "Volos. Do you get some sort of kick out of just throwing it all away?"

"I have thrown nothing worth keeping!" *Yet it is all falling apart.*

"You don't know shit about what's worth what. It's

no use talking with you. I'm going back to the hotel. I'm—"

"Just do what I told you. Cancel Pittsburgh. We are not going anywhere."

"You may not be," Mercedes said, and he swished out. Roadie's wife, bus driver, lighting man, and two guitarists—when had they come in?—all watched his exit with muted satisfaction. Someone, not Volos, said with dark amusement, "There goes Mercy out the door."

Angela seemed to have noticed none of this. She was in a daze made up solely of Mikey.

The night wore on. Volos watched, feeling separate and uneasy, as Angela tried again and again to reach her husband. As finally she phoned a neighbor. Ennis was away for the week, a sleepy woman told her. He and Reverend Crawshaw had gone to a revival somewhere, a rally against the evils of rock music.

He stood by her at dawn when the doctor made his report: it seemed to be Reye's syndrome, Michael had been admitted to Intensive Care, diuretics were being administered, intracranial devices would be used to monitor the pressure on the brain.

He walked with her as she went to look at the little body lying very still on the white slab of a bed, the pug-nosed face nearly obscured by oxygen apparatus, the wispy brown hair shaved to accommodate a cone of white plastic strung with a black lacework of wires.

Only when she turned to him and wept did he begin to comprehend that bittersweet brotherhood of mankind, that common bond called mortality. Then he could distance himself no longer, and knew to the marrow of his hard, ephemeral bones: flesh was frail. People had been trampled in the night. Mikey might die.

"Birdman will make Mikey get better," Gabe said to his mother. He had been saying it for a solid day, ever since Birdman had taken Mikey off to the hospital. Before that he had been saying, "Where's Uncle Texas?" But nobody had paid any attention to him then either.

"Mommy." She was sitting on the hotel bed as if he didn't matter. He tugged at her shirt to make her look at him. "Tell Birdman to help Mikey."

"He can't, honey," she said faintly. She pulled him up into her lap and held him hard, as if that would make things any better.

She didn't understand. None of them understood how real Birdman was. Gabe could tell they didn't, because they always said Volos, and Volos was just a rock star, a voice on the radio, a body in a video, a picture on a magazine page. But Birdman had flown to the Horsehead Nebula and back once on a bet. When he was bad, he was whipped with lashes of fire. He remembered when Adam and Eve were still alive, when angels came down and married human women and taught them how to make themselves beautiful and taught their children secrets. He remembered when people used to go up on top of the Tower of Babel and shoot arrows into the sky, trying to wing an angel, and it was good luck if the arrow came down red with blood. He had watched the archangels killing people in Jerusalem and Sodom. He understood every language anyone could talk in, even the language of birds. Once when he was baby-sitting Gabe and Michael and nobody else was around, he had called a bunch of pigeons in through the window and made them fly stunts. He liked pigeons because they were dandified and womanly like Mercedes, he said.

He knew some of the Princes of the Sefiroth to say hi to them. He could help Mikey.

"Make Birdman help!" Gabriel insisted to his mother.

He would have spoken to Birdman himself, but Birdman was pacing the floor and he couldn't get him to stop and listen. And it was no use trying to talk to him when his wings were that old-asphalt color anyway. The others were just sitting like his mother—Red and the rest of the band and the roadie lady and some of the roadies, just about everybody except Uncle Texas and grouchy old Mercedes.

"Mommy—"

"Hey, big guy," Red called softly to him. "C'mere."

He went to where Red was sitting in the squeaky hotel chair because he liked Red, though maybe not quite as much as he had liked Uncle Texas. Gabe missed Texas.

Red took him by the shoulders, gently. "Hey," Red said, keeping his voice way down, "take it easy on your mother. You heard what happened. The doctors say there's nothing anybody can do now."

From across the room Birdman said, "Gabe is right."

"Huh?" Red looked up in a dumb-cow way. So did most of the others. And Birdman was standing there with his wings flashing like coals afire.

"The boy is right. I must help. I am a coward if I do not try." Birdman crossed the room in two big strides and got down on his knees, right down on the floor, in front of Mother. "Ange," he said, begging, and she did an odd thing. She parted his hair with her fingers and kissed him on the forehead, and then she laid her hands on him, like Grandpa giving a blessing.

At the beginning of time, the Supreme Being had sat on his throne and emanations had issued from his right side and from his left. The ten emanations of his right side came to be called the Princes, or the Sarim, or the Archangels; they were the Holy Sefiroth, the most ancient and powerful and ineffable of angels, more puissant than seraphim and cherubim, older than the world. And the ten emanations of his left side came to be called the Adverse or Unholy Sefiroth, and they were the Angels of Punishment, more ancient and potent than Lilith or Lucifer and all the minions of hell.

They all had many, many names, as was fitting for such puissances, for the foundation of power is the Word, the name. Each Sefira had hundreds of names, only a few less than the thousand names of its creator. And the names of the angels of the Unholy Sefiroth meant "destruction" and "death" and "wrath of God" and "whip of flame," "pitiless" and "rigid" and "rod." The one to whom Volos needed to speak, the fourth personage of the Unholy ten, was called among other names Mashhit, which meant "death of children."

The less Mashhit was annoyed or inconvenienced, Volos knew, the better were the chances he could be cajoled into letting Michael Bradley live. Therefore, to summon Mashhit, Volos went to where Mashhit's presence already hovered strong: the Intensive Care Unit of the hospital, where Mikey lay unconscious.

It was after midnight. The monitors glowed at the nursing station, but the cubicles stood quiet and dim, labyrinthine in the shadows.

Angela walked before Volos, his psychopomp, leading him through mysteries. She was with him, she had told him, because he needed her to get him onto the floor. There were rules. He knew that, and he knew the rules were eyed mostly by those passing them by; she was not permitted to be in the ICU in the middle of the night either. It was one of the sweetest things about living with humans, the way the rules were there for bypassing, one of the things that made the world most unlike the bitter place from which he had come.

If any bitterness at all tainted his mouth, it was because the nurses would not have let him in without her. She was the mother, but he was the weird one with wings. He had seen them watching him.

He knew also that Angela would have come with him regardless, and that particular knowledge tasted like honey and made him brave.

"He's here," Angela said to him in a low voice, "isn't he?"

"Mashhit? Yes." The death angel's presence filled

the place, towering through the ceiling, passing through the walls so that the shadows overhead loomed like the spread of great dark wings.

In his bed Mikey lay, a white, broken fledgling, bedraggled and still. Angela went and sat by his head, laying her hand over his. Volos stood at the foot of his bed, centering himself so that the axis of boy and bed and his axis were one, making himself symmetrical and straight as a candle flame in a windless place. Flame was his courage. Darkness all around it was his fear.

"Mashhit," he said quietly. It was best to be calm and quiet with Sefiri.

Nothing happened except that, although the lights did not dim, the darkness increased.

"Mashhit," Volos invoked, lifting his hands in a priestly gesture that dated back to the Druids. "I, God's rebel servant, call upon and conjure you, spirit who slays without pity, by the most dreadful names: Soab, Sabaoth, Adonai, Jehovah, Elohim, Tetragrammaton, and I do exorcise and command you by the four beasts before the throne—" It was hard to keep the volume down. Fear kept twisting the knob. "—Mashhit, come to me peaceably and show yourself to me in a mild human shape without any deformity, and do what I desire of you. Now, without delay."

Before he could say the Latin words to complete the incantation, the darkness that hung below the ceiling of Mikey's cubicle shifted, and sifted down, and stood in approximation to the floor, taking the form of something that loomed man-shape and was black and wore chains made of black fire. Its wings were like those of a bat, like a doomster's storm-whipped cape, passing fleshlessly through walls. It filled the room. Its presence was huge. And its face was that of Mercedes.

"Mercy," Volos whispered.

"Yes, you had better beg for mercy. Fool." Mashhit

sounded dangerously peevish, like Richard Nixon at his very worst. In fact, much like Mercedes.

"I meant—" Volos let it go. He had never stood so close to a Power before, and the nearness was fearsome. He felt himself shaking, felt the room swaying. By all means let Mashhit think he had cried out for mercy.

"Thumbsucker. Infant." The specter's voice was cold but offhand. "You fancy yourself a hero, summoning me?"

"I summoned you . . ." Volos closed his eyes a moment, feeling the small flame of his courage go out, clenching his fists as if they could catch it. "I summoned you because I want you to let this child live."

"You do." Mashhit had not moved, but sounded more than ever mocking. There was a trick in his tone.

"I want Michael Bradley to live, and be well and happy, and grow old before he dies, and I want nothing bad to happen because of his living . . ." Trying to cover all the loopholes, Volos faltered. There were too many contingencies in the life of a mortal.

"Want, want, want." This was a game, and in a vicious way Mashhit was enjoying it. "Is it of consequence what you want? And do you want to be a martyr? Are you offering yourself in his place?"

If it had been a matter for hatred and fire and wrath, Volos could have handled it better. If there had been lightning he could have matched it with lightning, red fire with red fire, rage with rage. But it was all cold words and black wings, sullen indifference and a far-too-familiar scorn. Mashhit's cosmic contempt came to him on a bedroom scale. It was a petulence worthy of his former lover that he faced.

He whispered, "No."

"Good. Because I would not have accepted you, inchoate thing. Have you no idea what a botched job you are? A jury-rigged half-souled make-do? With wings of no more use to you than a cooked turkey's? Your mind is in your crotch, and you think that makes you human, but you are deluded. There are feathers on your back, and you think that makes you divine, but you are wrong. You are neither thing, you have not been able to choose, and you have failed at both. And you think of yourself as a rebel? Fool. You are just a runaway slave. Less than a scullery knave. Your worth is so small, your disobedience so insignificant, that the Supreme One cannot even be troubled to smite you."

Words are unaccountable things. Friends can speak lies, yet out of the mouths of enemies, hard and sharp as a raptor's bill, can come truth of a sort. Listening to the rantings of Mashhit, Volos heard such truth, and it stunned him. He tried to move his lips, but it was no use; words were power, and he had none. He could not speak. He could barely stand unsupported.

"Now, Volos with Half a Soul, it is time for you to fail at being a savior."

The Prince of Punishment moved a stride nearer, and Volos only just managed not to step back from him. Mashhit's presence was no longer pettish or indifferent. Now he filled the room with tangible darkness and unmistakable menace. His wings lifted, obscuring walls and ceiling so that shelter and safety became only illusions, so that in this room there were only death and Mashhit. His hands lifted, and they were tipped with black claws.

"Step aside, dolt. Yonder child is mine by right, and you cannot deny me."

Volos found that his beloved body was a traitor, a renegade out of control, a reprobate, limp and impotent in the presence of Mashhit; if he had put any liquid into it recently it probably would have wet itself. *So this is really fear.* Physical fear. He hated it.

He did not step aside, but what did that small defiance matter? In a moment he would fall.

"No!"

A strong voice. He wished it were his, but he knew it was not. This was the voice of a powerful entity, a voice with no hint of pleading in it, only anger and the grace to command. Then to Volos the world was made of relief and terror. How could he have forgotten how fearsome she was, the one who had come there with him to sit by her sick baby's side? It was she who had forced him to obey her when he would not obey God. It was Angela Bradley.

And she was on her feet, she had placed herself between Mashhit and her child like a she-wolf between the hunter and the den. "No," she ordered, "you shall not have Michael. Go away, Mashhit. Find some other prey."

"Well," said that personage in a soft, startled voice, and this time it was he who stepped back. "Well," he managed to add after a moment, "eternity is full of surprises."

"Did you hear me?" Angie spoke imperiously, as if to a balky child. "I said go."

"I hear, Lady of Angels, and I obey." The specter bowed his towering head. The face he had borrowed from Mercedes melted away, leaving only shadows behind. As if blown to tatters by a strong wind, he vanished and was gone. Volos could tell he was gone utterly. After Mashhit had left it, the small benighted cubicle seemed full of air and light.

In his white bed Mikey stirred and started to cry.

Volos understood enough about children by then to know that crying, when for too long there has been only silence, is the most welcome of good signs. He stood shaking and hanging on to the wall as Angie kissed her child and tried to quiet him and sprinkled him with warm, glad tears. As medical personnel came hurrying from several directions, brushed past a useless thing with wings, exclaimed over the patient, hugged the mother, and shook hands with each other. As Mikey struggled against the tubes and wires that had been sustaining him, and his wail grew to a full-throated, rebellious bellow of self-will.

"Volos!" Angie remembered finally that he was

there and came toward him, making him claw even harder for support because he felt his knees giving way under him, he would bow a suppliant before her again, his terror of her equaled the wonder and awe he was supposed to feel before the Throne.

"No," he whispered. "Please." Not even sure what he meant. No, please don't let me make a total asshole of myself . . . no, please don't be the one against whom I must rebel . . . no, please don't leave me.

She put her arms around him, and her embrace made him feel stronger, yet weak as water. He stood up straight, but held on to her with trembling hands and laid his head on her shoulder.

Angie had long since noticed one of the wry facts of life, that joy, even surpassing joy, lingers no longer than a butterfly, while problems and troubles settle into place like stones. At the time of Michael's healing she had felt as if she could never be unhappy again, but by midway through the next day she was haunted by shadows.

One of them was Volos. Wherever she went, to the hospital, her hotel room, the room where Gabe was staying with the roadies, the coffee shop—wherever she tried to find peace, he was following close to her side, very quiet, ashen under his dun skin. Even his wings were pale. Something had upset him as much as it had upset her. His anxious presence annoyed her more than comforted her, because he wanted some kind of reassurance, and she wanted the same thing herself—from somewhere. Still, she found herself dragging out the motherly questions.

"What is it, Volos? What's bothering you?"

"Nothing."

"There's something, I can tell. What is it?"

"Nothing, really, Angela. It is just that I am still shaking."

It was only a half-truth, and she knew it, but that was his problem. Maybe he was missing Texas, but if he could not say so, it was not up to her to tell him. He had not mentioned Texas at all since the blowup, and Angie had decided rather perversely that she would not bring up the subject unless he did. Once upon a time she might have tried to help him, but now she felt too thin and taut to help anyone.

Frightened. She had frightened herself badly, bullying Mashhit as she had done—not because of the results, which had been all she wanted, but because of the implications. It appalled and terrified her to find that she was so much like her father. She knew Daniel Crawshaw had power, and charisma, and a gift for righteous wrath; she knew he had the ability to speak with spirits. He called it praying. She called it cursing. And the last thing she wanted in life was to be anything like him. Since leaving him she had made up her mind that she was not the one going to hell: He was. Someday God would send him to hell and shut him and the devil in a room together, and God only knew which one would come out.

She stood at the window of her hotel room, feeling a need for sunshine, wanting to go outside and walk. If it were not for Volos she would have done just that, and maybe walked away some of her terror. But Volos could not go out on the streets with her, could not go anywhere in daylight without attracting frenzied fans. And she did not feel she could just walk out and leave him behind.

Volos . . . if she was Lady of Angels, then everything she felt for Volos needed to be rethought. Her life now was made of implications and contingencies. There was too much not being said.

Sitting on her bed, Volos mumbled to his hands, "I am a coward, Angela."

You're not the only one. But she did not say that. Instead, because she felt she must, she left the window and sat by his side.

Volos said, "It is a good thing you were there to deal with Mashhit. I could do nothing. I could barely stand up. If there was anything in me I would have shitted myself."

She touched his hand. Though she felt nothing except great weariness, she made herself be gentle with him. "You were the one who saved Mikey. I could never have summoned Mashhit. I didn't know it could be done."

Volos told his knees, "I knew before I summoned him that he would make a soft-on of me. It would have been surer and far safer if only I could have made myself pray."

Then within a heartbeat she was no longer making herself be gentle to him, but felt herself full of tenderness to her soul, all of it for him, because she understood. She said, "You couldn't make yourself do it."

"No. But I should have."

"It's okay." *I am a coward too.* She held his hand in both of hers but looked at the window as she said, "When I was trying to call Ennis, I knew I should have called my father as well. He loves his grandchildren. But I couldn't do it. I just couldn't bring myself to do it. I hate him."

"You are lucky. Hate makes it easier."

She turned to stare at him, feeling once again separated from him by a distance the touch of their hands could not bridge. Feeling far too much on her own. "You don't hate what you call father?"

"I think—I told myself I did. Hating was a place to hide in. But lately—thinking of praying—thinking of talking with him . . ." He let the words trail away.

Yes. She did understand some of this after all. Because with her hand on the warm plastic of the telephone, dialing Ennis, she had suddenly wanted to say more to him than just "Your son is very sick, you'd better come." She had wanted to ask him how he'd been. She had wanted to see his brown-eyed, ordinary face. Knowing that it would be wordless and full of an anxious love for her, like that of a large dog waiting on a doorstep. Knowing that he would come to her at once and almost without question if she called him. Wondering if he would kiss her and tell her he loved her. Wondering if he had changed.

She was still wondering.

So much had happened so quickly that Volos did not know on what hook to hang his pain. All he knew was that once upon a not-very-distant time there had been three who loved him and knew him truly: Texas, Mercedes, Angela. Then Texas had shouted hateful things at him and gone away, not coming back. And Mercedes—Volos knew there was something deeply wrong with Mercedes, knew that if he, Volos, had any human sense he should send him away as well. Yet he knew he would not do it. There had been enough bitter leave-taking already.

Now Angela—there he sat on her bed, not sure whether she would let him lie in it with her again, not sure of anything about her, like a child afraid to let her out of his sight, yet afraid to talk to her, to tell her any of the true things on his mind. She was the Lady of Angels. She was one who could, if she chose, make him do anything. Make him come to her, make him go away again. Make him lie at her feet like a worm on the pavement after rain.

She terrified him.

He adored her.

How was he to trust her not to enslave him? He had trusted Texas, and look what had come of it. He had trusted Mercedes, and—there was too much to think of besides Mercedes, who was a small, small man. He had trusted Angela, and thus far she had not betrayed him, but . . .

She was staring far away.

He pressed her hand. Out of the midst of his fear he blurted, "Angela. Ange. Please. Do not leave me."

At his words she turned her head and met his pleading gaze. Her eyes were large and dark and calm, like those of a pietà, transcending pain. She said, "I'm carrying your baby."

chapter
sixteen

Ennis had learned a lot from *Metal Mag* and *Star Gazer*, not all of it about rock music. But what seemed most useful to him was what he had learned about Mercedes. There had been considerable information, at first because Mercedes had taken every opportunity to be interviewed, trying to elevate himself by clinging to Volos's wings, and later because the gossip columns would not let go of him. He wanted a career of his own, the insiders said, and Volos wasn't going to help him get it. He was jealous of Volos's new (female!) lover. Only his expensive nose habit and Volos's sentimental willingness to tolerate him kept him with the winged star.

Also from the rock music magazines Ennis learned the itinerary of Burning Earth's tour.

Therefore on a Saturday night, late, on one of the sleaziest streets of a Pennsylvania city that had three times been flooded under just like the sinning earth of Noah's day, Ennis waited. As Volos rocked the concrete of the Johnstown War Memorial Arena and Angela stood backstage and mouthed the words along with him, Mercedes left the arena, as Ennis expected he would. The road manager, spurning his high perch amid the lights, was heading for a corner where his low-life instincts told him a drug dealer would pass.

Ennis saw him, touched Reverend Daniel Crawshaw's arm, and moved to the target's side. Mercedes stepped back quickly, but Reverend Crawshaw stood in the way. Both men were taller than Mercedes. Both wore white shirt, cross-of-Christ tie, black suit.

"We want to talk with you about Volos," Ennis said.

Reverend Crawshaw had made the will of God quite clear to Ennis. But it felt odd, even so, even though he understood his duty, to know that a few hundred feet away his wife was swaying her body to primal music, that in a hotel room within a few blocks his children were sleeping, and there he stood saying to a man he detested, "We want to talk with you about Volos." But there were priorities. Getting Angie back (if he wanted her back) was third priority. Getting the boys back was second. Making Volos burn in hell was first.

"He is a blasphemer," said Reverend Crawshaw. "We want him to die."

Ennis felt his shoulders wince, hoping that his face, like Reverend Crawshaw's, was hidden in the shadow of his hat. Reverend Crawshaw was outspoken. Even in daylight, Ennis felt sure, Reverend Crawshaw would have said the same thing. The man was a fearless soldier in the army of his God.

The sodomizer Mercedes looked very frightened, yet he was starting to smile.

"How?" he asked.

"He who lives by the sword will die by the sword. He who—"

Ennis, who knew what Reverend Crawshaw had in mind for Volos, but did not think it should be shared, said quickly, "We want to get him away from those crowds who adore him. Away from his bodyguards. Off by himself. Alone. After that we will take care of everything. We know you will help us. You despise him."

Mercedes began to titter, then giggled, then broke into high-pitched laughter. Like a mechanical toy jarred into action by his own noise, he walked. Ennis and Crawshaw flanked him, keeping pace with him. The street was empty, black and slick; it had started to rain, a shower strangely chill for the late-summer night. Perhaps another deluge was coming.

Mercedes said, "What's in it for me?"

"Satisfaction," Reverend Crawshaw boomed. "Salvation."

"Keep your voice down," said Mercedes, though there was no one in sight. "Not good enough. I want thirty pieces of silver. And don't expect me to hang myself afterward. You'll have to come string me up yourself."

Reverend Crawshaw said icily, "We will do no such thing. We are not murderers."

"No?"

"No. We are executioners for the Lord."

"The Lord likes to keep his hands clean? Well, that's good. It doesn't bother you two that I could incriminate you?"

"God will take care of us."

Ennis said, keeping his voice very low indeed, "You will help us?"

"Oh, yes."

They were passing through the red-light district. A young woman in fishnet stockings and a very short leather skirt beckoned from a doorway. Ennis shuddered, yet at the same time felt the devil take charge of the most private and depraved part of his body. He hated the devil, the never-sleeping devil, always waiting to catch him and make him unworthy of the trust Reverend Crawshaw had placed in him. But, in a few regards at least, he felt certain of himself and safe from the devil. No trick of Satan could make him fail to do God's will concerning Volos. Of that he felt certain. He hated Volos worse than he did the devil. The man had stolen his sweetheart and his poem.

"Yes," said Mercedes, " 'despise' is a very precise word for what I feel."

Ennis knew it was not; it was only a euphemism to dignify feelings far more savage. He knew this because he knew what he himself felt.

He asked, "Will it be hard to get to him?"

"No. Oh, no, quite easy. I have been thinking along the same lines myself. All that needs to be done is to take the woman. You know, Angie Bradley."

Both of them did know and showed no surprise. Ennis had briefed his father-in-law.

"And contact Volos," Mercedes continued, "and he will follow. He will do anything you say if you have her. He is besotted with her, can't stay away from her."

"Tell us how you would do it."

"I will give you a time," Mercedes said, "and a place. And I will meet you there and point her out to you if you like. But when it comes to dealing with him, do not expect me to walk up to him and kiss him for you. I am through with kissing him."

Time: Sundown.
Place: The fairgrounds, York, Pennsylvania.

Angie and the band had been planning this visit to the York Interstate Fair for weeks, since before Mikey got sick, since before Texas went away. They wanted to make it a treat for Volos. He had been to an amusement park once, where he had loved the roller coaster, but never to a real down-home firemen's carnival or county fair. And this was one of the biggest ones in the country, featuring Volos as Saturday night's grandstand attraction. So before the show, Angie and the others had decided, no matter how much of a security force it required, they were going to take him on the midway, let him ride the Screamer, get him to bet on a spin of the wheel, see if he liked the bumper cars.

Sundown, Saturday evening, with the sky streaked purple and the golden Ferris wheel lights just coming on—very beautiful, Angie noticed. And the mechanical music and the barkers blaring everywhere. With a small, excited son's hand straining at each of hers she walked on grass trampled into dust, smiling, feeling happy because there were friends all around her—except for Mercedes, of course, but no one minded Mercedes—and Volos was enjoying everything, with wings as bright as the sky and the lights. Every day Angie struggled to understand her feelings for him, unsure of what to do even though she carried his child inside her—but she had let all that go for the moment. There he was, walking beside her, a marvel, a delight, she wanted never to hurt him, and tonight especially he warmed her heart. He was as wound up as the kids.

"What am I to do here?" he exclaimed.

"Throw darts at the balloons," Bink told him. Bink had turned out to be the decent kind of person, not one to hold a grudge. It did not matter that he was none too bright. He and Volos had been getting along nicely since the fight. "Win a prize," he amplified. "It's a gyp, they all are, but what the hell. Try it."

"No, wait! What are those? Frogs?"

Whack the launcher with the mallet and see if you can get the big rubber frog to land on the lily pad rather than splash into the pond. Laughing, they all tried it, Gabe and Mikey too. Then it was test your aim, throw the ball, win a stuffed unicorn. Toss a dime into a goldfish bowl. Cisco, brawny-shouldered from years behind the drums, swung a sledgehammer and rang the bell to earn himself a cigar.

"Very phallic," Volos remarked. He aimed a water pistol at a hole and won a painted mirror featuring a truly astonishing bimbo on a motorcycle.

"What am I to do with this? I don't like Hondas."

"Give it to Mercedes," said Jack, the keyboard man.

Everybody laughed and looked for Mercedes, but he had gone off somewhere. Wet blanket. Who cared.

"I'll take it," Red offered. "Hey! Ice cream on waffles. You got to taste this."

"No, thanks."

"Aren't you hungry, man?"

"No. Why would I be?"

"But you haven't eaten." Red stared at him as if seeing him for the first time. He said slowly, "Don't you ever get hungry?"

"No. What is in that building over there?"

It was the poultry hall. Inside was all bird noise and the sinus-tickling smell of feathers and droppings. The birds were displayed in small cages stacked six feet high, aisle after aisle of them. Pigeons—pouters, carriers, fantails. Golden pheasants. Placid ducks. Chickens—Volos gazed intently at the chickens. Japanese long-tails. Frizzles. Silkies, with purple skin and feathers like fur. The bearded South American chicken that laid a blue egg. Squat hens, Leghorn, Plymouth Rock, Wyandotte, their feathers stippled, spangled, mottled, barred, laced. Strutting roosters with sickleform tails, black, gold, red. Fighting cocks, lean and tall and long-spurred, fierce and defiant in their captivity.

They circled their cages and their cries echoed under the rafters, yet they grew still and spoke softly when Volos came near. His feathers had gone muted, his eyes dark. He said, "Their wings are of no use to them?"

"No," Angie told him.

"But they should be flying things. They are so beautiful, but they are in cages. So many winged things in cages."

Angie asked him softly, "What is it, Volos?"

"I just—I just want things to be free."

"Can't always have that," Red said.

"Birdman, it's okay." Gabe tugged at Volos's hand. "Come on, Iwanna pony ride."

Soon it would be time to get back to the grandstand,

where a group called Bad Friday was opening. They all let the kids lead them out of the poultry house into the glaring, garish, noisy night. Behind a line of sweating security men, fans shrieked louder than Bad Friday, the barkers, and the rides combined. Mercedes wasn't back yet. Angie didn't care. Nobody cared.

It bothered her that Volos, like life, could dip so quickly from joy into sadness.

From behind the security cordon that encircled Burning Earth, faces shrieked like guinea hens. Volos went over to the edge of safety, touched straining hands, signed a few autographs. All the guineas scuttled toward him, so that his side of the circle sagged, heavily pressed, but all other parts of it bulged like a helium balloon. Angie found herself breathing more deeply, noticing that she could see out. Idly she looked at an Italian Sausage Sub stand, at a place that sold pastries called Elephant Ears, at the people milling between them, at a man walking toward her, a rugged sort of brown-haired man who looked startlingly familiar but did not meet her eyes—

He squatted a few feet outside the cordon, near the canvas side of a Vinegar Fry tent. "Gabe," he called. "Mikey."

"Daddy!"

They tore their hands away from her and ran to him, straight between the legs of the security men, who were instructed, after all, to keep fans out, not to keep small children in.... Even if she had wanted to, Angie could not have held the boys back, but she did not try hard. It was right, fair, that they should run to their father.

More slowly, she followed, slipping between the guards. Though she did not look back, she felt Volos's eyes on her. And he stood still and let her go. She knew he had meant what he had said about freedom. He would not cage anything.

She walked to Ennis. He tilted back his head to stare up at her, and his face might as well have been the face of a stranger for all the sense she could make of the look on it.

From behind the Vinegar Fry stand a man in a black suit lunged out and seized her.

His big hand had her hard by the arm, and the glare of his yellow eyes froze her. They were eyes she remembered all too well. Eyes no more forgiving than a snake's.

Ennis had stood up, carrying Gabe in one arm and Mikey in the other. "Say hello to your Grandpa," he told them. But they were silent, because something about Grandpa frightened them.

Angie's scream as they took her away was lost in the screaming of Volos's adoring fans.

Red did not realize at first what had happened. Nobody did. It was as if lightning had struck without even the warning of rising wind ahead of time. One minute he was looking at funny chickens and laughing, and the next minute the air had turned to knives. There was something wrong with Volos, the big guy with wings was standing like in front of a firing squad, and where the hell was Angie going?

Somebody had hold of her kids. Somebody had grabbed her.

Volos was on the move, heading toward her—

And then the security line broke, and the whole world was nothing but panting bodies and clutching hands and pleading mynah-bird cries.

They never did quite piece it together afterward, whether some of the security men had left their places to try to help Angie or whether one or more of them had been bribed to foul up. Whether disaster was allowed to happen from a good impulse or a bad. What the hell did it matter anyway, the result was the same. Red could hear Volos shouting at people to let him through, the winged front man sounded half insane, there were probably a hundred hands tearing at him, but Red couldn't move to help. He was entirely pressed in by breasty bodies, which was not nearly as much fun as it should have been. There were hands clawing at his face, somebody was trying to suck his mouth off, and he felt sweaty afraid.

"God burn all of you!" Volos screamed in a voice fit to stop the world. Red had heard at a party once that people frying at the stake used to cry out, "End, world! End!" And it never would. But this time for a moment it was as if the turning Earth stood still. The reaching hands hovered in the air. The imploring cries hung there.

Volos was flying.

It took him a few seconds to tear away from them all. He rose slowly, like a faulty prayer, his great wings beating heart-tempo only a little distance above a thousand upturned heads. Then he recovered and was gone within another breath. But memory remained with Red like a soul lingering after a body is gone. Memory of long legs in ripped jeans. Bare brown shoulders. Wings, pale as a jilted lover's face and beautiful in that carnival sunset's many-colored lights. Angel wings.

The fans had surged after him, stampeding between the food stands. Security had regrouped somewhat, so that Red stood in a small island of tranquility amid a sea of human trouble, looking up at the sky behind the fun house, Screamer, Bullet, Black Widow. Beyond the glare of the carnival rides he could see nothing else, not even a star.

Beside him Cisco said in morose tones, "There went our front man."

Red averred at the black sky, "He's—he's *real.*"

"Cripes, what did you think? He fucks and sucks same as the rest of us."

"No, but I mean—that thing about him flying in the hotel window, I thought it was just drunk roadie talk, and the way the kid got better, I just wrote it all off, I never—" Red gave up. Cisco wasn't paying attention anyway.

"There goes the show," the bass guitarist said. Dourly impassioned, he reached for the supreme expletive. "Goddamn motherfucking shit of a whorebastard, there goes the whole fucking band."

"You don't think he'll be back?" There was no reason to assume that more than one concert would be missed. Yet having seen an angel, Red himself had an unreasoning feeling that something huge had changed, that nothing would ever again be the same.

"Didn'cha ever stop to think things were going too damn good for a bunch of rejects like us?"

They stood looking silently at the darkness into which their lead singer had disappeared. The keyboard man joined them, his panic buttoned down the way his shirt collars used to be.

"Somebody has to talk to the office," he said. "Where is Mercedes?"

Nobody knew. Nobody had seen him for a while.

"To hell with him anyway," said Red with an anger he didn't know the source of.

Nearby, some fans were fighting over Volos's boots, which they had pulled off him as he rose, leaving him barefoot. They shrieked at one another like harpies. Leather still warm from his body heat was tearing apart in their hands.

Volos fought free and took to the air just in time to follow the kidnappers. Two cars. In the first, a brown Yugo, he saw two small faces at the back window. Gabe and Mikey were on their knees, fingers to their mouths, looking up at him. In the second, a gray Oldsmobile sedan, he could see two silhouetted heads in the front, and in the back, Angie lying across the seat, very still. Her knees were bent upward in a way that had to be uncomfortable, and her long hair hung down on the floor, but she did not move.

The York Fair was held on the outskirts of that city, along a modern highway on which taillights streamed like blood. Though cars honked, swerved, slowed, or even stopped as the drivers spotted Volos, this did him no good. The four-lane gave the Yugo and the Olds room to maneuver through the chaos. Two traffic lights and they would be on the interstate.

Red light. Please, Volos begged the air or the deities of electricity or perhaps even the one to whom such petitions are usually addressed, for suddenly he felt not too proud and angry to pray.

He could not say for sure that he was answered, but the light turned red. With the Olds behind it, the Yugo rolled to a stop, and Volos thumped down in front of it, making his body and wings a wall. If these people were going to take Angie and her children away from him, they would have to drive through him to do it.

The highway's sodium vapor lamps threw an orange glare by which Volos could see as clearly as if by fires of hell. Behind the Yugo's windshield a brown-haired, rugged-faced young man stared back at him with a look so dead, so wooden it made his skin prickle. It was as if someone had taken the insides out of Angie's husband and replaced them with circuitry. It was like seeing a mechanical man.

Gabe scrambled into the front of the Yugo and stuck his head out the passenger-side window. "Birdman!" he called. "Daddy's gonna take us home."

"Bye-bye, Birdman," Mikey sang from the shadows of the back seat.

People in the next lane and the approaching lanes were exclaiming and pointing and calling to him out of their car windows, "Volos!" As if they owned him. As if his life was a performance for them to watch. Showtime.

The light had changed. Behind Volos cars had pulled away, though the ones he confronted stayed where they were, blocking traffic. He had long ago learned of his ability to stop traffic ... good, but what next? If he moved from where he was, the driver—

what was his name—Ennis would just step on the gas and take off.

As he thought it, from behind the Yugo the Oldsmobile pulled onto the road's ample shoulder and accelerated past. Little more than arm's length away, Volos saw the two men in the front seat, the craggy face of the driver, fierce-eyed, glaring eternal torments at him, and—

Mercedes.

Mercedes!

Mercy, staring straight at him with a smile like a dog's snarl and lifting a hand to tell him Fuck You. The same hand that had once . . .

The Yugo backed up, skewed around him, and drove off after the Olds. People were getting out of cars and running toward Volos, their arms outstretched to touch him, clutch at him, get his autograph. He flew. Odd, he must have lost track of everything for a moment. The two cars were already through the next light.

Mercy. I cannot believe it.

He caught up to the gray sedan and the brown hatchback as they turned onto the interstate.

They picked up speed, and he flew above them. He did not know what else to do. Land atop one, block the windshield, make it stop? But then the other one would go on without him. Angie could not help him. He had not heard a thought from her since that first terror-stricken scream. She had to be unconscious—by some drug Mercedes had given her, he hoped, not by a blow.

God burn you, Mercy. What Texas did to me was lovingkindness compared to this.

Texas. It was easier for Volos to admit, now that he was in trouble, that it had been a mistake to drive Texas away and even more of a mistake not to try to make it right; why had he not tracked him down, begged him to come back? He had a good idea where Texas had gone. At the very least he could have called him and told him how much he missed him, missed his long-legged stride to walk beside and his soft-spoken advice and his absurdities. Missed his kindness ... Texas would have made everything better somehow if he had been there. If he had been at the fairground, he would somehow have kept this nightmare from ever happening.

Maybe not. Maybe it was time to see truth: Maybe even God could not stop the blackwing side of life.

Headlights, stabbing around turns, hurt his eyes. Made him blink.

He followed for an hour, grew tired. These people he was trailing were going sixty along the expressway. It was hard on him to fly so slowly. And all their other offenses aside, he decided, Bradley and Crawshaw were despicable for owning such boring cars, dull cars, difficult to see in the night, instead of something white and sporty.

Jenkins exit ahead.

They took the ramp, as he expected and hoped they would. Hoped, because there would be another chance for a rescue, another traffic light, maybe—

There was none. Overpassing the highway was only a small country road, the kind with domed asphalt and no lines. At the top of the exit ramp the Yugo went one way, the Olds the other. Volos groaned, thought fleetingly of physical dismemberment, for how else was he to follow both boys and Angie? But it seemed he had to choose. Swearing, he hung in the air a moment, then veered after the Olds and the Lady of Angels.

The road steepened as it wound up Jenkins Mountain, turning to a dark tunnel beneath overhanging trees. Volos flew low, his wingtips brushing the woods on each side, his bare, dangling feet nearly touching the gray sedan's roof. Feeling very much trapped.

Halfway up a long hillside the trees ended. Gratefully Volos swooped up into clean night sky and cir-

cled, watching from far above as the Olds pulled into
some sort of clearing and bumped to a stop.

There were no houses anywhere nearby. The place
was one of those run-down township parks, once
meant for family reunions and wienie roasts, now used
mostly for illegal camping and illicit activities. Its pic-
nic tables were gone, its pavilion roofless. At some
time there had been a nonregulation ball field, with a
backstop behind home plate, of which the supports,
two twelve-foot sections of telephone pole solidly
erected, still stood, as they might do until Stonehenge
fell. On one of them were glass reflectors embedded
in the gray wood, winking in the night like a three-
eyed cat.

About where the pitcher's mound might have been,
a bonfire blazed. Even after the Olds turned off its
headlights, Volos could see the metallic glints of several other cars parked in that place. Near the fire
stood men wearing rude black hoods that covered
their heads and faces, with slits for the eyes.

Cowards. No-balls.

In trees all around, a hundred thousand insects
shrilled, the crowd getting worked up in the cheap
seats. Overhead the stars watched in ineffable silence.

They are gutless. Why am I frightened?

The black-suited, craggy-faced man got out of his
car and dragged Angie out of the back seat, the rough
movements of his hands showing that he did not care
if he hurt her. Her father? How could he call himself
her father? He who sat on the Throne seemed kind
by comparison.

Slinging Angie over his shoulder, where her buttocks in their tight jeans appeared both indecent and
terribly vulnerable, Crawshaw strode the short distance to the bonfire. Looking up, he grinned like a
skull.

Volos knew then that despite open sky he was
trapped still.

As if in response to a pressing invitation, he spiraled

down the updraft of the—bane-fire, bone-fire, either way it spelled death. He did not want to die. He had not imagined himself to die until he had done much, much more living. Where was the blackwing power now that he needed it? But he knew it would not come to him. He had renounced it, he had imagined it out of himself. And in a way he could not say he was sorry. Blind anger was fit only for zealots such as these.

Ten feet above the flames he swooped away and landed atop the three-eyed telephone pole, teetering there, staring down at all of them. Careful, though, not to look at the small man who leaned against the passenger door of the Olds.

"Come closer, renegade," Crawshaw challenged him.

Clinging to splintery wood with his bare feet, Volos did not speak. It seemed to him as if the sound of his own voice would make what was happening more real than he could bear.

"You want to save this slut, unholy one? Then come here."

Texas, where are you? You never did teach me how to do the chin thing.

"Come down, you who like to wallow in perversion." As if slapping butcher meat onto a countertop, Crawshaw swung Angie down from his shoulder into the grasp of his hard hands, dangling her nearer the fire.

Volos felt his breath coming fast, his heart straining with a pain he could only dimly comprehend. *Rescue,* he thought, yearning to do it. But rescuer, savior, guardian angel—these were roles against which he had rebelled, for which he had not equipped himself. There were many strong men at the fire. He could not hope to fight them all.

"Pay the price of your sinning. Someone must pay. Choose! Will it be you or this fallen woman?"

Then Volos momentarily could not breathe at all,

and the summery September night went cold, and insect chatter was a roar that engulfed him, the roar of the mob rushing the sacrificial hill, the roar of the congregation as the knife poised over the scapegoat. It was not a fistfight that was required of him. It was not wrath, a rebel's black rage, no better than the ranting of a fanatic. It was instead the one stance he had sworn he would never take: It was submission.

He looked at Angela. In her father's steely grip she hung unconscious and helpless, limp as a broken wing.

"Blasphemer. Profaner. Come accept your punishment, or your Jezebel will."

"No," Volos whispered.

With his eyes shining like a wolf's eyes in the night Crawshaw looked up, then swung Angela so near to the blaze that her long hair hung scorching and sparking in the flames.

"Stop," Volos said.

The man with wolf eyes moved Angela perhaps an inch away from danger. "Are you coming?"

Volos said, "Yes."

He kicked with his wings, let them carry him toward the fire and the black-hooded men around it, down to the ground. His feet when they hit felt like lead. He tried to look only at Angie, not at anything else. Tried to think only of her. If he could feel sure she would live, it would not be so hard to do this thing.

So this is love.

His legs moved stiffly, carrying him forward, toward her. He stretched out a hand, wanting to touch her, to push her away from the flames, but his enemies seized him. Two of them gripped each of his arms. More grasped his wings. It was no joke, that he could have beaten them to death with the power of those wings, and they knew it. Through the feathers he could feel the sting of their hatred.

Crawshaw spat in his face. Staring despite himself, Volos saw that the man's eyes were fixed and soulless, like glass balls.

"Were you human once?" Volos asked him, afraid
not for himself but for everyone with a future, everyone mortal, if things like this could happen. "Did you
love her once? She is your daughter."

The man glared, then turned away long enough to
carry Angela the few steps to his car. He dumped her
into it, reached into a suit pocket with bony fingers
and handed Mercedes his keys. Smirking at Volos
across the night, Mercy started the car and drove
away.

"Blasphemer." Crawshaw stood in front of Volos
again. But Volos did not hear him. He was listening
to the sound of love being taken farther and farther
away, down the mountainside into the darkness.

Crawshaw backhanded him across the face. "Viper!
Unrepentant slave to sin! Do you know how to pray?"

Softly Volos said to him, "I have sung ten thousand
times 'Gloria, Gloria, Gloria' before the Throne."

His wings felt different than they ever had before,
far lighter, filled and uplifted by some passion that
was ardent and fiery yet soft and yielding as cloudstuff.
Puzzled, Volos glanced over his shoulder to see what
might have happened. There he saw a refulgence that
did not come from the bonfire. For the first time ever
in his incarnate life, his wing feathers shone a pure,
lambent white.

chapter
seventeen

The night of the League for Moral Purity bonfire, after helping lure Volos as far as the Jenkins overpass, Ennis took Gabriel and Michael to be baby-sat by their Grandmother Crawshaw. Though she had not seen the boys in nearly a year, she greeted them without much change of expression. She had been like that for as long as Ennis had known her: passionless, dutiful, supremely accepting of God's will. Years past, he had thought there was something wrong with her, something important missing, and had wondered how she got that way. But he no longer had such foolish thoughts. He understood now that what he had perceived as an emptiness in his mother-in-law was rather a spaciousness, a blessed purgation, the absence of sin. Hers was a life of obedience, an exemplar he tried to follow as day by day he grew more like her.

From her house he drove fast, reaching the park just as that treacherous sodomizer Mercedes was pulling out. Good. He had not missed much, it was just starting. By the fire he could see Volos, a tall sinner with white wings. Saw his father-in-law hit him. Saw how Volos stood on spraddled legs, like a gunfighter, and did not flinch.

264

His mind swerved at once away from grudging admiration. Reverend Crawshaw was the one to be admired, taking a strong stance against sin and sinners. Though Reverend Crawshaw, in his constant pity for human frailty, had allowed his followers to wear masks while performing this difficult task for the Lord, he himself wore none. Striving, as always, to emulate his spiritual leader, Ennis had decided to do likewise.

He parked the Yugo, got out, and opened its hatchback. He had some things in there that his father-in-law had asked him to bring from the house. Rope clothesline. An ax.

Hefting them, he walked up to the bonfire.

"Son!" His father-in-law greeted him warmly, then took the ax from him and turned back to the prisoner, displaying it horizontally on both hands. He spoke, chill now as a stone where no sun shines.

"He who lives by the sword shall die by the sword," he averred. His voice grew terrible. "And he who lives by the ax of rock and roll music shall die by the ax of God's wrath."

Watching Volos, this lowlife who had stolen his wife and taken happiness away from him, Ennis saw him sway a little, as if he had been struck a strong-fisted blow. Saw how he did not struggle or cry out or speak. His face looked pale even in the ruddy firelight, and in their sockets of shadow his eyes seemed huge, like a bewildered child's.

They took him over to where the two stubs of telephone pole stood and put a rope tight around each wrist and stretched him between them, cruciform, with his back to the fire.

This was a serious event, a culmination for the Crusade, and Reverend Crawshaw was treating it with befitting ceremony. "Show him what is going to feed the flames, men of God," he declaimed. Ennis was ready. Like an usher passing out Sunday morning bulletins he distributed the things: record albums, cassette tapes, compact discs, several hundred of them, all with the explicit lyrics advisory label, all with Volos's blue-winged back on the cover. All copies of *Scars*.

"So many. Thank you," Volos quipped, his voice struggling for the poise that would put him above what was happening. "I hope you got a discount."

"Fool!" Reverend Crawshaw's voice lashed like a whip. "You are going to die. Be silent and pray."

"*Sacre silentio*? No, thank you. The dead lie silent in their graves." Volos stood erect, Ennis noted, not hanging against the ropes that bound him. "I came here to live. To sing and love and speak and live." His dark eyes caught on Ennis a moment, then slipped past.

"Do not listen to him," Reverend Crawshaw told his sheep. "His is the voice of Satan. Go on about the Lord's work."

They circled, clockwise, from the prisoner to the fire, throwing his music on the flames. There had been stars before, but now the night went black with the smoke and fetor of burning vinyl.

Volos began to sing.

You want to fly
But you have walked by my side
You taught me to live
But now I have to die.

His voice—the voice that Ennis heard sometimes, despite everything, in his dreams—it defied darkness, it rose to the stars, quavering only a little.

I'm not afraid
I've seen the sunrise in your eyes
So what's a night ride.
It's just another road.
I feel your arms around me
For the night ride.

Walking in the black-hooded circle, Ennis felt him-

self slowing to listen. Of all Volos's songs, this was his
favorite, this tender love ballad, and Volos was singing
it with all his heart to Angela, Angela—unrepentant
sinner though he was, he truly loved her, he was willing to die to save her—

There was an eerie power in the prisoner's singing.
Several men had lagged or even stopped, listening.
"Keep moving!" Reverend Crawshaw barked, and
Ennis hastened his steps in quick obedience.

You are so very beautiful
Half angel
Half goddess
Your heart is a flying dove
Your thoughts are fire in the wind
And I am weak with love of you
I turn to you like a child
Please be with me.

Volos stopped, but without faltering. He had said
Amen, that was all. The song had been his prayer,
albeit to the wrong deity.

"Pagan," Reverend Crawshaw accused, and rightly
so. A pagan was anyone who worshiped something
other than what Jesus had called God; Ennis could
not argue. Yet he felt—but it was not his job to feel.
Feelings always hurt him. It was far better simply to
obey.

He stood with the others at his leader's back. The
Reverend faced Volos, only inches away, eye challeng-
ing eye, hefting the ax in his strong, long hands. Ennis
shuddered, then made himself stop it, ashamed.

"Heathen," Reverend Crawshaw said venomously
to Volos. "Worldling. No, it will not soon be over, O
ye self-proclaimed rock idol. You have offended God,
and you must suffer. Your hands will go, and maybe
that sexual organ you are so fond of flaunting, before
I am done with you."

Ennis saw Volos reach the limits of his courage, saw

his eyes go wild, watched him start to tremble and strain against the ropes that bound him helpless to the posts.

"But first to go," Daniel Ephraim Crawshaw said, "will be those mockeries with which you blaspheme the holy hosts of Heaven." He turned to his troops. "Son."

Ennis nodded and moved to take his place. As the Crusade leader's second-in-command it was his privilege to immobilize the condemned enemy's left wing. The assignment was coveted, and at one time he had felt honored by it. Now he just felt numb.

He placed himself behind Volos. A stocky man in a black hood, chosen to deal with the other wing, took position beside him. Reverend Crawshaw stood with raised ax behind Volos's shaking, straining right arm.

"Scream, Satan-lover," he said to Volos. "Now!" he told his assistants.

Ennis grabbed. He had expected that his task would be harder, that the prisoner would thrash and struggle, but Volos had more defiance in him than he would have thought possible. Defiance, or innate dignity, or mistaken faith—for whatever reason, the blasphemer did not fight. Ennis got hold of the wing easily—

And with a jolt as if the world had stopped turning, he found himself holding his own soul in his fingers. White feathers tingled in his grip, they were everything warm, kind, gentle, good that he had ever known in his life; they were his mother's hug, his father's last words before he died, his children's first steps, they were Angela—dear God have mercy, how could he ever have forgotten how he loved Angie? She meant more to him than—than anything. There was nothing he could not forgive her. Yesterday was not soon enough for him to be with her again. He felt his leathery armor of obedience split like a swollen wound. He cried out, feeling all the pain he had ever suppressed, all the anger, all the ardor.

Volos screamed.

Sweet Jesus suffering on the cross, no! It was all wrong, wrong, wrong, Ennis knew that to the fundament of his heart, and Crawshaw was a demon, and Volos was staggering and screaming out his agony as blood spurted and the ax lifted to strike again—

"No!"

Ennis lunged for the weapon. But the black-hooded man holding the severed wing stood in his way, he could not get to Crawshaw quickly enough, and he saw the flash of the heavy metal axhead, heard the sounds he would never be able to forget: the impact, and the snap of shattering bone, and the scream again.

Then he had hold of the ax, wrenching it away. His charge had surprised Crawshaw enough to let him do that.

"Ennis!"

"Shut up!" he shouted. "You are horrible!" He wanted to use the ax on the terrible old man, but he knew himself now, knew that he could not kill anyone. He swung, but not at Crawshaw, aiming instead at the rope snaking around the nearest post. It was a cramped, one-handed blow, but God must have been with him. The rope parted with one whack, and Volos did not fall, for Ennis had caught hold of his arm.

"Stay on your feet!" he yelled in the angel's ear, aiming the ax at the other rope. And Volos had more guts than anybody had a right to expect of anyone. Ennis could feel him responding, bracing himself, pulling the rope taut so that the ax could sever it.

The cruel thing gave way. Ennis had his left arm around Volos, felt angel blood soaking his sleeve, hot, felt Volos's hand clinging to his shoulder. And the night was full of blows and shouting and horror, there were two wings lying like dying swans on the ground and far too many men rushing him—he swung the ax at random to hold them off. Guided Volos toward his car. Wished fervidly that he had not parked so far away. The Yugo squatted well beyond the bonfire, that blaze of hatred which he was just now nearing—

Someone cuffed him hard on the side of the head. A voice he knew all too well roared, "Ennis Bradley! Heed me now, or hellfire awaits you!"

Ennis had no more time for murderous fanatics. With the flat of the ax he knocked Crawshaw out of his way and plunged onward, supporting the angel who staggered at his side. Behind him he heard a hoarse, barking scream. The air smelled of cloth burning, then of charring flesh—in his panic Ennis noted these things only vaguely. There was no time for them either.

For some reason people let him alone as he reached the car. He leaned Volos and the ax against it, then tore off his shirt and tied it around the singer's wounded torso as tightly as he could.

Volos said faintly, "Angie . . ."

"She'll be all right. I'll see to that. I promise you." Ennis got him into the front seat, leaving the ax on the ground. Started the Yugo, roared out of the dark and bloodied field, and already Volos slumped against the window, unconscious. Frightened for his passenger and frightened for himself, Ennis drove as he had never done in his life, taking the road down the mountain at a speed that several times had him airborne. He checked his rearview mirror often, but nothing except his own fear pursued him.

Angie awoke with a groan to find herself lying on cold concrete and looking up at darkness. Groggily she struggled to her feet. Alarm bells were ringing in her mind, yet she could not at first think what had happened or where she was—

God help her. That small, dim window overhead, she knew it, and the shape and damp smell of the room, and the glint of glass jars along the walls. She was in the basement of her parents' house, in the small stronghold where they kept the home-canned green beans and rhubarb. They had shut her in here sometimes as a punishment when she was a child.

I am not a child anymore, she told her terror. It helped just enough to keep her from blubbering.

She tried the door, already knowing what she would find. Locked. She tried the light switch. Nothing. They had taken out the fuse. She looked at the window, finding it barred and chicken-wired against hooliganism, as always. And as dark outside as in. Nighttime. She wondered how late.

Anger would help. In a hospital one night she had found that anger is a powerful ally. But how to use it? Summon Mashhit or some other spirit? She felt too weak and wretched, too much the Lady of the Basement, to risk dealing with such power. Not yet. Later, maybe, when things got even worse. She felt sure that things would, in fact, get worse.

She paced, knowing from childhood experience that no one would come if she shouted and slammed things around, that all the noise she could make would scarcely disturb the sleepers in the bedrooms two stories above. She thought of smashing jars against a wall anyway, as a gesture, then decided against it. Why ruin all her mother's work when nothing was her mother's fault, really? Her father was to blame, he and that snake Mercedes. Angie remembered the touch of his soft, ladylike hands as he had forced the drug into her, and she shuddered.

She wondered if Volos had seen them take her. He might not even know where she was.

"Volos," she called softly to the night.

Why did she hesitate to call again? He would be overjoyed to hear from her, frantic with worrying about her. Surely he would not mind her summoning him. Yet something felt different than ever before.

"Volos. I'm sorry, but I need you."

He had read her mind across a continent once, yet now she could feel no sense that he heard. For a black moment she wondered if he was alive, then pushed the thought out of her mind.

Cold, she hugged herself. "Volos. Please. Who will help me if not you?"

Because it would make him smile in that sweet way he had, she wanted to tell him that she loved him, but she knew it was not true.

"Volos?"

Then she froze, listening. Loud, hurried footsteps thumped down the wooden basement stairs, heading toward her. Without speaking she waited where she was as the old lock rattled. Winced as the door swung open and light stabbed in. For a moment the man in the doorway was only a dark shape to her. Then she knew him.

"Ennis," she whispered, and she stepped back.

"Ange. Please." He did not move toward her, but she could hear his voice shake with something close to panic. "I know I don't deserve it, but you've got to trust me. We have to get you out of here. Your father could get back any minute."

There he stood, the way he had always been before: earnest, awkward, very attractive in his shy way. Yet there he stood utterly different: shirtless, and unaware of it. Something had happened. Something huge had changed.

In three long strides she was out the door. "The boys," she said.

"Upstairs."

Because Ennis, a family male, had told her to, Angie's mother had brought Gabe and Mikey down from their beds. Obedient and unspeaking, she presented them. Angie said, "Mother," and hugged her, but her mother did not hug back.

"Ange," Ennis urged gently.

They ran to the car. Ennis carried the boys bobbing in his arms, which made them giggle. Once in the back seat they lumped together like puppies and went to sleep. Ennis headed toward the expressway, driving hard.

Angie waited until he was on the four-lane before asking him, "What has happened?"

He told her. Ennis was a man of few words and short sentences; he told her the story starkly, without flowers or excuses. His voice did not break until he had to explain how they had tied Volos to the posts. Then Angela looked over at him and saw tears running down his face.

"Ennis?"

"It was—when I held his wing—it turned me inside out."

She did not yet understand what had happened to Volos, did not yet want to know, but she began to understand what had happened to Ennis. She watched him steadily. Asked, "What did you feel?"

"I felt—I love you. I don't care what you did, I love you forever. And I knew—everything I was thinking and doing, everything I thought was right, it was all wrong. I knew I didn't want to hurt anybody."

After a moment she reached over and touched his hand. She said, "What happened then?"

He told her.

When she could speak she asked, "Is he—is he . . ."

"I don't know. I got him to the hospital and then I had to leave him there and come get you."

He drove fast, with the tears drying on his face. She could see them in the light of headlamps, illumination that sped by like happiness. In that same fleeting light she watched him, seeing as if for the first time the warm farm-boy planes of his face and the muscles moving in his bare shoulders. His body was very beautiful, as she had felt sure it must be. She felt two songs forming in her, one of Volos and terrible sadness, one of Ennis and hope.

Several miles farther down the highway, she asked, "Ennis, where are we going?"

"I don't know. Some motel someplace." She saw a blush start below his neck and flood his face as he heard his own words hang in the air. "I didn't mean that the way it sounded. I just mean I've got to get you and the boys someplace your father won't find you."

"Yes, I see. Let me think."

Her head ached almost as badly as her heart. From whatever poison Mercedes had given her, maybe. God burn Mercedes. Sitting with her chilly fingers pressed against her hot, lidded eyes, trying to sort things through, she asked, "Can you give me change for a phone call?"

He felt at his trousers pocket. "Yes. Sure."

At the next exit, without her having to request it, he pulled off and found a red-and-white booth at a gas station. Gave her money. Coins in hand, she got out, then looked back and saw how he sat bent over the steering wheel, hiding his face in his arms.

"Ennis?"

He looked up, then got out of the car and came with her, leaning against the doorpost of the old-fashioned phone booth. Once she had pressed the buttons for Information she put her arm around him.

"Persimmon, West Virginia," she told the nasal-voiced operator. "Robert McCardle." Her heart pounded. She repeated the number over and over to herself until she had dialed it and fed the phone more than two dollars in quarters.

It rang ten times, and she let it keep ringing.

"Hello?" A woman's faintly Southern-accented voice.

"Hello—" She almost called her Wyoma, as if she knew her. "Hello, Mrs. McCardle? I know I got you up, I'm sorry, but it's sort of an emergency."

"Who's this?" The voice was not unpleasant, even though it was four in the morning, just businesslike.

"Angie Bradley. I'm a friend of Texas'. Is he there, please?" God, please make him be there.

"Thanks for sendin' him back to me, Angie." There was a wry warmth in the woman's voice now. "Men, they just don't understand, but we love 'em anyways, don't we? Bob's sleepin' for a change, and I hate to waken him. Can you tell me what it's about? Somethin' go wrong with Volos?"

Because she had not really expected Wyoma to understand or be her friend, Angie found herself hugging Ennis hard, and smiling, yet near tears.

"He's hurt," she said. "Volos is. He's in the hospital."

"How bad hurt?"

"I don't know. I'm not with him. I don't even know if he's dead or alive." Her voice quivered. "I'm in kind of a jam."

Wyoma said in matter-of-fact tones, "You need some help? You and the little guys need a place to stay?"

"I sure do and we sure do. Thank you."

"Nothin' to it. C'mon down, honey child."

Volos awoke to find himself lying belly-down in a dim room and hurting more than he would have believed possible, body and soul. There were needles in his arm, taped to him, and tubes dripping fluids into him. The place smelled like the one where Mikey had been put in a white bed. Also he had faint, pain-skewed memories of the Emergency Room and the people exclaiming over him. All of which meant he was alive and in a hospital, not in hell after all, which should have made him feel better but did not. He felt wretched.

Far too much alone. Where was everyone? He would have welcomed even Mercedes's petulant face at his side ... no, perhaps not Mercedes. *God scar you forever, Mercy, what did I do to make you turn against me so?*

And what had Mercedes done with Angela? Sweet wounded Jesus, where was she, what might be happening to her?

I love her.

It seemed fitting yet very strange, that he truly loved

her, that he, Volos, heaven's dunce, had really wanted to save her. But all such salvation was doomed for mortals, he could see that now. Because even if he had died for her, what was to keep life from lashing at her like Chayyliel's scourge of fire after he was gone? And without making a cage of his arms, without making himself a prison for her, how could he keep her safe in his embrace forever?

Could even the fathergod do that?

Maybe not. Maybe nobody can save the ones they love.

He closed his eyes. Like firelight, images flickered within his mind: Caged pigeons. A parakeet nesting amid yellow flowers, waiting for frost. A hummingbird on the wing, gone within an eyeblink.

Gone.

Wings.

Gone, cut off. But how could that be? Perhaps Mercedes had been feeding him strange acids again, perhaps he had dreamed it all, the ropes, the fire, the madman with the ax, the ghastly pain—

No. The pain was still with him. Opening his eyes, trying to move, he nearly fainted from it. All he could do was slide a hand to feel the thick bandaging around his torso, then lay it down again. Where feathers should have been, behind him, there was nothing but hard cotton bedsheet.

But, without his wings—once he had told himself they were a bad joke, a nuisance, but now he sensed that they had been far more and everything had changed. What was he, who was he, now that they were gone? All he knew about himself was that he was a fool and he hurt.

Christ, he hurt.

Pain, partly of heart and partly of body, made him moan. A bosomy nurse sailed in, white ship of mercy in the night.

"Angie," he panted at her.

"I'm Bernice, Mr. Volos."

The leadhead. "No. I mean—Angie—is she all right?"

The nurse was checking his chart, his tubes, his pulse. "You don't worry about other people, now," she said in automatic tones. "You just think about getting yourself well."

He hated her, but persevered. "She's married to— the one who brought me here—" He remembered how it had felt, the shock of hope through his pinions when a goodhearted man had taken hold of his wing. He would never feel that surge again, but he remembered Ennis, and he badly wanted someone to tell him that Ennis had gotten to Angie in time.

"He dumped you here and took off again." The nurse's voice was crisp, disapproving. "I'll get a doctor to okay some more painkiller for you." She sailed out.

In a few minutes there were stupid questions and soothing inanities and another needle in his arm. With surprising quickness the world fuzzed over. Volos slept.

When he awoke, it was daylight, and this time he was not alone. There was someone sitting by his side. Someone with a crease-top Stetson and a string tie, with a kind face and worried eyes.

"Texas!"

"Kid, I—whoa!"

Despite pain, despite needles and tubes, Volos lunged up, reaching for him, nearly falling. At the sight of that familiar weathered face a hot reaction started in his heart and, having no wings to run to, swelled and heaved his chest. The upheaval hurt, yet he could not stop it, and he heard himself making uncouth sounds. He could not see properly, the pressure had reached his eyes and water was stinging its way through them somehow, running down his cheekbones into Texas' shirt. Volos felt all made of agitated water, wave after wave of salt tide. It was a good thing Texas had jumped up to support him, was sitting on the bed with his arms around him, holding him together.

So this is weeping.

Volos did not like it. The spasms made his wounds hurt clear to his heart and got in the way of things he urgently needed to say.

"They—took—Angie," he managed between sobs. Texas would go find Angie if Ennis had not.

"Shhh. She got away, she's fine. She and the boys are staying at my place." Texas was holding him very softly, careful of the bandages, stroking his hair. The weeping was perhaps almost worth it for the sake of the holding, the softness.

"You—sure?"

"Sure, I'm sure. Woke up this morning and there they all were. Don't try to talk, son."

But there was another thing he had to tell Texas, at once. "Texas—what I said to you, what I did—I am sorry—"

"Hush. Please."

Waters had begun to calm somewhat. Volos left the warm solidness of Texas's chest and shoulder a moment and sat up to look at his friend, because he had heard an odd distortion in Texas's voice.

"You are—weeping also."

Texas half smiled, despite the wetness around his eyes. "No kidding."

"But—I do not want that for you, Texas. This crying—it hurts." Volos felt dizzy with pain, and would have toppled if Texas had not still been holding him by the shoulders.

"I bet it does." Texas's voice wavered. "After what they did to you, it's gotta hurt like hell. Volos, you say you're sorry, I am so goddamn sorry I could spit. I never should have left you like that."

"It is all right. You are back home?"

"Yes."

"Has Wyoma stopped being angry with you?"

"Yes. It—it's going good, Volos. Better than it's ever been."

"Then do not be sorry. They can have my wings."

"Oh, Christ, kid . . ." The words broke like a heart.

Volos meant what he had said. He wanted to repeat it, with elaboration, but sensed that it would be merciful of him to be silent. Also, his voice sounded thick, and he felt stuff running down his face from his nostrils as well as from his eyes. Letting Texas support him, he explored it with his fingers.

"This crying—it clogs my nose."

Texas reached out one long arm for a Kleenex.

"It makes me feel sodden all over."

Still fumbling for the tissue box, Texas stiffened and gawked at him. "You mean—ain't you never done this before, buddy?"

"I—did not—imagine myself . . ."

"Kid, you can't do love without doing this."

"I—know that now."

Volos felt tears swelling in him again, because love was a two-edged thing. So be it; so let hurting happen. Love was like a sword, but also like a feather from an angel's wing.

He closed his eyes, let the tears run quietly, felt Texas dabbing at his nose with a wad of tissue. "Blow," Texas ordered.

"Pardon?"

"Snort air through your nose."

Volos complied. "Ick," Texas said. Volos sat still and let him take care of the cleanup. Then felt himself being gathered into a hug again. Gentle, Texas was being very gentle with him, as if handling a newborn. It was odd that a mortal could feel at the same moment so miserable and so much loved . . . The tall man with the kind eyes was cradling his head with one large warm hand. Speaking softly into his hair.

"Welcome to the human race, son," Texas said.

chapter

eighteen

After he got Volos settled down to sleep again, after sitting with the kid awhile to be sure he was resting quietly, Texas left the hospital and headed toward Jenkins. He drove his old Chevy pickup hard, thinking of what he wanted to do, which was to find the Reverend Daniel Ephraim Crawshaw and acquaint the man with intense pain. Being a cop—or rather, an ex-cop, for his attempts to get his old job back had failed—being a man who had seen a few things, Texas had long since concluded that in some cases swift justice had to supersede the slow workings of the law. And he was likely never to believe this more strongly than he did for Volos's sake.

The people of his West Virginia hills had a name for such swift justice: blood right, meaning among other things that vengeance belonged to kin. But Volos was a lonely stranger in the world, with no hometown, no family, and no better friend than Texas knew himself to be, even though as a friend he had screwed up pretty bad. Time to make up for that now. In Volos's case Texas figured the blood right was his.

That young fellow Ennis had wanted to help. Or maybe he had wanted to come back to Jenkins for reasons of his own, to face things that scared him. The guy had good instincts if that was the case. But there was Angie to be thought of, and for her sake Texas had made Ennis see the sense of laying low for the time being. Ennis had agreed to stay with his wife and kids.

Hands curled tight around the knobby old steering wheel, Texas sighed. It sure looked to him as if Ennis and Angie were getting back together. They had a lot of rough spots to smooth out, of course, but if they loved each other they'd do it, just like he and Wyoma were determined to do it. And it was a damn good thing for the Bradleys, he could see that in the way Gabe and Mikey hung on to their daddy and the way Angie looked at him. Good for all of them, but it was going to be goddamn hard on Volos. After what the kid had been through already, which was demonstrably enough to make a grown man cry.

Jenkins ahead.

It was a miserable place, Texas decided as he drove in and looked around. He guessed a lot of people would have said the same about good ol' Persimmon, West Virginia, with its sagging porches and scraggly lawns, but at least Persimmon had life. Marigolds in white-painted tire planters. Coon hounds doing ballet stands by fire hydrants. Men loafing, teenagers in patched-together Mustangs scattering gravel, bare-ass kids running around, women yelling at all of them. But this place, with its prim concrete porches, its shuttered windows, it looked like nothing was allowed to really live there. It seemed all buttoned up like a preacher's fly.

Angie had given him the address, and Jenkins was a small enough place so that he found the house without much trouble. He parked in front. A sort of a washed-out skinny woman answered the door. Yes, she was Mrs. Crawshaw. No, her husband wasn't home. She didn't seem to care who Texas was. Answered his questions with no more expression on her than a fish.

"When d'you think he's gonna get back?"

"Never."

Make that a baked fish, gutted and laid out on a plate. Texas recognized those dead eyes now, that flattened face. This woman had been through too much. Something had made her cold-out crazy.

He gentled his voice, tried approaching from a different angle. "Where d'you suppose he is right now?"

The question appeared to cause the woman some sort of difficulty. Disorientation, even. Her head wobbled for a moment, and then she started in a squeaky, unaccustomed way to laugh. "What do you want with him?" she asked Texas.

He saw no reason to lie to her. There is a basic honesty due to people who are drowning. Also, there was no telling how she would react to anything. Whatever he said to her, she could go either way. Quietly he laid it on the line: "I want to beat the tar out of him."

She did not so much as blink, but remarked, "Oh, is that what made him go up like that? Tar?"

One of the things being a cop had taught Texas was when to listen. Standing there on her clean-swept concrete doorstep, he just looked at her, and she kept talking.

"Well, I guess it might have been tar. Nice and black. But does tar go up in smoke if you make it hot enough?"

Cautiously Texas said, "It might."

"Well, that must have been it, then. Because they tell me when Ennis knocked him into the fire he turned all black first, and then he was like a tar cloud, and then he was gone. All black, and gone. And stunk horrible, they said."

Texas made an involuntary noise as comprehension knocked the breath out of him. This was evidently encouragement enough to keep Mrs. Crawshaw going.

"Nothing left," she confided. "No body. No way to have a funeral. See?" She began to titter again, squeaking rhythmically and horribly, like a harrowed mouse. "No body, no funeral. Nothing to bury. See?"

Texas saw well enough, but could not believe. "Excuse me," he begged, backing down her front steps, stumbling, nearly braining himself before he made his escape.

Once in his truck and on the move he realized where he was going, where he had been heading all the time. The Christian makes pilgrimage to a hill outside Jerusalem, the Jew to Auschwitz, and some people weep over a grave in Graceland. The cop visits the scene of the crime. In this case there was not much difference between the Christian, the Jew, the cop, the weeper—they were all Texas. He had to go see for himself, and he had respects to pay.

Driving up the mountain road, he felt chilled, as if facing something bigger than he could handle. It seemed odd to him, arriving, that there was no granite marker, no marble statue, no shrine to mark the site of an atrocity, the place where an angel had died.

But it was perhaps the place where a devil had died as well.

The park looked smaller than he had expected, and sleepy in the late-summer sunshine, yet warmly alive with grasshoppers and butterflies. Birds flew overhead, goldfinches, meadowlarks. Texas stared for a while, then got out of his car as if moving underwater. It was all wrong. Sky should have gone black. Earth should be screaming.

The ashes of the bonfire still lay in a sizable gray-black pile. Standing by it, Texas saw no sign that anyone had tried to clean anything up. Nobody felt any need, probably, because Jenkins looked like one of those places where nobody in their right mind was going to tell anything to cops or outsiders. And for once Texas was willing to go along with that kind of small-town cover-up. Glad the doctors at the hospital

were keeping very quiet about the strange bone stubs
they had removed from Volos's back. Grateful for any
kind of tacit conspiracy that would make things easier
on the kid, keep him out of court, help the smoke
blow over more quickly, and let him get on with life.

Some kind of life. God knew what.

Nope, nobody had messed with the evidence. Because if they had, they would have removed the
charred bone segments the fire had left behind, and
there some were, right on top—

Texas looked again, and swallowed hard, and folded
to his knees at the edge of the black circle. They were
not Crawshaw's bones, as he had at first thought. No
way had that sonuvabitch ever possessed these two
long, frail-looking, gently articulated limbs. Texas
knew himself to be looking at relics, holy remains, at
all that was left of Volos's wings.

Somewhere back in the dense, heavy, dark-green
trees that pressed around the clearing, birds and bugs
were singing as if nothing had happened.

After a while Texas got up, pushed his way to his
pickup through air that seemed far too thick for him,
and opened the door. He had a suitcase stuck behind
the seats, untouched. When he had heard about Volos
he would have been on his way to the kid in half a
minute, without even a toothbrush, except that
Wyoma had made him throw a few things into this
thing she called an overnight bag and take it along.
Trying to take care of him. He was starting to understand her better, to know how much she really loved
him, though sometimes she had strange ways of showing it.

The suitcase was going to come in handy now, anyway. Texas pulled it out, dumped its contents where
it had been and carried it to the dead fire. Carefully,
with hands that shook as if he were starving, he placed
the pieces of wing bone into its padded bed. Closed
it. Set it on the passenger seat, where it would ride
like an old friend and he could keep an eye on it.

After a few minutes he came back and started sifting through the ashes with his fingers. Methodically he searched through everything the fire had left behind, spreading its circle three feet wider than it had been before, making a mess of himself. The grime left by that fire seemed to crawl into his clothing and the creases of his skin, making its way everywhere, like sin. But he found nothing more, not even a button from an evil old man's black suit coat.

Damn, the fucker must be still alive somewhere. It was not possible that Crawshaw had burned to nothing at all.

Yet there had been something about the way his wife had laughed. . . . And there was so much that seemed not possible about Volos, about all the events that surrounded him, that it wasn't a big problem to believe a few things more. Just suppose the kid had more by way of kin than Texas had thought? A father, for instance, who could make a man go up in a puff of black smoke, with nothing left? Who could annihilate him?

Maybe the blood right had not been Texas' after all.

He got up, wandered into the sweet-smelling, sun-warmed grass and cleaned himself on it as best he could. With slow steps he walked the short distance to the stubs of telephone pole, the monuments that had been making the back of his neck shiver since he had seen them.

He went over there although he was not sure what he wanted or expected to find near them. Maybe he just needed to face—

Blood.

There, in a dark and random pattern on the ground. Texas knew it was blood. He had seen a victim's mark often enough to know it when he saw it. Knew how innocence left as much of a stain as sin did, soaking into the ground. Wildflowers would grow thickest in that place next year.

He stared. Circled around. Kneeled to touch for no reason. Got up, sighed, and turned to go away, to keep muddling along, trying to hold things together, aware that it was just a year to the day since he had first met Volos, aware that every year of his life he survived the unknown anniversary of his own death—

Like the breath of God, a warm breeze moved. Deep in the tall grass it stirred something that made a flutter of white, like a butterfly maybe, but too large.

It was probably just a piece of trash. But Texas stooped over, and parted the grass, and looked. And saw. Once he had found it he understood why he had come, what he had been looking for, and he felt his eyes sting as if from a black night's bonfire smoke, but all the heaviness seemed gone from the air.

Something had escaped that night, that fire. There at his dirty feet in their old roach stompers, there on the bloodied ground, shining white, lay a single perfect feather from an angel's wing.

Outside the hospital, news ghouls and Burning Earth groupies camped on the lawns or prowled around the building, looking for a way past Security. From atop a brightly marked TV van, men took footage of the exterior of the building. Several girls in unauthorized Volos T-shirts, immodest garments with rainbow satin cherub wings sewn into the shoulder seams, had gathered on the front sidewalk and were crying as if at a concert, screaming whenever they saw movement at a window, a shadow that might be their idol.

The hospital security staff guarded the place with efficiency verging on paranoia. Apparently some doctor had impressed them with the seriousness of the threat on Volos's life. Red had to show three forms of I.D., wave a magazine with his picture on the cover, and do some impassioned talking before they would let him in. Even then, a nurse's aide stood at the door-

way of Volos's room and kept an eye on him while
he visited.

It was not a visit he really wanted to make. At first
he just stood at the foot of Volos's hospital bed, not
knowing what to say to him. The star was sitting up
against pillows, looking out his third-story window at
blackbirds flying past. Not watching TV or listening
to music or anything. Just sitting. Not even noticing
Red was there.

"Yo, dude," Red tried.

"Hey, man!" Turning, Volos smiled, and Red had
to swallow hard, seeing the brutal bruise on his face,
seeing his haunted eyes. Volos, the hotshot, the superstar—Volos looked pale and fragile and flattened.

They talked awhile, awkwardly. Shop, mostly. Chit-
chat. Volos was so obviously and wholeheartedly glad
to see him that Red found it very hard to say what
he had come for.

"Things will work out, I think," Volos was telling
him. "My doctors are sensible. My surgeon in particular, she is a woman, she does not want other doctors
at other places to say she is crazy. So she will keep
her mouth shut, she has told me so already. And
Texas says that in the news I will pass over quickly, I
am just a publicity stunt, a hoax."

Red blurted, "The assholes. Why can't people understand you're for real?"

Volos's smile softened. "Once I would have wanted
that," he said.

"Goddamn it." Impulsively Red moved nearer,
touching a hand that had once belonged to an angel.
"I know, I'm so shit-for-brains dense, I could never
get it. Just like the rest of them. But I finally got it
through my head, and then they go and do what they
did—it makes me so goddamn mad."

Sad, really. Heartsick. And wishing he had the guts
to say that, and knowing he never would. Hoping
Volos understood.

Maybe Volos did. "It is all right," Volos told him.

"It's not all right. It sucks."

"Okay, it was hell. But I will be all right someday. It has made me real in a different way, Red. I cry now."

For a moment Red felt like doing likewise. He could not speak. Finally he managed to say, "Cripes, Volos. You call that an improvement?"

"You do not see? I get thirsty now, and drink Coca Cola. I get hungry, and eat."

Red was starting to get the picture, though not sure he liked it. "Huh," he complained. "Too goddamn bad you had to start with hospital food."

"This is what everyone tells me, yes. But Texas brings me Kentucky Fried Chicken. And soon I will be out of here. Red, there is this, too—I will be able to wear shirts. With slogans and brand names and things. I want to get myself a black leather jacket with gold chains."

"I'll get it for you," Red said.

"But why?"

"I want to give you something. Volos, you can say what you like, you're never going to be just another shithead human. You are the most special goddamn dude I've ever met in my whole fucking life."

There, he'd spilled his guts, and now probably Volos thought he was queer. Hot-faced, Red turned to go. Said, finally, what he had come for.

"I'll get it to you somehow," he told Volos. "But I dunno when I'll see you again. Me'n the band, we're all running low on cash. Got just about enough to head back to L.A. and line up a few gigs, maybe hook up with somebody else until you get your strength back and decide what you want to do."

"Wait." Volos looked bewildered. "You don't have to go away. If you need money—"

"No, man." Goddamn it, nobody had told him. Just what Red was afraid of. "I know you'd give it to us, but you don't have any left. Mercedes and Brett took your wad and split. They're probably out of the country by now, bitching at the servants in some villa somewhere."

Volos stared, blinked, then looked out the window again. "Red," he said after a while, "you are right. I must not be all the way human. For crying out loud, I cannot understand why Mercy has done these things to me."

"But that's part of it too," Red told him. "Not understanding things."

"Then I am very exceedingly human, yes? Because I scarcely understand anything."

When the phone rang, Angie was the handy one to pick it up. It was Texas, reporting in, as he did every night. "I'll get Wyoma," she told him.

"Just let me quick fill you in on your father. There's still no sign of him. No body has been found. No John Does in any of the morgues. I checked with the state police and the FBI and all the hospitals in five counties, and nobody knows anything. The sonuvabitch has disappeared."

"If my mother says he is dead, then it is probably true."

"I hope so. I don't want him showing up someday when he's not expected. And I hope this whole thing will just lay still the way it is right now. I don't want Volos to suffer no more on account of it. Don't want Ennis mixed up in it either."

Ennis was upstairs reading *The Cat in the Hat* to Mikey and Gabe. Before, such a dangerously imaginative picture book would have been on the long list of things forbidden. Now it seemed that the only thing forbidden was bitterness about the past. Angie could tell that Ennis felt very much lost in his new life, but hour by hour, piece by piece, in that patient, carpentering way of his he was putting it together for himself and her. Those days Angela saw Ennis as she had only dreamed of him before.

She asked Texas, "How is Volos?"

"A lot stronger. Eating pretty good." Texas hesitated, then added, "You should come see him, Angie. You and Ennis."

"Yes, I know," she said, meaning it. She knew this was something they had to face soon.

She handed the phone over to Wyoma and drifted upstairs, knowing there was one more thing she had to do for Volos before she told him good-bye, but not sure whether she dared.

Yet there was no choice but to dare. She owed him some daring.

"Ennis," she said softly at the bedroom doorway.

He had Mikey settled in a borrowed crib, sound asleep, and was rocking Gabe. Over the child's nestling head he glanced up at Angela with a lover's wide eyes.

"I'm going for a walk back in the woods," she told him.

It was nightfall, not a sensible time for taking a walk by any ordinary standards, but he said only, "Come with you?"

If she had said yes, he would have walked along with her and embraced her in the darkness under the trees. Let his hands explore her, lifted her T-shirt to find her waiting breasts. Maybe let her find something of his. Maybe made love with her right there in the backwoods darkness, though he no longer required darkness for lovemaking.

She wanted him, but said, "Some other time."

He just nodded. Ennis still had that same old gentle, wordless way about him that would not let him open his mouth and protest. But she saw the fear in his eyes, crossed the room in three quick blue-jeaned strides and kissed him, taking time to let it sink in before she left him there with a sleeping child in his arms.

It seemed like a long walk. She had only to get away from the house so as not to bother Wyoma or the children, but in the darkness she stumbled over every rock, every root, and the trees poked their branches at her face. It took her quite a while to reach the little clearing around the ruins of what had once been, she surmised, a moonshiner's still. But she kept going until she reached it, because she wanted to be sure there were trees rising all around her to keep from the innocents in the house any sight or sound of whatever might happen.

Once there, she breathed a moment, thinking. Then she made herself cruciform, facing the north star, conscious of the strength of her shoulders, of her long hair arrow-straight down her back, of her youthful buttocks and unbound breasts. She looked steadily into the treetops and said her chant.

"Dark angel, death angel, stranger to mercy, prince who flies on black wings in the night: I, the Lady of Angels, summon you."

She had written it out earlier in her head, as if it were a song. After she spoke she stood waiting and listening to the night. Nothing happened, but this did not surprise her, for she had known it would not be easy. The death angel would be made of more savage stuff than Volos, would probably be even fiercer than Mashhit.

She tried again. "Death angel. I call you, evil spirit, cruel spirit, lurker in cemeteries and dark places. You who take away healing from the sick and dying, obey me when I summon you! I, the Lady of Angels, command you to come to me."

It was as if in the night close at hand someone opened a freezer packed brimful of the hatred of the dead for the living. Angie felt the onslaught of bone-deep cold, and knew she was afraid. But nothing else happened. And fear was not a feeling in which she could indulge.

She said, "By all your many names, spirit of death, I summon you: Rogziel, Hutriel, Makatiel, Kezef, Azariel, Gamchicoth, Gog Sheklah—"

The night said to her, "I am here, little fool."

It was not a loud voice, yet it filled the hollows of earth and sky, coming from everywhere and nowhere, resonant yet not clearly either male or female; this was the mid-range voice of some cosmic singer. Bathed in that voice as if in a shower of ice, Angela stood rigid, knowing she was indeed a fool. She had neglected to command the presence to come to her "in a pleasing human form." The Prince of Death could have answered her summons as a winged python, a vampire bat, a black widow spider the size of the world, but instead, he—or she—had chosen to be a pressure on the chest, a chill in the air, a voice in the darkness, the smell of formaldehyde.

Angela said meekly, "So Death can indeed sometimes be merciful."

"Indeed," said Death in a voice like winter mist. "What is it you wish of me, Lady of Angels?"

If she made her business quick, perhaps she would live. She said, "First, concerning my father, Daniel Ephraim Crawshaw: where is he?"

"In my realm." Satisfaction in that gelid voice?

"Who killed him?"

"Are you claiming the blood right, little one?" The voice had turned to frozen steel.

Angela realized her mistake and made clear the truth. "No. No, I am glad he is dead."

"Then let him fry. What else?"

"Then, concerning Mercedes Kell."

"Ah, yes. The little snake from Kickapoo." Death sounded frostily pleased again.

"You know him?"

"I have known him since he was born and answered churlishly to the name his mother gave him."

Angela said, "I want you to go and inflict him with suffering. Put a knot in his belly and poison in his blood. Fill his lungs with water. Take away the use of that favorite toy of his. Blind his eyes. I want him to suffer first, and then die. Will you do this because I wish it?"

"My pleasure," said Death out of the black of night. "But beware for yourself, Lady of Angels."

"Why?"

"You have your father's power to enthrall and command."

She had already considered this. Because she could rule angels, she knew, she had the power to keep harm away from Gabe and Mikey and anyone else she loved or chose to help, for as long as she lived. In fact, if she managed it well, almost forever.

"Moreover, you are a beautiful woman. You could enslave men, more than he did, faster than he did. You could rule the lives of thousands, of hundreds of thousands. You could be a goddess."

She could be worshiped, as Volos had been worshiped.

"And you know what would happen in the end."

She thought of what had happened to Volos. She thought of her father, utterly evil, turning into the smoke of Satan's torch.

Angela stood swaying on the hard, sharp edge of thought, and Death did not hurry her. Death, she decided, had to be a woman, a sister, Lady Death. She could think of no other explanation for such patience.

Finally she asked, "You will do what I have said concerning Mercedes Kell?"

"Certainly. It would have been done regardless, though not so soon."

"And I will leave this place without being harmed?"

"Yes."

"Then I renounce the power of which you spoke. You are my witness."

"I am, and I bind you to your word. Summon me no more, little one."

The chill seeped out of the air. September night flowed back, filled with the warm yellow smells of grass gone to seed, of Jerusalem artichoke, of cornfields. But Angela found that she could not walk home through night air so yeasty with memories of life and sunshine. As if she had been leaning too long against the heaviness of Death's presence, she staggered a few steps, then fell and lay on the rich brown loam under the trees, too weak and shaky to move.

She did not faint. Nor did she feel afraid of her own unaccustomed weakness, her vulnerability. She lay where she was and made a love song in her mind, glad she could still do that, aware with quiet happiness that it was a good song, one of her best ever. She would write it down for Ennis, and it would be his and his alone, to replace the one Volos had so thoughtlessly stolen from him.

Resting, she knew she would be able to get herself moving again in a few hours, but also knew what would happen before then. Or rather, who.

He did. As if he had heard her song to him, Ennis came and found her, and helped her up with anxious questions, and walked her home, or rather to Texas' home, where he got her into bed and lay for a long time holding her in his arms.

chapter
nineteen

"Looks to me like your eyes are going to stay that way," Texas remarked to Volos.

"What way?"

"That sort of dusty-blue color."

Volos gave him a questioning look, then swung his legs over the side of the hospital bed, got to his bare feet and tottered toward the mirror. From the visitors' chair Texas watched silently, itching to help but knowing the kid would refuse if he offered. Volos was being so goddamn gutsy about everything, sometimes he was a real pain in the butt: proud, stubborn, and having a pisser of a time relearning how to walk. The loss of his wings had thrown him all off balance in more ways than one; leaning forward against the remembered weight at his back, he was constantly in danger of flattening his nose. Watching him try to get around was like watching a toddler taking its first steps, the difference being that this big guy had a whole lot farther to fall. It was hell to just sit and let him try.

At least he no longer had to endure the indignity of the open-backed hospital gown. He was wearing some pajamas Texas had brought him from Angie and Ennis's place, where Texas was staying to be nearby.

Texas figured Ennis wouldn't mind if the kid borrowed his PJs awhile. Figured the kid wouldn't want to keep them any longer than necessary, because sexy they were not. Even Texas could see that.

Achieving the mirror, Volos leaned on the countertop below it and studied himself, specifically his eyes.

"They have been that way since—"

"Four days. Yep."

"Well." Still with a hand on the countertop for balance, Volos turned around. "It is a good color. Warm blue." He smiled at Texas across the room. "They are just like yours."

Texas felt his mouth come open in an uncouth way and made himself close it. Felt his heart turn over and start pounding. There was something he wanted to ask Volos, and it was hard to find the words and the nerve. He worked up a sweat just thinking about it. Hadn't felt so scared in that particular way since the day he got married. Even talking with Wyoma about what he wanted to ask Volos had been hard, though she had understood better than he'd thought she could. She knew what the kid meant to him. The night he had come home to her, after she was finished crying and yelling at him and he got a chance to tell her about finding an angel, she had looked at him pretty odd. But all that first night long he had been either making love with her or telling her about Volos, and by morning she was looking at him in a different way.

Volos wobbled back to bed. "Why am I so tired?" he asked querulously. "Before, when I did not know how to sleep, the nights were long and beautiful. Now I sleep through everything. Is that all life is for you humans, eat and crap and sleep, eat and crap and sleep?"

"We find time for a little romance now and then," Texas said, and at once wanted to take back the words. He had been thinking of Wyoma, but had just reminded Volos of Angie for sure. Dammit. Texas looked hard at the toes of his lizard-skin boots, wishing they could come alive and crawl him away. He felt like a reptile. Sensed a dusty-blue scrutiny working on him.

"Texas," said the kid quietly, "tell me."

"Tell you what?"

"This thing that makes your eyes slip away. About Angela, is it not? Tell me. What is it? Why has she not been to see me?"

Texas mumbled at his boots, "I was hoping she'd come talk to you herself."

"But she has not. You tell me."

"Son . . ."

"I can guess," Volos said. "I have been afraid—she is leaving me."

Texas looked at him then. Looked at that bruised face and tried not to wince. Volos was facing him steadily, with only a little something shaky around the eyes. Okay, he and the kid were going to have a talk after all, but not the one he wanted.

Texas said, "All right, son. Looks that way to me, too."

"Has she said anything to you?"

"Yes. She's back with Ennis all right. They're leaving in a few days. Going west, as far from here as they can get, till they find a place to start over. Volos, I'm sorry."

"Do not be." The kid lay back against his pillows, staring up at the ceiling, and said to that cloudy whiteness, "Look, I can do it. If I could love her enough to let that lunatic take an ax to me, then—then I can love her enough to let her go."

Hearing him, Texas felt heartachy with pride, just as if he had the right to be proud. He felt the way he had felt watching each of his daughters walk across the stage on her graduation day. He wanted to say something, the important kind of thing some people can come out with when they propose a toast, but all he could manage was to gently tease. "What ever happened to no-halo-thank-you and not-anybody's-bloody-savior and no-flies-on-me?"

Volos turned his head and offered a small smile but said, "This joking thing, Texas—I never know what to say."

"Say, 'Gimme a break.' "

"Give me a break, Texas."

"Okay." Texas reached over and smoothed the coarse dark hair away from his forehead. "Can I get you something? Bottle of pop? Snickers bar?"

"I think I am not hungry right now."

"Guitar? Race car? Six bikini bimbos?"

"What is it you are supposed to give me? A break?"

"I really oughta do just that. Let you get some sleep."

Volos did not answer. His blue-eyed gaze was on the doorway, where Angie stood hesitating.

It felt to Volos as if dross after dross of him was being burned away, leaving only what was soul-true behind. The burning hurt devilishly. But as he loved her, he could not let Angela see that he was in pain. He had to let her go as easily as he could. Even through the flames he could tell that she knew what she had to do, that she had burned also and found her own truth.

He said to her, "Angela," and held out his hand. He said, "Where is Ennis? There is something I want to give both of you."

Still standing near the door, she faltered, "Down—downstairs. In the lounge."

"Why? I want to see him. He saved my life."

"He's with the children." Angie came in a few steps, as shakily as if she were the patient. "We couldn't get them past the nurse."

"Bernice the battle-ax." Texas had already unfolded himself from the visitors' chair. "I'll go sit the critters so Ennis can come up," he said as he went out.

She was there alone with him, the woman he loved.

She stood hovering near the foot of his hospital bed like a soul, his soul, reluctant to leave, knowing that if it did the body would die—

These were not good thoughts. Volos made his hand stop reaching toward her and laid it down on the bedspread. "Angie," he told her, "do not be so afraid. There is no need to say most of it."

"It's just that—I feel so bad." Finally she came and sat at his bedside, almost near enough to touch. Almost, but not quite. "I know now what I've done to you, but when I was doing it I didn't understand."

"How could you? Neither did I."

"I didn't know who I was, calling you."

Calling to him with every breath, speaking straight to his heart—it could not all have happened just because she was Lady of Angels. But he did not say that. Instead he said quietly, "Angela, I cannot hear you anymore, since the wings are gone. If you have written songs, I do not know them. When you are away from me I cannot tell if you are sad or happy or even if you are alive or dead. And that is good, if you are to be another man's wife."

Her eyes had gone huge with tears. She told him, "I never meant to lie to you. I really thought I loved you."

This part he truly did not understand. He lay very still and watched her face as she explained it to him.

"I—what it was really, you are so beautiful—I wanted to *be* you. I wanted to be able to sing, I wanted to sing the most wonderful songs in a voice like an angel so that people would listen to me and weep. I wanted to be tall and strong and free, like a god. I wanted—I wanted to have wings."

Lying in a white bed, listening to her, Volos remembered that first sweaty moment of incarnation when he lay on black grit, that first rooftop day when the City of Angels had spread at his booted feet and the Marlboro Man had galloped through the smog-golden sky and he, the winged newcomer, had raised his clenched fists, full of defiance and a godlet's posturing, not even understanding that he was staring straight into the sunset. Now he understood many things, but lay with his heart aching like his wounded back. Both would heal, but for the rest of his life he would bear scars.

Angela said, "I wanted to fly. I loved—I loved the way you were, and I didn't understand it was not the same thing as truly loving you. Volos, I am so sorry."

So what is this mystery they call love? She has taught it to me, yet she herself scarcely comprehends it.

"With Ennis and me, it is different. Especially now. I am all myself when I am with him, I am never afraid of losing myself in him, there is a comfort when we are together, there is—a bond . . ."

She was floundering, trying to explain. Volos said softly, "It is all right, Angela. You do not need to tell me everything. Perhaps someday I will understand."

"I hope so. I want—I want real love to find you. I want every kind of happiness for you, Volos."

Standing by the door, listening but staring hard at the floor, was the young man who had saved his life, the one whose touch had felt like holy wine on his wing. Despite everything, Volos was glad to see him. A good feeling warmed him like whiskey. "Ennis!" he called.

Ennis looked up. His sober brown eyes were haunted by shame. Suddenly Volos lost patience with life and humans. It was all shame and blame, Ennis was going to tell him he was sorry for something, and Volos was bloody tired of hearing it, everybody saying they were sorry about his wings, sorry about what had happened to him, sorry about breaking his heart.

"Damn it. Ennis, get over here, would you?"

Too tamely, Ennis complied. He came and stood by his wife, then opened his mouth and started to say it. "Volos, I'm—"

"Fuck it! No more goddamn sorries." Vehement, Volos sat straight up on his rumpled bed. "Ennis, you think I can't understand about you, the way you were before? Listen, it is the same where I come from, I *know*. The everlasting obedience, you feel like you have to do it, it's the only way, and it takes the soul out of you, it sucks you hollow like a bone. Look at me! Don't you see? What you did was like a miracle. Give yourself a break, would you? I felt your hand on my wing clear to my heart. You are a good man."

Something had happened. Vehemence could be of use after all, if it could drive away guilt. Ennis swallowed hard, but no longer needed to stare at the floor.

"Are you going to be all right?" he asked Volos.

"Yes. Christ. I did not come through all this just to lie down and curse God and die." Though the thought had occurred to him.

"Will you let me—do you trust me to be a father for your baby?"

The question took Volos's breath away. It had not yet occurred to him that he had some say as to the little one in Angela's womb. She was the Lady of Angels, to whom the Sefira bowed as if to the Holy Mother of God; who was he to say to her, I want my child?

Ennis said, "We talked it over, Volos. We want to keep the baby, if you will let us. To me it would be an honor and—and a blessing, like when Mary came to Joseph and told him she was carrying God's son."

That stung Volos into protest. "Ennis, I am not a god!"

"Could have fooled me." The young man stood looking at him steadily. "You're not the only one who felt something when I touched your wing."

He still does not quite understand. "Ennis no. If that was in me, then—then it is in all of us."

Sometime in the course of the conversation Angela had let herself lean closer, near enough to touch. Or perhaps it was he who, sitting up, intense, had come closer to her. Nevertheless, he startled like a deer when she placed her hand on his.

She said, "Will you let us keep the child?"

He knew already that it would be beautiful as only her child could be, with her dark, singing eyes, her quiet heart of a face; how could she think he would take it from her? He said, "Of course. But can—may I be a father also? Can a child have two fathers?"

"I think we could manage it. But are you sure it will not be too hard on you?"

"I seem to do things the hard way. Ennis?"

"Yes," Ennis said, and for a moment he also touched Volos's hand, so that the three of them were like a fire with three flames.

Volos looked up at him. "Listen," he said, "there was something I was stupid about. I took a song away from you. There is no way I can give it back, but I want to give you—no, shut up." As Ennis tried to protest. "I know what I'm doing. I have something I want to give both of you."

He brought it out of the bedside drawer where Texas had stored it for him: a shining white feather from an angel's wing.

Looking at their faces, he knew he had done the love thing not too badly, for an amateur.

In the downstairs lounge, Gabe played disconsolately with Legos, hating forever Bernice the Monster Nurse or anything that kept him from seeing Birdman. He badly wanted to see Birdman again, because his mother had told him Birdman had lost his wings, and this simply could not be true. When people talked like that, it made Gabe feel afraid Birdman was dead. He had heard the grown-ups saying in the night that someone was dead. And he worried that this must be Birdman, because Birdman could not be Birdman without his wings.

Sitting on the thinly carpeted floor beside him, Mikey banged plastic dinosaurs together. Mikey was stupid, sitting there playing as if nothing was wrong.

"Uncle Texas," Gabe said to the cowboy-booted feet by his side, "is Birdman dead?"

"No, son!" Texas slapped down his newspaper, grabbed Gabe under the armpits and lifted him to his lap. It was like being lassoed by a helicopter. "What the Sam Hill makes you think that?"

Gabe could not explain to him how ever since knowing Birdman he just knew things. Like he knew there was a baby inside his mother, and it was a girl, and she would be just like Birdman, like a dark fire angel, like she could fly without wings. And he knew Birdman was her father, but Daddy would be her father too. And he knew which people were really nice and which people, like Grandpa, only acted nice sometimes. And if he got close enough to hear he knew what the wild birds were saying. And even though he could not talk about them he knew Mikey knew these things too.

But he didn't know what had happened to Grandpa after the last time he saw him, though he knew something had happened, because there had been a black halo riding around Grandpa's head. And he didn't know what had happened to Birdman.

He said to Uncle Texas, "If Birdman's not dead, how come they won't let us see him?"

"You're too young, son, that's all. They don't let runny-nose kids upstairs. They're afraid of germs."

"But what's Birdman doing upstairs?"

"Getting better. He wasn't feeling too good for a while there."

"They cut off his wings?" Clearly impossible, yet the grown-ups kept saying this.

"Yes."

"Who did?"

He had asked his mother this more than once, but she only looked as if her head hurt and did not answer. And Uncle Texas was of no more use. He looked like he wanted to hide under his hat.

Gabe had heard Aunt Wyoma talking with his

mother about Uncle Texas, fixing supper together and telling stories about men the way women do. Aunt Wyoma had said, "He sure has changed. But it's all good changes. Everything I always liked best about him is right up front now. For a long time there it was hard, he was trying to be rough and tough, always hiding his heart—"

Mother had said, "Ennis, too."

"That so? You think it was Volos changed both of them?"

"It's not—with Volos it's not change, really. Wasn't, I mean. It was just a sort of—strengthening, when a person touched his wing."

"Honey, I ain't so sure. The whole bunch of you, there's a kind of warmth about you, a glow. The children, too. Like you got a golden light inside." After a little bit, Aunt Wyoma had said, "I wish I'd gone along for the ride. I wish I knew him. Volos, I mean. Before it happened."

Then they were both very quiet.

Uncle Texas might be the way Aunt Wyoma said, and he was an excellent person to ask for ice cream, but he was not being much help concerning Birdman. Gabe gave up on Uncle Texas and slid down from his lap to play again. But before he could grab the dinosaurs away from Mikey, the big doors to the lounge swung open and in came three people: Mommy, and Daddy, and Birdman in between them with his hands on their shoulders.

Birdman with a bruised face and a hurting walk and no wings.

Mikey started to cry first, but only because he got his breath first. It took a lot of breath to bellow as was called for. Half a moment later Gabe sent forth his own roar of grief and outrage to resound along with his brother's. Their father tried to hush them. They would not hush. They squirmed out of their mother's arms. Life was an affront to be defied with squalls of pain and rage.

"Got to admit," Gabe heard Uncle Texas remark to Daddy or somebody, "I know just how they feel."

"Michael. Gabriel." Birdman had wobbled down to sit on the floor with them, cross-legged, like an Indian. He gathered them into his lap, one on each side, and his hug they did not resist. He had the right to calm them. Also, it was good to find that his arms still felt the same, though he had no wings anymore to give them comfort with a touch.

"Listen, small ones. It is not so bad as you think."

"They—hurt—you," Gabe sobbed.

"Shhhh. Yes, it hurt, but it is over now. Listen. Do you remember how I told you about the Grigori? The angels who came down a long time ago to teach necessary things to the sons and daughters of Adam and Eve?"

Gabe remembered. There had been Sariel, who taught people about the changes of the moon, and Kokabel, who taught them about the stars, and Shamshiel, who taught them the signs of the sun.

"Armaros," Birdman said, "who taught women enchantments, and Azazel, who taught them the use of coloring tinctures to make themselves even more beautiful than before—almost as beautiful as your mother. And Penemure, who taught both men and women the making and singing of songs. Do you remember?" He rested his cheek against the top of Gabe's head as he spoke, so that the warmth of his breath stirred Gabe's hair. "And also Penemure taught children the bitter and the sweet and the secrets of wisdom. I have often thought it would be good to be like Penemure."

Gabe had quieted, because there were many things lying hidden in Birdman's words like faces hidden in a picture, and he wanted to find out what they were. Across Birdman's lap from him he saw Mikey sucking on his fingers like a baby. He checked on the whereabouts of his own fingers, and pulled them out of his mouth.

"You remember how the Grigori were supposed to go back to the sky, but they did not? They fell in love with mortal women and stayed on earth and became family with men. So they had to lose their wings, did they not? Mortals don't have wings."

Gabe began to guess part of it. "You—too?" he managed to say.

"That's right. I have become like the Grigori, that is all. Because I love the world and the people on it, and I want to stay here."

If what had happened to Birdman's wings was part of a pattern, a story with sense and a reason, it was after all not so cruel. But Gabe knew there was more, that Grandpa's black halo was in the story somehow, because his mother had not mentioned his grandfather at all since that strange evening when his father and his grandpa had come to the big fair. There was something she was not saying. Gabe could sense when his mother was not telling him things.

"Birdman tell me about Grandpa," he begged.

"Yes, okay. We think he has gone to be with the other fallen angels."

"Black angels?" Mikey put in, his voice sounding muffled and wet around his fingers. So he had seen it too, the black cloud like a smoke ring riding around Grandpa's head. Unless he just said that because Grandpa wore black suits all the time.

"Yes. Long, long ago, before there were Adam and Eve, some of the angels rebelled against the Father and went off with a prince named Lucifer to be in their own place." Birdman added more softly, "You know, that is just what I did, coming here."

"You did?"

"Yes. Rebelled, I mean. Now I have lost my wings, but we think your grandpa has found his. We think he has gone to be with Lucifer and the other fallen angels. So he is a fallen angel now, and I am not an angel at all anymore."

Gabe saw clearly that it had been fitting and necessary for Birdman to lose his wings, because Birdman might have been a fallen angel once, but he was not at all like Grandpa. "It's okay," Gabe assured him. "You're still—" But his voice faltered along with his thoughts. This tall person he loved was not really quite Birdman anymore.

And knew it, for he said gently, "I think you are to call me Uncle Volos now."

Late that night, after midnight, Texas got up from the Bradley's living-room sofa and headed toward the hospital. Angie and Ennis were upstairs, presumably sleeping, in a familiar double bed; they had come back to Jenkins for a few days to pack and do their banking and put their house up for sale before leaving the place behind. Gabe and Mikey were sound asleep in their cribs. But Texas was not getting much sleep, and he had a hunch Volos was not either. That afternoon, after the good-byes in the hospital lounge and after Texas had helped the kid back to his room, Volos had bellied onto his bed and fallen asleep as if he had been knocked on the head. Not a bad idea at the time. A good way to forget for a while. But he couldn't keep it up forever.

Outside, the weather had settled into a steady, warm early-autumn rain. In Texas' headlights the world shone slick as black leather with silver studs. Around the hospital, vacant expanses of parking lot lay wet and gleaming under security lights. The place was pretty quiet for a change. Some of the groupies had given up and gone home after the first day or two, and it looked like the rain had driven the others away. The reporters were mostly not around in the middle of the night, though they would be back at dawn.

Striding across the parking lot, Texas smiled, because he had just figured out how to sneak Volos past them when it was time for the kid to leave the hospital. Use a wheelchair—but for the kid to lean on, not for him to sit in. If Volos wore blue jeans and the western shirt and snub-toed Dingos Texas had bought him, and tucked his hair up under a Stetson, and pulled the brim down over his face a bit, he would be just another good ol' boy pushing Pa to the truck. Texas, hatless and blanketed and maybe drooling a little in the wheelchair, would be Pa. The news ghouls would be looking for a rock star in a wheelchair, not an old mountaineer.

Maybe pretty soon it would get so the kid could go down to the corner and shoot pool like a normal human being. Texas hoped so. He wanted Volos to be able to go see pig races and hill climbs and powder puff baseball. He wanted to take the kid snowmobiling and skeet shooting and coon hunting on muleback. He wanted the kid to raise hell at least once and need to be bailed out of the pokey. He had wishes for Volos.

Texas ducked past the nurses' station, walked down the hall as softly as he could in his hard-heeled boots, slipped into Volos's room without turning on a light just in case the kid really was asleep—

He wasn't. Against the sheen of rain outside, Texas could see him standing at the window, staring out, leaning close to the water-streaked glass.

Texas left the light off—no use bringing a nurse in, and anyway he had a feeling the kid didn't want a lot of light. Went and stood beside Volos at the window's other corner. "So you're up to your old tricks, buddy," he greeted him softly. "Going around with your shirt off." The kid stood there naked except for his bandaging and his briefs. "Not sleeping. Hound-dogging in the night."

Volos gave a faint smile but did not look at him. In the shadowy light from outside, the kid's face was as wet as the pavement, streaked like the glass. Silently and without moving he was crying.

"Oh, shit, son." Texas gave up on teasing, went into the bathroom and got a washcloth. Came back and tried to wipe Volos's face with it. "Dammit. Kid, how long you been like this?"

Volos roused enough to push the washcloth away.

Texas said, "I wish you would've called me."

"I am all right." Volos's voice sounded steady but desperately tired. "I think it is just that my eyes are practicing."

"Give me a break, Volos! You're so down, down looks like up." The kid was walking that lonesome valley, all right. If Volos had been playing a guitar, his fingers would have been skating over the frets like chalk on a slate, bending the strings stony-blue.

Silence. Volos leaned his forehead against the cool glass.

"Okay, so I am down," he said after a while. "Is this the way it used to be for you, Texas, at night when you were missing Wyoma?"

Texas nodded, wishing he could take the kid into his arms, hold him, and hug the pain away. But Volos wasn't letting himself be babied those days. Trying to get back on his feet, trying to be a man, he was full of his damn suffering pride.

"And when you wanted to find your father," he said, still staring out into the rain. "Texas, I wish I had done it for you."

"So I could beat him up?"

"But you would not have done that. You thought it, but—I know you, you would have tried—you would have wanted to love him."

It took Texas a moment to admit to himself that the kid was right. Only to himself. He had his pride too.

"You asked me to help," Volos was saying, "and I told you no. I cannot believe I did that."

"For God's sake, Volos, forget it! It was a bad idea."

Volos seemed hardly to hear him. Wet-cheeked, he was staring, and he said, "I would do it now in a minute, Texas. I would kneel in front of that Throne and say, 'I have been a wrongheaded fool,' because it is true, I am an ass. But—now that I could do it—the wings are—gone, and the sky is—so far away—"

"Whoa." Texas allowed himself to come a step nearer, and gentled his voice, keeping it very low. "You telling me you want to go talk with your Pa?"

The question snapped Volos's head up. "No. I hate him. But—I don't know. I should tell him—it is not fair that I blame everything on him. The wings—I thought they were his doing, but now I see—"

At least Volos was looking at him now. Texas nodded at him to go on.

"When I incarnated, I thought I wanted to be a mortal, but really I wanted everything at once, to be human and yet—not hungry, not weary, not weeping. To be—to be still a star." The kid's voice started to shake. "That is why I—had—wings, I gave them to myself, not knowing. And I cursed God, and hated them. But now—they are gone, but I—I keep feeling them hurting on my shoulders, like ghosts—"

"Whoa. Hush." No way could Texas let him tough it out any longer. He took the necessary two steps to gather him in, but Volos stepped back. Didn't want to be hugged right now. Wet-faced, but didn't want to sob on his shoulder. Pride. That was all right. Texas knew a lot about pride. Just now learning, now that he was past forty, when it was time to get past pride.

"You're no more a fool than any human," Texas told him softly. "Volos." The kid was gazing back at him with dusky-blue eyes, the same color as his. Maybe the God the youngster had always resented so was to thank for that.

"Son ..." Texas felt his voice start to slip, tried again. This was it. Scarier than anything else he'd ever had to ask anybody. "Volos—I'm one of the luckiest people alive, I've got a wife and daughters who love me, and when I went looking for trouble I came up with you instead ..." His voice went husky. "Kid, you might have noticed how I feel about you, and I wish there was some way I could make it official, but I guess all I can do is just say it: Would you let me take you home? Will you be my son?"

So there went pride for both of them. The question broke Volos down and wide open. But that was okay. A kid's entitled to do some messy crying in his daddy's arms sometimes. Texas held him, gentle, careful of the wounded back, and felt the hands clinging to him— hands that could make the music of an angel—and swallowed hard, and stroked the youngster's long, coarse hair, and dared to turn his lips to the side of that dark head close to his, dared to kiss. A father's entitled to kiss his son.

"But it's all I—all I ever wanted," Volos blurted when he could speak. "Just—a father—who loves me."

"Son, you got it."

Maybe more of it than he reckoned. Maybe more fathers than one. Back home, Texas had squirreled away something he had redeemed once upon a crazy time from an L.A. pawnshop, something he would give to Volos when he figured the kid was ready: a sort of four-petaled flower made of solid gold. Texas had a hunch the sky would not always seem so far away to Volos. Seemed to him he had heard someplace that once in a while even God wept. And outside, warm rain was falling.

epilogue

Volos sprawled on his bed, replete. He had been a month in the McCardle house, and to celebrate, Wyoma had invited the whole family, Starr, Merrilee, their husbands and their new babies, and had made Volos a devil's-food cake, which was so far his favorite, especially with double-chocolate icing. Usually he and Texas did most of the cooking (often with bizarre results) because Wyoma worked. But Wyoma had wanted to make the cake. She mothered him, in her way. That first day, within the first hour, they had understood each other. He had staggered in the door, and she had looked up at him with eyes that assessed the task before her.

"How long since you shampooed your hair?" she had demanded.

"Shampoo?" He had not imagined his hair to need such care. But since the incident which had caused the loss of his wings, his body was acting differently. Texas had needed to teach him to use deodorant. And his hair was growing in finer, less like feathers, more like Texas' hair. And oilier, more in need of washing.

"Didn't nobody never teach you how to take care of yourself?" Wyoma had grumbled, not unkindly.

Then she had led him upstairs, and scrubbed his head for him at the bathroom sink, and towel-dried it, and helped him totter to bed in the room she had prepared for him.

The bed, an old wooden thing with a wire spring, was the same little bed that had belonged to Texas as a boy. Volos had spent a lot of time in it those first few days, looking at the block letters Texas had scratched in the headboard with a penknife once when he was being very bad. RBM—Robert Balfour McCardle. At an awkward angle. Being mortal was an odd thing. In a way the boy who had carved those letters was as dead as Volos's wings, and in another way he would live on through generations.

Volos felt almost human now. He walked strongly, and the haunting pain was gone from his back. On the floor by his bed lay a big all-paws mutt puppy— Texas had taken him to the pound to adopt it, he had named it Raphael, and most days he and Raph wrestled in the grass and ran through the yellow leaves, out across the fields, past the family cemetery where his charred wing bones lay, then through the woods, down to the river and back.

In his room besides the dog were many good things: his guitar, and a radio shaped like a jukebox (a gift from Ennis and Angie), and baseball hats marked Agway and Persimmon Volunteer Fire Department and Mingo County Courier. And piles of magazines, *Metal Mag* and *Motorcycle Women* and *Bimboy*. And the balsa-wood airplanes and model cars Texas kept getting him, the silly oversized Teddy bear Wyoma had bought him, and a Corvette-shaped decorator bottle of Avon aftershave (not yet used, though the day seemed to be coming when he would need to shave) from the girl down the road. The room, like the house, was not large, and his things crowded it, but when he was in it Volos did not feel boxed in. Instead, he felt snug, as if the house itself, like the family under its roof, embraced him.

Soon, Volos knew, he would have to decide what to do with the life he had claimed for himself. He still did not seem able to think about money, about making a living, in the same way that other people did, and he knew this—but he also knew that a man could not be a boy forever and let his father and mother take care of him. Sometime he must leave home.

Texas and Wyoma kept telling him not to feel that way, that there was no hurry about anything, and he knew they meant it. Those two, they astonished him daily with their love, for each other and for him. Waking up every morning, he felt himself being born, blinking into the sunrise.

He knew only one thing about his life, really: He wanted to make music.

So sometime he would go back to L.A., maybe. Get together with Red again and maybe the others, see if they could become a band. Just to live and sing and dance in the night and sometimes do a little fucking, that was all he wanted. Maybe find a sexy guy to take his mind off Angie. Stay away from the junk, since he knew it could hurt him now. Stay away from record producers. The worst thing that could happen would be if he became a star again, but that did not need to happen. People probably would not recognize him. There was hair on his chest now, and his voice had deepened, there was grit in it these days, and his face had subtly changed. Like the rest of him, it spoke less of starfire and ether now and more of earth. It was a good face with soul in it, still his own but also somewhat like Texas'. Weathered, a little, by life and West Virginia. When he went back to L.A. he would call himself Flaim, and he would know where he was from, and who loved him, and who he loved. As if there were a compass in his heart, he would always know which way lay home.

From the kitchen down below he could hear Wyoma and her girls chattering. Texas was downstairs taking a nap with the TV on. As if he could see him, Volos imagined Texas stretched out in the armchair with his Stetson over his face and his booted feet propped on the coffee table. Atop the TV, standing in its frame, was a recent studio photo of Texas, Wyoma, Starr, Merrilee—and Volos.

He yawned and stretched, fingering initials freshly carved in his bed's headboard—VFCM. Volos Flaim Carson McCardle. Texas had loaned him the penknife to do it.

He stretched some more, then rolled over and patted Raphael's head. Reached over the dog for tablet paper and pencil. Chewed at the fingers of his left hand. It was still hard for him to write. He remembered three dozen languages—though not the languages of birds—but he still held a pencil like a first-grader. Use a tape recorder, Texas had suggested. But Volos wished to make songs as Angie would have done, and write them down.

So far none of his had felt like hers—but this time was different. Something within him had settled into place like a cowboy into a saddle, like a mountaineer back in the mountains, and now he could be whole, he could make music, really make it, like making a baby, from the fundament of his body and the penetralia of his soul. He sensed the song coming. Felt it snapping and clicking in him, electric. Could feel its heartbeat rhythm. Could almost hear the guitars.

Volos wrote:

Now I am made of fire
I blaze
through my numbered days
and all around me I see
the mothers the fathers the lovers
like candles aglow
with each other
one haloed in the other

melting in one another
above their shoulders rising
their invisible wings
of flame.

ROC   **⌀SIGNET**   (0451)

Fantasy Science Fiction BY JOEL ROSENBERG

☐ **THE SILVER CROWN. Book Three of the *Guardians of the Flame* Series.** In an effort to provide a haven for slaves, Karl and his comrades establish a stronghold called Home. But, caught between the slaver's forces armed with a new magical weapon and elves attempting to steal the treasured secret of gunpowder, they fear the walls of Home may not be standing for long. . . .   (159837—$3.95)

☐ **THE HEIR APPARENT: Book Four of the *Guardians of the Flame* Series.** Karl had gained an Empire—now what price must he pay to assure its future? He and his friends had freed many from the bonds of slavery, but now they were bound by the furious vendetta of Ahrmin of the evil Slavers Guild. . . .   (162129—$3.95)

☐ **THE WARRIOR LIVES: Book Five of the *Guardians of the Flame* Series.** When Karl is declared dead it is up to his son, Jason, to take on the responsibilities of leadership. But soon rumors surface of unauthorized raids . . . and a cryptic message is left on the corpses of the enemy— "The Warrior Lives!" Could it be? Jason must learn the truth.   (450019—$4.99)

☐ **THE ROAD TO EHVENOR, a *Guardians of the Flame* novel.** Where magic is creeping out of Faerie at the border town of Ehvenor, Jason Cullinane, son of the legendary Karl must ride to the rescue with his inner circle of warriors and challenge the forces of chaos before they gain a foothold in the human lands. (451910—$5.50)

Prices slightly higher in Canada.

If you and/or a friend would like to receive the *ROC Advance*, a bimonthly newsletter featuring all the newest and hottest ROC books and authors, on a complimentary basis, please fill out this form and return it to:

ROC Books/Penguin USA
375 Hudson Street
New York, NY 10014

Your Address
Name _____
Street _____ Apt. # _____
City _____ State _____ Zip _____

Friend's Address
Name _____
Street _____ Apt. # _____
City _____ State _____ Zip _____